Highland Wishes

Leanne Burroughs

Highland Press

High Springs, Florida 32655

A 2004 Published Laurie Winner!!!

Highland Wishes

To my husband, Tom, whose encouragement meant so much to me while I wrote this book and who decided I had to go to Scotland to actually see the places I'd done so much research on and was writing about!

ACKNOWLEDGEMENTS

Grateful thanks are due to Gary Newcomer, M.D., for medical information he provided – even though the time period was far earlier than he ever studied about in med school; to Jill Wilmot for her advice on English and Scottish meals; to Robert Clarke for answering my numerous questions about horses; and to the many people who were wonderful enough to listen to me and support me as I talked endlessly about my dream of writing this book.

Thank you to JO Bishop, who kept my computers running for me when they seemed to have a mind of their own, and who tried to answer my many questions of, "Why is it doing...?"

And a special thank you to DeborahAnne MacGillivray for answering numerous questions on Scottish history!

England and Scotland, March 1296

Chapter One

"Nay!" Victoria Blackstone shouted as she ran through the busy courtyard and into the house. Caring not what anyone thought, tears streamed down her face as she ran up the winding stone staircase to the family quarters. "I'll not do it. He cannot make me."

She rushed down the long, dark hallway to her grandmother's bedchamber, opened the heavy wooden door and peered around the corner. "Grandmum, may I speak with you?"

"Of course, child," came the frail, shaky response. "You are always well-come. What need you the help of your old grandmum for this day?"

Victoria stood silent and still and glanced at richly hued tapestries gracing the chamber walls. They blended with everything her grandpapa brought home from his many trips. Her grandmum treasured each gift that kept his memory close.

"Come, child," her grandmother broke the silence and patted the bed. "What has you so forlorn?"

Victoria climbed the three wooden steps to sit beside her grandmother. Bright red bolstering pillows rested against the headboard. Tiring quickly, her grandmother rarely left her room, but Victoria thought her a vision of elderly loveliness. Looking into pale blue eyes, Victoria took the frail, weathered hand and placed it tenderly within her own. "Grandmum, Father told me yesterday he betrothed me to Lord Bothington! Today he said I must wed that wretched old man Saturday next." She failed in her effort to hold back tears. They streamed down her cheeks.

Her grandmother's elegant silver brows raised in what could only be construed as disdain. "Nay!" Abigail Blackstone bemoaned, shuddering. "Not Percival. Your grandpapa did not trust him. He is wicked. His wives..."

9

She stopped, seemingly unsure what to say next. "Have you spoken with your father, dear?" Staring into Victoria's tear-streaked face, her expression softened. "Of course. He'd not listen. He can be most stubborn at times. 'Tis a serious flaw."

Though her grandmother's only child, Lady Blackstone no longer made excuses for his ruthlessness. She'd stopped doing so years ago.

Victoria nodded. "I went out to the rose garden. Father followed and we argued. He refused to listen.

Her father stormed into his mother's bedchamber, shooting a scathing glare in Victoria's direction. "'Tis as I thought," he railed. "I knew you'd run to your grandmother. She caters to your every whim." A tall, barrel chested man with black hair and brown eyes, the pulse in Gerald Blackstone's neck throbbed as his anger mounted.

From his look of hatred, Victoria thought she could read his mind. His look clearly indicated she'd defied him for the last time. He'd wed her to Bothington and be rid of her once and for all.

"God must hate me to give me a worthless daughter rather than the son I wanted." Blackstone approached, grabbed Victoria's arm, and dragged her from the high bed. The instant he looked at her face, Victoria knew she was in trouble. He'd always told her crying was a female trait he hated. Releasing a curse, he backhanded her. Victoria felt his ring dig into her skin and tasted blood on her lower lip.

A cold wave of fear rushed over her.

"Gerald, nay," her grandmother yelled. "Leave the girl alone."

Blackstone shot his mother a look of disgust. "Stay out of this. You have no say in anything."

Victoria brushed away blood as he stormed, "I'll gain vast lands from this marriage, girl, and have no intention of giving that up for your whims. The alliance is also beneficial to our king, so he approves."

He pushed her towards his mother's bed. "You've been the bane of my existence your entire life and 'tis time I benefitted from having to endure your presence."

"Gerald!" her grandmother moaned. "Enough!"

Blackstone glared at them both with undisguised hatred. Ignoring his mother's plea, he warned, "Do not think to disobey me on this or you'll regret the consequences. You shall marry Percival on the date stated, and I expect you to meet him after the

10

nooning meal on the morrow to accept his generous offer." He pinched her face, drawing it close to his, hurting her with his fingers. "Remember, daughter, no decent man will offer for you. I made certain of that."

He turned to stalk from the room. Reaching the door, he repeated, "After the nooning, daughter, or the beatings I gave you in the past will seem like soft caresses compared to what you'll feel in future." He slammed the door shut behind him.

Victoria's grandmother opened her arms and held Victoria close when she flew into the welcoming embrace.

Tears streamed down her face as she rested her head on her grandmother's thin shoulder and sobbed. "I'll not do it, Grandmum. Oh, if only I could be somewhere else. Anywhere."

Victoria rose and paced, inhaling the soft floral scent wafting through her grandmother's bedchamber. "Grandmum, I must leave. Do you not see? I must head farther south—into England. I cannot stay where hatred brews—or be wed to Bothington. He'll beat me, Grandmum." Unable to hide her anguish, Victoria rushed back up the bed's steps and fell to her knees on the padded straw mattress. "'Tis rumored he beat his first two wives to death." When she saw her grandmother's look of shock, she ruefully added, "Aye, Grandmum. I knew already. You would not have told me anything I'd not already heard. I did not think anyone could be worse than Father, but Bothington makes my skin crawl. I hate everything he stands for." She gently clasped her grandmother's hand rubbed her thumb over the pale, translucent skin, willing her grandmother's understanding.

Victoria rose and stared wistfully out the arrow slit, watching the breeze brush branches against the side of the Hall.

"Tory," her grandmother began, "you know I shall not live much longer." Victoria vehemently shook her head when her grandmother used her pet name and hastened to interrupt, but her grandmother stopped her with a troubled look, her breaths rapid and weak and her frail voice cracking. "Nay, child, you know 'tis true. In truth, I am not loath to the thought. Your grandfather awaits me in Heaven and I have missed him these many years."

Victoria fought her mounting tears. She loved this gentle woman so much.

"I would do aught to see you happy, but I have no say in your future." Her grandmother shook her head sadly. "Your father makes such arrangements, whether you wish him to or not. He always has, as all men do. No more talk of running away, now.

Your father would search, drag you back, and be far more brutal than before."

"Nay," Victoria sighed in desperation. "I cannot allow that. I have no illusions of finding love, Grandmum, thanks to Father's actions." She added firmly, "He took everything else from me, but I'll not relinquish my happiness to him. Why, Grandmum? Why can I not find love? You did." Victoria gazed into her grandmother's soulful eyes and changed her mind on giving up on love. "You told me you and Grandpapa had a special love and love like that does not come along often. I want that, Grandmum. I want a love like you and Grandpapa shared. I wish I lived anywhere but here. *With anybody else.* I wish—"

"Do not say such things, child." Her grandmother squeezed Victoria's hand in a weak grip. "Only God knows your destiny. Be careful what you wish for. One never knows when wishes will be answered, and God may not grant them the way you hoped."

Victoria drew a calming breath. "Rest now, Grandmum. I'll not do anything without weighing my choices. Truly. Everything will work out. You shall see."

Victoria placed a light kiss on her grandmother's aged cheek. Taking the woman's frail hand within her own one last time, she kissed it before lowering it to the bed. "I do not want to lose you, Grandmum," she said in a rush of words as tears welled in her eyes.

"That will never happen, luv," her grandmother added tenderly. She tapped her finger lightly against Victoria's breast. "I'll always be in your heart."

Victoria walked slowly to the chamber door and turned one last time. She knew she'd never see her grandmother again.

Seeing a worried look on her grandmother's face, she thought of perfect parting words. "I love you." She choked back tears, rushed back to the bed to give her grandmother one final hug. She removed herself from the embrace and whispered, "Remember that always, Grandmum."

Grant Drummond stormed into the Great Hall and headed for the high table. The only thought to cross his mind was that the English would bloody well pay for what they'd done! Over seventeen thousand people dead!

He'd returned home immediately upon receiving news of his father's death. Stalking past his fellow clansmen, Grant grabbed an empty goblet and headed for the ale barrel. He dipped it into the keg, tipped back his head, and downed the contents before coming up for air. Slamming the goblet on the trestle table, he boomed, "Angus! You son of a dog, where are you?"

Captain of Drummond's castle guard, Angus' weathered cheeks and flaming red hair, sprinkled with liberal grey streaks revealed most of his two score years. Injured during a previous battle, he'd been unable to accompany Grant the last time King Edward plotted his usual skullduggery.

"Here." Although he had a limp from his injury, he walked steadily toward his new chieftain.

Grant felt tired. He'd pushed his men and their horses to the edge of their endurance.

"I received your message. Tell me what happened. Tell me every last bloody detail of how those dogs of Satan killed my father."

Angus strode the remaining distance and patted Grant's shoulder, then helped himself to nearby ale. "Och, lad, 'tis good to have you home, but I regret the circumstances."

Grant acknowledged the comment with a nod.

Warwick, a slender silver-haired man who'd been not only like a father to Grant, but also been his mentor, placed his hand in a reassuring gesture on Grant's shoulder. "We sent information in the missive, lad. Why torture yourself?"

"Because I want the facts burned in my memory afore I take my revenge," Grant gritted though clenched teeth.

An awkward silence followed, broken only by the hearth's crackling red and orange flames.

"'Tis rumored," Angus began in his usual gruff fashion, "King Edward stopped at Hutton. As usual with that son of a dog, something dinnae settle right in his craw and he decided to kill a few thousand people."

Men grimaced, tilting their heads toward Grant. He needed facts, not personal feelings and vindictiveness. "We imagine he chose Berwick since 'tis our most important Border castle. That *foosty scunner*, Edward, besieged the castle, but its guard stood prepared." Angus shrugged, using the derogatory term to describe the English king. "They jeered Edward, taunted him about his parentage, and made obscene gestures. When they defied Edward to do his worst, little did they know he'd do just that. He abandoned the castle and entered the royal burgh, ruthlessly killing men, women, and bairns." He shook his head dejectedly. "All noblemen dead and women raped afore the bloody English

13

murdered them."

"Edward murdered everyone?" Grant's mind refused to accept the horror of what he heard. His heart thundered and anger mounted as he waited for his question to be answered. He turned to Alexander.

The young man picked up the tale. "Not everyone. Not the bloody English, but thousands of Scots were murdered. 'Twas naught but a two-day rampage to maim or kill everyone in their path."

"Edward thinks he's good," Grant roared and slammed his fist against a table, "but he is not that good. How knew he who was Scot?"

"Edward had men living in town." Grant handed Alexander a fresh tankard and the young man took a fortifying drink. "'Tis obvious they pointed out English homes to be spared."

With such distasteful information, Grant couldn't bring himself to accept the facts. "And Da went to this bloody city? *Why*? It makes no sense. Why go to the Borders?"

He'd known it would hurt to hear facts surrounding his father's death. He just hadn't realized how much. It struck a chord of dismay in his heart. He let his thoughts drift. Clan Drummond's great chieftain dead! His da, Malcolm, had been a great warrior and a fair and honest man. There simply had to be a mistake. Mayhap if he prayed hard enough, a miracle would happen and his father would walk through the door.

Grant knew he looked like his da, with dark hair, wide shoulders, and a hint of a cleft in his chin. His father had dark eyes, though, whereas everyone told him his were more the shade of his mam's—the grey of a slow moving burn on a cloudy day.

He shook his reverie aside when Angus began again. "A messenger brought Laird Malcolm a missive. He dinnae take us into his confidence, but assured us he would tell everything when upcoming dealings were concluded. We accompanied him, mind, but he insisted on doing everything his way. You know how stubborn he could be when he set an idea in his mind. He thought to be gone a mere fortnight."

"What happened?" Grant's hands were clenched so tight, his knuckles turned white.

"Ran them to ground, Grant," his clansman shuddered in remembrance, weariness in his green eyes.

"After seeing the slaughter in town, Berwick's captain thought it senseless to resist, so he surrendered, knowing the castle's earth and wood ramparts would be too easily overrun."

Angus stopped when a buxom serving girl brought some roasted pig and more ale from the kitchen. As the succulent aroma wafted through the air, Grant watched as his tired, hungry men greedily reached for refreshments and settled themselves at tables.

Alexander spat into the rushes. "Edward wished to lay waste our dreams of independence, but that will never happen." He raised his tankard to Grant in a toast. "I drink to the brave men that died at Berwick."

Grant took a long draught of ale. Upending his goblet, he downed the last of it without drawing breath. He looked expectantly at Alexander, then gestured impatiently for him to continue.

"That's all we know. After the slaughter, billows of smoke and the smell of death were everywhere." The young man changed thoughts and looked at him pensively. "You know how sad we are about your da."

"Och, aye," Grant said in a ragged voice as he threaded his hand through his hair. "Everyone thought Da a good man—and a good chieftain. I do not think I can do what he did." He turned away and gathered his strength, determined to remain in control of his feelings. He added in a halting voice, "I'll miss him, but he will remain in my memory forever."

Warwick approached him with a look of concern—likely mirroring every man's thoughts. "We have no doubt you will be a good chieftain. You have your da's fine attributes." His eyes scanned those gathered. "You know you will have our fealty."

Grant didn't immediately answer. Instead, he looked to a large portrait of his parents hanging on the grey stone wall behind the raised wooden Great Table. It looked so lifelike he almost felt their presence. *Father hated posing for that portrait,* he fondly remembered, *but Mam pleaded until he could no longer deny her.* Although a large man, everyone had known his tiny lady wife had him wound around her delicate fingers! A scowl had darkened his father's face. "'Tis not manly to sit for someone like that. We know what he's really like—and I dinnae want a bloody pederast in my castle." As always, his mother won out and Grant treasured its presence in his Hall, being one of his few remaining possessions of them both.

Shaking off his reverie, he turned when he heard someone ask a question. Ian leaned against the grey, stone wall. "What wish you to do, Grant? Head back to Berwick?" Troubled eyes watched him closely.

Hands fisted at his sides and legs braced apart, the scowl on his face could leave no doubt in anyone's mind this would be one long night.

"Och, aye," Grant growled. Settling themselves around the long, wooden trestle table, men waited for him to join them. "We will repay them in kind. 'Tis back to their bloody town, and this time we'll give *them* a taste of what they did to us. They'll wish they'd never been born! Edward and his bloody English will pay for what they did to Da." His body trembled with suppressed rage.

Chapter Two

Heavy mist swirled like a cat wrapping itself around its master's leg as they reached the final stretch to Berwick. Gently rolling hills in Leith belied the tension surrounding the Border town.

Now Grant knew the traitor's name and was on his way to seeing his plan through. They rode fast, barely stopping. He planned on confronting the man most people blamed for the massacre—Gerald Blackstone. Grant planned to see to him personally. Regardless of who wielded the sword, he blamed Blackstone for his father's death. And he would have his revenge.

His thoughts turned dark and he had no doubt he'd see the House of Blackstone destroyed.

Victoria gathered clothing for her journey. She wished she could wear the blue mantle her grandmum gave her at Christmastide, but knew she'd be too easily spotted. Thinking it the last gift she'd receive from her grandmother, she placed it carefully atop folded clothes. Remembering eventide's chill, she wrapped and tied the bundle with a blanket.

She planned to head to the stables once everyone was abed. In one of his crueler moments Father had forbidden her to ride her beloved gelding, Galahad, but she needed the horse now. Knew she must distance herself from Blackstone Manor. Certain her father would search for her, she wouldn't get far afoot. He wouldn't search because he loved her, but because he hated her for being a girl and wanted to make her life miserable. He always had.

Planning to head south to London, Victoria planned to slip out without the tower guard seeing her. Gilbert guarded the gate, and although kind and gentle, he feared her father, as did most everyone. He wouldn't let her leave for fear of recrimination. Father ran his home based on fear, not fairness or kindness.

Victoria delighted that Gilbert liked Evalina, a young scullery maid, and had in recent days secretly allowed her in the tower. Victoria hoped this night would prove no different. She needed to keep a watchful eye on the tower steps, thinking tonight her only chance to make good her escape.

She snuffed out the candle and glanced around her moonlit bedchamber one final time before quietly exiting. Part of her feared leaving the only home she'd ever known. Other than belongings in the blanket, everything else she owned would remain in this room. Setting her goals firmly in mind, Victoria believed her freedom worth far more than a few possessions.

She edged cautiously against the stone manor walls, ensuring she remained in shadows as she wended her way down the long, dark corridor.

She tiptoed into her younger sister's bedchamber. Her sister slept so soundly, their battle cannon could be fired and Ashleigh wouldn't hear it. Smiling, Victoria kissed the young girl farewell. So far everything had gone as planned. She hated leaving her beautiful sister, but knew she'd be safe. For some reason her father didn't abuse Ashleigh. Victoria thought it odd, but her father barely acknowledged the blonde-haired girl's existence. She and her sister looked nothing alike.

Eyeing her surroundings one last time, she silently departed her home. The horizon was blanketed in the darkness of night. She stared at emerging stars and wondered what the night held in store for her. The eerie sound of rushing wind gave an ominous portent to the night.

She shuddered.

In the faint glint of moonlight, Grant motioned Angus closer. "Just a bit longer afore we head forward. I saw a lass head up to yon tower, so mayhap their guard will be distracted until we are too close to be stopped."

Men close enough to hear Grant chuckled. "Mayhap we could bide awhile on yon tower afore raiding the keep. I could use the attentions of a wench myself." Duff leered and grabbed his crotch in a suggestive motion.

Other men guffawed, but Grant reproached his scruffy looking clansman. "Get your mind out of the dirt, Duff. We have no time for that. Once we arrive home, you can have all the lasses you want."

Grant turned and scanned the section of wall illuminated by muted moonlight. He watched activities surrounding their ultimate destination and felt confident his men would be safe if they remained cloaked in the darkness of night. Soon the men he sent to town earlier returned. The time for retribution had arrived. Rage tightly controlled, he waved his hand and yelled, "Now!"

Following his lead, men pressed forward toward the magnificent Norman doorway to take the manor and its inhabitants by surprise. The blood-curdling Drummond war cry rent the stillness of the night.

Enroute to the stables, Victoria heard commotion in the courtyard. Too late, a hoarse call of warning sounded. Men in all states of dishabille rushed from the hall and barracks. Victoria took refuge behind the largest wooden barrel and crouched behind it.

She thought she heard something ramming the main door. Were they under attack? Surely no one would be foolish enough to attack her father.

High-pitched screams filled the air. In fear, she crouched lower. Could she do aught to help? Her breath caught in her throat, pinioned by fear. She fought rising waves of panic upon realizing she had no weapon. Only thinking of necessities like food and clothing, she'd not once considered protection.

What had she been thinking?

Soon the fierce clanking of swords sounded near to hand and something jostled the barrel where she sought refuge. Who was on the other side? Her father's men? Brazen attackers? Would she be killed? She'd disguised herself as a boy, so they'd never think her a woman. These attackers might kill everyone, similar to what many said the king had done in town.

She shuddered and thought of all she'd heard had been done in the name of her king. Surely it couldn't be true. The English wouldn't really have slaughtered so many.

Why were these people here? More important, *who were they*?

After repeated curses and screams, fighting stopped, quiet reigned. Had they left? Or were they dead? Surely everyone would be safe. Victoria couldn't imagine anyone foolhardy enough to attack her father's holding. Known for his ferocity in fighting, he wouldn't be considered a kind man. He fought the way he lived his life—cruelly.

As anxiety coursed through her, Victoria peered around the barrel. Seeing no one, she thought herself safe. Off in the darkness she heard voices. Anxious to check on her grandmum and sister, she peered once again to determine if she could leave the safety the barrel afforded. Suddenly someone grabbed her from behind and jerked her from her hiding place. Howling winds sent a chill down her spine not only of cold, but fear. The ruffian dragged her to the courtyard's center and tossed her at a man's feet as if little more than a sack of grain. When her efforts to fight proved fruitless, the first stirrings of alarm swept through her.

"Found this lad hiding, Grant," the man ground out. "Should I run him through?"

Realizing the blackguard towering above her seriously considered the man's gruff question, she uttered a terrified gasp.

"How auld are you, lad?" the blackguard questioned sternly. Nudging her with the toe of his heavy boot, he seemed to stare into her very being.

She stiffened and lowered her lashes as a knot of fear lodged in her stomach. She dared not speak. If she made that mistake, they'd instantly know her for a woman and she didn't want to find out what these pigs would do then. By the lilt in their voices, Victoria knew they were Scots. Filthy Scots her father always called them. That meant they'd killed her father's men and would soon rape the women. She'd been told often about barbarous Scots. Gathering her courage, she lifted her eyes. Battle-hardened faces confronted her.

Her eyes darted wildly and looked for a means of escape. Finding none, she inched to a standing position. She had to get back to the house. The man before her made no motion to stop her, yet his grey eyes bored into hers. Having met with success in standing, she backed up, but met with firm resistance. A *large* man's body stood behind her.

"I asked a question, lad," the man said. "How auld are you?"

Howls erupted when she refused to answer. "Mayhap he is deaf, Grant—like Colin—or daft."

Realizing the prospect of escape looked dim, she hoped the soot she rubbed on her face earlier hadn't come off during her scuffle with the scoundrel. She'd piled her long hair beneath her hat before leaving her chamber. With it pulled low enough to conceal most of her face, she hoped they wouldn't peer at her too closely. Mayhap they wouldn't kill someone they thought a mere boy. The blackguard narrowed his eyes and continued staring.

Behind them someone yelled, "Kill the bloody pig, Grant. It matters not how young he is. If he's a Blackstone vassal, he should die. He may have been with the ones that killed your da."

Men hurled insults and obscenities.

As she surveyed the group of men surrounding her, her stomach knotted with a sense of foreboding. Instinct warned to

20

escape right away—and to keep her disguise in place. She fumbled frantically to adjust her shapeless hat, pulling it lower on her face.

Her movement caused Grant to pause.

The thought crossed his mind that the attire before him belonged to a young stable ghillie. Yet something about the coarse trews, smock, and ill-fitting brown jerkin didn't appear true. Narrowing his eyes in scrutiny, he strode closer with deliberate purpose. His eyes never left the young lad's face—or the long black lashes gracefully framing brown eyes. He thought them the most beautiful eyes he'd ever seen. Certainly not the eyes or lashes of a lad!

A smirk crossed his face.

In terror, Victoria watched his approach. If he got too close, he'd know. She drove her elbow with deliberate precision into the man behind her, turned and ran. She got all of two steps before he grabbed her shirt and jerked her back. She flailed furiously, causing her cap to fall off in the ensuing scuffle.

The solidly built man twisted a handful of her hair around his beefy hand. He jerked her against his chest and plucked her off her feet for a moment as rage surged in his eyes.

Panic welled in her chest as she winced in pain and bit back a scream.

The cap dislodged, her long-flowing chestnut-colored hair draped gracefully around her shoulders, down to her waist.

"'Tis a lassie!" a gasp of surprise sounded.

Closing her eyes, she swallowed hard and did the only thing she could.

She prayed.

Grant chuckled as Angus rubbed his meaty hand over his stomach and glared. "A gel caught you off guard, did she, Angus? Or could it have been her great beauty—with all that dirt on her face?"

Angus scowled at Grant and dragged her face closer to his by again wrapping her hair around his hand.

Indignant, she tried to jerk free, but failed. She grew more furious by the minute.

The burly man hissed with evident displeasure and placed his face in front of hers. "Lassie or no', if ever you do that again, you'll be dead." Allowing the threat of his words to penetrate, he unwound her hair and shoved her.

When she stumbled into Grant, he grabbed her by her upper arms and steadied her.

"What will you do with her, Grant?" a young man shouted.

Someone referred to as Duff offered the lewd suggestion, "Let us see what she has aneath that shirt." She felt a chill wash over her.

Looking into her soft brown eyes, Grant saw an attempt at bravado. Though tall for a lass, the top of her head didn't even reach his chin. He saw a look of defiance blaze from the depths of her eyes and almost laughed. Most men were afraid of him, so a lassie certainly should be. He guessed this one didn't know that—or didn't care. She should be quaking in her borrowed boots right now. After all, he held her life in his hands. He instilled fear in men much larger and braver than this wee wisp of a girl. His unwavering eyes searched her face.

Leave her. That's what he'd do.

He hadn't come to take prisoners. He traveled to Berwick to kill Blackstone, and that he'd done—*with his own sword.* He didn't need to kill everyone as the bloody English did a few sennights earlier. Those were their filthy tactics, not his. He'd had his revenge.

Aye, he'd leave her and she could fend for herself. On her back from the looks of those lovely brown eyes.

He continued looking as if staring into her soul. He wondered how he ever could have mistaken her for a lad, even if only momentarily. From what he could now see beneath the soot, he imagined her quite pretty. She returned his glare insolently, yet her breaths came heavy with fear. She drew her tongue between her parched lips.

The effect on him proved immediate. "Fetch her," he shot over his shoulder as he released his grip on her arms and walked away. His men looked after him, stunned, and the young woman stared in mute horror, as if not believing she'd correctly heard his words.

"Nay!" she yelled, aghast. Her eyes grew wide with terror.

Grant heard the desperation in her voice. With one last searching glance he looked at the wide-eyed woman and reaffirmed his resolve.

"Grant?" Alexander queried in obvious disbelief.

"Fetch her, I said," he answered without looking back or sparing the woman in question a second glance. He struggled not to break into a wide grin. Failing, a hint of a smile crossed his face as he walked away and found his mount.

'Twas the first time he smiled since hearing the terrible news about his father.

Victoria grumbled as Angus dragged her along, the punishing force of his fingers digging cruelly into her arm. She tripped, but regained her footing. It didn't seem to disconcert him that she tried to thwart his efforts.

How dare that man say *fetch her*? As if he thought her no more important than a sack of grain. The pompous jackanapes! She'd *not* go with them. She had other plans for her life, and these bloody Scots wouldn't stop her now. They didn't know whom they dealt with yet.

Although feeling defenseless at the moment, she'd never give in without a fight. She'd defended herself against her father her entire life. She wouldn't give up now.

Chapter Three

They traveled through hills for what seemed an eternity. Victoria heard *him* saying they must ride hard and fast. Did these creatures never need to stop? Didn't they have to attend to personal things? She'd burst before asking them to stop. She grumbled and cast *him* an accusatory glare. For the moment she rode with a lad who ignored her, an improvement over men she rode with during the night. They'd thought it great sport to torment her, caressing her breasts through her shirt and rubbing their meaty hands up and down her legs. She fumed in anger. Since they were Scots, she should have expected no less.

She heard them talking about endless rumors abounding.

"Edward must be stopped. His interference causes havoc and we cannot lose sight of danger he poses," the lout Angus injected angrily. "I hoped it would not come to this, but it now seems war is inevitable."

The brigands' leader used little-traveled roads, so she'd seen all manner of landscapes. She'd never traveled north of Berwick, only father south into England. She forced herself to keep her eyes open, but riding for endless hours, she found herself tiring.

Their leader discussed circumventing Jedburgh. "Think you we are far enough ahead of anyone following us that we can stop at the abbey William the Lion founded? We could refresh ourselves whilst there."

Winter refused to release its tenacious hold. As they journeyed north through the rolling countryside, strong, cold winds buffeted her. It took all her strength to sit straight, but she refused to lean back.

Not against the likes of *them*.

North of Jedburgh's abbey, that *creature* shouted for them to halt. After conversing, they rode deeper into the woods. The leader dismounted with little effort to give his steed a brief respite, then strode purposefully and picked her off her mount. Too unnerved to fight, she merely glared.

He smirked as he faced her. "I imagine by now you must attend to personal ablutions?" Angry and tired, she pulled away and shot him a scathing glare as if his question was ludicrous and the answer should have been obvious after all these hours.

24

He ignored her as if no more than a bothersome midge and pulled her farther into the woods. "Stop jerking, lass, or I'll drop your britches here afore my men—or would you not mind that?"

His taunting smile startled her. She swallowed, and felt herself turning red at the implication behind his words.

"Mayhap the town slut wouldn't mind. Mayhap that is what you want."

Breathing deeply, she muttered in anger and quit struggling. She'd attend to her needs, then flee. Before anything else went awry it, would behoove her to escape this monster. She had to return to check on her grandmum and sister. He'd never find her within the dense woods and overgrown thicket. Shoulders back and head erect, she tamped down an urge to strike him as she stalked away.

Close behind her, the sound of his laughter sounded indulgent. "Tread lightly, lass. You think me so daft I would let you go alone? Methinks not. I'll escort you, then we will continue our journey."

Her shoulders sagged, but she shot him what she hoped proved to be a glare of pure defiance while allowing him to lead her deeper into the woods. She heard the sounds of a rippling river in the distance.

Muttering threats, she informed him in no uncertain terms, "I am not the town slut!"

Mortified at his closeness, she felt his mocking gaze as she saw to her needs. Ooh, how she hated him.

Nevertheless, too soon she soon found herself seated in front of him on his huge, black destrier, his sinewy forearms wrapped around her. Why did he have her on *his* horse? She inhaled sharply as she felt the strength and breadth of his hard body. *How did one ignore that*? Until they stopped, he'd paid her no heed. Why now?

To her dismay, she found out when he commanded in his strong, even voice, "Lean against me and rest."

"I'll not! I want naught to do with your filthy, heathen body." With reckless abandon she tossed her hair so it hit him in the face, then turned forward and bristled, "And I am not the least bit tired."

Grant smiled at this bit of misinformation as he saw her eyes blaze with fury. He hadn't let her observe him watching, but he'd been aware of her every movement and had assessed how far she could travel before she collapsed. They still needed to distance themselves from Berwick, so they were unable to stop. He wanted to ensure the English didn't learn his identity or destination.

Without her knowledge, he eyed everything about her, from the sun glinting off her long, brown hair to the liberties his men had taken. Time after time she'd slapped their hands away, their actions seeming to bother her. Not what one would expect of a lightskirt. His men knew better than to do more, yet something didn't settle well with the liberties they'd taken. For some ridiculous reason, he felt honor-bound to keep her safe.

He just didn't understand why.

She was but his prisoner— and a Sassunach to boot.

Nevertheless, he often switched with whom she rode before settling on Hamish, the lad responsible for tending horses. The tall, gangly boy seemed to know what his chieftain wanted and ignored the lass. That, or the lad, who was but five and ten summers, still felt too shy to follow the the other mens' actions.

Regardless of her stubborn mutterings and her belligerent demands, he knew she had to be exhausted. Smiling, he witnessed her try to stifle a broad yawn. Even his men were tired, and they were battle-hardened warriors used to riding hard. He'd seen her sag against Hamish, then jerk forward, forcing her back ramrod straight to leave space between her and the young man. He thought she had a lot of spirit.

Even though he couldn't stop riding, he determined to make her rest, no matter how much she fought him—and he had no doubt she would. She did seem quite stubborn. Feeling she'd hate him more than she likely did, he utilized the one tactic he'd noticed raised her ire the most.

"Lean against me, lass." His voice brooked no opposition.

He pulled Victoria close, and as expected the stubborn woman pulled away. He pulled her back again and she immediately jerked forward. Doing this once more with the same expected result, he moved the hand holding his reins closer to her belly. Ensuring he had a firm hold, he closed his free hand over her breast.

Her head whipped around and her eyes turned murderous.

Horrified by such an intimate touch, Victoria shrieked in surprise and outrage as she tried to jerk away from him. "Take your filthy hands off me!"

Despite the sun's warmth, a chill settled over her.

Seeing his smug look, she wanted to slap it off his face.

"Och, but lass, I know that must be what you want. After all, you are placing it right where my hand is."

Again she tried to jerk away, but had little success when he pulled her firmly against his chest. When he removed his hand, she leaned forward, her breaths coming faster.

Grant responded with a harsh bark of laughter. "Lass, we can play this game all night if you wish, but I assure you, I'll win. I would advise you not to keep making me repeat myself."

Her breathing increased. She jabbed her elbow into his side and jerked forward. "Do not touch me!" she bristled at his unwanted attentions. She raised her chin in an act of defiance and saw everyone laughing and leering.

She hated them.

Amused, he let her sit for a minute untouched, then reached beneath the fabric of her shirt and clamped his hand onto her bare breast. She jerked with such violence he thought she might unseat herself as she tried to escape his touch.

He struggled to keep her in front of him while she railed. "Stop!"

He lowered his head to her ear and whispered, "I told you that you wouldn't win, lass. Now, lean against me. You will be safe if you do as I say. Should you continue to fight, you will spend the remainder of this trip with my hand where it is."

Enjoying the feel of her soft breast, he lightly kneaded and added with a confident laugh, "Now I would enjoy that, but I doubt you will. The choice is yours, of course, but you will not be given a different one. I suggest you make your decision." He felt her tremble.

Glancing down, he saw her hands fisting in her lap. He wondered if the cantankerous woman might hit him again.

"You sir, are a horrid person," she informed him testily.

He wasn't bluffing—and she knew it.

With a tortured sob, she leaned back tentatively, defeat riding heavily on her spirit. By dint of will she clearly refused to let him see her cry. She uttered no sound, but tremors wracked her body.

She finally acquiesced and leaned against his chest, but Grant felt her whole body tense. He heard her take and release deep calming breaths, but didn't think the technique helped. Keeping his end of the bargain, he removed his hand from her soft, full breast only to feel a bolt of lust shoot to his groin.

Bedamned, he didn't need this.

27

The cold wind intensified, and the lass couldn't stop her body from shivering. She wrapped her arms around herself to stay the chill.

Crossing the Eildon Hills near Melrose, he felt her shivers and knew the stubborn woman had to be freezing. It had been warm during the day with the briefest hint of emerging spring, but as darkness fell the chill of a lingering winter returned, and winds had been blowing forcefully for the last hour. He wrapped his *plaide* around her, only to have her shove it off.

"Get this off me," she stormed, not turning to face him. "I need nothing from you." Though clearly setting her mouth in a grim line of determination, she couldn't stop her teeth from chattering.

With a clearly dubious smirk, Grant disagreed. "Aye, lass, you do. 'Tis cold and you are freezing. Now quit arguing and leave my *plaide* be. I know this weather and know what is best for you."

She made a scoffing sound.

Grant tucked his plaide around her again and pulled her against him while he guided his horse along Melrose's treacherous terrain, formerly Roman encampments.

"But—"

"*Wheesht*, woman," he snarled.

"What does that mean?" she snapped. "Do not shout your foreign words at me and expect me to—"

"Silence!" he roared in exasperation, cutting off her protest. He needed to concentrate on their journey and ensure his men's safety, not be arguing with the wisp of a woman in his arms.

"You, sir, are a frustrating man. Why did you not say that in the first place," she grumbled as she unwittingly moved closer to the warmth his body emanated.

"I did," he ground out. He shook his head in aggravation and spurred his mount forward. He suddenly felt like laughing at the indignant look he'd seen on her face when she turned to look up at him.

The warmth of his plaide and the heat of his body made her acquiesce. The combined warmth felt far too good to continue fighting.

After several moments of silence, she piped up, "I want you to know I'm not being quiet because you told me to. I merely have naught further to say to one such as you." Giving him a sidelong glance, she faced forward with a haughty look that told him she thought she'd won that round.

After venting her feelings, despite her obvious fears, she snuggled against his chest and rode toward her unknown fate.

As he shook his head and rolled his eyes heavenward, Grant didn't deign to answer her ridiculous comment. He thought her a stubborn wee spitfire—a soft, curvaceous spitfire.

Though maintaining a grueling pace, he felt her gradually relax. Her even breathing told him she'd fallen asleep. He smiled at her stubbornness.

In the quiet of night, with only the sound of horses' hooves on the newly thawing earth, he held Victoria and urged his mount forward.

Warwick brought his horse abreast. He glanced at the young woman in Grant's arms and with raised brows said, "'Tis not often a prisoner falls asleep in her captor's arms, laddie. The wee lassie may not know it yet, but she trusts you."

"Blatherskite," Grant grumbled as he digested Wick's words. While he protected her from branches looming low in their path, to his mentor he merely added, "She is tired."

"Nay," came Warwick's assertion as he spurred his steed forward, "she trusts you."

A smile formed on Grant's lips as he peered at the stubborn woman in his arms. He felt a strange sense of satisfaction at the implication behind Warwick's words.

When Victoria awoke, the grey light of dawn surrounded her. Soon the rising sun washed the sky with a hazy pink light. A new day had begun. *Blessed Holy Mother*, she thought in alarm, *did I fall asleep? Wrapped in this man's arms?*

"Good morrow, lass," he said as she stirred. "Did you have a nice sleep?"

Instantly awake at the sound of his voice, she stiffened. "I did not fall asleep. I merely..." she responded in a grumpy voice, trying to think of something that sounded plausible, "...rested as you ordered."

Grant smiled. "'Tis glad I am to hear you did as I asked."

"You did not ask. You ordered," she huffed.

The bloody man laughed at her! She ought to kick his kneecap—or someplace higher. He wouldn't be laughing then.

"Then 'tis glad I am to hear you always do as ordered."

To her surprise, they stopped. She wondered if it would be for a moment or if they'd rest. Were these men inhuman? Based on past actions, she felt they wouldn't be considerate enough to let

29

her rest in comfort. Although if honest, the muscular chest she leaned against hadn't been uncomfortable.

Grant dismounted easily, gripped her by her waist, and lifted her from his horse. He slid her down the front of his firm body and held her face in front of his to stare into her eyes. Her limbs ached so badly she stumbled against him when her feet touched the ground. He braced her by wrapping his arm around her waist and pulling her close. Too close. She felt his firm chest against hers and tried to pull away, but her knees buckled. When he drew her close again and chuckled, she shot him a scathing glare. She knew only too well he used his strong, hard body to intimidate her.

With a long, lazy smile, he assisted her away from the horses, his arm intimately encircling her waist. "Rest, lass," he said, releasing her with great reluctance, "and do not move until I return. See if you can work your limbs out and I'll take you into the woods." He rolled his eyes when she shot him a glare. It did nothing to ruin his good mood. He did fancy teasing this woman. "Do not be getting ideas, such as trying to run away. You would not get far, mind. You would do well to heed my words."

He hoped the look he shot her made his message quite clear.

"Do you always speak like such a heathen?" she asked, trying to show no reaction to the implied threat.

"There are no heathens here, woman. Only free Scots." He gave a derisive snort. "Who will settle no longer for being under English rule. Would it be us you speak about?"

Victoria glared without answering, looking all the while at the broad expanse of his chest. It had felt so good to rest against him last eve. Although hard and firm, she'd fit against him perfectly.

She'd never admit such a thing though!

Grant tethered his horse. Young Hamish would take the animals to the nearby burn to ensure they were watered. Glancing sideways at his young hostage, he saw her ignore his warning and inch her way towards the forest. Bedamned if the woman didn't think she could run away! He shook his head in amusement and tried to hide his smile at the winsome lassie's audacity.

Grant turned to speak to Angus. Though shaky when she rose, from the corner of his eye he saw her dash on wobbly legs into the overgrown woods. Angus jerked his shaggy red head towards the woods and Grant nodded.

"I know Angus, I know. Wish you to chase her this time? Och, the woman's tongue is as prickly as a thorn and I have fought her enough this day."

Angus responded with a broad smile. "'Twould be a pleasure." He strolled to the edge of the Midlothian forest and burst into a dash.

When she heard crashing sounds, Victoria glanced behind her and saw Angus. The thought crossed her mind, *not that behemoth again!* She tried to zigzag around trees to evade capture. Seeing the water's edge a short distance in front of her, she increased her speed. She could swim well and hoped these brutes couldn't.

This might be her chance. If she made it to the water's edge, she could perchance get away. As she rounded a pile of leaves, she heard a *whoosh* and abruptly found herself pinned to the ground. The slam of the huge body knocked her breath from her. She couldn't move or breathe and the brute was crushing her ribs!

She released a groan of protest.

Several bone jarring hours later, with distant hills bathed in the setting sun's glow, Grant ordered his men to stop. After tending to their horses and personal needs, the men quarreled.

"Nay," Angus argued. "We must keep going."

Grant's gaze wandered to Victoria. "We cannot. We have pushed her too hard. She must rest the night."

"She is but a prisoner—"

When arguing continued, Grant stood motionless, his eyes moving to take in each man. In a low voice, he said, "We camp for the night. I'll hear no more on the subject."

Dismissing them with a flick of his lashes, he strode to his horse.

The subject was closed.

"We should be safe until the first light of morn. We can cross into Edinburgh in the morn. Do not wander from the wood's safety, and only light one campfire."

They backed off the argument, but grumbled amongst themselves. They stopped to let his prisoner rest. Rubbish.

Victoria scowled as she listened to their discussion. The bloody heathens had her tied to a tree. How dare they? They milled about setting up camp and ignored her. However, she thought that better than having the likes of Angus on top of her. She couldn't think of a part of her that didn't ache from where he'd

31

crushed her earlier. They acted as if she didn't exist—and she imagined they wished she didn't.

Although if truly the case, why didn't they release her? They already had their fun with her. At that another thought sprang to mind. *What else do they plan to do*? She focused her energies on tugging against her bonds, hoping they might have loosened since she tried only moments earlier. They hadn't.

She mumbled, "Oh, Grandmum, what could I have been thinking? You were right. You always are. It certainly wasn't prudent of me to have tried to flee home."

As first stars of evening emerged, she watched as men sat round the fire, crackling flames merrily casting shadows on their weary shoulders. They looked as tired as she felt. She cared not one whit. Hadn't they dragged her along until every bone in her body ached?

Now she wondered if they planned to starve her. She couldn't eat with tied hands. Neither had they offered food. Aggravated at being caught in such a predicament, she again tried and failed to loosen her bonds.

Although tired of having jagged bark dig into her back, she sagged in exhaustion against the tree. Her eyelids drooped, and she started when someone touched her shoulder. She looked into the grey eyes of the brigand whom she'd spent the last day and a half riding with. The men clearly considered him their leader. Why had he forced her to ride with him? At first he'd paid her no heed and now he wouldn't leave her alone. She preferred being ignored.

She peered up at him through lowered lashes. He wasn't bad looking for a bloody heathen. Tall, with dark hair, she considered the breadth of his shoulders. The man exuded power. She'd watched him as he helped to set up the camp. His muscles pulled taut and shifted beneath his shirt as he moved everything where he wanted it. "That matters not at all," she mumbled under her breath. She wanted to be away from him—as far away as possible.

He ignored her mumblings, offered her a trencher after cutting loose her restraining bonds. Though hungry, she wondered if she dared eat. Mayhap they poisoned the food after they ate.

"Nay," she said with a grimace of distaste. She rubbed her chaffed wrists and returned his level gaze. "I want naught from you, except to be released. Indeed, you have wasted enough of my time and I vow 'tis time you ended this farce." She acted with bravado as humor glinted in his eyes.

"You are quite loathsome," she muttered, masking her fear and inner tumult.

He shrugged with indifference and spoke in a dry, testy voice. "It must be true, lass, since you keep telling me that. Howbeit, considering I do not plan to release you, I would eat 'twere I you. Our *cuisine* may not be fancy, but you will not starve. And to answer the question in your bonny brown eyes, nay, 'tis not poisoned. Scots do not waste food."

He set the plate beside her, then returned to his men, carrying himself with the grace of an agile warrior. The men discussed their trek from Edinburgh to Stirlingshire on the morrow.

"I am not hungry," she deliberately commented to his retreating back. Her stomach chose that moment to growl. *Traitor*, she thought and sighed in acquiescence. *Just this one meal.*

She noted in derision that he didn't loosen her ankle bonds. That horrid man thought such a minor detail would keep her from running away? Not bloody likely. First chance she got, she'd be gone and they'd never find her.

How had she gotten herself into such a predicament? Of even more importance, *how would she get out of it?*

Despite vehement protests, Victoria found herself again fastened to the tree. They expected her to sleep like this? Rubbish. She'd never lower her guard enough to fall asleep near *that* man. As soon as she figured out how, she'd run as far from these brigands as possible, even though she had no horse. Galahad had been left at home—as had the belongings she so carefully packed.

She couldn't believe the audacity of this man, giving her the option of sleeping beside him or being tied to the tree. Bloody man said he felt too tired to stay awake ensuring she didn't run away. She'd told him in no uncertain terms, "I would never lie with the likes of you. Not while I have a single breath remaining."

He'd mocked, "And why is that? You think I would satisfy my lust this night with the likes of you? I think not. Which is it, lassie, are you afraid of me—or yourself?" He'd cocked that eyebrow of his in such a condescending manner. She wished she could scratch out his eyeballs.

So now she found herself tied to the tree again. If only...

Too tired to watch her? Well, she'd see about that. As soon as they fell asleep she planned to raise a loud din and wake them.

They'd get so tired of having her around they'd be pleased to see her leave.

She did feel tired, though. Perhaps she'd close her eyes for a moment and then start harassing them.

She fell sound asleep.

Colin poked Grant in the ribs when her head nodded.

"And the lassie said she would not sleep," Grant jokingly told his old friend. "Said she did not trust us enough. She's a feisty lass."

"You going to keep the daffin lassie lashed to the tree?" Colin questioned.

"Nay," Grant responded. He'd noted her exhaustion and the stubborn way she tried to fight sleep. He laughed at her antics of the last day, then turned serious. "Afore I bed down I'll lay her on the ground. 'Tis best we keep her tied, though, in case she wakens. I am tired and wish to sleep. Angus has the main watch, but he will not have time to keep a constant eye on her. She's one stubborn lassie."

He shook his head as he looked at her, his shrewd gaze running the length of her body as she slept. She looked as innocent as a newborn bairn as her head lolled in sleep. He certainly knew that for a falsehood. Hadn't he listened to the sting of her wee tongue this day?

Before he bedded down under the stars, he unlashed Victoria. Och, she may have looked like an angel as she slept, but the soft, lush body he cradled in his arms felt very human. He definitely didn't want his mind taking that track. He imagined she must have driven the young men in her keep wild with desire. Of a certainty she played havoc with his senses. He wanted naught but to run his hands over her lush body. He placed her on his plaide, then retied her wrists before lying beside her.

He hadn't planned to sleep like this. He'd rather be miles away from her curvaceous body, but he had no other way to protect her from the cold. Since he hadn't planned on taking prisoners, he'd brought no extra furs. He knew he shouldn't care if she felt cold, being only a prisoner, yet he couldn't afford to let her get a chill.

At least he tried to convince himself he had no other reason to feel concerned. They still had a day's ride before arriving home, and he didn't want a sick woman to slow him down. Truth be told, he felt a tug of protectiveness. With a stream of lurid Gaelic oaths, he rolled over and wondered for the umpteenth time why he'd brought this stubborn woman with him. She'd proven naught but trouble.

Her scream pierced the night.

Men grabbed their dirks and jumped to their feet. They spun around, searching, but saw no one. She mumbled something that sounded like, "Do not hit me. Pray do not hit me anymore." What ruse did the lass play?

Grant knelt and peered warily at her slumbering face, but found it difficult to see her with no light save that of stars twinkling in the night sky. The moon remained hidden behind clouds. His brows drew together in a frown of bewilderment. The woman appeared to sleep, yet thrashed about. Laying his hand on her forehead, he brushed hair from her face, causing her to still. When he removed his hand, she again thrashed and moaned. He untied her bonds and smoothed the hair from her face. "She's having a bad dream, men. She sleeps." He gravely shook his head.

"Go back to sleep." His gaze remained rapt and his voice somber. To their surprise, he lay back on the ground, stretched to his full length, drew the troubled lass into his arms, and wrapped his plaide around them both. She calmed immediately, and the men, shaking their heads, drifted off to sleep as the stars in the heavens dimmed and morning grew closer.

She fit him perfectly.

Chapter Four

Victoria awoke the next morn as telltale colors of dawn encroached the darkness, surprised to discover herself on the ground rather than tied to the tree. *When had they done that? Who'd done so? Had she really fallen asleep?*

The man called Grant hunkered beside her and released her ankle bonds. "Do I carry you like a sack of wheat, lass, or will you walk with me?" His meaningful look let her know he planned to do just that. She shrugged, giving an indifferent assent, and he helped her rise. She stretched her sore muscles before the blackguard aided her into the woods. He gave her a mocking bow and held her arm with a firm grip.

She felt the full force of strength emanating from his body and thought him such a contradiction—nice one minute, cruel the next.

She felt affronted when he stayed within the copse of leafless trees, but at least he had the decency to turn his back. Considering how inconsiderate he'd been throughout most of the trip, she wondered at this small kindness. Her eyes shifted about the dense forest. Could she escape? She had to make her move soon. She knew not where this dreadful man planned to take her, but instinct warned it would be easier to escape before they reached their final destination.

As though reading her mind, he tried to divert her thinking. "By what name are you called?" He looked at her through narrowed eyes, his face masking his thoughts.

Afraid to answer, she faltered. No one had asked anything personal since kidnapping her. Did they truly not know her identity? If she gave him her name and they didn't already know Blackstone was her father, they might kill her outright. If they did, this might be a test to determine if she'd lie. "Tory," she said, momentarily flustered. "My name is Tory. What's yours?"

The sun hadn't yet had time to warm the earth and it still felt frosty. She wrapped her arms around herself and rubbed them briskly to ward off the chill.

"Tory? I do not believe I heard that afore. 'Tis an interesting name, that," he said with a veiled expression.

"Aye," she responded. A hint of a smile tugged at the corner of her lips even though she tried her best to stop it. "My grandmum told me I am an interesting person."

"Och, aye, lass, you are. That is one of your better attributes."

"I care not what you think of me." She glowered at his choice of words. This man could be so irritating. Obviously he tried to unnerve her. She'd never admit it worked.

"Och, but you should," Grant chuckled in an amused voice.

She had the grace to blush. "Might I ask you a question?" she suddenly queried and tried to ignore his insinuation about her character and the indecent look he gave her. She flicked him a reproachful glare. "Howbeit I noticed straightaway you did not have the decency to respond when I asked your name."

He slanted a smile. This woman fascinated him. Her eyes burned with such anger he thought she looked cross enough to try and slit his throat with his own dirk. Never had a woman spoken to him in such blunt fashion. Most were either afraid of him because they knew him as a Drummond or were busily trying to seduce him to their bed—usually for the same reason. A sudden thought occurred to him. *I wonder how those luscious looking lips would taste?*

He shook off what he considered an absurd thought. "My name is Grant, and to the other, you may ask, but that does not mean I'll answer."

"I am aware of that," she said tartly. "Indeed, 'tis quite apparent you only do whatever you wish. Not what anyone else desires."

With a smirk, he told her, "If 'tis an answer you want, I would suggest you start by being civil. Not your usual tart tongue." Seeing her exasperated frown, he continued, "What is your question? Go careful, mind."

Clearly trying to hide her true feelings, he watched while she pondered what she wanted to say. "You may find it presumptuous of me to question your motives since you seem so certain of yourself, but why did you kidnap me?"

He kept his expression inscrutable. In truth, he tried to focus on what she asked. He seemed unable to get his mind to register anything past the word *desire* she'd used earlier.

He pulled himself from his reverie and chuckled. "Well, now, you will not fancy my answer." He taunted as he saw the question in her eyes, "When you reached up to keep your bonnie wee cap on

37

your head, you revealed a few *bumps* most *laddies* do not have. You gave yourself away whilst trying to keep your wee disguise intact."

Anger smoldered in her eyes.

"As to why I took you, I cannot answer. 'Tis something I have asked myself a hundred times o'er since listening to the bite of your mighty wee tongue."

He muttered sourly, "To you we are heathen Scots. To us, you are murdering English. Leaves us in a quandary does it not?"

"I never murdered anyone," she said in a soft voice and lowered her head so he couldn't see her eyes. She guessed he thought of the massacre weeks earlier. She'd cringed when she heard of purported atrocities. She even heard Edward hadn't stopped his blood bath until he saw a young girl giving birth to a child while being hacked into pieces!

Surely that couldn't be true. No one would do something so heinous, and certainly not her fellow Englishmen.

Of a sudden it dawned on her she'd never discovered who'd been killed. Her father? Her grandmother? Her sister? A feeling of intense dread swept over her and her heart hammered. She had to get back home to check on their safety.

Without thinking, she threw herself at Grant and beat her fists against his chest.

He grabbed her hands in his, a low chuckle in his voice. "My answer was not that bad."

She should pull away and set some distance between them.

She couldn't move.

Not to be deterred, she questioned boldly, "Whom did you kill?" Her fingers toyed unconsciously with the seams of her breeches after he released her hands.

"What speak you about?" he questioned, taken aback by hands that again beat soundly on his chest. He grabbed them and stilled her by wrapping his arms around her. Struck by the beauty of her soft brown eyes that widened with alarm, he looked into her upturned face. She trembled. Why?

"The night you kidnapped me," she whispered. "Whom did you kill?"

"I did not stop to introduce myself nor did I bother asking names," Grant responded with a dry chuckle.

A light breeze wafted through nearby trees and ruffled her long, curling hair.

"But," she hesitated, her voice sounding strange and unnatural as she looked into his stormy grey eyes, "why did you attack in the first place?"

"Och, now," he answered with confidence, "*that* is easy. That black-hearted Earl of Blackstone murdered thousands of people at Berwick." With memories his statement brought back, he loosened his hold on her body. "One of them was my da."

A momentary pain crossed his face.

"My fa...The Earl of Blackstone killed no one!" Victoria yelled in defiance, freeing herself from his embrace. "He told me he did not kill anyone."

Sunlight filtered dimly through the branches as she heard Grant's ruthless laugh. He raised a brow in reaction. "And you believed him? You were on such close terms with the blackguard he would have revealed everyone he murdered?"

She treaded on dangerous ground. She'd come perilously close to revealing her relationship with Blackstone. How could she avoid that and still find out what she needed to know? "Nay, he said naught. I am only a woman after all, and he has no use for women."

Grant took note of the quick rise and fall of her breasts under her large, filthy shirt. "Not even for the usual reasons?" he taunted and saw by the rising blush to her cheeks she understood his intent immediately. Odd, but he found that blush appealing. He gave a slow, sexy smile and ran the tips of his fingers over her lips.

"Oh," she evaded, but her face paled. "Of course, for *that*." She shot an accusing glare. "Is that not the only thing men consider women good for? 'Tis certainly not for companionship or intellectual conversation."

"Keep a civil tongue behind your teeth, woman," he retorted in derision. He detected a note of bitterness—or was it pain? Had Blackstone abused her? Is that why she'd become a lightskirt? The thought flashed through his mind that he wanted no other man to ever touch her. It angered him that someone else may have, although he had no idea why. He tried shaking that disconcerting thought off.

He thought back to the previous night when he held her while she'd had her night dream. Why had her da skelped her? One didn't often have nightmares about spankings. She truly seemed terrified.

Brushing those thoughts aside, his answer was ruder than he meant for it to be. "Aye, lass, women are only good for one thing—

and I bet you're quite good at that. After all, most ladies do not go around wearing breeches in England, do they? Did you live there or were you visiting from the nearest kittle-hoosie?"

Victoria caught her breath and tried to disregard his hurtful words. Brothel, indeed! She wanted nothing more to do with this insufferable man, but must know the fate of her grandmother and sister.

"You did not answer my question," she said quietly. "Know you who you killed? They were my fam...friends." She caught herself before saying family.

"Methinks that is not something you should remind me of, but nay, I know not who died." He looked pensive. "Other than the person I went to kill."

"Who was that?" Her voice caught, and of a sudden she feared making eye contact.

"That Son of Satan, Blackstone, of course," he spat out.

She wondered if he'd accomplished his goal. She tilted her head to look into his warrior's face, but couldn't voice the question. Her blood chilled with the hatred she saw in his eyes when he spoke of her father.

"Were any women killed?" She shouldn't continue asking questions, but she needed to know. She took a deep breath and held it while she awaited his answer.

"You do grave disservice to my person with such a question, woman," he reproved. His sharp tone startled her, yet she breathed a sigh of relief that her loved ones must be safe. "I am not a bloody butcher like your rotten king."

"But," she continued to probe, although knowing it unwise to do so, "I heard Edward only attacked Berwick because a band of English sea merchants were killed by renegade Scots."

Grant paused before they entered another cluster of leafless trees and his watchful gaze searched her face. "And you believe that stramash?"

She shrugged uncertainly as she walked beside him.

"Why so many questions? What was your position at Blackstone Manor?"

Now she'd done it. Asked too many questions and aroused the blackguard's suspicions. She shrugged with what she hoped looked like nonchalance. "No one they considered important. I doubt they will miss me over much."

She'd never let this man know the depth of truth in that statement. She tried to change the subject and blurted, "Did you know the name Grant is Norman? It comes from the word grand, meaning large or tall. I studied names in my free time and find the subject quite fascinating."

Grant looked at her as if she'd lost her mind.

With Wick flanked at his side, the weary group finally approached the castle. Dusk began to settle and the sky appeared multiple shades of grey. Grant inhaled and took a deep cleansing breath of Highland air. He glanced at the surrounding verdant mountains and breathed a sigh of relief. He was home.

And he had his prisoner safely ensconced within the confines of his arms.

Chapter Five

Serving maids and household servants streamed from the castle and threw themselves into the arms of returning men. Her innards swirling with turmoil, Victoria watched in wide-eyed amazement at the bustle of activity. Wherever this was, she had no doubt it was far more fortified than her old home. She should have already escaped. How would she ever flee from someplace this secure? This man would have to release her.

She still couldn't understand why he brought her to the Highlands. And why had his men given her such strange looks? She'd seen their furtive glances throughout the day. What had she done to garner such attention?

Drummond's kinsmen were dumbfounded, and murmurs continued throughout the night. Laird Drummond took someone prisoner? Unbelievable. He killed no one unnecessarily, and *never* took prisoners. He always left people to fend for themselves and rebuild.

Minus a few head of cattle and some horses, of course.

What had he been thinking? And a lassie at that. That made it even more confusing to everyone. They might have felt sorry for her were she not English. Since she was, hate her they would—with all their being.

Grant relaxed and spent his evening listening to the story of Blackstone's rout. He ignored Victoria. Tied in a corner, people paid her scant notice, with the exception of several who kicked rushes on her as they passed by.

Her bruised, reddened wrists hurt, since her bonds were much tighter than they'd been during the trip. Mayhap if she hadn't attempted to run out the door immediately after being brought inside, they might have left her alone. *Too late to contemplate that now*, she grumbled in frustration as she thought of her penchant for acting before thinking things through.

Whisky flowed freely, and everyone drank copiously of *ùsigue bethea*, as she heard the Scots call their whisky. She glanced around the huge stone room with its tall ceiling and observed several serving wenches seemed *extremely* glad her captor was home.

42

Although her home had been a large manor built by early Normans, this room looked larger than any she'd had there. A large painting of a man and woman hung on the grey, stone wall behind the high trestle table. She thought they made a striking couple and noted the imposing man in the portrait appeared an older version of the brute who'd dragged her here.

Weapons were displayed in abundance, although they seemed primitive. To her surprise, several brightly colored tapestries also graced the walls. She decided a woman must have hung them, since they didn't depict battle scenes men were so wont to display.

Grant rose to retire for the night. Advancing, he pulled her to her feet, his words slurred. "Come, lass. The hour grows old."

She thought he'd forgotten about her.

He led her upstairs, guiding her swiftly past spacious rooms. Her eyes barely had time to adjust to the hallway's darkness before he opened a chamber door and pushed her inside a dimly lit room. In rising panic she spun to face him. A chill coursed through her as she looked into his steely grey eyes. "Nay," she yelled with barely controlled fury. "I'll not stay here!" Her entire body shook from anger.

He drunkenly laughed. "You have no choice in where you stay, woman. You are naught but a prisoner, not a well-comed guest, and will do whatever I say. You have no more freedom. Best you get used to that idea." Of a sudden his tone changed to one of irritation. "Now remove your clothes."

"Remove my...?" She backed away. "Nay, I will not!"

Her response no less than expected, her refusal infuriated Grant nevertheless. He moved closer and deliberately eyed her from her toes to the top of her head, aghast at her boy's clothes and all they'd revealed to his men. As planned, he could tell his gaze completely disconcerted her. Her eyes widened in alarm. "No problem, lass. If you do not remove them, I shall."

"Nay!" she screamed and her cheeks filled with color. "I'll not let you rape me! I'll kill you first." Her breath caught and caused her voice to break.

"Rape you?" Grant sneered, laughing without humor. "I want naught to do with your bloody body. I would not bed you if you were the last woman in this castle. The possibility of touching you makes my skin crawl, and the thought of you birthing my byblow simply would not do. I would kill the bairn afore I let a bloody Sassunach be its mam."

43

He took a menacing step forward. "And never threaten my life again or you will regret it."

His grey eyes appeared cold as ice.

His cruel statement stopped her cold. She thought men would bed any woman within arm's length. Men back home certainly had. It was a silly response, but of a sudden she felt offended he didn't want her. "Then why?"

Grant suppressed a yawn and gave an unreadable look. "Because I am muckle tired. Not that I owe the likes of you an explanation. We had a long, arduous journey and I am home now. I wish to sleep. I do not plan to worry about you doing something daft like trying to escape. Now do as I bid."

She eyed him warily and started to say something, but Grant waved her off. "Do not try to deny it. You know you will and I know you will, and I am not in the mood. Late or soon, I plan on taking your clothes. 'Tis merely an observation, but I suspect even you are not daft enough to try escaping naked through my Great Hall with my men sleeping there. They may not have touched you afore, but I assure you if you go down those stairs naked as the day you were born, my men will not hesitate pleasuring themselves with you."

She shuddered and glanced anxiously toward the door.

"The choice is yours," Grant said coolly, "but I am not in a patient mood."

"P...please," she beseeched in a hushed tone, feeling a sense of alarm. Her voice strained with the effort to conceal her fear. "I'll not try to escape tonight. I pr...promise."

"You think me daft enough to take the word of a Sassunach?"

"Then tie me like you did before," she pleaded. Tears pooled in her eyes and desperation sounded in her voice. "Do not make me t...t...take off my clothes."

"That is the only choice you have," came Grant's frigid response. In an instant his smile hardened to a sneer. "Howbeit if you continue aggravating me, I may tie you up *after* you remove your clothes."

Deaf to her pleas, he gestured he expected her to begin to disrobe.

When Victoria didn't move, except to back away, he reached her in two long, quick strides. In an unexpected move he grabbed her shirt. When he forcibly jerked her forward, the neckline tore. Saints knees, he'd not meant to do that. He just wanted to make her realize he meant his words. Instead of backing down, he demanded, "Now, will you remove those filthy breeches or will I? I cannot imagine any decent father letting his daughter dress thusly. Or is this what well dressed Berwick whores wear these days?"

"How dare you!" she shouted. She raised her hand to slap him, but he easily grabbed it and stopped her. "I am not a whore." Although she raised her voice, a look of vulnerability crossed her face. "How many times must I tell you that?"

A fierce expletive broke from beneath his breath. Making a supreme effort to bite back his anger, he ground out, "The rest of your clothes."

In a bid to stall, she looked around the room and noticed moonlight seeping through the arrow slits. It did nothing to lessen the feeling of dread seeping into her bones. "Where am I to sleep?" The large, sparsely furnished area looked a man's room, having no feminine touches. It had a male, musky scent to it. *His scent.*

"On the floor," Grant replied, his face a hard mask. "Where else would a prisoner sleep?"

Victoria saw a pallet on the floor beside the massive four-poster bed.

After what seemed an interminable silence, she motioned toward it. "May I remove my breeches there?"

He felt a hint of a smile tug at the corner of his mouth when he thought of what would soon be revealed. He had to admit he thought her comely. If she only knew everything he told her earlier had been a lie. He wanted nothing more than to bed her.

Her eyes wide in panic, they pleaded dolefully.

"Aye," he answered, raising his eyes heavenward in aggravation. "If 'twill speed this nonsense up. I wish to go to bed. Now!" He saw the indecision in her eyes. Startled to action by his yell, she lowered herself to the pallet and tried to remove her breeches while she attempted to cover herself. Her torn shirt hung down her arms and barely covered her breasts. Enjoying the view, Grant didn't deign to bring that to her attention.

As if she sensed his thoughts, Victoria folded her arms across her chest to shield herself from view, but the motion only pushed the curves of her breasts to greater prominence. He thought it odd she didn't turn her back in an attempt to cover her nudity, but sat fully facing him.

Her eyes searched for a cover when she set the ragged clothes aside. "Might I have a fur?" she questioned tremulously, unable to conceal her terror. Her face ashen with fear, her voice cracked and she fought back tears.

Grant made a supreme effort to tear his eyes from the luscious curve of her breasts. He didn't fancy the thought this wee slip of a girl could affect him so deeply. But affect him she did—clear to his loins. Regardless of what he'd told her earlier, he wanted her so much his body shook. He took a deep breath to steady his turbulent emotions.

"Nay," he retorted icily, trying to break the spell he felt she'd cast over him. "You are a prisoner. You belong to me. Now lie down and quit yammering."

He fisted his hands by his sides and tried to talk over the lump growing in his throat as his eyes slid over her curvaceous body. Actually, it wasn't merely the lump in his throat that had his body in misery right now, since it hadn't been the only thing that had grown while looking at her. He feared sleep would be impossible this night after all.

Victoria shivered. Though pleasantly warm during the day, Highland nights grew cold quickly. She wished she'd had a bath after her long journey, but considering no one bothered to offer her food, she assumed she'd get nowhere asking for a bath.

She wouldn't sleep. *Not with him in the room.* He was as naked as she. She'd seen him—all of him—before casting her eyes downward. She made the conscious decision not to sleep as long as he stayed in the same room, and certainly not while he remained naked!

But he said he didn't want her.

That would make her father happy. Hadn't he told her repeatedly no decent man would ever want her? She knew only too well he'd made certain of that. Several men offered for her, but she hadn't really been interested. Having little love in her life, she always dreamt of finding someone who'd love her like her grandpapa loved her grandmum. Everyone told her men didn't wed for love, but she continued to dream. The few times she thought herself interested, Father sent her suitors away. Then he came up with the idea of wedding her to Bothington. How could her own father hate her so much? She'd done nothing wrong except to be born a daughter. Could he really consider that such a slur on his manhood? She tried repeatedly to make him love and accept her, but he only repaid her efforts with abuse. Offering her to Percival Bothington exceeded anything hateful he'd done in the past. He had to know Bothington would kill her. Thinking on the situation, she guessed it his intent.

She sobbed quietly. *I won't let this place, this man, defeat my spirit. I shall bide my time, then find a way to flee.* No one could keep her where she didn't want to be, and it was painfully obvious from everyones' actions that no one here wanted her. *I shall escape soon, mayhap on the morrow. Tonight I'm just too tired.* She fell into a troubled sleep and lapsed into another troubling dream.

Grant lay motionless, his body in turmoil. Saints toes, he only wanted to sleep. Not be tortured by visions of a winsome lassie with captivating brown eyes and soft brown hair lying on the floor beside his bed. A hint of a smile played about his lips as he thought of her sitting defiantly on his horse. He remembered how she'd felt in his arms.

He heard her troubled sobs a scant while after his preparations for bed. Suddenly Tory screamed. Now what tricks did she play? He tried to ignore her, knowing no one in the castle could hear her. His wooden door was too thick for sounds to penetrate. His immediate guardsman might hear, but he wouldn't interrupt unless summoned. If anything, he'd think Grant enjoying a wonderful romp. *Och, there was that thought again,* he thought in frustration!

She'd quiet down. Yet why did she seem so tormented? He didn't think it had anything to do with the journey here. Had it?

The young woman instantly took that thought away when she mumbled, her dark nightmare having returned. "Nay, Father, do not lock me in here! I did not mean it. Truly. I'll not do it again. I promise. *Please* do not beat me!" Her body wracked with sobs and he could stand it no longer. Slipping from bed, he lifted her and placed her beside him, soothing her with more tenderness than he understood. She calmed, but still shivered. He wondered if she shivered from cold or her tormented thoughts. He covered them both with his fur pelt and stroked her back. Without conscious thought he pulled her closer and cradled her in his arms. Her bottom fit neatly into his groin, and already in a state of semi-arousal from her near presence, he became instantly hard. *Just what I needed*! Again!

Within a few moments her breathing quieted, and blessedly, the next thing he knew, he awoke to morning.

He placed her on the mat without a sound. He'd done nothing but hold her during the night, but something seemed changed.

"What will you do with her this day, Grant?" Warwick had always been as close as a father. He'd also been one of Drummond's closest advisors.

"She is but a prisoner," Grant proclaimed with a shrug. It bothered him he'd again consoled the lass. Why did her torments bother him so? Why did he feel such a need to protect her? *Nay*, he thought, setting what he considered daft thoughts aside. *This day I'll stop this nonsense.* He was determined to ignore the strong urge that pulled him toward Victoria.

"She will work outside." He thought for a moment and shot an amused glance at Wick. "I am certain the dog pens need be cleaned, since no one else wants to do so." He laughed at what he considered a wonderful idea. That would put the lass in her proper place. He only hoped his dogs wouldn't tear her to pieces. He glanced at her and noted how she looked in the rough brown shift he'd provided for her. Much as he hated to admit it, she looked bonny even in the ugly shift. He felt certain its rough material must bother her, since the prissy thing probably wore soft garments back in England.

She'd be too stubborn to utter a single word of complaint. When he awoke this morn and returned her to the floor, he gathered her boy's clothes and burned them. No lass would dress like a lad in his home. Images of all the breeches had revealed of her soft curves flashed through his mind.

"Grant!"

Grant drew himself back to the present and cut Wick off with a lazy grin. "Nay, Wick, I do not wish to hear your comments. She is my prisoner and I'll treat her as such."

"I was not going to talk you out of anything," the wise man said, his tone icy. "Though truth be told, I dinnae know why you brought the gel here, since she seems a stubborn wee fiend. Howbeit, since you did, I only thought to suggest mayhap you should feed her if you dinnae wish her to collapse. I dinnae believe she has eaten since yestermorn when we broke our fast on the road. No one gave her food last night. The lassie must be fair starved."

Grant started at this information and decided Warwick had the right of it. A wicked smile lit his face. "Thank, you, Wick, 'tis a wonderful idea you give me." *This will put the wench in her proper place. No more uncomfortable feelings after this.*

"Wish I to know?"

"Probably not." He moved away from Warwick and back to the table, a smug smile on his face. He motioned for Warwick to bring Victoria. "*Do mi*, lass." When she just glowered, he translated, "To me. There are a few rules you must learn." He arched an eyebrow. "You've not been properly deferential since I came upon your person."

The look on her face clearly indicated she had no intention of changing a thing.

"In future," he said, pointedly ignoring her glare, "you will address me as 'my lord.'"

"Never," she stormed, her face flushed with anger. "You are not—nor never will be—my lord."

The fury in her eyes angered him. Upset at her act of defiance, he ordered, "Sit on the floor, woman. Here!" He pointed to the foot of his chair by the trestle table. His hard fingers on her arm dragged her down in an expression of his displeasure.

Her long, wavy hair fell in disarray about her shoulders as he jerked her down.

Warwick furrowed his brow.

"Wick, have Cook fetch my prisoner food." The old man went to accomplish this request, probably thinking he'd gotten his chieftain to agree.

He returned with a small trencher and informed Grant, "Kitchen staff refused to provide food for a bloody Englishwoman, so I fetched some." He placed it on the table when Grant stopped him.

"Nay, Wick," Grant laughed ruthlessly. "On the floor. Pets eat on the floor."

"Pets?" Victoria and Warwick questioned simultaneously.

Victoria's head shot up and her eyes focused intently on Grant's. She had a feeling she wouldn't fancy his response and a chill of dread shot down her spine.

"Aye," he bluntly answered, a dark gleam appearing in his eyes. "Methinks I could stand having a new dog around."

"Dog?" Victoria and Warwick voiced in unison again. They looked at him with unspoken questions.

Victoria couldn't seem to follow this man's strange train of thought. "What are you talking about? I do not—"

"Aye," Grant said in a voice of pure ice.

"You know, a bi—" he began as Warwick drowned out the rest of the word by yelling, "Grant, nay!"

Men in the Great Hall guffawed. Warwick's glare appeared menacing.

When she found it, Victoria's voice sounded devastated. Color rose furiously to her cheeks and hurt shown in her eyes, as though his hateful remark had been tantamount to a slap on her face. When he saw her pain, he instantly wished he could retract the crude remark, but his men were present and he wouldn't back down in front of them. *She was English after all.*

"You're cruel," she said, her voice sounding hurt. A hint of tears glistened in her eyes, but she refused to give in to them. "But I have been insulted by better than you before this."

He sat unmoving.

"I am not a *dog* and will not eat like one."

He could hear the tension in her voice. She tried to jump up and run, but he reached out and snared her arm, jerking her back. He stared coldly.

"You will eat as I say," he growled in a hardened tone, "or you'll not eat at all."

"Then I'll not eat," Victoria bristled, anger reddening her cheeks, and pulled her arm forcefully from his grasp. She raised her head in a show of defiance. "If you wish to starve me, so be it, but why did you drag me all the way to this Godforsaken country to do so? Why did you not kill me when you found me? 'Tis what you really wished, is it not?"

"Get her out of here," Grant growled, even though he knew she'd balk at his comment. And Warwick had been correct. She needed to eat. He had his pride, however, and wouldn't back down in front of his men.

Not for a Sassunach.

"The dog pens need to be cleaned, woman. Get you to that and do not come out until they are finished." He whirled on her and grated out, "Do it now, or you will pay for your actions." With a roared Gaelic oath, he pushed her toward the door with so much force she tripped.

The roughness with which she was jerked to her feet by his men made her think her arm might have been dislodged.

"Unhand me!" she screamed, anger surging through her. She tried to fight as they dragged her out the door. It did no good.

The men clearly delighted in giving orders and their hands trailed greedily over her body.

One of Grant's men, Archibald, particularly hated anyone English, his parents having been murdered while yet a child. He'd

50

vowed never to forget, and remained most vocal against them. He'd been furious upon discovering Grant brought English *trash* home with him.

He pulled Victoria behind him with so much force she repeatedly fell to her knees. Too soon they reached the area where the dogs slept.

"Enough of this tripe," he glowered as hatred emanated from every pore of his being. "Get you to work, woman." Incensed, to torment her further he bent and picked up a handful of waste and threw it at her.

"Is that enough of a hint, *wench*," he snapped as he towered over Victoria. Making use of the well-known English term, he sneered, "Or should we rub some over you so you know exactly what you are supposed to clean? Then again," he slapped his knee and laughed uproariously, "you will never finish 'til you get rid of yourself. I would be willing to do *that*, mind." Men guffawed while he pushed Victoria into the first pen, causing her to land on her hands and knees, skinning them.

For a moment Victoria felt her courage falter when she saw the wicked gleam in his eyes. This man would go out of his way to inflict all manner of cruelty upon her. She needed to remain alert around him at all times. He made no effort to hide his derision.

She moved within the pen and began to clean with the few supplies available. For the most part she had to use her hands, which was her captors' intent. She paused between pens to mop her brow, then moved between the areas as guards followed and made lewd comments. These men were as disgusting as conditions in the animal sleeping area.

Growling at her approach, many dogs didn't seem pleased to find an interloper in their pens, and several bared their teeth. She tried not to show fear and spoke quietly when a huge dog drew near. It tilted its head and stared while the uproarious laughter of nearby men roared in her ears at what they considered daft comments.

She glumly wondered how many pets these people owned. Tired and hungry, at the nooning meal her guards took turns entering the Great Hall. Not once did anyone mention bringing her food or tell her she could go inside, although they remembered to jeer at her. She'd never heard so many obscenities and she'd certainly heard her share from her father's men.

As the sky darkened, she feared she might have to remain outside. The brisk wind heightened and blew across her face and through her loosely tied hair. She shuddered.

As she neared exhaustion, the man she remembered as Warwick came to escort her inside. Still and silent, she watched his approach. He had such a kind visage she had to remind herself he was naught but a Scot. After he led her into the kitchen, he sat her down in the corner, brought her a full trencher. "Eat, lass." He reminded her, with a not unkind smile, "'Twould be in your best interests to not be seen by our chieftain in the Great Hall right now if you wish to eat."

The thought of eating without first washing was abhorrent, but she decided to do so before he changed his mind. Hungry and tired, with a small sigh she let her body begin to relax.

For some unknown reason she thought this man had been named appropriately. He did seem to be a defender and champion. She didn't know why she trusted him, but she did. The weak smile she gave him for his kindness held an edge of exhaustion.

While Warwick urged her to eat, Cook stood behind him and ranted. "I want naught to do with this filthy Englishwoman. Remove her before her English stench soils my kitchen."

With that reminder, Victoria turned to Warwick. "Where might I have a bath?" Since she'd skinned her hands and knees repeatedly being shoved to the ground, she felt certain if she couldn't cleanse the areas they'd become infected. Her captors might not mind that, but she would.

Kitchen servants broke into gales of laughter and tormented, "Faugh, the Princess has want of her evening bath." They bowed to her and mocked, "And what else might we get thee, Princess? Should we wipe your shoes with our hair?" Cook stopped a moment before continuing. "Och, our mistake, *Princess*. That would mean you had shoes."

With a small sigh of frustration, she tried to ignore their hateful comments.

During this taunting, Grant summoned Warwick. He knew well the cruel comments, as well as the physical abuse, she'd received this day had taken a toll, even though she tried to not show it. Though she looked guarded and uncomfortable, the lass had impressed him with her spirit. Warwick thought she showed a great deal of courage thus far. She'd certainly held her own against endless verbal cruelty.

Warwick remained as unsure why Grant brought the lass to Drummond Castle as did everyone else. Since he had close ties emotionally to the young man, he had a vested interest in seeing which of the two willful young people relinquished their stubbornness first. He began to think Grant had met his match.

Chapter Six

Ready to depart the Hall, Grant looked for his prisoner. Not seeing her, he questioned Warwick, "Where is the lass?"

With an indifferent shrug, Warwick responded, "I left her in kitchen when you summoned me." When Grant glared at him, the old man returned the glare in kind. "The lass had to eat, mind. I'll not be party to you starving her to break her spirit."

Grant ignored that comment and headed to the kitchen. He saw his prisoner nowhere and turned to Cook, a bald massive bulk of a man. "Where is my prisoner?"

"Och, m' lord," the burly cook began, "the mighty Princess wanted her royal bath. Thinks herself too good for the likes of us, mind." He continued with a wicked laugh, "So, Archibald has been kind enough to accommodate her request like the proper good English trash she is."

Grant frowned. By the saints, he couldn't imagine anyone fetching in a tub and enough hot water for a bath without his direct order. Most still thought bathing would make them ill.

"Where is she then?" Grant sent Cook a chilling look, glanced around the huge kitchen, but saw a tub nowhere.

The burly man could obviously no longer contain his glee. He threw back his head and laughed, revealing several missing teeth. Hands holding his large stomach, Cook chortled, "Why down at the loch, mind. We thought that fitting." His eyes were as cold as his smile and gleamed with a triumph he made no effort to conceal.

Grant rushed down the winding path to the loch. What could his men be thinking sending the lass there? With the Highlands just getting over their cruel winter months, she'd freeze. His men were used to such weather, but the woman might catch a lung ailment and die. He conceded they probably hoped that would happen.

His pace quickened.

With few stars out this eventide, it was dark. He hoped the lass wouldn't slip in the loch and *badh*. He hadn't brought her here to have her drown. Unbidden, the question came to mind, *why did you fetch her?*

54

Grant shook off that disconcerting thought, hurrying forward. The loch could be dangerous at night, and he didn't know if Archibald would help if she slipped or try to make such an accident occur.

The lass sat shivering on the bank. Her lips quivered and her arms were wrapped around herself in what had to be an unsuccessful effort to ward off the cold. He saw Archibald lazed against a tall, willowy tree. The man had been brooding and ill tempered all day, and Victoria's presence could be the only cause.

"What are you doing, Archie?" Grant demanded as he bent to help Victoria stand. Sweet merciful heaven, the wee lass shook so hard he had to steady her. Archibald must have thrown her in the loch. Her shift was drenched. He couldn't imagine her being daft enough to walk into the water on her own. Not with its freezing temperature.

"Why, staring at our beautiful sky this fine even," the tall, sullen man said. Although too dark for Grant to see his expression clearly, he heard the smile in Archibald's voice. "I thought the wench might enjoy a view of a fine Highland sky."

"As she froze to death?" Grant hotly retorted. He grew angrier by the minute. Archibald didn't respond, but shook his head. Grant swore violently. He glared at Archibald, but said nothing as he gathered the lass into his arms and wrapped his plaide around her. Her wet shift clung in a most revealing fashion to her long, shapely legs and he tried to keep her as warm as possible while he rushed her back to his keep. He wouldn't carry her past his men looking like *that*.

"Put me down!" she stormed through chattering teethd. "No one has carried me in years and I do not need you to start now." She tried to look fierce, but shivered too much for it to have the desired effect.

"And have you freeze to death taking your sweet time returning to my keep?" Grant retorted as he lengthened his strides. "I think not."

"I need no—" she stubbornly began and tried to break free from his hold. His grasp remained too firm to be broken.

"*Wheesht,* woman," he cut in as he ignored her demands and struggles.

Grant stormed past his men and went to his bedchamber.

After setting her on the floor, he knelt on one knee beside the hearth to kindle the peat fire. Firelight soon danced and flickered against the stone walls. He rose to get drying cloths, then returned and gently dried her arms and face while the heat from the fire warmed her. Her glance slid to him and she tensed when he pushed her kirtle up to dry her legs. She looked up several times with questions in her eyes, but never spoke. She said nothing since her initial protestations over him carrying her.

He had to remove her wet kirtle, but knew she'd panic. Giving her no time to react, he leaned her forward and pulled the raiment over her head.

Before she could fight him, he wrapped her within a blanket. A broken moan escaped her lips and she bit her lower lip to try and stay her tears. Failing, her eyes widened and two teardrops rolled down her cheeks. Pulling her to his chest, he cradled her in his arms until warmth from the fire and his body made her drowsy. Her eyelids sagged beneath the weight of her fatigue and she fell asleep ensconced in his embrace. His body, on the other hand, remained vibrantly awake from her squirming in his lap.

He lowered her to the pallet. Since he'd cradled her soft body, he again felt a familiar stirring. In an attempt to ignore it, he moved away before the urge to pull her back into his arms became too strong to ignore. Instead, he hunted for a fur pelt in his wardrobe and covered her, then put as much distance as possible between them. He snuffed out the flickering candles and lowered himself to his bed. There remained no question in his mind it would be another lengthy night.

What about the girl stirred him so? Grant admitted he wanted to tangle with her atween the sheets. Mayhap it had been too long since he bedded a woman. He chuckled. Nay, that wasn't the problem. He never had a shortage of willing partners to his bed, although lately no one interested him.

Until now.

It seemed as if he'd searched for something special, but hadn't found it. Maybe because he knew not for what he searched. Perhaps being home would change that. Grant realized after years of being away, he didn't want to travel anymore.

Every day he ensured Victoria received jobs no one else wanted around his keep. Unconsciously he tried to see how far hc could push her before she broke. Thus far it hadn't happened and he'd been amazed at her endurance.

Several times she gathered herbs to use on the cuts and scrapes she inevitably obtained. These barbarians did seem determined to push and shove her. It seemed they'd made it their purpose to torment her.

Victoria quickly learned not to balk, since it only made things worse. Gradually the guards allowed her more freedom and didn't remain on her heels to taunt her. She mused they must be getting bored. The novelty of making her life miserable seemed to be wearing off.

The last vestige of winter seemed unwilling to release its tenacious grip when she again found herself outside cleaning dog pens. Even Grant's men hadn't wanted to remain in the freezing cold. When Archibald headed inside to the warm keep, he ordered, "Stay outside and continue cleaning." He sneered when he took the light cloak his chieftain had given her as well as her shoes. He hated her, but it seemed he refused to be the one that let her escape.

As the nooning meal drew to a close, Grant glanced around the Hall. Not seeing Victoria, he inquired to her whereabouts. An awkward silence followed.

"She is outside," a red haired man named Torchil finally informed him with an overabundance of smugness, "as you ordered."

Grant again glanced around his Hall. "Who guards her? Everyone is inside."

"She is alone." Torchil gave an unconcerned shrug.

Grant shot to his feet and started toward the front door. "Alone? And you did not think the daffin lassie would run away?"

"Nay," came a nasty chuckle. "I am certain she'll not go anywhere."

Spinning to face the young man, Grant's eyes narrowed. "Why?"

"Because Archie took her shoes," Torchil declared with an emphatic nod of his head. "Even she's not daft enough to run away in this weather with naught on her feet."

"What?" Grant exploded and strode to the oaken door of his keep. "She'll freeze to death." He threw open the heavy door and angrily strode outside. When he didn't see Victoria, he rushed over to the pens and scanned the area. The thought flashed through his mind he'd do serious bodily harm to his men if she escaped.

He wouldn't let her go yet.

He heard sniffling and headed in the direction of the sound. He glanced inside the pen, saw her crouched in a corner. She looked miserable and shook all over. To his amazement, the young

57

woman wasn't alone. Four of his dogs—his vicious attack dogs—were silently curled around her. To warm the lass?

He'd heard rumors the daffin lassie spoke to his dogs like they knew what she said. It appeared they might.

Grant cursed and didn't bother with the gate. He placed his hand atop the pen and vaulted himself over in effort to reach Victoria. His dogs rose, teeth bared, until they recognized him. Did his animals truly protect the lass?

He bent and scooped her in his arms, then kicked the gate open with his booted foot. He strode toward his Great Hall, fuming. His woman could have frozen to death. She didn't even have on the cape he'd given her. Did his men hate her that much?

Through chattering teeth she said, "I am all right."

Grant said nothing as he looked at her. She didn't look all right.

He swore profusely as he entered the Hall. "Fetch my personal tub and buckets of hot water to my chamber." The stormy look on his face as he took the stairs two at a time told his men they'd best fetch the water without delay.

Grant wrapped Victoria in a bed fur until enough water had been poured into the tub. "Leave," he growled, dismissing everyone. He slammed the door shut before helping her to her feet. He removed the fur and her shift. Her teeth chattered so hard he doubted she could have protested.

When he placed her in the water's warmth, her eyes shot open. Grant hoped it wasn't too hot. "Your temperature must return to normal to ward off frostbite."

After he submerged her in the tub, he sponged water over her. She didn't protest, but watched his every move.

Gently leaning her forward, he washed her back. He'd not paid attention to it before. Blessed Saint Michael, someone had lashed it. He opened his mouth to query her, but when he skimmed his fingertips over the scars, she tensed. Though questions burned in his mind, he said nothing. He'd discover his answers soon enough.

Within hours the young woman looked flushed and began coughing. Her forehead smoldered with fever when he felt it.

Cursing, he left his chamber and stormed down the hallway to his mother's old herbary. He grabbed a single torch to light his way. His mother had been a gifted healer, and he knew he'd need her medicaments. He stopped before entering the room. Took a deep breath. He hadn't been here since her death. With no windows, the room looked darker than he remembered. The lone torch did little to light the room.

He'd never paid much attention to what herbs his mother used to help people, but the one treatment he remembered was for an ailment such as this. Duncan MacThomas had been his best friend as a young lad. He'd fostered with Grant's family while very young. He smiled at the memory. A tall, skinny boy, Duncan had bright blue eyes and dark hair. To see him now, one would never believe he'd been a sickly child. Grant's mother often made poultices for Duncan's chest to draw out his cough, as well as other herbs to lower his fever. It being the only illness he knew how to treat, he determined to do just that for the woman in his bed.

She would *not* die!

Before returning to his solar, he stopped for a tankard of ale, knowing it would be a long night. Furious his men had mistreated the lass, he sorely needed a drink.

For days she tossed about with fever, talking in her sleep. He felt guilty listening, but wanting to know more about her, listen he did. He even asked questions and at times he thought she answered, but whenever he mentioned her back she babbled about her father.

Relieved to discover her fever had broken, he felt her forehead when her eyes opened. Taking no chances, he sponged her with mint water to ensure her fever wouldn't return. He looked at her anxiously since the pale cast of her cheeks still worried him. She was quick to blush when upon discovering she wore nothing beneath the thin covering. He saw the mortification in her eyes, but continued to sponge her body.

Throughout her recovery, he rarely left his chamber. Once when he broke his fast, he informed his men, "In future, the lassie remains inside. I did not fetch her here to torture her." He spun on his heel and returned to his bedchamber before anyone could utter a word, although many asked themselves —*why had he brought her here?*

The only other person he allowed to treat Victoria was Warwick. Still afraid she'd die, he didn't want her alone, and although he tried his best, at times sleep won out. Warwick tended her faithfully, although he left the personal care to his young chieftain. Grant thought his friend tender with the young woman— as tender as a gruff old man with battle calloused hands could be.

When she felt well enough to sit, Victoria said, "Thank you for saving my life—again. You seem to do quite a lot of that." With a pointed look she added, "Although I must confess, if you'd let me go you'd not need do so anymore. Indeed, your men seem determined to kill me, yet you seem just as determined to save me. Why?"

Unable to come up with an appropriate response, he merely grunted, "Hrrmph!"

Victoria's eyes flashed in indignation. "What do you want of me?"

He had no answer.

When Grant allowed Victoria to go downstairs, he carried a fur to wrap around her. Caring not what his men thought, he refused to risk her having her relapse.

Victoria entered the Hall and shivered. He escorted her to the hearth and moved a chair closer.

"Nay, I but wish to sit before the hearth to warm up." She sat with the fur wrapped around her and was soon surrounded by four burly dogs. They encircled her and lay with heads raised on alert, closely protecting her.

Grant wasn't pleased to witness this. These were his attack dogs. Why were they guarding his prisoner?

A female dog ambled into the Hall. She recently had a litter and her pups were finding their feet. The dog headed to the hearth's warmth, her pups close at her heels. As she stretched before the fire, five pups nursed. The tiniest dog tried to work his way in, but the larger pups butted him out. Looking forlorn, he turned toward Victoria.

She smiled at their antics.

He scurried over to her, repeatedly tripping over his own feet. Victoria leaned over to scoop the animal up and squealed with delight when he licked her chin. Grant glanced around the Hall at this unexpected sound of happiness and noticed his men watched as she cooed and giggled at the puppy. Their glances didn't look as malevolent as usual.

Grant had never seen Victoria react like this, usually remaining reserved around his men. Eyes alight with excitement, the smile she gave the pup dazzled everyone. She looked like a child with a prized toy.

Unaware her actions caused a stir, Victoria questioned, "What will happen to the puppies?" Freya, the pup's dam, came closer and snuggled beside her. Reaching for the tiny pup, she placed it beside his dam so he could nurse.

She leaned down to place her face by Freya's and murmured, "You did a good job little mother. Your babies are beautiful." She rubbed her hand over the dog's furry head, petting her with a light touch.

Grant shrugged. "Most will go to families in my keep. The little one you had will be drowned."

"Nay," Victoria yelled in shock, shifting her eyes from Grant to the pup and back again. "You cannot kill him!" Eyes pleading, she begged, "Please do not let that happen. He is but a babe."

Grant sounded rueful. "'Tis but the runt, lass. Colin is in charge of our dogs and usually takes the runt to the loch." He didn't understand her upset. They didn't want tiny dogs to suffer, and Colin thought it most humane. As she'd seen, runts rarely got an opportunity to suckle.

"Nay." With a horrified look she gathered the tiny, furry animal into her arms. "I'll not let you do that. I'll care for him myself." Her eyes pleaded with his. "Please, Grant, let me have him. I swear I'll take care of him."

"But, lassie..." he protested and rubbed his jaw. She'd never used his name before.

"Let me keep him," Victoria begged as her eyes welled with tears. "I never had a pet of my own. Please..." She tried to rise with the pup in her arms, but still too weak, she started to sway.

He caught the stubborn woman in his arms, pulled her close and held her against him long after it became obvious she regained her footing.

Breasts pressed firmly against his chest, Victoria's breathing soon became as ragged as his. What was he thinking? This woman was his sworn enemy—his prisoner. Yet only one thought coursed through his mind—he wanted to kiss her.

What an absurd thought.

Something wet against his arm returned Grant to the present. He chuckled as he glanced down. The wee pup happily licked his arm. He quickly regained his wits and moved Victoria away. What hold did this young woman have over him?

And what could she be thinking? He'd never consider such nonsense about keeping a dog.

When he saw the glow in her eyes, Grant didn't have the heart to naysay her. He sighed in resignation. "All right, lassie. You may keep the wee mutt."

Several men who sat at the large trestle table exchanged glances and shook their heads. What had Grant done? Whoever heard of a prisoner being given a pet?

When he saw her tire, he removed the animal from her arms, set him down on the rushes and ordered, "Go you up the stairs to take a kip." He reached to pick her up, but she evaded his hold and scooped the small dog up again.

"Lass—"

"Nay, Grant," she interrupted. "I'll not leave my puppy downstairs." She turned and glowered at Colin. "Something might happen to him if I am not around." Her implication couldn't be mistaken.

"Woman, I will not have an untrained dog in my bedchamber," Grant reasoned as he rubbed his forehead, concentrating. "Put it down."

She gave an endearing smile. "If he wets in your chamber, I'll clean it."

"Not *if*," Grant grumbled, "you mean *when*." Though he tried to out-stare and intimidate her, he succeeded on neither account.

Brow raised, he growled, "Woman, if my men disobeyed my order like you have, they would not live long enough to boast about it. Do not mistake my hospitality for weakness."

Biting her lip, the stubborn woman met his stare and refused to set the dog down.

Grant rolled his eyes and grumbled under his breath, but picked Victoria up without another word. He vowed to address her disobedience apace.

A winsome smile spread over her face as he carried her upstairs. She cradled the tiny dog in her arms and stammered, "Thank you m...milord."

Grant's head swiveled in surprise, but he said nothing. A smile of pleasure crossed his face and he promptly forgot about correcting flaws.

The next morning she rushed her puppy outside, her praise profuse when he did what she hoped. She didn't plan to mention he'd done the same thing in Grant's bedchamber. She only hoped Grant hadn't noticed.

Grant insisted she rest, so she took advantage of the time to play with her pup. He laughed when she told him she named him Lancelot.

"Och, is he your knight in shining armour?" Grant teased.

She stiffened. "Nay, I believe not in faery tales." She averted her gaze and looked at the floor. "My father made quite certain no prince or knight would ever want me."

She picked up Lancelot and hurried away, thinking it a perfect time to change those wet rushes.

Grant frowned as he watched her depart. What had the gel meant by that strange comment?

Chapter Seven

The early April day dawned cold and rainy. Rather than go outside to the lists, the area in every keep where warriors did their daily training, Grant let his men remain inside after breaking their fast. They chose to stay in the Great Hall to listen to their neighbor. A tall, strapping young man with unruly bright red hair, Geordie and his companions were offered ale and a hearty meal.

"May God give you a good day, Laird Drummond." He gratefully accepted a full tankard and took a hefty swallow of ale.

"What news?" Grant questioned.

His mouth full of food, the young man said, "Edward's bloodlust was not assuaged after Berwick. He sent John deWarrene to conquer Dunbar." He brushed crumbs from his face before continuing. "Men guarding Dunbar Castle were ready for a siege, Laird Drummond, but their main army remained outside its walls at Spottsmuir." He took another sip of ale to wash down his food. "Edward's lackey, Warrene ignored the castle and fought troops outside. Our men fought bravely, but they hurled themselves at English troops and Welshmen retaliated with thousands of arrows."

The young courier steepled his fingers and shook his head in disgust. "Da said the Earls of Atholl and Mar dealt the death knell." Grant's men looked puzzled, but he continued, "Our men couldn't win without their forces, and the Earls pulled out at the last minute."

Grumbles sounded throughout the Hall. Grant tried to silence them so the courier could finish his tale.

"Confused, our men wound up trampled by Warrene's cavalry. Da said our men were so upset after the earls' defection they swung their swords in anger rather than precision, making it impossible for them to win. Da said over ten thousand Scots were slaughtered on the battlefield. Many of those injured were lying helpless on the field before being massacred. He sent me to warn you, since surely we'll take up arms against the dastardly English again."

While the young man relayed his information, another courier rushed into the inner bailey. "I have an urgent message for Laird Drummond."

Grant told his guard, "Admit him."

As soon as he stepped inside the Hall, the man doubled over, trying to catch his breath. "Laird Drummond, I bear evil tidings." As every eye in the hall swerved to him, he nervously shifted from foot to foot before delivering his chilling message. "Baliol's surrendered!"

Grant's men leapt to their feet and the young man valiantly tried to catch his breath. When he finally sat, he calmed himself enough to relay, "King John surrendered to the English after the battles of Berwick and Dunbar."

The sense of unease in the Hall seemed palpable.

The distraught courier reported, "Baliol and Edward met at Montrose. In front of English and Scottish courtiers, Edward had Baliol's coat of arms ripped from him and thrown on the floor to ensure Baliol's humiliation." The young man reached for the cup of whisky handed him. "They *escort* him now by sea to London's bloody Tower."

The overwhelming silence in the room sounded deafening.

The young man rose. "Thank you for your hospitality. I must depart posthaste and continue to relay my sad news. 'Tis imperative everyone knows." Grant had Alexander show the weary man to the door and bid him Godspeed.

When the tumult in the Hall subsided, Grant swore at the newest revelation and turned to his neighbor and escorted him to the Hall's front door. "Georgie, tell your da we'll be ready to ride whenever you need us. 'Tis our responsibility and privilege to fight for our freedom."

After the massacre in which his father had been murdered, the thought crossed Grant's mind that he shouldn't be surprised at the English's horrific actions. "I regret nobles have been taken prisoner. English always keep high ranking Scots alive so they can torture them later. We must free them as soon as possible."

Geordie'd reported Sir Andrew deMoray of Bothwell and his son, Andrew, were hostages. Andrew the younger was a new acquaintance and had recently gotten married. Grant met Andrew through Duncan, and the three became fast friends.

Whenever together, Andrew animatedly mentioned his beloved lady wife. When he received the invitation, Grant attended the wedding along with Duncan. Andrew told everyone, "I hope to begin a family right away."

Being the best strategist Grant knew, Grant wanted to meet with Andrew as soon as possible to map out battle plans. With Andrew's current incarceration, he'd first have to rescue his friend.

Busy with visiting couriers, no one paid attention to Victoria. Grant had her scrubbing walls in his Hall. With the torrential wind and rain, she felt surprised he didn't have her doing something outside, so she might drown.

She hadn't been told Grant no longer allowed her outside.

Several times during the courier's report, Grant's men glanced in her direction. They didn't trust her and probably wondered if she could hear the courier. She had no intention of revealing she could. Clearly this version was slanted and incorrect. Englishmen would never do such horrendous things.

Too soon the visitors departed.

She felt bone tired when she finished cleaning the wall, but she'd wanted to stay and hear everything. She carried the filthy water to the great portal door, thinking to dump it and return for a brief respite.

She didn't reach the door before Archibald saw her. He strode over and peered into the tub.

"Where go you, wench?" His eyes narrowing, he growled out the English term as an epithet.

"I'll be right back, Archibald." Victoria rolled her shoulders in an effort to hold the heavy tub. "I assure you I am not trying to run away. I'm too tired and am merely discarding this." She nodded to indicate the water.

"And waste good water?" he jeered, pushing her back into the room.

Victoria blew out a frustrated breath and answered with a patience she didn't feel. "Archibald, this water is filthy. 'Twould serve no good purpose to anyone. Let me pass. I vow, you are the most difficult man I ever met."

In spite of her protests, he blocked her path. With a low, guttural chuckle and a gleam of hate in his eyes, he said, "You know you'll want your damnable bath again this eve. Might as well get it over with now."

He stepped forward with a menacing gait, took the huge tub effortlessly from her hands, and dumped the murky water over her head.

Victoria sputtered in indignation under the vile onslaught. Without thought to repercussion, she lowered her head and ran

66

headlong into Archibald's stomach, knocking the breath from him and causing him to stumble backward.

He released a howl of fury and grabbed her by her wet hair before jerking her around. He pulled her arm and twisted it behind her.

She screamed and feared he might break it.

"Stars!" the angry man ground out. His lips close to her ear, he threated, "Do not ever attack me again, slut."

Victoria felt his massive chest heave in anger as he pulled harder on her hair and arm. He released her by flinging her so hard she flew into the opposite stone wall, sending white flashes behind her eyes and the remainder of her body exploded in pain.

"Do you ever touch me again, woman, I'll kill you!"

Before she passed out, she saw him storm away, a stream of curses resounding through the Hall as his expression darkened with each step.

From a corner of the room a small girl stared spellbound at the unfolding scene. She witnessed the entire act of cruelty.

When Victoria didn't rise, the girl cautiously approached the other children. It was a momentous step for Annie, since she always tried to remain unnoticed. But this was important. She got someone's attention by pulling on her arm. With frantic motions she motioned to Victoria, causing all the children to rush to the unconscious woman.

Soon men joined the children to see what the commotion was. Warwick joined the group of gathering men, and shook Victoria in effort to awaken her. When she didn't budge, he told the children, "Fetch me a bowl of water."

Grant walked into the Hall as Warwick splashed water on Victoria's face. He crossed the Hall and pulled a face at the sight that greeted him.

When Victoria tried to sit, she became dizzy. She held her head in her hands to still the spinning room and her stomach lurched. Before she could stop herself, she threw up.

"What is amiss?" Grant asked, backing away. When no one answered, he faced her. "What is wrong, lass? Why do you not get up? Why are you on the floor?"

From the corner of her eye she saw Archibald return and lounge against the wall in outraged silence, his lip drawn back in a glare of hatefulness. She inhaled sharply and diverted her eyes. Doubled over in pain, she stammered, "I f...fell, milord, and hit my head. Naught else." Her wary eyes flew back to Archibald, whose own eyes revealed pure hatred.

Though she tried to be discreet, Grant perceived the direction her eyes traversed and knew she hadn't told him the truth. To her he elevated one brow. "Best you be more careful, lass. You would not wish to injure yourself more. Hie you up the stairs and rest now."

Victoria rose stiffly and her knees buckled. Warwick shot out an arm to steady her. "I must put the cleaning supplies away, but—"

"Woman," Grant growled in exasperation, his frown remaining formidable. "I said go up yon stairs. Do not argue."

"But—"

"Now!"

Eyes wide, she turned and fled upstairs, her small dog scampering at her heels. Warwick watched from the bottom of the stairway. Since she had difficulty maintaining her balance, she swayed awkwardly as she mounted the steps at a slow pace. If she lost her balance again, she wondered if the tenderhearted old man planned to break her fall. When she reached the top landing without falling, Warwick rejoined the others in the Hall.

Grant said not a word, but glared in outrage.

Finally he broke the silence.

"We must get some things clear." He began with great deliberation, "When yon lassie arrived she had bruises on her body and a split lip. Though not pleased to see them, I could do naught about what happened afore she came into my care. Nor did I know their cause." His ferocious look encompassed everyone in the room. "I can do something now. Somehow the lass keeps getting injured. It could be she is clumsy and falls—like she said she did this day. The alternative is she's being treated none too gently. That might account for bruises I continually see. Mayhap she is being grabbed rather than watched."

From the rear of the room Archibald shouted, "How can we be too rough? She is naught but your prisoner." No humor showed in the tilt of his lips.

Grant maintained his patience. "Aye, you have the right of it. She is a prisoner, but she is *my* prisoner—not yours. I told you to watch her, not abuse her."

His look of fury included every man in the room. "I do not want her to escape. That requires she be watched, but it does not require force. So, let me make myself perfectly clear one last time. From now on she had best have no new bruises."

When no one uttered a word, Grant cocked a brow. "Comprehend you my intent?" His tone of voice left no doubt in anyone's mind what he meant.

From the back wall Archibald again growled, "She is naught but English trash."

Grant spun and glared at his friend. "She is *my English prisoner*, Archibald. In future no one save me will punish her." He narrowed his eyes. "I strongly suggest you heed my warning."

Glaring eye-to-eye with Grant, Archibald spat in the rushes and walked away.

"Archie!"

"Och, aye, Grant, I understand your intent—and I dinnae fancy it one bit." The harsh exchange between the two men hung in the air, but Archibald never broke his stride as he left the room.

That eve Victoria sat on the floor near Grant, her food served in a small trencher. Though he didn't allow her a knife, he fashioned a utensil she could use from a small twig, and made no more disparaging comments about pets.

She smiled and petted her small dog as it lay dutifully at her side.

While men discussed the couriers' visits, Victoria flexed her neck. Despite the brief respite Grant allowed earlier, her neck obviously still ached.

Ever aware of her presence, Grant saw her movements. He turned his chair, stretched his legs in front of him, then pulled her between his legs. Not breaking conversation, he checked her neck and shoulder.

She glowered and pulled away. "Stop that. My neck hurts and I have a blinding headache."

"I know, lass." Grant frowned. He'd only meant to help. "That is why I—"

"I do not want you to touch it. I need no one to—"

"Woman! *Haud your wheesht*," Grant roared to silence her midsentence. "Do not tell me one more time you do not need anybody. Must you argue with everything everyone tries to do for you?"

He muttered, "I never met a more ornery woman in my entire life." He grabbed the stubborn woman and pulled her between his legs again, ignoring her protestations. "Now be silent. I wish not to hear another word out of your mouth."

"Is that what those strange words 'hud whatever' means? Silence?" she badgered. "Why not say what you mean instead of making people guess what you're saying?"

"It means keep quiet—or in your case, shut your mouth, woman," Grant retorted in aggravation. How dare she make fun of his Gaelic?

"How dare you?" she yelled in exasperation. "I vow, I cannot believe the audacity of..."

Grant pushed hard with his thumb on a particularly painful area, which caused her to take a deep breath as pain shot through her neck. When she glared up at him, Grant probed her neck and shoulder as if he hadn't been interrupted.

"My mam did this for me when I injured myself as a lad." He chuckled and ignored the fact she railed at him. "Which happened quite often I might add. It seemed to help at the time. 'Twill help you, too, if you will but trust me for once and quit your infernal fighting." With that he massaged her neck.

Victoria gasped from the pain and instinctively grabbed his leg. Taken aback, Grant couldn't stop himself from laughing. Not able to turn her head, she shifted her eyes to glare at him. "'Tis not funny, milord. It hurts."

"I am not laughing at your pain, lass. I would never do that. I laugh at how familiar you've become." Grant chortled as Victoria made a face and frowned. "I did not think you would accost my person in front of my men."

Still she frowned. *What did this man mean?*

She found out soon enough when Grant continued to laugh. "Your hand, lass. You have rucked my kilt up with the firm hold you have on my body."

When she realized her hand clenched Grant's bare thigh, she moaned in shock and withdrew her hand in humiliation. She'd never in her entire life been so forward. What must he think of her?

In an effort to get him to quit laughing, she grumbled, "You, sir, are no gentleman or you'd not mention such a delicate subject in front of so many men." Her attempt backfired when he laughed even harder.

When he thought her distracted, Grant tilted her head so it rested on his leg and continued to massage the sore tissues. She seemed too embarrassed to fight him any further and he realized his purposeful distraction worked. The muscles in her neck and shoulder relaxed and he lightened his touch. Not once did he stop the conversation. Soon her even breathing told him she'd fallen asleep.

As he rose to carry Victoria to his bedchamber, Warwick smiled. "The wee lassie does trust you, lad. 'Tis as I told you afore, she'd not so readily fall asleep around you if she dinnae trust you."

Grant said naught. Though the depth of his current feelings surprised him, he smiled as he walked away.

When Grant disappeared upstairs, his friend, Ian, rubbed his chin thoughtfully. "He is going to keep her."

A collective shout of "*What*?" filled the room.

"The lassie," Ian reiterated. "Grant is going to keep her."

"That is not amusing, Ian," came a growl of disbelief. "She's English."

"Och, aye, she is," Ian laughed at the obvious. "But have you not seen how he watches her every move? He's captivated with her. She is charming, mind."

"He'll get over it," Angus grumbled. "She is naught but a momentary distraction."

Ian shook his head adamantly. "She may be a distraction, but I vow there is naught momentary about it. Mark me, men. He is going to keep her. Were she not English, I bet he would wed her."

"Nay!" men shouted in unison and stared in horror in the direction their young chieftain headed.

Archibald shouted, "Thank God that will never happen."

Ian said no more, but smiled and arched his eyebrows with a knowing look.

Warwick looked at the young man a long time with a satisfied smile on his face, then turned and left the room. He looked as smug as a cat having trapped a mouse.

Chapter Eight

Sennights later Victoria sat in the Great Hall near Grant. She hated sitting on the dirty rushes, but it allowed her a chance to rest and Grant tended to ignore her. So, she acquiesced with little fuss, although she didn't understand why he remained adamant about having her nearby. It seemed he wanted her at table, but couldn't figure out how to do so and not lose face with his men.

Seemingly unaware of his actions, Grant stroked his fingers through her hair while he spoke with his men.

Victoria used the time to play with her small dog.

Concentrating on her pup's antics, she remained unaware of the attention she garnered as she giggled in delight. Men smiled and watched her interaction with Lancelot.

A short, dark, stocky serving women glared at Victoria and stalked back to the kitchen grumbling, her eyes hardening with each angry step.

A short time later a young lad brought a trencher to her and placed it on the ground. He set a cup of whisky beside it. She didn't fancy alcohol and couldn't imagine them sharing their water of life with her. She'd learned if she didn't comment, Grant let her eat in peace. So, she didn't draw his attention to the whisky.

She ate while men discussed comments from another courier. With all the recent battles, they'd had many visitors over past days.

She could tell Archibald was incensed when he muttered, "Can you believe Edward exiled our king after his surrender and stole our Stone of Scone? Took it to bloody London." Archibald spat in the rushes with open contempt. "The *foosty scunner* had the audacity to have hisself declared King of Scotland on our holy stone."

Grumbles told Victoria everyone shared Archibald's feelings. What could be so special about a stone? It should be an honor to have anything placed in magnificent Westminster Abbey. As a child she'd delighted in her visit there. Its lavish interior boasted a treasure trove of art, with tiered sculptures lining its walls. The highlight of her holiday had been the leisurely cruise down the Thames. Her father hadn't been pleased with her presence during the London holiday, but her grandmother had insisted she join them. It had been the only time her grandmother prevailed.

Grandpapa told her when Romans inhabited the mighty town they called it Londinium. Formerly a royal castle, London's imposing Tower now served as a dreaded prison. These Scots weren't pleased Baliol had been taken there.

Finishing her meager offering, she drank some whisky, doubting she'd like it. She made a face after a few sips and set the metal quaich down. She'd have much preferred tea like her grandpapa used to bring Grandmum from China. Her grandmum even had a special caddy she kept locked, insisting tea was costly. She was determined to lose none of the special spices. The caddy even had a special compartment where she could blend the tea to her own taste. Victoria always loved watching her prepare the special drink and especially loved it when Grandmum shared it with her.

Grant's favorite dog ambled over and plopped beside her. Patting his furry head, she lowered her mouth to his ear and whispered, "I know not if dogs should drink, Thor, but they share everything else with you. Would you fancy the rest of this? It seems a shame to waste something your master thinks so highly of." The mutt looked as if he understood her words, causing her to smile. It delighted her that to Grant's chagrin his dogs were friendly with her. At least someone—or something—fancied her. She moved the cup closer and watched as Thor lapped the liquid. Like owner, like pet, she grinned impishly.

She'd have given some to Lancelot, too, but her pup chose that moment to chase a cat. Quick to catch it, the two romped in the rushes.

Soon she felt tired and had difficulty keeping her eyes open. She couldn't leave the Great Hall, lest Grant anger that she left before him. She'd discovered that lesson when she tried to storm away when he wouldn't listen to reason--again. Feeling sleepy, she decided to use Grant's huge, fluffy dog as a pillow since he, too, seemed to be resting.

It didn't take long before she fell asleep.

Hours later Grant stood to head upstairs. The sound of Tory's puppy whimpering annoyed him. What was wrong with the animal? Lancelot usually didn't whine. Grant nudged Tory with his foot and told her to quiet her dog. She didn't move. He nudged her again. When he shook her, her head slid off Thor and landed in the rushes, causing Lancelot to whimper louder. Growing aggravated,

Grant told Colin to take the larger dogs outside. He pulled her by her arm and she stirred, but didn't awaken.

She felt as limp as a wet rag.

Colin shouted, "Thor's not moving." Almost deaf, every conversation he held was at a near yell.

Grant's head shot up and he bent his knee to the floor to check his favorite dog. In an instant he knew something was amiss. He feared his dog wouldn't survive the night. A knot of fear formed in the pit of his stomach. Turning back to Tory, he shook her. "Woman, wake up."

Again she stirred, but didn't awaken. Grant raised her to a sitting position and she opened her eyes, but closed them again when her head lolled to one side.

"Something is wrong with them both. Mayhap poisoned." A surge of alarm shot through him. He stood and gathered Tory in his arms and rushed two steps at a time to his chamber. Emitting a low growl, he shouted over his shoulder, "Bring something to purge the poison."

His men looked as if he'd spoken in a foreign tongue.

Warwick followed. "Lad, we know naught of how to help the lassie. None of us know about herbs. Your mam took care of such things."

Raking his hands through his hair, Grant gazed at Tory. He'd placed her atop his bed and she looked as pale as death. Shaken by her stillness, he knew if they didn't do something soon, whatever ailed Thor might kill Tory as well. Anger boiled within him. Clenching his fist, he turned to Warwick. "Have someone fetch that strange woman that lives in the woods. 'Tis said she knows about healing."

"The witch?" Angus queried, eyes wide in amazement.

"Och, she is not a witch, auld man," Grant answered in exasperation. "Just strange. Hurry." Upset, he walked to the ewer and basin and moistened a cloth to use on Tory's warm forehead.

Going to the castle wasn't what Agnes planned for her evening. She'd have been happy to never set foot there. She hadn't been given much choice, though. See if she'd help them with some nonsense of healing someone!

Pulled up to Grant's solar, Finlay pushed her inside. Grant turned as he heard the commotion. "You came."

Spitting into the rushes, the old woman grumbled and glared at the large man who'd dragged her from her house. "As if *he* gave me aught choice! Pulled me right out of my house, he did. Threw me over his shoulder like I was naught but a sack of wheat."

Grant glanced at his men, who merely shrugged.

"You said to fetch her," Finlay answered, "and she dinnae wish to oblige."

Finlay resembled a fierce Viking and used whatever means he thought necessary to accomplish a task. The large man had long blond hair and sky blue eyes. One look at his size and ferocious appearance usually made people acquiesce to his wishes. If they didn't, he took his threats one step further. He never failed.

In effort to ease the growing tension, Grant directed the old crone's attention to Tory. "This woman has been poisoned. I need you to give her a purgative to remove the poison. Whatever someone gave her almost killed one of my dogs as well. I needs you to heal them both."

Agnes looked at the bed and again spat in the rushes. Grant frowned at the crude gesture as she asked, "Is this the English I heard about?"

Grant nodded. She certainly wasn't very ladylike, although that should have been obvious from her disheveled state. In total disarray, her clothes were filthy and her hair hung limp and stringy. Although her face looked weathered, her eyes were striking and clear.

"And you want her saved?" she queried incredulously.

Grant again nodded, gazing at her in stupefaction over what he considered a daft question.

The old woman approached the bed and looked at Victoria, then turned and looked as closely at Grant. "Why do you want her saved? Why not let her die? From what I hear, 'tis what everyone wants."

Grant absentmindedly brushed his hand over the top of Tory's head. "My reasons are none of your business, auld woman. She is my prisoner and I want her alive. That is all you need know."

Agnes studied him anew before moving. The look on young Drummond's face revealed far more than he knew. Amusement lighting her wrinkled face, she cackled and reached inside her shift, pulling out a small bag attached to her corded belt. She selected several herbs and told Grant she'd need hot water. Grant dispersed Alex. Upon his return, she stirred herbs into the water and approached Grant's bed.

75

When Agnes raised Victoria's head so she could swallow the foul smelling liquid, Grant stayed her movements with his hand. A threatening look clouded his eyes. "Do not give her anything that will make her worse, auld woman. You will not like the outcome if you do."

Without a word of acknowledgement she ignored Grant. She poured the foul tasting liquid down Victoria's throat, then placed the young woman's head back on the pillow. Within minutes Victoria groaned in pain and threw up everything she'd eaten earlier.

Grant watched as the bossy woman pushed filthy grey streaked hair from her eyes and ordered everyone to leave the room. She didn't have to tell them twice! Grant remained, steadfastly refusing to budge. Again Agnes poured the foul smelling liquid down Victoria's throat with the same expected result. She continued until dry heaves wracked Victoria's body.

"Take this with you," she'd told Angus as she handed him the foul smelling potion. "Use it on his lairdship's dog." She assumed he was having the same outcome with Grant's dog.

She removed Victoria's clothes and cooled her heated body with water from the nearby ewer and basin.

Grant came closer. Even though worried about the young woman on his bed, his body reacted to her nakedness. He knew it was the last thing in the world he should be thinking right now, but blessed St. Michael, though ashen, the woman on his bed was an absolute vision.

Agnes chose that moment to glance over her shoulder. She teased, "Och Laird Drummond, does it excite you seeing the lassie naked as the day she was born?"

Grant shot her a look of scorn. Drat her for noticing. He already knew how inappropriate his reaction was. "Of course not, auld woman," he blustered over his embarrassment. "Do not be mouthing such nonsense. I am watching to make certain you harm her not."

"Och," she cackled with a mischievous twinkle in her eyes, "so that rise in yon kilt is not your manhood?"

Grant shifted uncomfortably and glared.

"And I thought you brought me here because you cared about this woman."

"Rubbish," Grant boomed, his brows creased together in a line of disapproval. "I told you she is my prisoner, naught else."

"Aye, I can see that." A pointed glare at his crotch and an amused smile made her mouth twitch. Blessedly, her glare made his body finally relax. He needed to concentrate on the well-being of the young woman in his bed.

What was it about the girl that made his body react when his mind knew full well the inappropriateness of such thoughts? Here she was, lying near death, and his wayward mind could think of naught but how much he wanted her healed so he could take her to his bed.

Nonsense! Such musings were the thoughts of an inexperienced lad, not someone as worldly as himself. She was his prisoner, naught else.

He fooled no one but himself.

The pain in Victoria's stomach felt unbearable. She heard people talking, but couldn't understand them. Why couldn't she focus?

"Can you do naught for her pain?" Grant sounded worried. Her eyelids fluttered open, but immediately closed.

"I imagine her belly is quite painful after the poison," the wizened crone sympathized. "Someone in your keep has a mighty hate for the wee lassie. A warmed stone might help. We could heat one in yon hearth and place it on her belly. The warmth should alleviate some pain, but 'twill be difficult to keep it there. Any time she moves, she will knock it off."

"Warm the rock, auld woman. We will think of some way to keep it there."

To Grant's dismay, Agnes proved correct. The flat stone wouldn't stay in place since Victoria tossed about too much. Exhaling in resignation, he gathered the fragile woman in his arms and sat in his favorite chair before the hearth. Though he felt discomfited as Agnes watched his every move, he cradled Victoria in his lap, placed the warm stone on her belly and held it there.

Victoria calmed in his arms. Agnes warmed stones, swapping them for ones that cooled. They continued this throughout the night. Come morn Grant placed the deathly ill woman on his bed and stretched to work the kinks from his body.

Over the next days Agnes remained close to her chieftain's young captive. She bathed Tory's skin every day with mint water in an effort to break her fever, and witnessed with glee the tenderness the young man showed the lass when he thought no one watched. If he left the room for any reason, he always returned with the same question, "How does the lass now?"

Prisoner, my foot, she thought wryly, experiencing a degree of amused satisfaction.

Finally Tory's fever broke and she could sit abed. Her small dog needed no invitation to join her. At her first movements to rise, he bounded onto the bed. Tory smiled and rubbed the small animal's head.

Greeting Agnes with warmth, she enquired, "Thank you for your efforts. Why have I never seen you around the keep?"

"Because I dinnae fancy it here," Agnes began with more than a hint of sarcasm, "and most folks dinnae want me near them." With a mischievous glint in her eyes she added, "They think me a witch."

Victoria's eyes widened. She cocked her head to assess the wizened old woman. "Are you?" she asked doubtingly.

Agnes' mocking snort provided all the information Victoria needed.

"I did not think so." Victoria gave Agnes a long penetrating look, then smiled and impulsively placed her hand atop the old woman's weathered hand. The woman shot her a surprised glance. "But you do know a great deal about the healing arts."

A non-committal grunt proved the only response Victoria received.

Agnes prepared to leave Drummond's home and return to the safety and solitude of her small hut. She gathered her remaining herbs into her small pouch. The dense forest surrounding her home provided the quiet she preferred. With the lassie mending, there were far too many people in this castle for her liking. She'd been away from her home too long and looked forward to the peacefulness it afforded. Bone tired, she ached and fought to keep her eyes open. She hadn't left the young woman's side.

Agnes felt something special about the lass. She thought her pleasant. The wee mutt fancied her as well and animals usually had good instincts. He hadn't left Victoria's side the entire time she remained unconscious. Then again, neither had young Drummond.

Agnes thought that quite telling.

She approached her young charge one final time and leaned forward to look into her bright eyes, taking her true measure. An aura of mystery surrounded the lassie.

Agnes could feel it.

She patted Tory's cheek and chuckled. "Young Drummond thinks I used magic on you to make you better. I think you are the one who holds the magic and has our chieftain spellbound."

Tory started to protest, but Agnes cut her off. "Nay, dinnae be denying it to an auld buzzard like me. These auld eyes see far more than people think. I dinnae sit alone with you day in and day out, you know." When Tory wrinkled her brows, Agnes saw she truly didn't understand. "The young chieftain sat with you every day."

She added with a mischievous cackle, "It would almost make it worth living inside this bloody keep to see this play itself out. I dinnae misdoubt things will prove interesting."

Chapter Nine

The call to arms Grant expected came several days later. The time had once again come to place his peoples' lives in harm's way. He made plans for half his men to aid in the protection of their country, the other half would stay to tend his castle—and his prisoner. Prior to his departure, he determined to ensure her safety. It didn't take him long to determine who'd poisoned her, nor to oust Elfrieda from his castle. He hoped this would serve as warning to everyone the lass wasn't to be harmed. Jealous women, indeed.

Warwick planned to accompany Grant, so while Grant rushed around making final arrangements, Wick made a few of his own. He gathered together men who would remain to guard the castle, met them eye-to-eye and bluntly said, "Best you plow no seeds in the laird's garden whilst we are gone men. Mark my words on that."

Several pointedly stared at Tory as she sat in a chair before the hearth. A young man looked at her with undisguised lust. "English or not, I would not mind giving her a belly."

Warwick glared with contempt. "You'd best not be getting the lass with child, fool." He warned, "She's a comely lass, men. Dinnae underestimate our laird's feelings. Keep your hands to yourselves." Amidst grumbles, he turned and issued the same order to the Captain of the Guard. Warwick determined Grant's young charge would be safe.

For reasons he didn't understand, he felt protective.

After completing endless chores, Victoria walked out to the courtyard. She enjoyed being outside after being cooped inside the castle so long. She glanced to the fields in the distance and saw a child fall. When he didn't get up and run around, Victoria rushed to where he'd fallen. Unable to rouse him, she picked him up and carried him back to the keep.

Thinking her trying to escape, guards grew violent.

Angered by their actions, Victoria whirled on them. "This boy is injured and I plan to tend him. Do not think to hinder me." Her tone and combative stance caught the guards off balance. In control, she dismissed them.

"Take your filthy hands off me. Now! I have work to do and you'll not stop me." Victoria shot them a defiant glare, jerked her arms away, and proceeded into the Great Hall. The guards seemed so shocked with her unexpected take-charge attitude they let her pass.

Victoria ran upstairs to Grant's solar and grabbed her small basket. She'd gathered herbs whenever the guards left her alone. Those moments had been rare.

She carried her basket so she wouldn't spill precious herbs and returned to the Great Hall where she'd laid the injured lad on a table. The floor would have been preferable, but she thought it too dirty. With dogs ever present and men spitting in the rushes, Victoria didn't think it an environment conducive to injuries. *I must address that with Grant*, she thought as she hurried toward the injured lad. The current state of the castle's cleanliness—or lack thereof—simply couldn't continue.

Victoria noticed she'd acquired an audience. One wrong move and she'd be dead. She had no doubt their explanation would be more than sufficient for their laird.

As she checked the boy's injuries, Victoria recognized him as Iain. He was Cook's son and Cook hated her almost as much as Archibald.

Iain would have a headache from the lump on his head, but his predominant injury appeared to be a broken arm. Since she only had a small amount of boneset, the small boy's size pleased her. She thought him about five or six summers. As she mixed herbs, from the corner of her eye she observed men gathering. All the better to drag her off and torture her. She rubbed the back of her neck to ease the tension.

The small boy wailed when he regained consciousness. Victoria leaned closer. "'Tis all right, Iain. I shall fix your arm and you will be quite as good as new." His wails intensified. Restraining him, Victoria diverted his attention and swiftly set his arm. His shocked look and loud yelp told her the distraction succeeded. After she applied medicaments, Victoria fashioned a small cast.

Knowing a small boy would never hold his arm still, she tore the bottom of her kirtle and fastened a small sling. She'd have used her chemise, but she didn't have one. She'd have to go around with a torn kirtle from now on. She doubted anyone would care enough to replace this one. She cradled the sobbing boy, then rocked and talked to him in a soothing voice until he calmed.

Iain's parents stood nearby frowning. Victoria shifted Iain so he couldn't see them. He needed to calm down and the hatred on his parents' faces wouldn't help. Cook looked ready to tear her hair out by its roots. From the dark looks he shot her, he'd probably be happy to do so, but for some reason his wife restrained him. Mayhap she wanted the honors herself.

When he relaxed, Victoria motioned Iain's mother closer. She transferred him to his mother's waiting arms. "I shall mix an herbal potion so he will sleep." The boy needed rest and her datura mixture would be what he needed.

She gave his mother a pointed look. "I know you do not like me, but please let Iain drink what I shall give you. Do not think to spite me by not doing so. 'Twill not be me you hurt, but Iain. He'll be in pain without it." Gracefully rising, she went upstairs to return her herb basket to Grant's large master solar.

She carried only the datura down with her.

Victoria smiled when she saw children crowded around wee Iain, looks of unconcealed awe on their faces. He'd be important the next days with his cast and sling. Soon things would return to normal for the small boy. She said a silent prayer of thanks.

She also thanked God for making Grant's men allow her to treat the boy. She'd felt certain they would try to stop her.

The next day children shadowed Tory, having a million questions. Where had she come from? How did she know how to treat Iain? Could they help gather herbs?

She felt certain their parents would soon call them away, but while they were with her she answered their questions as honestly as possible. "I shall be happy to let you gather herbs if you are around during my free moments." To her surprise, an outspoken lad named Adam with strawberry colored hair brazenly approached the guard. "Can Laird Grant's prisoner take a wee break to gather herbs?"

Douglas surprised her when he shrugged. "Aye, if she does not take too long." In his early twenties, he had wide shoulders and sandy brown hair.

The children grabbed her by her hands, then ran ahead of her until they reached the herb patch. Sounds of children's laughter echoed throughout the keep as they ran and played. More herbs could be found outside the castle gates, but she'd never be allowed out there. The children ran in circles, but were careful where they stepped once she cautioned, "You might trample tender herbs."

Victoria glanced around the keep and saw a young girl watching from a distance. When she asked her name, the children dismissed the information as unimportant before saying, "Annie."

A small girl with dark curly hair named Sorcha told her, "Annie is strange. I never heard her speak. She saw you fall that day in the Hall and got Rhiannon's attention."

After more prodding they told her, "Annie's parents are dead. We know not where she lives." They thought nothing odd of her staying on the outskirts and dismissed her from their thoughts while all tried to speak at once.

Enjoying her moment of relaxation, Victoria tried to discover as much about the children as possible. She delighted Rhiannon when she told the legend behind the young girl's name. The children sat entranced while she regaled them with the story.

Rhiannon mentioned, "Mam told me the tale before, but you know even more of it."

Since she didn't want to take advantage of the young guard who let her take this unprecedented break, Victoria informed the children, "We must return to the courtyard. Thank you for helping me fetch herbs. I hope I see you on the morrow."

She doubted it would happen.

The next day children again shadowed her. Victoria worked inside the Great Hall after she asked her tall, handsome young guard, "May I concentrate on the floor? The rushes sorely need changing." She worked while children scampered and played. They constantly ran over to her and asked questions which she laughingly answered.

Douglas glanced her way upon hearing her lilting laugh.

When Victoria stopped to rest, the children gathered around her and begged for another story. Surprised at their request, she delighted in doing just that. The children sat in rapt attention while she wove her tale. From the corner of her eye she saw Annie watching from a distance.

Exhausted by day's end, Victoria dropped down on her mat in Grant's bedchamber. The children seemed to like her. Smiling, Victoria fell into a deep peaceful sleep and didn't stir until early morn.

Following days continued in much the same fashion, with children easily approaching and spending time with her. She looked forward to their time together and wove tales every day.

Annie always stood close enough to watch and listen, but never close enough to participate. Victoria's heart went out to the small child. In many ways Annie reminded her of herself as a child. She'd always been on the outskirts, too, since her father wanted nothing to do with her.

Adults also seemed friendlier. Though they didn't seek her out as the children did, they no longer tormented her. When Gavin, one of Grant's men-at-arms, received a gash on his arm during daily sword training, the children asked her to treat him.

Victoria didn't know whether he'd allow her to tend him or not, but she gathered her herb basket and sought him out. After his initial surly refusal, Gavin grudgingly agreed. He was a handsome young man with dark brown hair and eyes as blue as the sky. Daily she checked his arm for infection.

Soon Gavin spoke on a regular basis. She treasured those moments and noticed other men were no longer quite as abrupt either.

To her surprise, one morning Iain ran to her. "Lady Tory, Da burned his hand when hot water tipped over. He needs your help, but will not ask." Knowing how much Cook hated her, she doubted he'd let her anywhere near him. Nonetheless, she rushed upstairs and gathered hyssop, goldenrod, and coneflowers.

Entering the kitchen, she approached Cook with an assurance she didn't feel. "I would like to look at your hand. Iain asked me to tend you." Eyes wide, the small boy stood to the side and nodded, confirming the fact. Cook's injured hand was wrapped in old rags and cradled in the palm of his other hand. Even though he kept his expression stony and blank, she could see his pain. When he didn't speak or shout obscenities as she'd anticipated, she moved closer and reached for his hand. Although she fully expected him to slap her with his uninjured hand or to verbally assault her, she unwrapped the cloths. She paled.

When he didn't pull away, but met and held her eyes, she led him to the nearby table. He lowered his massive bulk into a chair. She took her basket to the counter and mixed a poultice from the three flowers. She knelt beside Cook. "'Tis of utmost importance this burn be kept clean and dry. Where might I find clean cloths?"

Cook spoke for the first time. "To the right of the hearth, on the top shelf."

She got them and tore them into strips.

When she finished treating his injury, she gathered her herbs. "I'll be pleased to change your dressing on the morrow."

Without another word she headed out the door and up to Grant's solar, smiling all the way. Cook hadn't thanked her for her attentions, but neither had he kicked her from his kitchen.

After she told the children their daily story the next day, Victoria thought it the perfect time to check Cook's hand. She decided to try something she'd mulled over for hours. She turned to the children. "I am going to check Cook's hand. I shall see you on the morrow." Stopping in her tracks, as if in afterthought, she turned back and sighed. "I seem to have forgotten my herb basket. Annie, would you run up to Lord Grant's solar and fetch it for me? 'Tis in the corner near my mat. You cannot miss it."

The small girl's eyes grew wide with surprise and she began to retreat. Several children volunteered to retrieve the basket, but she calmly asserted, "Nay, I appreciate your volunteering, but I wish Annie to help me this day. Perhaps you could take turns doing things, but only if Annie is willing to help us start this game."

Victoria smiled at the child and beseeched, "Will you do that, Annie? Will you help me and start a game of assisting with a new adventure?"

Annie stood still as a rock, staring wide-eyed from her safe distance. Her mouth twitched in indecision. Holding out her hand to the little girl, Victoria smiled in encouragement. "I need your help, Sweeting. Will you aid me?"

She felt heartened when Annie suddenly smiled back. To everyone's surprise, Annie nodded and ran into the keep. Within minutes she reappeared, carrying Victoria's herb basket. She handed it to Victoria with a smile that dimpled her cheeks, then once again retreated to the edge of the group. She returned the young girl's smile. "You did such a good job, Sweeting. Thank you for taking such good care of my herbs and not spilling them." Smiling, she turned and walked into the kitchen.

She no longer dreaded getting up each morn.

With green clad hills rising sharply behind him, Grant approached his castle. Och, it felt good to be home. He drank in the sight of nearby mountains. Evidence of their harsh winter had quickly faded, with few mountaintops covered with snow. Gorse appeared in full bloom and created a bounty of yellow splotches amidst the hills' green backdrop.

The call from Geordie's father came sooner than Grant hoped—and things hadn't gone well. Tired and dirty, at least his injuries weren't too bad. He couldn't say the same for his men. Dougal seemed mortally wounded and others were grievously injured, with arrow wounds and sword slashes.

Past days' events had been a disaster.

Edward's men had been on a rampage. After their win at Berwick, it seemed they couldn't be stopped. Edward's onslaught captured Dunbar, Roxburgh, Jedburgh, and Dumbarton. Tension escalating throughout Scotland seemed unbearable, as vile atrocities were committed along the way. They couldn't lose sight of danger Edward posed. He was ruthless, evil.

It hurt to admit Edinburgh Castle, commanding a strategic site on Castlerock, had been captured. Built in the eleventh century, the imposing castle had steep cliffs on three sides and a long descending ridge on the fourth. It sat amidst a backdrop of dramatic hills and valleys. Perched atop the basalt core of an extinct volcano, it had been the royal residence of Scottish kings. Now the bloody English held it.

Grant envisioned the English destroying tiny St. Margaret's Chapel, Edinburgh's oldest building. Built in honor of King Malcolm III's saintly lady wife, the chapel had been around since 1100. Grant prayed the English would leave the old chapel alone. He snorted in disgust, doubting that would happen.

Edward's demands and destruction were unbearable. He cared only about laying waste to Scotland.

Passing heather-clad, craggy hills, Grant's men entered this fray, joining brave troops. Ill-disciplined Scots broke rank and hurled themselves at English troops, allowing the English army to storm across the field. Cut down by English soldiers, they were quickly showered by thousands of Welsh arrows. Mutilated bodies soon littered the battlefield. Armed with little more than fierce determination, it had been a miracle anyone escaped. The thought made Grant sick.

Afterward, Edward returned to England, convinced Scotland had been subdued. Riding south, he'd been overheard making the insufferable comment, "It does a man good to rid himself of such shite." Grant had no doubt he'd been referring to Scotland and its people.

Chapter Ten

Grant rode home to Crieff, or *Craobh* as it was known in the Gaelic, its name meaning 'among the trees.' Holding the area's most important cattle market, Highlanders came far and wide to sell to lowland buyers. Known for hanging lawless Highlanders, Grant suspected Murrays in the area oftened wished those with the name Drummond were included in those being hung!

The current situation in Scotland seemed abominable. Edward had truly become a power to be reckoned with. Grant's thoughts roiled in turmoil as he neared his home. Built on a volcanic rock by King Alexander I, Stirling Castle had been lost now, too. Whoever controlled the towering fortress guarded the River Forth's lowest crossing point and held almost all of Scotland. Because of its importance, Stirling changed hands more than any Scottish castle since William the Lion had been captured there. Grant grumbled, "They won that battle, men, but we shall win the war. Mark my words on that."

He regretted no one at home had the calling of a healer. His men were grievously wounded and his mother no longer lived to tend them, God rest her soul. He flinched when reminded how much he missed her.

He cringed when he thought of sustained injuries. These men were his responsibility, his family. How would he see them cared for?

While men rode under the portcullis, people streamed from the Great Hall. Women wailed when they realized the seriousness of their men's injuries and mourned the passing of those who hadn't returned. They were used to wounds since their men were always off fighting somewhere. That could only be expected since they had a reputation for being the best warriors in the Highlands.

These injuries were worse.

While Grant removed his helm and mail shirt, injured men were carried into a room to the left of the Great Hall. Women rushed around gathering water and strips of material to bind wounds. Grant watched the proceedings, unable to rise from where he'd slumped against the wall. Tiny hands tugged at his sleeve. He glanced down and saw Rhiannon standing shyly at his side. A tiny sprite, her smile charmed everyone. Grant guessed she must be about seven summers now. He wondered why the wee lassie had come outside. She was too young to see so much blood.

Grant tried to rouse himself to shoo her away, but Rhiannon shook her head. With light brown hair and expressive blue eyes, she implored, "Laird Grant, do not send me away. Da is here."

Rhiannon's father was the most severely injured. He'd always been one of Grant's faithful younger men. Dougal rode with him with nary a grumble and had repeatedly proved his fealty to Clan Drummond.

Heaving a deep sigh, he remembered a skirmish in nearby Wales. Dougal thought he'd fallen in love with a young Welsh girl he'd seen in town. Though only six and ten, he'd pleaded with Grant to let him kidnap the young woman and fetch her to Castle Drummond. Grant thought it the daftest thing he'd ever heard since Dougal just met the lass and Grant thought him far too young. Dougal wore him down and had, indeed, brought Gwenhwyfar back with him. In hindsight, Grant thought it hadn't been such a daft idea considering their present happiness; however, at the time she screamed and fought all the way to Drummond Castle.

No different than the way my Tory fought to get away from me while fetching her to my home.

He shook his head. Why think of his prisoner now? He'd thought of her constantly while away from home. No matter how often he tried to shake her from his thoughts, her image continually reappeared. It had been disconcerting when trying to sleep after a long day's ride only to have his body think of her *that way*. Those thoughts made it virtually impossible for him to sleep.

Shaking his reverie aside, he faced Rhiannon. Dougal's only child, she was his pride and joy. To Dougal, the sun rose and set on the wee poppet.

Grant had been told the lass' name meant Great Queen, after a Celtic deity—the one who rode a white horse and always had gentle birds around her. She'd been falsely accused of killing her firstborn child, but had been acquitted. During her trials she endured horrible treatment with pride and dignity. *Like my Tory has since being here.*

Grant glanced toward Dougal. Gaping wounds on his left arm and thigh screamed of violence they'd witnessed. Grant drew Rhiannon close. "I know, Sweeting, but you shouldn't be out here. The men are sorely wounded and there is naught you can do to help."

The young girl nodded violently. "Och, but I can, Laird Grant. I can truly."

He looked at the sprite quizzically. "Rhiannon, what speak you of? You know naught of healing."

"Och, I know," she rolled her eyes with obvious exasperation at the absurdity of his comment, "but Lady Tory does. She would help if I but asked. Should I get her?"

At Rhiannon's words, his head shot to attention. He hunkered down painfully to her level and looked into her solemn blue eyes. He asked less than patiently, "Speak you of my prisoner?"

His eyebrows raised in skepticism.

The little girl nodded more slowly now and bit her lower lip. She looked up into Grant's face and cast him a fearful glance, clearly doubting the wisdom of coming to him. She said so softly Grant barely heard her, "Aye, Lady Tory is a great healer."

Grant shifted position and sat on the ground. Och, how his body ached, yet he gently lifted Rhiannon into his lap. "Tell me what you speak of, lassie. How would you know such a thing?"

Rhiannon bit her lower lip and stilled, watched her father being carried into the Hall with other injured men. Her mam walked beside him, holding his hand. He attempted to allay the child's anxiousness and fears by smoothing hair from her face. She seemed such a sweet, good-natured child.

"Whilst you were gone, Lady Tory spent her free time with us we'ans." When Grant looked at her questioningly, Rhiannon hastily continued. "She did not shirk her duties, truly. She stayed muckle busy and always finished her chores. Please do not be angered."

Grant found it amusing the lassie worried about his prisoner. *Lady Tory?* When had they begun calling her that? He'd have to get to the bottom of what happened while he'd been gone. Right now he needed to find out about this healing thing.

"'Tis all right, Rhiannon. Tell me what my prisoner did."

"Ooh, she tells lovely stories," the child clapped her hands and smiled an impish grin. "She even knew about my name! She told me more than I ever heard afore."

Grant could tell this really impressed the girl, but he still had learned no pertinent information. "Och, Sweeting, that is fine, but tell me about this healing." He tried to temper his impatience so Rhiannon wouldn't be frightened.

She glanced toward the door where her father disappeared. "Cook's son fell and landed on a large rock and Lady Tory saw him. No one else did, mind, and he would have lain out there. *He might even have died*!" she exaggerated in her childish way. "Lady Tory dashed to Iain and gathered him into her arms. The guards ran after her, mind, thinking she tried to run away again." Pausing, she added in a conspiratorial voice, "You know how she always insists on leaving."

Grant grimaced. Even the children knew Tory tried to escape. Rhiannon broke into his musings. "She'd already started back toward the keep when they caught up with her, but they grabbed her and jerked her arm. They were so mean." She shook her head sadly as she remembered. "They tried grabbing wee Iain from her arms, but she pulled away, glared and stomped her foot." When he smiled, she continued in an impish whisper, "Lady Tory yelled at the guards."

Smiling at the vision this conjured, he could envision Tory stomping her foot and yelling. She'd done it with him enough times when demanding he let her leave his castle. He felt glad for once someone besides him experienced the sting of her sharp tongue.

Oblivious to his thoughts, the tiny girl made a face. "She told them she knew they hated her, but the wee laddie was injured and she planned to tend him whether they fancied it or not. She stormed into the Great Hall and up to your bedchamber. We all followed to see what she would do, mind." She drew a deep breath. "She reached into a corner and brought out a wee basket, then went back to the Hall to treat Iain."

Rhiannon's eyes widened with excitement as she warmed to her topic and shared the rest of her news. "She'd gathered herbs whenever allowed to rest in the courtyard. We thought she fancied pretty flowers. Laird Grant," she gasped incredulously, "she had a whole basket full! She drew things out of her basket and healed Iain. Truly." Her excitement grew. "Iain broke his arm, and she fixed it! Lady Tory used plants and made a fine cast for his arm.

"After she finished, she sat on the floor and croodled him in her arms 'til he quit his yammering. While she held him she told him his name meant 'appointed by God.' Is not that wonderful?" came her awed question. She stopped for a minute and held her breath. When Grant said nothing, she continued in a rush, "Of course, I know not what *appointed* means, but that matters not. Wee Iain were really mean to her afore, Laird Grant, because his da and mam hate her." She shrugged her shoulders and added sadly, "Because she's English, you know."

Grant nodded and tried not to reveal his growing impatience at not learning the information he so yearned to know.

"Do you not see?" she blurted. "If she healed Iain and he were mean, mayhap she would heal my da, too, even though you have all been mean." She said this last with a displeased frown, clearly thinking everyone should be wonderful to Tory since she'd been kind to them. "Please, Laird Grant," the lassie implored and lifted her bright eyes to his. They brimmed with tears. "Please ask her to help—or let me. I know you'll not approve, but 'tis liking her I am. She lets me spend her free time with her whenever I want and says I am not a pest. Please!" She burst into a round of fresh tears. "Please, Laird Grant, Lady Tory is so kind and gentle."

Gentle? Tory? *His Tory*? Could wee Rhiannon really be talking about the wildcat he'd left the morn he and his men rode out under the battlements? The quick-tempered woman who'd stormed at him again and again that he must release her?

Why couldn't she understand he wasn't of the mind to do that? After a pause, Grant asked himself a different question. *Why wouldn't he even consider her plea*? He shook his head. He didn't have time for such thoughts right now. He'd visit Cook and get his side of Rhiannon's story. Surely it couldn't have happened as the lassie said.

In astonishment, Grant slowly exited the kitchen. He tried to hide his surprise with a satisfied smile. Cook verified Rhiannon's story. "Och, aye. The wee princess was a saint. She mixed three flowers into a poultice when I burned myself."

It appeared his Tory had indeed tended people in his absence—from wounds, to lice, to colds. Gavin, one of his men, let her treat a gash on his arm—and apparently had been more than willing to do so. Not to mention her treating Iain.

His lass had been busy indeed.

Cook called her a saint! The man hated her, yet now called her a saint. When Grant left for Dunbar, Cook called Tory 'Princess' in a derogatory fashion. Now, he called her the wee princess with a sense of awe.

He heard Tory might be in the garden, which explained why she hadn't heard the commotion of approaching horses. His mother had always loved the garden's serenity. His grandfather built it in a location that would remain peaceful and away from the busy fortress' noises. He felt a pain as he remembered the garden both his mam and granddam loved so much. He shouldn't have let it get overgrown, but going out there brought back bittersweet memories. It just plain hurt. He'd loved his mother so much. Everyone had. She'd been the kindest, gentlest woman he'd ever known, and his home hadn't been the same, nor had a healer, since her death. He missed her.

A muscle flexed in his jaw as he thought of her death, and an aching sadness turned to hatred as unbidden memories flooded over him.

Stepping around the opening into the enclosed garden, he drew up short. Tory knelt on the ground pulling weeds near a stone wall, her small dog scampering playfully at her side. Her face glistened in the midday sun's heat, and tendrils of dark hair stuck to the side of her face. His heart skipped a beat at the sight of her.

Och, it felt good to be home.

Tory'd begun to bring his mother's garden back to life. *Why?* What did she care what it looked like? It certainly hadn't been on the lengthy list of chores he'd left for her in his absence. The garden was the last thing he'd have thought about. Rubbing his jaw, he shook his head and admired the garden's beauty and peacefulness. No wonder his mother had loved it so.

His grandfather originally laid out the garden for his grandmother, who'd loved plants and flowers. The stately copper beech trees and yews planted years before still flourished. As they did every year, the leaves on the copper beech were turning from olive and tan to burnished copper. The bright leaves brought a riot of color to the garden. His mother always exclaimed, "How delightful!"

His grandfather had statues from Continental Europe brought in for his lady wife, since she loved angel statues. When Grant's father wed, Grant's mother had taken as much interest in the garden, which pleased his granddam. His father expanded it and even surprised her with a carved stone sundial which stood in the center of the massive garden. Though only a lad, Grant remembered the joy on his mother's face the day it had been delivered.

The thought flashed through his mind that the garden and Victoria were both exquisite. Without a conscious thought his body responded to the luscious curves of her body. She seemed such a contradiction, this woman—at times tough enough to stand up to anything and other times vulnerable and in need of protection. *His protection.*

She looked like a woodland sprite amongst the garden plants and Grant stood enthralled. He thought mayhap he'd have new statues brought in for Tory since she seemed to care for the garden as much as his mam and granddam had. A walkway around its outer boundaries would be the perfect addition. He made a mental note to get Tory's ideas on it.

He had no doubt she'd be there to see the project completed.

Studying her avidly, he approached and saw a smudge of dirt across her cheek and nose. Somehow the lass always managed that, almost being worse than the lads in his courtyard. They always had dirt on their faces, too.

When he hunkered down beside her, Victoria stilled. For no discernible reason her heart pounded. To her annoyance, his nearness always set her senses awhirl. "I did not hear you return, milord. I am glad you are safely home. Is everyone well?"

Victoria couldn't take her eyes from his handsome face. She'd thought about him so often while he'd been gone, although she knew not why. Of course, she'd never tell him that. He'd get a swelled head and read something into it that certainly shouldn't be there.

He looked tired.

"Nay lass," he began in a subdued voice, a pained expression crossing his face. "We are not. Our men are sore injured. I am here because I have heard remarkable tales of *a sweet lass* in my castle healing people in my absence." He said the last with a grin.

She felt herself blush while he rubbed the pad of his thumb lightly over the dirt on her cheek. She hoped she looked unaffected by his words.

Grant sobered. "Is it true, lass? Are you a healer?"

Victoria stilled and cautiously answered, "Aye." She knew not if he'd approve. Mayhap he'd be cross. "But I never shunned my work. I prom—"

He waved a hand to cut her off. "My men have not been the most courteous to you," he admitted apologetically.

Victoria shook her head slowly in agreement, wondering what he meant. Courteous indeed. They'd been downright hateful.

Grant quickly answered her thoughts. "Would you consider tending them in spite of that?"

He seemed reluctant to ask.

When she didn't immediately answer, Grant continued in a defeated tone, "I will not force you. You could do more harm than good if even I tried, but my men have families that love them." He sighed deeply. "I love them as well, and would not wish more harm to come to them than already has."

His eyes troubled, he paused then cleared his throat, probably to continue, but Victoria no longer listened and started rising. She took in his weary, dusty appearance. "I'll do whatever I can. When Grandmum taught me the healing arts, she made me promise never to use my gift to hurt anyone."

Looking askance she laughed shakily. "Of course, she never dealt with the situation of healing one's captors." Growing silent, she murmured, "Your men may not wish me to treat them, though, and I'll not do so if they are against the idea. I'll help anyone I can, but will not force myself on them."

Grant nodded in agreement while they walked from the garden. The breeze blew lightly through her hair and he desperately tried not to conjure up a vision of that last part of her statement. *Force herself, indeed.* He'd bed her in a heartbeat, but wouldn't tell her that. Unfortunately, certain parts of his anatomy weren't in total agreement and responded on their own.

Chapter Eleven

After rushing up to Grant's bedchamber, Victoria gathered her herb basket. She washed her arms and hands in the basin, then hurried to where Grant waited at the foot of the stairs. He escorted her into a room where a flurry of activity prevailed and men moaned in excruciating pain. The air hung fetid with blood and infection.

Rhiannon threw her arms around Victoria's legs, looking wet-eyed up at her friend. "You came. I knew you would. Did I not tell you, Laird Grant?" she purred victoriously as she grinned at him. "I told you she would come." She grabbed Victoria's hand and drew her towards her father. "Look at my da first."

Victoria tried to glance at everyone as she approached Rhiannon's father. Her stomach and mind rebelled at the depth of misery she witnessed, dried blood everywhere, and the putrid smell that encompassed the room. When she took inventory of Dougal's wounds, he pulled away. His eyes searched for Grant, found him standing at the foot of the pallet.

"'Tis up to you, my good friend," Grant answered the unspoken question in Dougal's eyes, "but I hear from several people, your Rhiannon amongst them, that Tory truly is a healer. She is the only one we have and I admit I would fancy seeing you healed." Grant paused when Dougal didn't respond. "Will you at least allow the lass to look at you?"

Dougal's wife, Gwenhwyfar, laid a hand gently on his brow. "Aye, Sweeting, 'tis true. The lady has the power of healing. Let her treat you for meself and our we'ans."

A young woman with a pleasant face, she had brown hair and large eyes the blue of a sky on a cloudless day. She'd been kind since Iain's accident and the children had taken to accompanying Victoria. Rhiannon joined them daily.

Through his pain, Dougal's head snapped towards his beloved wife's face, his eyes asking a silent question.

"Aye, Sweeting," Gwenhwyfar lovingly responded to her husband. "I said we'ans. Rhiannon and a new wean on the way." She gently stroked his cheek. "I beg you let the lady help. I believe she's a *bandruidh*. Aye," she solemnly clarified at his questioning glance, "a white lady, a healer. God has given her an amazing gift."

With a tear coursing slowly down his cheek, Dougal met Victoria's eyes and nodded his assent. She didn't know if the tear came from his pain, fear of her treatment, or the wonderful news he'd once again experience fatherhood.

She rather hoped it the latter.

Never had she been faced with helping so many injured people and she questioned her skills, feeling uncertain. Feeling the tensions rising in the room, she nevertheless determined the extent of each man's injuries, receiving glares all the while. The unmistakable stench of rotting flesh told her she must act quickly. Inspection completed, she approached Grant. "Might anyone be willing to assist? 'Twill be impossible to treat everyone at once, and the longer we wait, the worse their situations will get."

Heading to the Great Hall to gather recruits, he assured her, "Many will work hand-in-glove to assist."

Upon their arrival Victoria announced, "I shall need warm water and clean rags." She didn't have the heart to tell them she couldn't use the ones already gathered.

Duncan asked, "What need we do first, lass?"

She furrowed her brows, thinking. "I only have a small basket of herbs, naught enough to treat all the injuries. Even if you escort me outside the gates to gather more, we have no time."

Grant looked at her evenly, his face impassive. He seemed to be making a decision. "Mam had an herbary. If you wish, I'll escort you there to see if there is aught you can use."

"Grant," she exclaimed excitedly looking around the small, cluttered room, "your mother must have been quite gifted." At his nod of agreement she rushed on, busying herself with gathering herbs. "Surely anything we need is here. I'll take some things. If I need more we can return."

Walking back to the sickroom, she warned, "Willow bark needs be brewed to dull the men's pain. It tastes bitter, but 'tis important they drink it."

For reasons he couldn't explain, a measure of tension left Grant's shoulders as he walked side-by-side with the young woman.

Back with the injured men, Grant asked, "What need we do?"

She shifted her eyes between men lying on the ground and those waiting to assist. Biting her lower lip, she hesitantly but firmly said, "They must be stripped."

To a man, mouths gaped and an appalled response resounded, "What?"

A wry smile touching his lips, Grant calmly eased her away from the others.

"Nay, milord," she said, jerking her arm from his grasp. "Do not try to dissuade me. It must be done and must be done now. I need them washed to assess their wounds. As 'tis now, I cannot tell which is a wound or merely dried blood."

Grant's men glowered.

Clearly frustrated with their lack of assistance, her patience wore thin. "Look, I bloody well care not what they look like beneath their clothes, but it must be done. Now either help or get out!"

Grant shot a frown at her use of words, but said nothing.

Still in shock, but at an almost imperceptible nod from Grant, his burly men moved toward their fellow warriors and did what the bloody Englishwoman wanted. She suddenly seemed far too bossy.

Once men were bathed with a wash of pressed garlic and mint and covered with light cloths to protect their modesty—or hers—she checked each person's injuries. Reaching Archibald, he pushed her from him with his little remaining strength, radiating fury.

"Nay!" he yelled, spewing Gaelic curses. "I'll not have this bloody witch touch me. I would rather die. She'll poison you, not help," he spat in derision. "English only know how to kill and maim!"

Uncertainly she looked at Grant and he shook his head. "Nay, lassie, we agreed only those that wanted your help would be the ones you treat. If Archibald wants not your care, that is his decision. You would only exacerbate his hatred."

Shoulders slumped in resignation, she approached Rhiannon's father. Closer examination revealed his wounds far worse than she'd originally thought. Already infected, she'd need to reopen both wounds before treating them. How? She wasn't a chirurgeon. Did she have enough comfrey? She'd need it not only for those injured, but to calm her own nerves.

She turned to Grant, fearing his reaction. "I shall need a knife."

Again, from around the room, she heard a resounding, "Nay!"

"Nay, lassie." Grant took silent assessment of her. "I cannot allow that, mind." His expression made it clear he wouldn't change his mind or brook any argument.

"Then you do not really want me treating them." Victoria stubbornly shot back, coolly ignoring his glare and giving him another glimpse of her stubbornness. "If that's the case, I might as well leave. Moreover if you think I care one whit what you think of me, you are sorely mistaken." She shrugged as if she had no care in the world and nothing they said mattered.

How far from the truth!

Approaching her in two long strides, Grant dragged her to the side of the room, and in response to her declaration said menacingly, "But you should, lass. Your life depends on what I think. Naetheless, I cannot give you a knife. My men would not allow it. I must naysay you."

Ready to explode, Victoria explained slowly, as if talking to a child, "I understand your feelings. You have made them perfectly clear since fetching me here. Howbeit, these wounds need to be cleansed, and cleansed quickly."

She waved her hand around the room. "I understand the situation. If I do naught, most will die. Their wounds already fester. Neither can I guarantee what I do will help. I can only try. No matter what, you will not think it good enough."

Grant opened his mouth, no doubt to roar at her, but Victoria cut him off with her own raised voice. "But this is not about winning and losing. 'Tis about saving lives. If I do not treat them, they will die. 'Tis as simple as that, *Laird Drummond*. And, if I treat them and still they die, you will blame me." She paused, wetting her lips. "I know if that happens, you will probably kill me."

Lowering her voice, she glanced around the room, saw men nodding. "I accept that, but I believe Dougal may have chain mail imbedded in his wounds. To remove it, I must cut the surrounding infection. You asked me to help, but are not allowing me to do what 'tis necessary. I believe this is what God would have me do. 'Tis what my grandmum taught me years ago. Pray let me try," she whispered hoarsely, perilously close to tears.

She knew the importance of time and they wasted that precious commodity arguing.

Grant stared at her a long time without speaking. The silence in the room seemed deafening. He drew out his dirk. Clenching his jaw in fierce determination, he ignored grumbles around him.

Eyes riveted on her face, he held Victoria's wrist and placed the dirk in her palm. Conversation muted, he leaned forward and said between gritted teeth, "Do not make me regret this decision. Do nothing that will purposely harm my men, or..." His words trailed off.

Victoria swallowed, nodded her agreement and walked briskly to the fireplace, knowing precisely what he'd left unsaid. Fighting back a shiver of dread, she placed the dirk's blade in the pot of boiling water. Trying to further cleanse it, she held it over the hearth's flame. Steeling herself, she returned to Dougal. "You must hold him."

Though terrified, she tried not to show it.

After giving him a healthy dose of whisky, someone placed leather in Dougal's mouth for him to bite. Several men held him to keep his body from thrashing. Bending over Dougal's pain wracked body, Victoria poised to make her first incision when Angus cursed and grabbed her wrist. Breath ragged, her eyes spun to meet his. His dark grey eyes blazed and narrowed.

"Dinnae do anything you shouldn't, woman. If you do, you will not get out of this room alive. Mark me on that."

"I know, Angus." Turning to begin her incision, her hands shook and sweat broke out on the back of her neck. She hoped since Dougal's name meant God's messenger, God would take a particular interest and guide her hand. She needed His guidance.

Indecisive about her ability, she hesitated. Taking a deep breath, once she started, her hand moved surely and swiftly. After cleaning away much of the infected area on Dougal's thigh it still appeared too red. Though unable to express her concern, she didn't like the look of it. Knowing all eyes bored into her, Victoria leaned over Dougal again and dug deeper with the dirk's tip. The man let out an excruciating yell, then blessedly passed into unconsciousness. Men grumbled behind her.

Soon, the dirk's tip hit something hard. Carefully probing, she let out a whoop and slowly extracted a piece of mail imbedded within the wound.

Several men nodded their heads in approval. Her relief was so great, she felt faint. She needed to sit, had no time. Too many wounds remained.

"Drink," she croaked, running her tongue between parched lips. "I need a drink."

Alexander asserted, "I'll get some ale, or whisky if you prefer."

99

"Thank you Alexander, but I shall need my wits about me this night."

Clearly thinking that a barmy statement, he fetched her something other than ale or their water of life.

Victoria breathed deeply. "I fear his wound will need needle and thread put to it. 'Tis too deep to close on its own."

Grant nodded acknowledgement.

Her face shining with beads of sweat after suturing the injury, she hurried to the counter and mixed a poultice of comfrey, flax, and yarrow. Soon a tankard was handed to her. Accepting it gratefully, she downed it in three gulps as men often drank their ale.

Returning to Dougal, she applied the poultice to his wound and gently wrapped strips of cloth around his thigh to bind it. She hoped it would stem the bleeding and promote healing.

After treating his slashed arm, she thought told Grant, "Though infected, it does not seem as bad as the leg." Back she headed to the boiling water.

Returning, she saw Dougal had regained consciousness. Drat. Why couldn't the bloody heathen stay knocked out? Then he wouldn't feel the pain as badly. Once again, she placed the leather strip in his mouth. Dougal tried giving her a wan smile, but she thought it never quite made it to his lips. She nodded at him, indicating she understood, and concentrated on cleaning out the infection.

Glad to have that ordeal over, Victoria verily hoped Dougal would be her worst patient. Bone tired, she didn't think she could treat too many injuries like that. Evening shadows darkened the room as she walked among the men, tending wounds. Tension dissipated, but still she felt their mistrust.

Hours later she finished, thinking the worst over. Although she'd tend them throughout the night. Too much chance of infection setting in.

Exhausted, she thought she might pass out.

His arm around her weary body, Grant escorted her into his Great Hall. "You have to eat."

She sat heavily. Working for hours, she'd far exceeded the point of exhaustion, had shadows under her eyes. Too tired to make the effort to tie it back again, her hair had become unbound and cascaded down her back.

Men milled around the Hall waiting to hear about injured comrades. Glancing toward them, she noticed Stiubhart's arm bleeding. "What happened to your arm?" She leaned forward to get a better look.

His volatile temper erupted. "'Tis naught but a wee cut. Naught to worry about."

Exhausted, she rose from her chair to check his arm only to have it rudely jerked it away.

"I said 'tis only a scratch!" Stiubhart growled.

Moved to anger, she lost her temper, had an overwhelming urge to scream. Having tended the worst of their companions, things obviously would return to how they'd been before—despising her again. After hours spent treating those most injured, she couldn't take any more anger.

With a willful tilt of her chin, she yelled, "I just spent hours tending your friends with *scratches*! I'll be damned if I'll let you sit here untended because you're too stubborn to ask for help!"

Grant rose at her outburst. "Woman! Do not speak thusly to my men. Women do not use such language in my home! Neither God nor I approve."

Eyes wide, she sank slowly into her chair and burst out laughing, extreme fatigue causing near hysteria. Her laughter earned another glare from Grant.

"God does not approve of a woman using a bit of profanity?" she sputtered sarcastically. "Rubbish! Your men spew garbage from their mouths daily. You think God approves of that? I think not! Besides," she switched thoughts, defending her actions, "I only tried to help. It matters not if a cut is large or small. If untended, it can become infected."

Grant ignored the last part of her dissertation. "'Tis all right for a man to use profanity. 'Tis expected. I repeat, 'tis not proper for a woman, and I'll not tolerate it. Another such outburst and I shall beat you, and there is the end to it."

Paling at his words, Victoria turned away. She thought it no more than she should have expected. Just because he hadn't beaten her before, she should have known his true colors would be revealed in time.

He was, after all, a man.

Turning back, she mumbled a half-hearted apology. "I am willing to tend anyone who only has *minor cuts and scratches*." Softening her words, she reiterated, "It will not take long and would be in your best interest."

101

Grant nodded agreement and sent one of his vassals into the darkness of night to tell anyone injured they should return to the Hall if they so wished. He remained by the hearth, one hand on the mantle. He frowned. *Was that fear in her eyes?*

Grant reconsidered the recent conversation. She'd been her usual argumentative self, standing up to him as she always did. She seemed fearless, quite headstrong, yet the moment he'd mentioned spanking her, her entire demeanor changed.

He wondered at the abrupt change. Surely a lass as stubborn as his wee prisoner wouldn't be afraid of a spanking. He envisioned her getting as many in her youth as he had. Once the present crisis abated, he'd get to the bottom of this mystery. He felt too tired right now.

How could one lassie be such a bossy piece of goods?

Victoria peered up from her trencher and saw most of Grant's men heading into the Hall. They didn't appear happy about being summoned, but they all looked injured! Merciful heavens, what had she gotten herself into? One by one, she tended them. Many only required vinegar and St. John's Wort to cleanse their wounds and staunch minor bleeding.

"'Tis important this be kept clean. Come see me at the first hint of infection or if binding cloths need changing."

As the wee hours of morn approached, everyone left the Hall and she sank beyond exhaustion into the closest chair. She didn't think she could possibly stay awake, yet turned to Grant with furrowed brow. "Milord, am I to believe you were the only man in the entire battle not injured?"

He grimaced.

"Come now," she teased with a tired sigh. He'd been too quiet by half while she tended his men and hadn't moved from the hearth, gripping the mantelpiece. "Would you do less than you asked of your men?"

Glaring, he inhaled sharply, walked slowly to the table and sat heavily on the chair beside her. He inched his kilt up to expose his left thigh. Her eyes widened at the deep gash. Merciful saints, he hadn't been casually leaning against the mantle. He held it to try and ignore his own pain. Neither had he planned to tell her. Eyebrows knit in worry, she cleansed the area and put a poultice on the wound.

Stubborn man!

Chapter Twelve

Victoria wrapped clean strips around his thigh. Grant said nothing throughout the entire process, but his eyes never left her face. He'd forgotten how much her touch affected him.

"Is that your only injury, milord, or have you other wounds you do not wish to tell me about?"

He grumbled about her forwardness, but lowered his plaide and tried to remove his shirt. She stood to help. "Your chest!" she gasped. "The slash is worse than your leg."

He again sat and Victoria knelt in front of him, gently cleansing the wound. He winced and exhaled heavily, but wouldn't admit the extent of his pain.

Her fingers moved gently over his chest while she applied a poultice. Finally he could stand it no longer. The pain in his chest felt unbearable, but the soft touch of her fingers was driving him to distraction!

He fought to ignore her, but failed miserably. Leaning down, he framed her face with his hands. Tilting her head back to face him, he lowered his lips to hers and brushed them with a feathery kiss.

Victoria gasped, but didn't pull back as a shudder of awareness coursed through her. She neither responded to, nor resisted his advances, but her look of shocked innocence gave him pause. Certainly not the reaction one expected from a town whore. With a growl of desire that tore from deep within his chest, he pulled her head to his.

He tried to part her lips with his tongue, but Victoria blocked him, appearing flustered. The lust in his body traversed to his manhood. Saints alive, the lass obviously had scant experience kissing. At least it seemed as if she didn't know how to return his kiss. He couldn't explain the delightful rush that brought him. He'd teach her, of that he felt certain, and he had all the time in the world.

In that instant he knew he'd never let this woman leave his castle.

He pulled away slowly from the kiss and looked deep into her eyes. She tried to lower her head, but he refused to let her. A flush rose to her cheeks, but neither said a word. He stared into her eyes, as if reaching to the essence of her being. His lips again seized hers and he pinned her against his firm, hard body, ignoring the pain caused when she brushed against his wounded chest. When she gasped, he thrust his tongue inside her mouth before she guessed his intent.

Her senses were awhirl as she felt stirrings she'd never felt before. Victoria pulled away from his embrace and tried to bring herself back to reality, her breathing rapid. What just happened? Why had he kissed her? More important, why had she let him?

It felt wonderful.

Turning, she reapplied the poultice, then picked up cloths and completed dressing his wound, trying not to look into his eyes. That felt too personal—like he could see more than she wanted. She had to get away. Now! She needed time to figure out what happened and why she felt as she did. Her inexperience in no way provided answers to the bewildering and wonderful feelings he provoked in her.

She had to flee.

Finishing her ministrations, she picked up her basket and without a word returned to the sick room trying to fight the strange fascination that drew her close to him.

Grant didn't follow. He, too, wondered what he'd done. And just as Victoria had questioned—why had he done it? *And why did he want to do it again?*

Most of the men were up and about within three days. After their initial reluctance to having Tory treat their wounds, many of his *brave* warriors returned over the next days to let her change their dressings. He laughed, knowing their seeking his lass out had naught to do with the state of their wounds.

Archie worsened daily.

Victoria said, "If Archie does not receive treatment soon, he'll die. His fever dreams increase and no matter how many times the men to cool him with mint water, it has been to no avail."

She finally determined she'd tend him herself. She couldn't let him die.

She gathered her herbs and walked toward Archibald as Grant entered the room. With a measured tone, he asked, "What are you about, lass? Archie does not want you near him. 'Twould be most unwise to ignore his wishes."

Victoria's head jerked when she heard his voice. She took a hasty step backwards before retorting, "But he'll die from his stubbornness and I refuse to let that happen. I must try and help him."

"Nay," Grant said, his face tightening in displeasure while he moved closer, "you will not. Archie specifically said—"

"I care not what he said," Victoria challenged, rounding on him in anger. "And I am going to treat this stubborn oaf. Howbeit why I certainly know not. 'Tis probably too late. You cannot let one of your men die, Grant Drummond, simply because he is pigheaded.

"Besides," she said, her nerves stretched taut, "if I treat him while in his fevered state, he'll not know I had anything to do with it. Let the bloody heathen think he healed himself! Indeed, he may think himself invincible, but he's not. You should know that by looking at him."

She placed her hands on her hips. "If you're going to try and stop me, you will have to drag me from this room, because otherwise I *will* treat him." Frustration lanced through her as they glared at each other before she ordered, "Get out of my way."

After a few minutes of neither budging, Grant gave a barely imperceptible nod and moved to let her pass. His face held amused approval. Bloody heathen probably couldn't believe she'd had the audacity to tell him off.

Removing the linen covering Archibald's body, she thought she'd be ill. Two of his wounds had festered to the point she no longer held any hope for his survival. As she'd done with Dougal, she heated Grant's dirk and cleaned Archibald's wounds.

Grant held his friend, knowing pain would be intense, even if Archie didn't appear to be conscious. They'd waited too long. He couldn't blame this death on the girl. Archibald brought this upon himself. The fact she'd saved all his men had been a miracle.

God verily had guided the lass in her healing.

He shook his head, struck by the fact he'd never met a woman like her. She now tried to save the person who'd been cruelest. She seemed a complex creature, his prisoner. At times she had a sense of fear and underlying insecurity and at other times—like the way she'd taken charge and cared for his men—she exuded calm and confidence.

Archibald didn't regain consciousness. For days she tended him, placed new poultices, changed binding cloths, and tried to cool his body of its debilitating fever. Since mint water hadn't worked, she switched to elderflower water.

The remaining men were mobile and even Dougal had almost recovered. As Grant surveyed the room, he realized they all had much to thank her for. She'd been brave in the face of surrounding agony.

The following day Victoria leaned over Archibald to change his binding cloths. She was alone with him, since everyone had recovered enough to return to their homes or sleeping areas. Her eyes were red-rimmed from lack of sleep. To Grant's frustration, she refused to leave the room while anyone remained.

Archibald's eyes opened. Through the charged stillness in the room, he jerked himself out of bed and grabbed her. Fisting his hand, he knocked her to the floor and flung himself atop her. Flattening her beneath him, he choked her. She desperately tried to fight, but the man seemed mad. She tried to scream, but no sound emerged since Archibald choked her too hard.

"I told you I dinnae want a bloody English witch touching me."

The loud commotion brought people running into the sick room. Seeing the tussle, Grant dashed towards Archibald, grabbed him by the hair, and yanked him off Tory with a solid jerk.

She rolled away, gasping for breath. Her neck hurt and her breath seemed pinioned there by fear. She raised her hands to her neck to ensure Archibald really didn't have her anymore. The next thing she knew, Grant scooped her in his arms and rushed her from the room. She tried to look back to see what happened, but had no strength.

She'd have ordered Grant to put her down, but it felt too good to be held. She felt safe. This one time she wouldn't raise a fuss.

Heading to his bedchamber, Grant took the steps two at a time. He opened the door with one hand and kicked it shut once inside. He lowered Tory to his bed. "Are you all right? Faith, woman, I told you not to touch the man, but nay, you always must have your way. This time it almost killed you!"

His last words came with a glower.

She tried to answer, but failed to get her voice to work.

Grant brushed her hair from her face with his roughened fingers while she took in large gulps of air. She looked so pale. Why wouldn't she answer him? He needed to know if he should do anything. Stubborn woman! In vexation, he shouted louder than he meant to. "Are you all right? Answer me!"

She slowly nodded, wheezing harshly. "I...I am all right. I just must catch my breath. And aye, I already know you were right, so you need not rub that in my face." After taking several more breaths, she queried, "Is Archie all right?"

"My men are subduing him," Grant answered, anything but pleased with her at the moment. "When Archie gets angered, 'tis muckle difficult to calm him." He smiled ruefully. "We might need to give him one of your wee potions to knock him out again."

Victoria nodded, but made no move to rise.

The door flew open and Ian strode into the room.

"Is she all right?" At Grant's quick assent, Ian told him, "Took six men to subdue Archie. We did it, though."

He turned towards Victoria. "I do not think it a good idea for you to go down the stairs for awhile, lady. Have you roused Archie enough for one day." He shifted his eyes between Grant and Victoria. "The next time we may not arrive in time to pull him off you."

"Please tell everyone thank you," Victoria said softly and sincerely. "Indeed, I appreciate all you did." She hesitated briefly. "I know 'twould have been easier for everyone involved if you let him kill me, but I thank you for not allowing that to happen."

Before the tears building in her eyes could spill over, she said, "I think I fancy being alone. I vow I need time to gather my wits about myself."

At Grant's silent approval, Ian left the room. Grant, however, didn't.

"Please leave." Her voice quavered. "I really wish to be alone. I think I'll have a bit of a lie down."

"I know you do, lass." Grant gathered her gently into his arms and enveloped her in the circle of his embrace. "I'll stay just the same."

Unable to hold her emotions back, tears fell. Gulping air between great choking sobs, she fell into the comfort of Grant's arms while he whispered soft words in the language his men often spoke. She understood nothing, but it sounded peaceful.

When Grant felt the shudder of her sobs subside, he loosened his arms.

Victoria looked through tear-brushed lashes and asked into the awkward silence, "Why do I muck everything up? Father was correct after all. I can do naught right."

Victoria's eyes shifted to her hands, but not before he caught a glimpse of their pain. "I only tried to help."

"Och, but Archie did not know that, lass," he consoled as if speaking to a child, his expression softening. "His body has been wracked with fever for well o'er a sennight now and I misdoubt he thought clearly when waking to see you above him. When I naysay you in future, best you heed me."

She worried her hands in the fabric of her kirtle. "But what if I make a mistake again?"

With a tenderness that surprised even him, he smiled. "You will, lass." At her look of shock and surprise, he explained, "That can happen when one helps people like you have. You'd not be human if you never made mistakes."

He wondered why she always mentioned killing her. She seemed to expect it.

Needing a diversion, he went to the washstand, then wrung out a cloth to wipe her face. With her body pressed to his, he felt in danger of losing control. Taking a deep breath, he gazed at the young woman on his bed. With dirt smudged on her face, she looked like a lassie playing in his courtyard.

Unbidden, the thought came to him, *my wee lassie.*

Grant had no trouble finding chores for Tory inside his keep. Her assignments seemed endless. To her delight, one day he assigned duties in his library. Though unusual for this part of the country, his father had amassed many books. "I want the room and its contents cleaned and dusted." He seemed surprised when she smiled.

After hours cleaning, she glanced at the books. Since Grant didn't place as many guards on her when she stayed inside his castle, she remained alone. She approached the floor to ceiling bookcases, leaned down, glanced at several books on a lower shelf and selected one.

She settled on a chair, opened the book, and perused it. Engrossed, she didn't realize how much time elapsed, or hear Grant open the library door and enter the room.

"I did not let you stay inside to shun your duties. I expected you to see to your chores."

Shocked, she jumped to her feet, dropping the precious book with her actions. Quickly bending to retrieve it she rushed to reshelf the tome.

"I finished. I just...wished to glance at the lovely drawings," she stammered in panic. She tried to think of a logical excuse for her actions. "The cover looked so lovely, I but wished to see if there were drawings inside."

"It looked like you were reading." He looked at her quizzically.

Paling, she tried to laugh off his words. "I am just a woman, milord. Surely you could not have thought that."

Grant frowned and looked uncertain. "Finish quickly." Shaking his head, he exited the room.

Her knees shook in delayed reaction.

Chapter Thirteen

A loaded wagon trundled into the courtyard while Grant worked his men in the training lists. Auld Gofraidh came by once or twice a year to sell his herbs and wares.

Grant shouted to the children gathered around Tory. "Fetch Cook." Though expensive, he liked his food well seasoned. He started to return to his practicing, but stopped. A delight to behold, he always enjoyed watching Tory.

Once again his young prisoner had children gathered around her. He laughed when he saw one youngster looking at her with undisguised adoration. The young lad—all of four summers—obviously had a case of calf's love. Her sunny disposition seemed to draw children like a wave to the shore. He couldn't begrudge her the time with them, though. She always completed the chores he set forth daily, usually doing more than ordered. Lately, she spent much of her time healing people. No matter how many chores he assigned, she made time for the wee ones and they adored her for it. Even though parents warned them about the hated Englishwoman, they only saw someone willing to spare time for them when no one else would. Even their parents began to come around. Now the bairns had Tory playing peevers and tag. The air abounded with giggles and shouts as children chased each other.

Wee Annie stood at the group's edge watching, a look of yearning in her eyes. Though she never joined in, she never seemed far from Tory, as though bonding with his prisoner in her own fashion. Tory had asked him about Annie, but he really knew little about the girl. As chieftain, he needed to check into such things. He was, after all, responsible for all his people's welfare.

Tory kept his home spotless. She tackled things he neither demanded nor dreamed she'd do. Things no one else would do. Rarely resting, with everything she did around the keep she always seemed in a state of near exhaustion, yet never denied the children any of her time.

She'd cleaned his Great Hall, though he'd thought that impossible. Since his mam's death, that huge room had been deplorable. Victoria removed the old rushes and added new ones, generously sprinkling in garlic to rid the room of fleas brought in by dogs. She added rose petals to fragrance the Hall whenever stepped on. Now the children could play without being bitten by fleas and his men could roughhouse. They used to love wrestling each other and could do so again. The lass made it a pleasure to be home.

He finally admitted he'd wanted her to fail. To his amazement she hadn't. She rose to whatever task he assigned, no matter how unpleasant. And she did it all with grace.

Most of his people had picked up the children's habit of calling her *lady*. That irked him. She was his prisoner.

How had this feisty woman turned that around?

He turned back to his lists when Victoria rose and walked toward the Great Hall.

He turned at a loud shout and saw the grizzled old man move from his wagon. The man called out again and glanced at the Hall. As he walked toward the wagon, Gofraidh called, "My lady! Is that ye?" Grant couldn't imagine whom the old man thought he saw. As he decided the man daft, the peddler shouted, "Lady Victoria, is that really you?"

When Tory paused before entering his Hall, he stopped cold.

Turning, she saw the peddler calling out and waving. She strained to see him better, then raised a hand to her mouth and gasped, "Oh!" in surprise before running back to the courtyard and into the auld man's arms. She flashed a rare and ravishing smile and threw her arms around his neck. He spun her around and joy lit their faces.

The two laughed loudly and spoke in unison. "Is it really you, my lady?" and "What are you doing this far North, my good friend, Godfrey?"

He didn't fancy this turn of events. She'd never laughed like that for him, or flung her arms around his neck. Striding towards them, he jerked Victoria away from the peddler. Without thought to his words, he boomed acidly, "Dare you touch my woman without my permission!" He rounded on Victoria. "How know you this man?" The girl obviously hadn't been as open and uncomplicated as he'd thought. He shot her a reproving glare.

Catching the peddler totally off guard, the old man stammered as he jumped in fright and broke into a nervous sweat. Victoria said nothing, but stilled and met Grant's angry gaze before his eyes moved to the peddler.

The peddler eyed Grant warily and waved his gnarled hands. "I knew this lovely lass her entire life, Laird Drummond. I meant no harm."

Grant pressed, "I asked how you knew her?"

With Victoria standing behind him, Grant couldn't see her. She silently warned Gofraidh to say no more. Fear froze inside her that her friend might reveal her identity.

"I sold my goods to the cook at her manor, my lord," the old man said hesitantly. Victoria could see the fear in his eyes. 'Twas almost like she could read his thoughts. *What is the wee lady trying to tell me with those strange looks she keeps giving me? Doesn't she know I must answer the laird's questions or possibly forfeit my life?*

"She helped Cook decide which herbs needed to be purchased for the fine fare served at Blackstone Manor."

That answer seemed to quell Grant's curiosity. He calmed and turned to Victoria. "You helped in kitchen?"

She tried to stall and carefully phrased her words. "Well, between us, Cook and I were good judges of what we needed. I enjoyed helping compile his list."

Grant nodded and pushed her towards his kitchen. "Good, then for the nonce be gone and come back with Cook's list for *my* kitchen."

Thinking herself safely out of danger, Victoria eagerly rushed to the kitchen.

As soon as she left earshot, Grant spun on his heels and glared at the peddler, his voice hard. "Where do you really know the lassie from? I saw you looking at her for answers. 'Tis the truth I want, mind."

"I have known her for her whole life, Laird Drummond," the old peddler anxiously said, tumult and the first inklings of real fear showing in his eyes. "That is the truth of it."

"You know her well?" Grant's eyes narrowed.

"Och, aye, I do," the peddler proudly stated as a grin lit his wrinkled face. "Och, the things I could tell you about that sweet lassie—"

"That is precisely what I wish," Grant stated with an edge to his voice. He turned to Warwick. "See Gofraidh gives Cook everything on his listing. Then, take him and his wagon out beyond the forest. I shall join you there, for I wish to hear these things he can tell us about the *sweet lassie*. In her presence, send him on his way as if the transaction is completed, but let them not be alone. I want no messages leaving here from her, mind."

An hour later he met Warwick and the peddler in the forest, safely out of view from anyone looking from the castle's battlements. Seating himself on the ground with a stately copper beech tree behind his back, Grant stretched his long booted legs in front of him.

"Now, auld man, tell us how you know her." When Gofraidh didn't immediately respond, Grant urged, "Come, come, man, I have not all day. How do you know her?"

Gofraidh released a muffled groan of resignation. "Och, Laird Drummond, Lady Victoria is a sweet young woman." He shrugged and tried to smile. He didn't succeed.

"Hrmmph!" Grant snorted. "That remains to be seen. I find her quite willful. What did she at Blackstone Manor?

Looking shocked at Grant's request, the auld peddler, or *ceard,* responded quickly, "Ran the whole manor she did. And her being so young. She is seven and ten, mind, but she ran it about five years already. Her da expected her to do everything. A harsh unpleasant man he was. Punished her mightily if she did something he dinnae fancy." The old man wiped perspiration from the back of his neck even though a cool rain lightly fell.

Grant wondered about her age, had thought her considerably younger than his nine and twenty.

"She pitched in with anything that needed to be done," Godfraidh continued in a conspiratorial tone, warming to the subject. "One never would know her for the auld laird's daughter from the way she acted. She is too kind by far to be related to that bloody blackguard."

Grant stiffened at Gofraidh's surprise statement.

"What did you say?" he said, voice controlled. Those around him looked as shocked as he felt. Grant's anger mounted. Had the lass played him for a fool?

"One would never know Lady Victoria is Blackstone's eldest daughter if they dinnae know her well." Grant's hands fisted tightly beside him as the peddler continued, "They were as different as night from day—he being black-hearted, mind, and she having the heart of an angel."

A lying angel, Grant thought, his stomach clenching as tightly as his fists already were.

Blackstone's daughter? Saints knees, how could that be? More to the point, how couldn't he have known? He should have been apparent immediately. Now things she'd said—or tried not to say—made sense.

Perception dawning, his jaw tightened. "Tell me about her and leave out nothing." With a look that brooked no refusal, he rejoined, "Were she and her blackguard of a da close?"

Shaking his head rapidly and not realizing the full import of what he'd revealed, the auld *ceard* quickly told Grant, "Nay, Blackstone delighted in terrorizing his daughter. He hated her because she had not been born a son. His treatment of her was appalling."

Flushed with anger, Grant motioned for the peddler to continue. Questions racing through his mind caused his muscles to clench.

"Ever since she was a wee bairnie, Blackstone beat her. The drunker he got, the worse her punishments. 'Tis only through God's grace the lassie still lives."

"What did she do to warrant beatings?" No emotion crossed Grant's face as he leaned forward to catch every word.

"Och, the lassie dinnae have to do anything but be in the auld man's way. Then again, if he couldn'te find her whilst in his foul mood, he searched for her, growing angrier all the while. He seemed overfond of beating her. 'Tis passing strange considering he's not laid a hand on his younger daughter," he mused. "And the lassie's mam dinnae lift a finger to help. Blackstone hated his wife for the wean being a gel and that worthless excuse for a woman took her anger out on wee Victoria. Her mam dinnae beat her, but never stood up for the lassie." He shot Grant a wan smile.

"Yet through everything, the bonnie lassie maintained an inner strength. God surely touched her. Only her granddam ever treated her kindly, yet Lady Victoria is the kindest, sweetest tempered lass you ever saw. Always sees the best in others. Lady Victoria's granddam adored her and did her best to make the lass' life normal. Called her Tory."

Kind? Sweet tempered? Surely this man spoke of someone other than the hellcat living in his castle.

As the storm increased, they moved to a location affording more protection.

Hours later, Grant smiled tightly and bid the peddler farewell. The auld stooped man didn't need a second offer. He rose and brushed leaves and twigs from his clothes. Taking his leave he told the young chieftain, "Keep you well, Laird Drummond."

Grant didn't respond. What he'd learned was shocking. The lass obviously experienced a good deal of unpleasantness in her

114

life. Now he needed to determine what to do with the garnered information.

"Explains a lot," Warwick said as he drew his mount abreast on their return to the keep.

Rain poured down in sheets and the day's darkness matched the darkness of Grant's mood.

"'Tis good her da is already dead or I would kill the blackguard myself for what he put her through. Certainly explains the nightmares that torment her," the old man continued sadly, shaking his head. The fact Warwick never had a child of his own yet yearned for one made it all the worse.

"Aye, it does," Grant stated, his face revealing nothing of his inner feelings. Truth be told, he felt perplexed. "But what do I with this knowledge? Ignore the fact she's Blackstone's daughter? Ignore she did not tell us the truth?"

Warwick looked at Grant with the wisdom of his years. "You dinnae go to destroy Blackstone's daughter, lad. You went to destroy the man, and you did that. Remember, the lassie told us her intent had been to flee." Pursing his lips, he added reflectively, "Mayhap you dinnae take the lassie by chance. Mayhap there is more happening than any of us are aware of."

"Such as?"

"I am not certain, but methinks the girl has been placed in our care for a reason. My auld mam always told me God never makes mistakes, and from what the peddler said, it appears God has taken a special liking to her." As they dismounted and gave their horses to the groom, he added, "Mayhap you were not so daft in fetching her here after all."

"She is not in my care," Grant groused. He flung open the door to the Great Hall, causing it to crash open with a resounding bang as rain blew in from the force of the wind. Tension in every step, he headed to the ale and grumbled, "She is my prisoner!"

With a hint of a smile, Grant's companion teased, "Are you certain she's the prisoner? Mayhap your wee prisoner has her captor wrapped around her wee finger. My auld mam had another good saying," he added with a chuckle when Grant almost exploded. "She used to say you must always give a stranger a chance, otherwise they will remain strangers and never become a friend."

"I do not want her as a friend," Grant snarled as he slammed his tankard down on the table. "And I do not wish to hear any more of your mam's sayings. The woman does not have me

115

wrapped around her finger. She is my prisoner, naught more. Do not read things in where they do not belong." Grant pushed his tankard, causing it to careen to the floor.

"She is not Maeri, Grant," his mentor said softly. "You must let that memory go."

Grant rose, placed his face in front of Warwick's and hissed, "*Haud your wheesht,* auld man! I told you never to mention her name again." Turning on his heel, he left the room, his voice thundering a string of Gaelic curses throughout the Hall.

"You can tell me to be silent all you want, son," Warwick retorted to Grant's fleeing back. "It changes naught. Your lassie is here for a reason."

Chapter Fourteen

Grant found Victoria in the kitchen, neatly arranging newly purchased herbs. He couldn't believe Cook let this woman in the kitchen. He never let anyone touch what he considered his personal items. Without saying a word, he took her arm and dragged her from the room, pulling her up the narrow stone steps to his bedchamber. She tried to jerk free, but his fingers dug deeper. When he reached his chamber, he pushed her into the room and slammed the door firmly shut behind them.

"What is wrong with you?" she yelled, spinning to face him once he released her. "What think you I've done now? How dare you drag me about this keep like you were a barbarian?"

Ignoring, her storming eyes, he kept a tight rein on his emotions. "I am a barbarian. Best you not forget that." He held out his hand and demanded, "The list you gave Gofraidh earlier, woman. I wish to see it."

Victoria paled. "List?" she croaked. "I have no list." She tried to back away, but for each step she retreated, Grant advanced one. Soon the back of her knees bumped against his bed. Trapped!

Squaring her shoulders, she lifted her chin in a false display of courage.

Grant said nothing, just kept his hand extended and leaned closer. He stood so near she could feel the warmth of his breath.

"Milord, let me leave," she faltered as she tried to inch around him. "I still have things I wish to do. I have not finished arranging the spices we got from Godfrey."

Babbling, trying to think of anything to change the subject, she said with a feeling of growing desperation, "It seemed odd hearing Godfrey's Gaelic name. I knew him so long by the other, you know. Did you know his name means God's peace?"

She stopped for a moment, shocked to see what looked like longing mixed with anger in Grant's eyes. Surely she must be mistaken. He stood so close she felt the heat of his body.

By Saint Michael's sweet soul, she could be one exasperating woman! "Do not gainsay me now, woman," Grant said tersely, gripping her by her shoulders. "You have not until now and this would not be a good night to start. That is correct, is it not?"

His eyes narrowed.

"You have not lied to me ere now?" Grant didn't wait for her answer, but pushed her until she sat on the edge of the bed, which rucked up her kirtle and afforded him a view of her calves. With his hand still extended, he demanded, "I want it now."

She regarded him for a tense moment. Her round, solemn eyes watched his foot tapping impatiently. She blanched and reluctantly reached into the pocket of her shift before handing him the folded paper. He searched her face, unfolded the paper and looked down at the long listing of herbs. The hand was none he'd ever seen and his brow rose in question. "Who wrote this?"

No response.

Aggravated she didn't immediately answer, Grant shot a reproving glare. "I asked a question. Did you write this?" Color fled her face and though she clearly tried to contain them, twin tears gathered, but didn't spill down her smooth cheeks.

"Do not defy me, woman."

Her defenses crumbled. She slowly nodded. It obviously hadn't been an easy admission.

When Grant's gaze shifted back to the list, she thought he'd begin yelling or strike her. To her amazement, he did neither. "'Tis a lovely hand."

Her head jerked up and she stared at him incredulously. He sat beside her, a hint of a smile lighting his face. "Thank you," she said softly, before fear returned and she floundered, "b...but—"

"But what?" Grant interrupted and held up his hand to silence her. "You thought I'd be angered you read and write?"

Hesitantly she nodded and looked at him with both fear and a question in her eyes.

"Never be ashamed of anything you learned, lass," he said with a bit of wonder in his voice. "What angers me, is not that you read and write— but that you hid it. Not many women know how." As an afterthought he added, "Not many men do either. How learned you?"

"I cannot," Victoria said, suddenly in a panic as thoughts of her father returned to haunt her. She looked at him with renewed fear and pulled away to rise from the bed, but Grant stayed her with his hand.

"You can. And you will." Grant's eyebrows rose, emphasizing he meant what he said. "Do not tell me you cannot read, woman. Not only have I seen this list, but I caught you reading in my library. I want to know what happened in your childhood. Tell me." Gentling his tone, he cradled her hands between his two larger ones.

She shook her head wildly, stared at him a long time without answering. Grant only nodded his affirmation and again raised his eyebrows. Hesitantly she began, "But I...I cannot. Father made me promise—"

"Your da is not here. He's dead. Tell me," Grant persisted as she hesitated.

She swallowed and bit her lower lip. She'd always guarded what she told her father. Shouldn't she do that now as well? Dare she tell this man what he wanted to know? Would he beat her if she did? It didn't dawn on her to question how he knew of her father's death, although her head spun with questions. Cautiously she began, keeping her voice steady. "My father did not fancy me. Actually," she laughed hollowly and tried to put her thoughts into words, "that is an understatement. He hated me. He wanted a son and never forgave me for being a girl."

She glanced at Grant to see how he'd taken this information. "I wanted to prove myself as good as any son, so I tried to do everything better than boys in the manor. I always thought there would be one thing I might do so well Father would realize how much he loved me."

She laughed harshly. "Of course, that never happened. I guess I was not intelligent after all to believe it would ever happen, but I foolishly kept trying. Instead of pleasing him, I angered him even more. While the boys attended classes, I hid in the room and listened. I studied alone at night trying to learn what they'd been taught. When I could read and write as well as any boy, better then some, I told my father, envisioning the pride on his face."

She stopped and wrapped her arms about herself. Misery and confusion mixed on her face.

"What happened instead?" Grant asked softly as he ran his hand gently over her arm.

Tears pooled in her eyes, but she fought to hold them back. Drawn by the allure of Grant's gaze, she couldn't force herself to look away. "First he laughed, then shouted. Said men didn't want women who could read and write. They only wanted them in their beds." She stopped and whispered, "That is all he used women for. He yelled it was highly unacceptable for a woman to have schooling and insisted from that day forth I tell no one of my folly."

119

Her voice lowered until barely audible. "I have not until now."

Her body shook and voice cracked. "He beat me and locked me in a storeroom. He...he'd done that before, but never like that time. He got drunk and forgot about me, left me in that t...tiny room all night."

She looked at Grant through tear laden lashes and whispered haltingly, "I...I was so afraid." She admitted this so softly Grant lowered his head and strained to catch her words.

"When he finally released me, he told me he'd decided to take my horse away from me as well. He forbade me to ever ride him again." Victoria sobbed and added mostly to herself, "I loved him so much. Galahad was the only animal I ever owned. Father knew it one of the cruelest punishments he could mête out." She stopped as memories flooded through her and she remembered the pain of that day.

Grant gave her a considering look. He should have figured everything out himself. He'd seen her perusing the books in his library. Her actions had been suspect even though she tried to convince him she'd been looking at drawings.

Not sure how Grant would react to her information, she rushed on in a flurry, "Being surprised to see Godfrey today, I did not think about not writing the list when you mentioned it. Of course, I...I really cannot write much."

Seeing her torment and knowing this last assuredly a lie, Grant felt lost. Although he didn't understand such protective feelings, he raised his hand to her face and rubbed his thumb over her quivering lower lip.

He'd protect this woman for the rest of her life.

Grant framed her face with his hands and slowly lowered his lips, pressing a kiss to her brow, then brushing her lips with his. "Aye you can. Do not ever feel you must lie about it again."

Her skin tingled where his lips touched hers. His words and actions caught her by surprise and it showed in her response. When she didn't pull away, Grant wrapped his arms around her and pulled her closer, growing more intense with his kiss.

"Open your lips," he groaned huskily, instantly feeling the effects of her body pressed against his. This woman pushed him to his limit. "And relax. I'll not hurt you. I promise."

There was no mistaking the lust in his eyes. With only slight coaching on his part, Victoria parted her lips to his insistent tongue. He drew her closer and deepened the kiss, making love to her with his tongue. He unfastened the ribbon tying her hair, causing it to tumble down her back in loose waves. He combed his fingers through them, unable to get enough of her.

Soon his hand cupped her breast and heat surged in the deepest, most private part of her. Her one layer kirtle provided little in the way of protection and she felt his burgeoning manhood against her belly.

She felt suddenly breathless.

Her feelings had her mind in a jumble. How could a kiss make her feel so many emotions? A shiver of awareness coursed through her, flooding her with feelings she didn't know she possessed. Grant pushed her down so they were lying on the bed. His hand glided up the inside of her thigh when someone pounded on his door.

Grant pulled his mouth away from hers and released Victoria reluctantly, then rose to his feet and cursed fluently while striding to the door. He threw it open and raggedly ground out, "Who goes?"

"Grant," Ailean, began, stepping back quickly, "Ian sent me to tell you a courier arrived." A flush crept up the young man's neck when he saw his young chieftain's tousled hair and the disheveled state of his plaide. He stammered, "'Tis sorry I am to disturb you, but Ian thought you'd want to come down the stairs."

Grant looked back at Victoria and saw the passion-filled look in her eyes. Merciful St. Columba, he'd put that look there.

And he wanted to do more—so much more.

He massaged the back of his neck and heaved a resigned sigh. Storming out the door with a mutter of disgust, he slammed it shut behind him. What the deuce had he been thinking! She was his prisoner, not his lover. He'd taken her upstairs to yell at her and force the truth out of her, not make love to her. He'd not make that mistake again.

Muttering an eloquent curse, he headed to the Great Hall and grabbed a tankard from the table, downing its contents quickly.

"What message have you, Ian?" he blurted in frustration, mainly with himself. Had he not been interrupted, he'd have thoroughly loved to the lass. "What needed you that you interrupt me?"

Ian showed Grant the note that just arrived. He tipped his head toward the ale barrel to let Grant know the messenger awaited a reply. Once again, they were needed to fight against

Edward's men. Grant ensured the tired messenger, "My men and I shall leave on the morrow."

Not only would they put Edward in his place, he'd put as much distance as he could between himself and the lass. The timing couldn't be more perfect.

Soundly stopping Edward's forces during the battle, Grant pulled his men aside. "I have a side journey I wish to take. 'Tis personal, so you may accompany me or head home."

His men heartily joined him on his brief sojourn.

A mere sennight after they detoured from their journey home, afternoon guards on the ramparts yelled, "Riders approach." Activity bustled in the courtyard and word quickly spread that Laird Drummond approached.

Soon men rode in under the battlements, followed by twenty beautiful horses. A smile came to everyone's lips. Their great chief had been reiving again.

Rhiannon dashed into the Great Hall. "Laird Grant's back." Everyone rushed outside to well-come the men home. Rhiannon saw Victoria hesitate, grabbed her hand, and pulled her towards the door. "You too, Lady Tory. Come well-come our men home."

Victoria followed, hesitated at the door. She doubted Grant would want her greeting him.

Rhiannon released Victoria's hand when she spotted her father and went flying into his arms. Dougal looked healthy this time, as did most men. Quickly spotting Grant, she released the breath she'd been holding until she saw him. He, too, looked fit. Her medicaments wouldn't be needed overmuch this day. She breathed a pleased sigh of relief and smiled.

Grant spotted her immediately when she reached the door. He witnessed her happy smile and saw her hesitance about coming forward to join in the festivities. *She doesn't know where she fits in.* She reminded him of Annie, always standing on the outskirts of activities.

Dismounting his great steed, he tossed the reins to his page and walked resolutely to Victoria. Her eyes shone, but she lowered them demurely. "Well-come back, milord. 'Tis glad I am to see everyone all hale and hearty this time."

"Och, aye," he responded while his eyes roved over her body. He'd missed her. Although determined to keep her from his thoughts, she'd crept into them every day, and certainly every night. "We are much better off than the last battle we returned from."

Grant swept his hand in the direction of the courtyard. "We took a side trip, too, to obtain some horses." Never taking his eyes from hers, he continued with a teasing glint, "Would you fancy seeing them?"

With a look of surprise, she took a steadying breath and nodded in agreement. "Aye. They look quite beautiful." Grant wrapped her hand in his large one and pulled her after him down the steps. They joined the mingling throng of people who admired the new horseflesh and moved smoothly through the crowd.

As they approached several animals, she noticed how exquisite they were. "Where did you buy these?" she asked breathlessly and looked up at Grant in awe. "They are truly of rare quality."

Around her, men guffawed while Grant glared at them to silence them. His piercing eyes took in her body's every movement.

"We acquired these fine steeds from several locations south of here." He watched her closely as he carefully walked her around several horses.

When they approached a fine steed, Victoria *oohed* and *aahed* over the lovely horse, exclaiming over its beauty. A horse behind her whinnied and pushed her forward.

She tried to ignore the interruption while she continued to caress the chestnut mare's neck, but the horse behind her remained persistent. Becoming exasperated, she rounded on the animal to scold it and stopped dead in her tracks. She stood stock-still and stared at the lovely horse now before her. It whinnied, and lowered its head to nudge her.

Without saying a word, she flung her arms around the animal's neck and laid her face gently against it. "Galahad," she whispered, "is it really you?" As if in answer to her question, the horse lowered his head so she could more easily caress it.

She bit her lips and tried desperately not to cry. Surely this couldn't be possible. How could her beloved horse be here?

Behind her, Grant watched her every move with a smile. He watched her place her cheek upon the horse's mane and couldn't stop himself from reflecting how much he wished she'd do that to him. That she'd run her smooth hands over his naked body and not over the horse's. Lust flared in his eyes—and his loins.

Feeling eyes upon her, she turned to Grant and asked with a trembling voice, "Where did you get this horse?"

"Why from your auld stables, I believe," Grant said with a smug look as he continued to eye her hungrily. "You did say the horse belonged to you, didst you not? We got the correct one?"

"Aye, but how—?"

"Some questions are best left unanswered, lass," he chuckled and his mouth curved in a wry smile. "I thought you might fancy having him around. Mayhap I'll let you ride him sometime, if you'd like."

Seeing a sparkle appear in her eyes, Grant ventured, "Mayhap on the morrow?"

Without a thought, she flung herself at Grant. She twined her arms around his neck and kissed him firmly on the mouth. "Ooh, thank you, milord," she said with a grin that lit her entire face. Grant had never seen her so lovely. "Thank you so much. Oh, Blessed Mary, I missed Galahad so much."

After she saw the shocked look on Grant's face, she realized what she'd done and tried to disentangle herself. She hoped no one else had witnessed her faux pas and surreptitiously glanced around. She saw everyone in the yard watching with arched brows and licentious grins.

Face flaming, her smile faded. Victoria stammered, "Grant, I am sorry. Pray forgive me. I did not think. I vow I just..." Words failed her, and Victoria wished she could crawl into a hole and hide. She turned away and buried her face in Galahad's mane. How would she face these people again? What had she been thinking?

Grant on the other hand thought she could greet him like that any time she wanted.

Chapter Fifteen

When Grant finished his training the next day, he searched for Tory and found her working in the herbary. "Wish you to go for that ride we spoke about yesternoon, lass?"

Grant saw her indecision. He knew she did, but after she kissed him in front of his men she'd tried to remain as distant as possible. That hadn't relieved his problem. All he could think of while lying in bed had been that she lay near him again instead of being miles away. Not to mention the numerous delightful things he wanted to do to her beautiful body. Instead he'd lain alone for hours.

Now he felt determined to get her away from the keep. Alone.

Finally, Victoria's desire to ride her precious horse prevailed. *Now if only she'd ride me*, Grant thought silently! Grant shook his head to bring him back to the present. He needed to stop these constant thoughts. They were driving him insane.

When they arrived at the stables, both horses were ready. Grant helped Victoria mount, but kept her reins in his hands for an awkward moment. Before handing them over, he cautioned, "Do not make me regret this, Tory. Do not try to run away when we get out the gate."

So excited to be riding her beloved horse, she willingly agreed. There would still be plenty of time to leave later. She need not do it now.

As they rode in silence, Grant changed course toward a small, peaceful glen. Stopping, he helped her dismount. He held her a trifle too long, and thought he'd never seen her so relaxed.

Nor so beautiful.

"'Tis a lovely spot, Grant," she glanced around, her face lit with eagerness. "And riding Galahad again has been wonderful. I cannot thank you enough for fetching him here – even though you will not tell me how you found him." She gave him a brilliant smile.

Grant finally admitted, "Your granddam told me which one belonged to you."

Her eyes widened in amazement. "You saw my... grandmum?"

125

Grant nodded.

Overcome by emotion of the moment, she rushed on, "Oh, how is she? Is she well? Did you tell her where I am? Did she ask about me? Did she...?"

Grant laughed at her onslaught of questions.

"Whoa, lassie. One question at a time. Aye, I saw your granddam, although it took skill to figure out her room without alerting the entire manor. On the journey here you sounded concerned about her and your wee sister, so I thought 'twould be good to ensure they fared well. She is fine, although weak. I do not think her health is good, but that is probably due to age."

She nodded wearily. "I do know. She didn't feel well before I left. If I could have brought her with me, I would have done so, but I knew 'twould never be possible. Such a journey would have been too taxing." She admitted sadly, "Oh, but I did hate leaving her and my sister. I love them so much. They're the only people that were ever kind to me."

Grant frowned at her words, but interrupted. "She did ask about you, lass. We did not have much time, since we did not want to be discovered, but I answered as much as I could without revealing all. I am certain I did not tell her everything she wished, but knowing you are alive and well seemed sufficient.

"Although tired, she led us down the hall to your sister's room. The lassie slept soundly, but she is a bonny wee thing. I can see why she means so much to you. Your granddam said to tell you your sister is well and growing like a weed.

"Although too weak to accompany us to the stables, she gave good directions on how to find your horse. She seemed pleased you would be reunited with him." Grant noticed Victoria growing weepy-eyed. "Fret not. Your granddam is fine and much happier since being assured of your safety. She wanted me to tell you servants are taking good care of her. Said she feels like a queen with ladies-in-waiting." Though the words were spoken lightly, he could see a great weight lifted from Tory's shoulders.

The auld peddler had been aright. Tory and her grandmother were obviously close.

Suddenly, Grant surprised her with a basket of food. "I thought you might be hungry after our ride. Join me." He took her hand within his and pulled Victoria beside him.

Grant leaned against the large oak with legs outstretched and crossed at the ankles. He watched Victoria avidly look at the spectacular view stretched before them. The fragrance of blooming flowers wafted through the air.

Eyes lighting up, she looked at Grant's tanned face and excitedly said, "Your land is beautiful. I would love to see it all someday."

Grant grew pensive. "Well, lass, that is up to you."

"I do not understand. Why do you say...?"

Grant interrupted. "Have I your promise you will not try to run from my castle? I cannot let you ride around my property if I must continue to worry you will disappear. I must have your promise afore I'll begin making such concessions."

When she didn't immediately answer, Grant pulled her close. "Think carefully on your answer, Tory, for will I solemnly hold you to your word."

"But, I...I cannot—"

"Aye, lass, you can," Grant stopped her as he rubbed his thumb lightly over her lower lip and tamped down an urge to kiss her. "I know you still hope to leave. I also know that will never happen."

Her eyes flew to his face and he let the impact of his words sink in. "What is freedom around my keep worth, Tory? Will you promise to stay so I can allow you to move around more freely than you do now?

"I cannot grant privileges if I must continue to hold you as a prisoner. I would rather you thought of this as your home."

His words taking her aback, Tory didn't respond, but stared into his eyes. Could she give up her dream of escaping? Truth be told, did she really want to leave anymore? She'd started to feel comfortable now that people began to accept her.

Could that be enough of a reason to stay? Were she honest, was that the *only* reason she wanted to stay?

She rose to her feet and paced. "Grant," she began hesitantly, wringing her hands in the folds of her kirtle, "you simply do not understand."

She turned and found he stood behind her.

"Aye, lass, I do. I know how difficult it can be to give up on something you thought you really wanted. I lost something I wanted a long time ago, too." He drew closer still and ran the back of his hand lightly over her cheek. Eyes dark with desire, the jolt that shot through them felt like a thunderbolt and caught them both off guard.

Astonished by the depth of his feelings, he pulled Victoria against him, cupped her buttocks, and held her firmly against his hard, lean body. He rested his head lightly on her hair and smelled the light rose fragrance she always used. He gently touched her chin and tipped her head up to face his. He tentatively touched his lips to her trembling mouth, which caused his pulse to increase. No longer able to stop himself, he lowered his mouth to hers and claimed it with an urgency he hadn't anticipated. He'd waited too long to do this, but knew he should stop.

She hadn't yet said she'd be willing to stay.

He lowered her to his plaide and his hands roamed over her lush body. Lightly down her arm, gently at the nape of her neck. She responded to him eagerly, yet tentatively, like she had when he'd kissed her the first time. He could sense her nervousness, but the soft whimper which emanated from her throat proved to be his undoing.

Lust conquered reason. He wanted her, and naught else mattered. His mouth slanted over hers again and again. Victoria panicked, yet felt awed at the same time. His musky male scent overwhelming her, she'd never known such ecstasy.

When he unlaced her shift at the neckline, Grant's hand moved until it lightly cupped her exposed breast. He heard her inhale sharply and felt her slightly pull away from him and start to say something, but he quickly drew her close again and covered her mouth with his own to silence her.

Although her mind raced with unanswered questions, soon her mouth softened and surrendered as the first stirrings of passion within her intensified.

Any thought of stopping him quickly disappeared. She moaned as Grant's mouth gently moved down her neck and placed small quick kisses everywhere his hands explored. His mouth latched onto her breast, and she thought her world would explode.

When he raised his lips again to hers, she shivered at the loss of his mouth on her breast and her body arched. In that instant Victoria felt his hard male member press against her belly and panicked. She glanced down and noticed his rucked up kilt. Merciful heavens, he looked huge! There would be no way she'd be able to...

She pulled away in panic, inhaled deeply, and stammered, "Please, Grant, I cannot. I..."

Grant pulled her back into his arms and silenced her with another kiss, his tongue stroking her gently. He forced himself to roll over and stand up, and held his hand out to help her rise. It took every ounce of strength he had to keep from tossing her to the ground and mounting her right then. By the saints, that is what he really wanted to do. Bury himself in her. Breathing raggedly, he said instead, "I'm sorry, lass. I planned only a leisurely ride." He noted she didn't catch the double meaning of his words.

While he shifted his stance uncomfortably, Victoria noticed he still appeared aroused.

Her emotions were in turmoil. Kissing him felt so good. Why did she have to be such a coward? She'd obviously never find anyone who would wed with her. Not after what her father had done. Did she really wish to spend the rest of her life alone?

It appeared the door to her past waited for her to close it, but the question rose as to whether she'd be brave enough to move ahead through the new door standing ajar.

Shaking her head, she knew she had no choice. Unless he forced her, God's principles her grandmother had instilled in her wouldn't allow her to become his mistress.

She breathed heavily and murmured sadly, "I am sorry, Grant. Truly. 'Tis that I cannot..."

She couldn't finish her sentence, but as he looked into her eyes, she clearly wanted him as much as he wanted her. Bloody hell, what would he do about this?

Upon return to the keep, Grant received word Duncan traveled enroute from Rhiedorrach and sought Highland hospitality. Grant thought it just the diversion he needed. Knowing Duncan, he'd have an entire entourage with him. The man did nothing simply.

Grant immediately tried to dismiss all thoughts of Victoria from his mind. Now if only other parts of his anatomy would follow suit.

After he broke his fast the next morn, he double-checked to ensure all plans were finalized. In a low, cold voice he'd assigned Victoria the task of readying spare rooms for his guests. He also told her he wanted her to confer with Cook about menus. Now would be a good time to try out those expensive spices she'd been so excited about.

He soon found he had nothing to fear. With the ease of one used to running a large home, Victoria had taken care of everything. He felt surprised at her thoroughness.

Upon Duncan's arrival, Victoria ensured everyone was settled into comfortable surroundings. Grant laughed as he saw all the men milling about his keep. They'd have a fine time this week.

A slow smile replaced the scowl he'd worn since he and Tory returned from the glen. Aye, he always enjoyed Duncan's visits.They were as close as brothers. They fought well together in battle, too, and had done so far too many times.

After telling Grant that Edward won another battle down at Ayr, the two men settled back to catch up on old times.

As they drank and lazily reminisced, he watched his friend's eyes gravitate toward Victoria. That shouldn't have surprised him. Duncan always scouted his newest conquest. Suddenly it occurred to him he might have the perfect solution to his immediate problem. He groaned aloud at that thought, since the word *problem* described his predicament so aptly. It seemed he could no longer be anywhere near the girl without wanting to bed her.

As the thought entered his mind, the lady in question crossed the Great Hall and headed toward the kitchen, moving with her usual grace. He wondered again how she'd made this day run so smoothly. Everything had been perfect for his guests' arrival. When he gave her the news, she acted immediately, and everything had been completed to perfection, as if it required no extra effort. She ran everything from the background and never drew attention to herself. Just seeing her enter the kitchen set his body aflame again. He couldn't take his eyes off her, nor obviously could Duncan. His friend seemed quite fascinated with the girl.

Shifting uncomfortably in his chair, he felt the same rising problem he always experienced in Victoria's presence.

He settled the matter firmly in his mind, called over a buxom serving lass, and quickly gave her instructions. A look of alarm crossed the girl's face. "Are you certain, m'lord?" she asked in shock. "I do not think Lady Tory—"

"Aye, Ginny, that I am. Very certain indeed, and 'tis my orders you follow, not hers." His tone chilled her, and with a cavalier wave of his hand he affirmed, "Get you gone and carry out my orders, lass."

Only he didn't feel the least bit certain of his actions now the wheels were set to spinning. His insides churned as he gave the order. Did he really want this?

Giving a brief curtsy, Ginny left the room with a strange look on her face and headed to the kitchen. She quickly found Victoria and relayed Grant's orders.

"He wants me to what?" Victoria asked with disbelief and incredulity.

"Aye, lady. 'Tis Laird Drummond's orders. He said he specifically wanted you to serve this night. Said you should borrow clothes. I do not think I have anything that will fit, mind. Mayhap Seonaid might have somethin' for you. She is smaller on top than me." Giggling, the heavy young girl hurried off to find Seonaid and relay the message.

Chapter Sixteen

Victoria couldn't understand Grant's motives. He'd had her do many things around his castle since he brought her here, but had never had her serve his men. And there would be great feasting this night with their many guests, which meant freely flowing whisky. Victoria already heard bursts of laughter coming from the Great Hall. Instinct warned this could lead to potential problems.

Well, she thought, somehow she'd have to make the best of this. Pausing to compose herself and rearrange her borrowed clothes one final time, Victoria bravely headed to the tables with Cook's capon and goose to serve the men she knew well. She felt half exposed with as much breast as this blouse bared. The looks of shock on the men's faces as they eyed her across the wide table told her none of them had prior knowledge of Grant's orders. She felt her cheeks grow hot at their bold stares.

To their many questions, she could only shake her head and answer she didn't know why he had her serving this night. She saw many men had trouble keeping their eyes from her half exposed breasts. She again thought the clothes Seonaid loaned her didn't particularly cover a great deal. She feared if she leaned over too far she might spill out of the blouse.

She tried to avoid the head table where Grant supped, but soon discovered that didn't fit his strange plans. He ordered she alone serve the head table.

Gathering her courage, she set her turbulent thoughts aside and took over the serving chores from Ginny for the remainder of the meal. She felt all eyes on her as she approached the main table.

Duncan, seemed quite taken with the new lass, and raised his eyebrows in question to Grant. "And why have you kept this tasty morsel away from us? Keeping her all to yourself, I would wager." He eyed him sagely and slapped Grant on the back. The look he saw in Grant's eyes gave Duncan all the answer he needed, even though Grant himself didn't.

Duncan appeared well on his way to being deep in his cups – and Erwin, an upleasant man in Duncan's party, continually ensured Duncan's tankard remained filled. Looking at Grant in a most thorough fashion, Duncan nodded to himself and smiled. Aye, he had all the answer he needed.

Grant ground his teeth in silent frustration as he watched Victoria try to avoid Duncan's hands while clearing the table. She found it exceedingly difficult to do so. He saw his friend nuzzle her neck as she bent to remove an uneaten trencher from the table. Later he saw Duncan place a proprietary arm around her shoulders to draw her closer.

His own hands firmly grasped the side of his chair when he saw her breasts almost spill out of her blouse. Duncan's eyes were about to bulge out of their sockets from leering at the lass' lovely attributes. He could only imagine what his own were doing.

He'd arranged for entertainment after the meal, and everyone settled in to enjoy the festivities. With whisky flowing freely, several men enjoined serving lasses to dance with them. Victoria tried to stay out of everyone's way as much as possible while still ensuring tankards remained filled.

Once when she ventured to the head table, Duncan grabbed her around her waist, rose from his chair, and swept her onto what now served as a dance floor. He held her so close she could barely breathe.

"Please, milord," she said breathlessly while Duncan whirled her around the floor. She could feel her long hair flying freely behind her. "'Tis not seemly for you to hold me so closely." His already swollen member pressed hard on her belly as her green kirtle whirled around her with soft rustling sounds.

"Och, but lass," Duncan, began drunkenly. His words slurred together and his hand caressed lightly down the small of her back. "You feel much too good to be lettin' go of." He tightened his arm around her waist and pulled her firmly against him.

While she danced with Duncan, Grant's men drunkenly asked permission to dance with her as well. He glared, but surprised them by nodding his assent, and Victoria glided from man to man during subsequent dances. With them she at least felt more comfortable, although in several instances she felt acutely aware of their physical presence as she had with Duncan.

Thinking her incredibly graceful, his eyes followed Victoria as she glided across the Hall. He felt a pang of jealousy that he couldn't hold her while she danced, but knew he couldn't do that. He'd sworn never to dance again, and hadn't since that fateful day with Maeri.

Duncan looked extremely handsome in his clan plaide, but Victoria didn't feel comfortable around him. And she thought his men far too rowdy! She wished Grant would let her leave the Hall. She was having fun dancing, but everywhere she moved she felt Duncan's eyes on her, and if she got too close, she felt his hands! She didn't know why he disconcerted her so much, but he did, and the man who sat beside Duncan had such evil looking eyes. She tried to avoid looking at Erwin, but felt his eyes boring into her. She squirmed under his scrutiny and felt like he literally undressed her with his eyes. A shudder of revulsion coursed through her.

Taking a break from dancing, she caught her breath while she served more ale to the head table. Why wouldn't Grant look at her? A few times she'd thought she felt him watching her, but when she glanced in his direction, his eyes remained carefully averted.

Had she truly done something wrong in the glen? She'd obviously offended him. But he'd kissed her; she hadn't asked him to do so. Mayhap he felt disgusted she didn't know how to kiss properly. She'd happily learn as long as he taught her. *Oh merciful heavens, where had that thought come from?* It was true, though, she ruefully sighed. She wanted nothing more than to kiss him again. It didn't matter though, since she doubted it would ever happen again. He'd most definitely avoided her since then. Which, she thought, made it even more of an oddity that she now served his table.

Duncan appeared so deep in his cups he could barely stand. As her saintly grandmother would have said, the man looked totally foxed. He clutched at Victoria the next time she walked by and pulled her down onto his lap. He held her tightly with his sinewy arms, and pulled her closer for a kiss. As he ground his hips against her bottom, Victoria could feel his enlarged manhood.

She tried to pull away, but he became angered and Grant heard his loud mutterings, "Nay, Sweetheart, do not pull away. You shall grace my bed this eve and I wish but a taste of what's to come."

He didn't remember the man ever being so loud.

Shivers of apprehension coursed though Victoria as she yanked herself forcefully from Duncan's arms and glared down at him. Anger flared in her voice. "I certainly will not grace your bed this night, my lord, nor any other. You think far too highly of yourself."

She pulled away and dashed over to Grant. "Please let me leave the room." To her shock and dismay, he glared and declined her request. She didn't understand why, but he suddenly looked cross.

"Please, Grant," she said breathlessly, swallowing back her fear, "the men are far too tipsy. I fear the situation may get out of hand. Lord Duncan is becoming too…"

His voice harsh, Grant turned away and shot instruction over his shoulder that she'd entertain all of his guests in whatever manner they wished. Struck by the harshness of his words, she frowned.

"But Grant," she beseeched, her voice aghast and trailing off as she met only his disappearing back. Before she could question his odd behavior, she felt herself again swept onto the Hall floor. She was whirled and twirled until she could scarce catch her breath.

Grant watched from the corner of his eye, and set his jaw firmly, his expression uncompromising. He'd done the right thing this night. He knew it. It would be best for the lass if she went to a different castle. *'Twould be best for him.*

Tension pounded at his temples. Duncan wouldn't hurt the gel, just bed her. And he felt certain Victoria had done that enough times before. Once again the thought of her being with another man wrenched his stomach inside out. The thought it would be his best friend this night did naught to dispel his uneasy feelings. He ruefully admitted he alone wanted to bed her.

Warwick joined him and frowned in disapproval. "You shame yourself this night, son. I never thought to see you, of all people, playing the coward."

"Watch your tongue auld man," Grant shouted. Anger flared through him as Warwick's words struck too close to home. "You go too far. I'll not listen to your nonsense."

His old friend grabbed him by the arm to stop his exit. "Och, aye, you will. What you are doing to that wee lassie is a great injustice. You are doing it out of fear, and I never thought to see you act the feckless fool."

When he angrily protested, Warwick stopped him. "Nay, dinnae interrupt. You have pulled away from any type of commitment since young Maeri's accident – and 'twas an accident. I am thinkin' she dinnae die because you planned to meet at the dance. You must quit blaming yoursel'. If you dinnae, you will never have a relationship. You are nine and twenty, lad, and 'tis time you—"

"Not to blame?" Grant inhaled sharply, his gaze locking angrily with Warwick's as his voice rose. "Of course I am to blame. Had we not planned to meet at that dance, she would not have been on the road when footpads murdered her! Not to blame? You think Maeri's family has forgiven me? Nay! And neither will I. Be silent and leave me be, auld man. I know what I am doing. And," he further spat, "I do not wish a relationship. Leave me in peace!"

"Nay, I dinnae think you do," Warwick persisted, his voice thick with disapproval and an accusatory look in his eyes. "Is it only whores you plan to spend the rest of your life with? What about an heir? Do you wish the Drummond line to die out with you? You owe it to your people if not for yourself."

"The Drummond line will not die out! You know that only too well."

Warwick continued as though Grant hadn't interrupted him. "You have a bond with this lassie if you will but admit it and quit trying to fight your feelings. You need her." Grant looked ready to explode, but Warwick continued, "She's brought out a side of you none of us have seen in a long time. A side you kept buried far too long.

"Mayhap you may not mind torturing yourself, but look about you. I believe there's not a man among us that believes you do the right thing by the poor lassie. If you really wish to be rid of her, let one of your own men have her. Many here would gladly take her to wife. Or," his mentor said in a parting shot as he closely watched Grant's reaction, "is it that you cannot bear to have her so close? Is that the true problem? I have seen how you look at her when you think no one watches. We all have. You want her – and you know it. Are you too much of a coward to admit it?"

"Be gone," Grant shouted in foul temper, "and do not come near me again this night!"

"For the love of God, man, will you not reconsider? Tory is a rare woman. When you look back on this night years from now," came Warwick's persistant plea, "do you wish to look at the chance you took or the one you let slip away?"

He strode away from Warwick and saw Duncan had Victoria up against the stone wall, his pelvis pressed firmly against the junction of her thighs. He was doing his best to kiss her, and she desperately tried to fend him off. Why did she fight Duncan so hard, he wondered in frustration? Most women would be pleased to be chosen by Duncan. They'd drag him upstairs themselves if given the opportunity. He'd always been a favourite with the women of Grant's keep. Why did his lass have to be so obstinate?

Och, there was that thought again – *his lass*.

Victoria broke Duncan's hold and rushed over to Grant, her voice tremulous. "Grant, please, this is madness. I beg you to let me leave. I cannot stay in the Hall any longer!"

"You can and you will, woman," he said with an edge to his voice. The nerve in his neck twitched as he tried to keep his emotions under control. "Leave me be." He grappled with questions whirling through his mind to which he had no answers. He turned away from her, only to find Warwick at his elbow.

"I told you to stay away from me, auld man," he growled, his eyes dangerously narrowing to small slits.

"I find it most interesting you know so little about one so close to you," the old man chuckled and completely ignored Grant's threats. At Grant's frown, he continued, "Have you not noticed how predictable Lady Tory is?"

He rushed on before Grant could answer. "When she gives an answer she does not deem important, 'tis always 'milord.' When she thinks you should pay close attention, 'tis 'Laird Grant.' But when she really wants your attention, or feels what she is saying is of utmost importance, then you are plain auld 'Grant.' I have often thought that interesting. I doubt she is even aware she is so predictable." With a casual shrug Warwick walked away and left him to ponder his words.

Suddenly he wanted this eve to end. As much as he enjoyed the man's company, he wanted Duncan's visit to end and Victoria to be gone with him. He knew his friend's tastes in women only too well, and knew one night with Tory in the man's bed wouldn't satisfy his lust.

Just as he knew one night with her in his own bed wouldn't be enough. He wanted her for a lifetime. It was why he reacted the way he did whenever around her.

Duncan would request permission to take her to his own castle.

Why couldn't it just happen? Why did he have to watch? Och, his feelings were all tapsal-teerie right now.

He sat in his chair and drank without stopping. Mayhap whisky would take his staggering pain away. Naught else appeared to work. Fraught with self-doubt, he couldn't stand the beseeching looks Victoria threw his way. Not to mention the glares he now got from most of his men. Archie would probably be the only person who would congratulate him on his plan to remove Victoria from his keep.

As he quaffed down another tankard of ale, he heard Victoria's scream. His heart froze. Duncan had thrown her down on the table and drunkenly tried to kiss her. He heard Duncan growl in low, rich tones, "If you will not go upstairs, lass, I'll take you right here on the table." He motioned for his men to hold her down. Erwin, to Duncan's left, seemed to enjoy his participation in this debacle far too much.

He frowned, his mind in turmoil. What was Duncan doing? He'd never been unthoughtful before and never forced a woman in his life. He'd always been most considerate.

Tears streamed down her face as Victoria turned her head wildly trying to locate him. She beseeched, "Grant... p...please!"

For one terrible moment he witnessed Duncan begin to use force to make her acquiesce. Again the thought flashed through his mind, why would Duncan do this? It was so unlike him. Erwin, Duncan's aide, leered at Tory like he wanted her to slake his own needs.

Grant had to grab hold of his chair to stop himself from going to Victoria's aid. This had turned into a nightmare! Not at all what he envisioned when he came up with this *brilliant idea*.

He thought Tory would be swept off her feet by Duncan's charm and good looks and willingly throw herself into his bed. Most women would. Usually, all Duncan needed to do was smile to have women swoon at his feet. They thought him handsome and gallant.

Suddenly he realized that thought didn't please him either. If Tory thought to do any swooning, he wanted it to be over him. *Damnation, is this what I really want?*

He groaned and could bear no more. Why did Duncannot take Victoria upstairs so no one – he in particular – had to watch?

He glanced back in time to see Victoria struggle futilely as Duncan slowly, but methodically, raised her kirtle. And he saw the exact moment realization dawned on her that he wouldn't be coming to her aid. With a low cry of defeat, she looked at him with wounded eyes and her body crumpled as she quit fighting. She finally accepted he would do nothing, nor would his men. Tears streamed down her face.

A quick glance at his men showed most had risen from their seats. All eyes were on Tory and they were poised to protect. They merely waited for his order, and frowned when it wasn't immediately forthcoming.

God help him, he couldn't do it! In that instant he knew what he told himself the night he kissed Victoria the first time had been correct.

He'd never let her leave his castle.

The stubborn woman wormed her way into both his heart and his life, even though he'd tried to keep her out of both. And he wanted her in *his* bed, not his best friend's.

Swearing in exasperation, he jumped up and launched himself across the empty chairs that separated him from Victoria. Anger flared in his eyes as he grabbed Duncan by the scruff of his shirt and pulled him roughly away from his woman. "Gorblimey! Enough!" he stormed as his strong hands kept Duncan away from Victoria.

Foxed, Duncan stumbled back a few steps before he caught himself and straightened.

Grant gathered Victoria close and held the sobbing woman protectively. He pulled her firmly against him as she hid her face in his red plaide.

"What is gnawin' on you, Grant?" Duncan smiled and asked drunkenly and struggled to maintain his balance. "'Twas a wee bit of fun we were having. Right, lass? Never have you denied us women in your keep afore."

"Nay, Duncan, I have not, but until this eve you always chose willing lasses. I will not tolerate rape in this keep, and well you know it." He tried to push Victoria behind him, but she clutched his plaide too firmly to get her to move.

"Nay, please hold me." She fought down the impulse to fling her arms around his neck and never let go.

He looked down at Victoria's vision of innocence, he turned back to Duncan and emphatically added, "And this night you have chosen the wrong woman. I'll allow no man to touch my lady wife!" There was now ownership in his hold on Victoria.

A collective gasp filled the room.

"What are you speaking about?" Duncan asked with a strange smile as he continued to bait him. Grant had the odd sensation he should wipe that smug look off the man's face. "This woman is not your wife. She is but a serving lass. You have no wife."

"I do, and she is," Grant retorted irritably. "Have I not said so in front of this hall full of people?"

139

"Lass?" Duncan slurred, his brows seeming to raise in speculation and the hint of a smile spreading on his face as he leaned forward to peer at Victoria.

Victoria trembled. He leaned close to her ear and whispered gently, coaxing her. "Tell him you are my lady wife, Tory." When she stared in non-understanding with frightened eyes and didn't immediately answer, his fingers tightened around her arms.

Victoria looked up at him uncertainly. She drew in a deep calming breath and slowly nodded as his fingers continued to tighten. He watched the myriad of emotions flitter across her face.

"Answer Duncan," he prompted, his fingers digging into her upper arms. "Say the words."

Victoria noted his face suddenly had a determined look on it.

She nodded once again, inhaled deeply, and let out a breath as she looked over at Duncan and said in a voice barely above a whisper, "Aye, he is my husband."

Again a collective murmur passed through the Great Hall and everything seemed to go still and silent as every pair of eyes locked on the scene enfolding before them.

Sobering quicker than Victoria thought possible, Duncan moved close and muttered an apology. She moved closer still to Grant, who wrapped his arms protectively around the soft womanly curve of her belly to steady her.

"'Tis sorry I am," the drunken young man said with dark intense eyes that seemed to gleam with some unspoken secret. "Why did you not say something sooner? I would never have made such a fool of myself this night over this lovely lady." His mouth edged upward at one corner.

To Victoria he said with feeling, "'Tis sorry I am, my lady. More than you will ever know. Please accept my heartfelt apology."

Grant looked at his longtime friend and knew the fault was his, not Duncan's. "We accept your apology. Next time, make certain the lass is willing. You always find plenty that are."

With that, he picked Victoria up in his strong, muscular arms to carry her to his bedchamber. When he looked around, he saw the startled yet relieved looks on his men's faces.

At the side of the room, Erwin glared with loathing, but no one paid him heed.

Warwick stood at the foot of the staircase. He said naught, but as Grant headed upstairs, a wide smile spread across the auld man's face.

Curse the frachetty auld dog!

Chapter Seventeen

Grant gently laid Victoria on his bed. Her lips trembled as he brushed away tears with the pads of his thumbs and stared long and hard at the look of pain he'd inflicted. In her own way she seemed such an innocent. He vowed to himself that if at all in his power, never again would he intentionally cause this wee woman any pain. He owed that to her.

Blessed Mary, how would he ever tell her what really happened this night? Would she ever understand? *Would he?*

"God keep you the night, Sweeting." He gently rubbed his thumb over her lips.

"Grant?"

"Snuggle yourself down on the bed. You are safe in this room." Leaning down, he held her in his arms. Finally he broke away. "I must go back to our guests. I'll come back up later."

Striding to the door, he looked back at Tory one final time and shook his head before firmly closing it.

What had he done?

He paused a moment outside his heavy door. He had some fences to mend downstairs, and he certainly had a good many questions to answer.

If only he had those answers.

When Tory awoke the next morning, she found herself alone. She'd apparently fallen asleep and didn't know if Grant returned last night or not. She hadn't heard him if he had.

What a nightmare! Thank goodness the evening had finally ended. She wished she could speak to Grant, since so many questions whirled through her mind. She lay in bed and tried to remember how long he said his guests were staying. She guessed they'd have to maintain this farce the entire time they remained.

Could she do it? Aye, she could pretend for a short time, but what made Grant say such a ridiculous thing? Why hadn't he pulled her away from Duncan and left it at that? Men! Who could understand them?

She wondered whether Grant regretted his lie. What if he told Duncan the truth? Would she have a repeat of the previous eve?

Panic set in when she set about her morning ablutions. If Grant kept up the tale, what would she wear? She certainly couldn't go downstairs in her hideous torn brown kirtle. Duncan would never believe them wed if she appeared in that ugly thing. Nor could she wear the outfit she wore to serve tables last night. It would never be proper for morning wear. Tory hoped she never saw that outfit again. Seonaid was more than well-come to have her clothes back.

Should she stay in Grant's bedchamber? How could she get word to him to find out what he expected?

She sat up and brushed her hair as a knock sounded at the door. Scrambling out of bed, Tory wrapped the blanket around her shoulders and went to open it. She thought that strange, since no one ever paid any attention to her privacy and usually barged in. They only knocked if Grant happened to be present. When she peered out the door, she saw a young kitchen maid standing with an armful of clothes. She stepped inside when Victoria moved.

"Laird Grant told me to fetch these to you, my lady, afore you came down the stairs to break your fast. He said to remind you that guests are still in the castle and to make certain you wore one of these dresses."

The young girl worried her lip. "He said I could stay to help if you wished."

"Why would you stay?"

"To help you dress and fix your hair if you fancy it," she responded shyly and gave her lady a considering look. "I would be honored if you'd allow me to do so. At least for today, until you can choose someone you prefer."

"Oh, of course," shea answered thankfully, assuming Grant wanted to keep up the pretense of being wed. "I would be most appreciative of your help. I am sorry, but I am not certain of your name. 'Tis Triona, is it not?"

"Aye, my lady," the young maid said, immensely pleased Tory had made the effort to remember her name. Only being a lowly kitchen maid, she hadn't thought this lady would notice her. Turning to the kirtles she brought, Triona selected one she thought would look well on Tory.

"Laird Grant said he is sorry you have no clothes of your own, my lady," she said happily as she hung the remaining clothes in Grant's tall wooden chest. "He said to tell you if these did not fit properly, he will have the sempstress alter them until he can have kirtles of your own made."

"Goodness," Victoria smiled brilliantly, "why all the fuss? These will do fine for one week. Lord Grant certainly need not have kirtles made merely for the duration of Lord Duncan's visit."

Giving Victoria an odd look, Triona shook her head and walked over to the fireplace. Before she could stop her, Triona threw her neatly folded brown shift into the blazing fire.

"Triona!" Aghast, she rushed to try and salvage the kirtle. "Why did you do that?"

Triona rushed over to calm her. Tory moaned, "Triona, Lord Grant will beat me when he discovers what happened! He'll blame me."

"Beat you? Nay, my lady," came the young woman's emphatic reply. "'Laird Grant told me to burn yon kirtle.'" She seemed determined to allay Tory's fears.

"B...but why?" she asked in bewilderment and studied the young girl keenly. "I'll need it again next week."

Triona looked at her askance and assured her she need not worry about the kirtle.

Nervousness mounting, Triona told her, "Sit, so Ican style your hair." She'd never done anything like this before for the lady of the keep. She hoped Tory fancied it. If she did, mayhap she'd let her remain to help. Her elevated status would be such an honor and make her mother so proud.

As she handed Tory the small looking glass in Grant's room, Triona nervously showed her the hairstyle she'd created. She held her breath while her lady studied it.

"Ooh, Triona, 'tis lovely," Tory beamed at the young girl. "You did a marvelous job!" She observed her reflection in the looking glass. "If you are quite certain Lord Grant does not object, I would love you to dress my hair this week. I could never get it this lovely. I usually just pull it back with a ribbon – but then you know that, of course. You have seen it all this time." She smiled at the young maid tentatively.

Clasping her hands to her mouth, Triona looked clearly relieved and jumped up and down with glee, belying her five and ten years. "I would love to, my lady! Thank you!" She felt like hugging the lovely young woman, but knew she didn't dare. Tory was lady of the house, after all.

With growing trepidation Victoria gained the stairs, slightly raised her flowing emerald green kirtle, and walked down the cold stone circular steps with tension gripping her. Could everyone pull off this charade? Would they be willing? Aye, they'd do it for

143

Grant. *Well,* she anxiously thought as she rounded the curve approaching the Great Hall, *this is it.* She drew in a deep, calming breath.

When she reached the foot of the stairs, Grant noticed her immediately. He rose to escort her to their guests and stopped dead in his steps, staring speechlessly. The woman looked a vision! He couldn't believe his eyes. But then, all he'd ever seen her in were filthy breeches and that hideous brown shift. Now she had on one of his mother's fine côtehardies and her hair curled stunningly atop her head, anchored in place by ribbons. He noticed Triona had topped Tory's hair with a lace kertch, befitting her station as a married woman. Grant could only think of running his fingers through those lovely tresses.

And doing many other things of interest to that magnificent body.

He quickly regained his senses and strode to the staircase. He removed her kertch, which released a slight scent of roses from her long tresses. "I love your hair. Do not cover it." She looked taken aback by his compliment and started to respond, but he stopped her flow of words when he leaned forward and planted a kiss on her lips. "Good morrow to you, lady wife." Taking in her beauty, he noticed the burning flush which rose to her soft smooth cheeks after his surprise kiss.

Hoping to keep her off guard, he presented her with his arm. To her credit, she stepped toward him gracefully and took it as if it was the most normal thing in the world and she did it routinely. She wouldn't cause problems after all! Praise the saints. Knowing her as well as he did after the weeks she'd been with him, he'd been certain she would. He couldn't believe his good fortune.

He walked back to the raised great table and saw the stunned looks on everyone's faces. They looked speechless. Aye, he thought with a chuckle, she had them already under her spell, too. But then, he admitted to himself, she'd had him bespelled since the first moment he'd seen her.

Grant seated Victoria between Duncan and himself at the head table. She deftly patted the graceful folds of her emerald green kirtle. Duncan looked quite ill this morning. He also looked extremely uncomfortable and watched Tory with an expression of concern. Her cheeks burned as memories of the previous evening's events flooded her memory. She wished she could flee, but Duncan quickly apologized for his actions the previous evening. She decided when not foxed, he had a firm, masculine voice and

144

appeared quite well mannered. She also thought Erwin, now seated to Duncan's right, looked totally unapologetic about last eve's events. In fact, he looked fairly disgruntled.

She tried not to dwell on the burly, unpleasant man and held up a quelling hand. "Lord Duncan, I accept your apology. Truly. Consider the incident forgotten."

"Och, but lovely lady you have not forgotten last eve's events," the handsome young man said evenly as he watched her closely.

"I did not say that." She averted her eyes.

"Indeed, lady, you do not need to," Duncan said. "I can see the truth in your lovely eyes."

She blushed. "Forgetting would be difficult, I am afraid. I only ask, sir, that in future you never again place a woman in the predicament I found myself."

She saw a look of doubt and concern cross his azure blue eyes and handsome chiseled face as he cocked an eyebrow, which caused her to laugh in a lovely lilting tone. "Nay, m'lord. I do not ask that you become a monk. I can tell by the look of shock in your eyes that is what you must think. I ask only in future you seduce women who are willing. With your handsome looks, you will have no problem finding such women."

Grant frowned as he heard her call Duncan handsome. He didn't fancy that comment. Tory focused her attention on Duncan and didn't notice his reaction. As if to assure Duncan further, she swept her hand around the room to infer most women present would be more than willing to spend time with him.

She saw Duncan visibly relax, and he kissed her hand. Grant again frowned and put an arm around her waist, pulling her closer.

Duncan noticed, but made no comment. He merely said, "Thank you for being so gracious, Lady Drummond. *Slàinte*," he smiled as he toasted her. "To your health."

While he smiled at Grant, he gave her a wink. "Were I you, my lady, I'd have serious words with your husband about the joke he thought to play last eve."

Perplexed, Victoria asked, "Joke?"

"Of course. Who but Grant would think to have his own lady wife act as a serving lass?"

Before Tory could say a word, Grant said through gritted teeth, "I am certain I'll hear about it in future!" The thought flashed through his mind that as often as he'd perplexed his mother, 'twas probably fitting he had chosen a woman who definitely didn't have an even-tempered disposition. His mother probably laughed every time she gazed down on him from Heaven.

As if verifying that fact, the next words he heard were, "And well you should, milord husband." She said this teasingly and then turned her attentions to the food she shared from his trencher. Tory amazed him at how quickly and easily she slipped into the role of lady of the keep.

Tory turned her gaze back to Duncan and began to ask, "Lord Duncan, how is it—"

He interrupted tersely, "I am not a laird, my sweet lady. That honor is bestowed on my esteemed father." The tone of his voice and thunderous expression made her pause. The thought flashed through her mind that the words weren't meant kindly.

She felt Grant gently place his hand on her arm, and rightfully took it as a warning not to pursue the subject.

She glanced into Duncan's suddenly cold eyes, gave him one of her warmest smiles, and reached across the table for the pitcher. "Would you fancy a bit of ale, sir?" she asked as if nothing seemed amiss. "I would offer you a spot of tea, but I fear my h...husband has none in the entire keep. I pray I'll be able to remedy that some day, since I am use to the tea my grandpapa used to bring my grandmum from the East. She kept it in the most charming tea caddy. In meantime, however, my lord husband does have plenty of ale."

She hoped Duncan hadn't noticed she stumbled over the word *husband*.

A glint of humor returned to Duncan's eyes. "Aye, sweet lady, I would." He swung his eyes to Grant's and chuckled.

The week passed quickly and everyone enjoyed the visit. As the week progressed, Tory felt Duncan did, after all, live up to his name. She certainly wouldn't have believed it while he'd been deep in his cups and totally randy the night she met him, but after getting to know him better, he did seem to be a steadfast friend as his name implied.

She enjoyed the stories the two men shared. It seemed they'd known each other most of their lives. She heard rowdy tales of obnoxious young boys as well as tales of heroic deeds performed as young men. She soon found herself impressed with their tales – as well as both men.

Staring in amazement, she laughed at the many pranks they used to play on each other, and thought them as close as brothers. They joked with each other the same way she and her sister had.

She made a conscious effort not to call Duncan lord again, but she slipped one other time. When she saw his eyes cloud, as he was about to comment again, she quickly apologized, "I am sorry, Duncan, but it has been ingrained in me to call all men of rank *my lord*. I'll endeavor to do better in future."

Behind her Grant glared. Unable to stem his curiosity, he spun her around to face him. "What do you mean you call all men *my laird*? When you came here you adamantly refused to call me that."

Smiling with pleasure, the wicked gleam that appeared in Tory's eyes supplied all the answer he needed. "You vixen! You did that apurpose to aggravate me." He glowered when she smiled sweetly and pretended she had no idea what he meant.

As the week of visitation ended, Tory and Grant went out to the courtyard to bid their guests farewell. Before he mounted his great steed, Duncan asked Tory if she'd allow him to kiss her goodbye. She looked taken aback by his request, but before she could formulate an answer, Grant cut in and glared. "You may not." He put his arm around Tory's waist and pulled her close to his side, effectively whisking her from Duncan's proximity. He shot his friend a ferocious glare.

Duncan hid a smile as he mounted his steed.

As Duncan rode out the gate, Grant turned to her and gave her a hug, catching her completely off guard. She'd expected him to immediately revert back to his previous actions. Instead, he smiled, "Thank you for a truly wonderful week. I know not how you kept everything flowing so smoothly, but you are a marvelous hostess, and the food Cook served surpassed my expectations. Truly you do know how to use those spices you bankrupted me with awhile back."

She stilled and she gasped. "Did I really? You said I could get whatever I wanted! Why did you let me do that? Oh, Grant, I am-"

Anxiety edged its way into his lady wife's eyes. He determined to remedy that. He didn't like seeing fear there and wouldn't let her apologize for something he'd only been teasing about.

"Nay, wife, I merely jest. Although spices are quite costly, I would hope I am better situated than buying a few wee spices would bankrupt me." He smiled and swatted her backside lightly.

"Grant," Tory let out an exasperated sigh, "our guests are gone. You no longer need call me wife. Now I must change out of these lovely clothes. I thank you for letting me borrow them. Your mother had exquisite taste."

Panic suddenly set in and her eyes flew to Grant. "Oh, I forgot. I am sorry, Grant, but I fear you are going to be quite cross."

"What is wrong, my lady *wife*?" He found he enjoyed calling her wife. This arrangement might work out after all.

"I believe Triona must have been so excited about helping me with my hair and clothes this week she got carried away." She paused and then rushed on before she lost her courage. "Triona threw my kirtle into the fireplace. I...have naught to wear!"

"Naught would look extremely lovely on you, lass," he teased, trying to allay her fears, but not being able to pass up the opportunity to tease her. Seeing her blush, he took pity on her and assured, "You have plenty of clothes to wear. I ordered Triona to burn that kirtle."

"B...but why?" she questioned, a thoughtful frown fleetingly crossing her face.

"I cannot have my lady wife dressed in hideous clothes such as you had afore," he teased again in a warm voice. "Howbeit if I am truthful, I must admit that on you even that ugly thing looked good."

"Grant, stop this nonsense. Duncan is gone now, and there is no further need for this charade."

She started to turn away and sighed. "You may go back to being your usual inconsiderate self." She said this with a hint of teasing as she smiled ruefully, yet with a slight sag to her shoulders.

Grant winced at the truth in her words.

"Lady mine, methinks we had best go up to our bedchamber. I needs explain some things, and best it be done in private." He took her hand, pursed his lips in a frown, and led her up the staircase to their chamber.

"We are what?" Victoria shouted with a gasp of outrage, disbelief written all over her face after Grant carefully explained they really were wed.

"You are standing here, straight-faced, telling me the fiasco the other evening was my wedding ceremony?"

When he nodded, Victoria burst out haughtily, "I think not."

He closed the distance between them as Tory shot him a withering glare and continued to rant. "I did not risk life and limb trying to run away from my home in an effort to avoid marrying someone I did not love to wind up a captive here and being tricked into marriage with someone else I do not love. *With someone who hates me!*" Agony and despair echoed in her voice.

"I am sorry, wife," he said haltingly, trying not to pay attention to the fact she'd emphatically said she didn't love him. That declaration bothered him, but he tried to ignore his feelings.

Instead he continued, "According to Scotland's laws, we are wed. Ask anyone. Marriage by declaration is perfectly legal here. I declared you my lady wife in front of my Hall full of men, and that makes it fact." He tried not to smile at the glower on Tory's face. "Plus, you confirmed it when you agreed and willingly told Duncan you were my wife."

"Willingly?"

Tory sat on Grant's bed in exasperation and looked for something to throw at him. The man could be totally frustrating. "Rubbish! Lest you forget, sir, you were gripping my arms like a vise. You gave me no choice. I had to agree."

"Nay, you did not," he told her softly, but regretfully. "You certainly could have told Duncan otherwise, but then most assuredly you would have wound up in his bed."

He said the last with more bitterness than he meant. Although he'd never show it, it really bothered him having heard her say in no uncertain terms she didn't love him.

Tory bit her lips. "I vow, you are the most frustrating man I have ever known. This cannot be true, and 'tis cruel of you to keep pretending 'tis so. I refuse to accept this. Where is Warwick? He will stop this bloody nonsense."

With a growing sense of alarm she rose and sprinted from the room, running all the way downstairs without stopping, her hair flying out behind her.

"Warwick! Where are you?" Not seeing him in the Great Hall, she bolted out into the courtyard to see if the men now trained in the lists. They were, and heedless of their training she ran over to them and called Warwick's name.

"My lady," the old man said with quiet reproach as he rushed over to meet her. "You shouldn't be out here. You could have been sore injured had I not heard you calling. Training lists are no place for a female, mind."

"Warwick, please," she rushed on, ignoring his lecture and oblivious to the chaos she created with men training. "Tell Grant to stop this nonsense. He says he and I are wed. Tell him to stop this charade now! I vow, 'tis no longer amusing."

Grant raced after her and paled when he saw his young bride run headlong into the lists, heedless of danger. He thought his heart would explode with relief when he saw she hadn't been injured after racing full speed into the midst of his training men. The thought of her being injured made his knees go weak, although why that bothered him so much seemed truly disconcerting.

Pretending naught was amiss as the terror he felt slowly ebbed, he came up behind Tory, arms akimbo on his chest. Warwick looked bemusedly from him to Tory. The men present quit training and stared. Any one of them could have been responsible for her death, and the thought numbed them.

Warwick turned back to Tory, looked at her as if humoring a child, and said at last, "Lady Drummond, did Laird Drummond not explain everything to you?"

"Indeed, I daresay he gave me a lot of rubbish about declarations and Scots law, but 'tis time for this farce to end. Now tell the truth and you can all have a good laugh on the *daft Englishwoman*." Her eyes beseeching him, she nodded sharply as if to give Warwick permission to speak.

Warwick shifted his feet nervously as his eyes lit with a tinge of sympathy for the young woman in front of him. He ruefully informed her, "My lady, I dinnae quite know how to tell you this, but what Laird Drummond told you is the solemn truth. You are legally wed. You are Lady Drummond, mistress of Drummond Castle."

"Nay!" Tory cried in disbelief as her eyes swiveled from Warwick to Grant.

"Aye, my lady," the kindly old man assured her. "Marriage by declaration is quite legal in Scotland. Since we are so spread out in the Highlands, not everyone has easy access to a priest, so there are several ways for us to wed. One, of course, being an actual kirk ceremony. Another is hand-fasting." When he saw she didn't understand, he explained, "That means you would be marrit by mutual agreement for a year and a day." Seeing the questioning look still in her eyes when she frowned, he added, "At that time if you both wished to stay wed, you could be wed by a priest. The last way is marriage by declaration, and that is what Laird Drummond did. He declared you his lady wife, and he did so in front of a gathering of men. That is all he needed to do. And considering how many men were in Hall and heard him that night, there is no doubt about it. You are truly wed. All assumed you knew that, lass. You did, after all, confirm it to MacThomas."

Feeling a wave of unease sweep over her, Tory grasped at any idea she could think of and blurted, "But I am not Scottish. I am certain 'twould not be accepted in England."

"Aye, lass, it would," came the old man's somber reply. It pained him to see the lassie so upset. "England may not fancy Scot systems, but it does recognize our forms of marriage. Plus, lass, you no longer live in England. You are in Scotland, and are wed to a great Scotsman. And if I know our chief, which I do quite well, he will not be letting you go back to England." After a pause, Warwick added, not unkindly, "Ever."

Tears streaming down her face, she turned to Grant and pounded forcefully on his chest. He didn't try to stop her.

Realization filled her eyes with pain and she choked out, "How could you do this to me? How? I tried to run away from my home so I could find someone to love me and now you go and do this!

"But you hate me!" she declared with aching emotion and sadness in her eyes. "Why would you do this? Why would you saddle yourself with me? I understand you do not think I could have any feelings, but I do." A look of anguish shot across her face as she finished, "My wedding is supposed to be in a lovely little kirk filled with lots of beautiful flowers. 'Tis what I dreamed of. But most importantly, the man with whom I wed is supposed to love me. Surely you could have thought of something else – anything else. I hate you! I hate you! *I hate you!*"

"I know you do, lass," he said in resignation and looked over her head into the worried faces of his men. He hadn't expected a reaction quite like this. He'd expected anger and disbelief at first, but somewhere in his mind he expected her to be glad. He only saw pain reflected in her eyes. "I know you do."

With that, he stilled her hands and lifted her struggling body into his arms and carried her inside the keep and up to their bedchamber. She needed to be alone with her thoughts. She'd come around and accept this.

Would she not?

At the same time, Tory thought forlornly, "*What have I gotten myself into?*"

Chapter Eighteen

After fortifying himself staunchly with whisky, Grant strode upstairs to his bedchamber later that evening. He assumed Tory must still be cross, since she hadn't come down to share his meal with him. The sooner she accepted they were wed, the sooner his keep could return to normal.

His men had been in utter turmoil earlier. Not only were they upset over Tory's distress about her current situation, but she'd stormed headlong into their training session. The stubborn woman could have been killed or maimed. His men were aghast at the thought it could have been any one of them who dealt the deathblow.

His mind slightly blurred, Grant thought the best way to end this awkward situation would be to bed his young bride and end this standoff once and for all. Truth be told, he'd wanted to bed her since the night he took her captive. Blessed St. Ninian, he could feel himself becoming aroused just thinking about her in his bed.

Grant entered his bedchamber and saw Tory sitting on the bed brushing her beautiful brown hair. She looked so lovely with her hair down. Why did women think it practical to braid their hair or pile it atop their head? According to tradition, now that they were wed, she should no longer wear her hair unbound. Since he preferred it down, he told her that is how he wanted it. He didn't mind the curls Triona styled for Tory occasionally, but he really just wanted to run his fingers through her hair.

At least she stopped wearing the silly kertch married women were supposed to wear. Everyone on his lands knew they were wed, and nothing else mattered. He realized he did want everyone to know she belonged to him. Never before had he had such feelings of possessiveness.

When he approached the bed, Tory scooted away and settled herself on the floor. Grant followed and pulled her back up. "Nay," he began gently, not wishing to frighten her. "You will share my bed from this night forward. You are my lady wife, Tory. You must accept that." He raised her head with his hand and gently stroked her cheek.

Grant stared at her and said nothing for a long time. "Come, Tory," he said gently, "'tis time we come together as husband and wife. I have waited for this a long time."

Understanding his intent immediately, she panicked and tried to pull away. "Nay, Grant, please. I cannot..."

Grant misunderstood her plea and became cross. "Aye, you will. You are my lady wife, Tory, and will do as I say. 'Tis time you accept we are wed."

"B...but..." she stammered, shaking uncontrollably. Grant thought her response a rejection.

"No more stalling," he said and began to remove his clothes. Growing wide-eyed, she tried to hide beneath the furs and fought the urge to close her eyes. "I would prefer you to be willing, but willing or not, we will consummate our marriage this night," Grant added as he saw her look of shock.

Lying beside her, Grant looked at Tory with fierce longing. She clutched the fur tightly and held it around herself as if a protective armour. Grant pulled her close, and kissed her. His tongue gently parted her lips and probed within her mouth, and his hand brushed firmly against the swell of her breast. Far too impatient to possess her to go as slowly as he should, he'd waited too long for this moment.

Why didn't she respond, he wondered in frustration? He knew from past experience that she wanted him as much as he wanted her, so why did she seem so reserved now? He could ignite the fires within her if she'd only relax. He wanted her soft and pliant in his arms.

Suddenly a thought flashed through his mind. *Could she be thinking of another man? Someone from her past?* Glaring, Grant stormed, "Were you going to meet some other man the night I found ye?"

Tory didn't know how to answer. While she hadn't been going to meet a <u>specific</u> person, her heart's desire had been to search for someone who would love her.

Grant hadn't waited for her answer before he removed her nightrail and his hand closed over her bare breast. Unlike previously, she panicked, not allowing herself to relax and enjoy his touch.

"Well..." she finally began.

Having imbibed in too much whisky, Grant became angered with her delay in answering. He took it to mean she had been meeting someone. Had she coldly responded like this with men in her old house, too, or had she been the wanton? Once again, the thought of any other man touching her proved more than he could bear. Images conjured in his mind of her legs wrapped lovingly around a nameless, faceless man.

His mood no longer felt pleasant.

With far too much whisky consumed, and thoughts of other men with Tory uppermost in his mind, Grant pushed reason aside and affirmed he'd make her his once and for all. He rose above her and parted her legs with his knees. He didn't miss the fear in her eyes. What could that be about? As his wife, it was her bounden duty to please him. Why did she seem afeard? Women were only too willing to share his bed.

Too worked up to stop, he'd make her forget whatever man she'd been thinking of. He'd waited too long for this moment, and his enforced celibacy since meeting Tory wore thin. She'd be his – now! She'd accept their marriage soon enough.

His powerful body poised above hers, with one sharp thrust he entered her and froze in amazement when he broke through her innocence. Her scream filled the room and Grant stared down into huge tear filled eyes.

Blessed Saint Michael, she'd been a maiden!

No other man save him had ever touched her. Buried deep within her softness, Grant felt surprised and pleased he'd been gifted with the miracle of her virginity. Of a sudden it dawned on him what he'd done. He'd taken his young bride while she'd been totally unprepared for him. She hadn't been thinking of another man. She'd been afraid of what was to come.

Merciful saints, what he did was no better than what he'd stopped Duncan from doing a week earlier. Although his legal wife, that didn't make it right.

No wonder she'd been afraid. She must hate him. Grant rolled to the side, raised himself on his elbow, and stared down at her, wiping tears from her cheeks.

"Why did you not tell me, Tory?" Grant asked in a voice filled with amazement. "Why did you let us believe you a whore?"

Sobbing hysterically, she glared and muttered huskily, "I did tell you! I told you over and over, but none of you ever believed me."

As anger built, she sobbed bitterly. "Nor did I know you were going to force yourself on me this night, or I would have been certain to reiterate the point." She flung the words at him in anger and desperation, heedless of consequences. Her voice sounded

154

strangled as she added, "Well, you got what you wanted all along. Now get out of here and leave me alone!"

Sobbing, she jerked out of Grant's grasp and rolled away. She turned her back to him and reached frantically for her nightrail or his robe, whichever she found first.

Grant's emotions were in turmoil as he redressed. He glanced at the spot on the bed she'd rolled from and saw the bloodied sheet. He paled. What he'd done had been wrong.

He stormed out the door and slammed it soundly behind him. Grant ran his hands through his hair and sagged against the door while wondering, *what have you done?*

Inside the bedchamber Tory lay curled on the bed. Crying, she wondered how he could have done that. Why had she been foolish enough to think he cared about her? Hurt and humiliated, she swore out loud, and yelled words Grant wouldn't allow had he still been present. She no longer cared. Right or wrong, she didn't think God would judge her too harshly right now.

Heart heavy with shame, Grant stormed down to the Great Hall and headed for the whisky. Several men remained in the Hall and were surprised to see him return downstairs. They thought their young chief had gone up to bed his beautiful new wife – and thought not to see him for several days.

"Grant," Warwick began questioningly, "why are ye—?"

"I do not wish to discuss it, auld man," Grant boomed. "Leave me alone whilst I drink myself into oblivion."

Grant quaffed down his drink and dipped his goblet to refill it. Before he could raise it to his lips, Warwick stopped him with a light hand on his arm. "What gnaws at you?" Seeing his chieftain ready to cut him off, the old man wisely said, "Nay, lad, dinnac tell me naught is wrong. A young buck like you does not go off to bed his young wife and come stormin' back down the stairs if naught is wrong."

"I do not wish to speak of it," Grant growled. "I told you to leave me be."

When Grant glared, but said nothing else, Warwick patiently waited, his eyes asking unspoken questions. Whatever Grant thought wrong must be of great import, and his young chief would eventually tell all.

Muttering a string of Gaelic expletives, Grant glowered, "Mucked it up, I did, Wick. I did everything wrong. I wanted the lass so much, when she did not immediately agree, I acted no better than a fumbling laddie. I waited not, but plunged ahead and bedded her."

Grants shoulders sagged as he looked into the eyes of his old friend. "She was a maiden, Wick, and I nigh unto forced her." He stopped and shook his head in anger over his own actions, and added in disgust, "Nay, I did force her."

Wick paused with his tankard raised halfway between the table and his mouth and quickly lowered it back to the table.

Men gathered in the Hall gasped in surprise. They never thought to hear their young chief say something like that. Neither he nor his da afore him tolerated the debauching of innocent maidens.

"Och, Wick, I doubt she will ever forgive me."

"The lass still had her maidenheid?" the elderly man asked in surprise. At Grant's disgruntled nod, Warwick hid his surprise with a satisfied grin. Liking the gel as he did, he felt quite pleased with that information. It didn't surprise him in the least.

Grant rested his arms on the table and leaned his head atop his hands. "What should I do, Wick? I do not want to lose her. Nor do I wish to force her every time I want to bed her. And," he stopped momentarily and raised his head slightly, "truth be told, all I want to do when I am around her is bed her. 'Tis surprised I am you have not seen my kilt flapping wildly every time I am around her, since my manhood always seems to be proudly saluting her whenever she is near!"

"Well, I agree 'tis not the best of beginnings, lad," the old sage began, thinking pensively, yet clearly envisioning the mental image his young chief had drawn for him, "but you also dinnae have to let it be the end."

Grant raised his head slowly from his hands to peer at his mentor and frowned, "What do you mean? What can I do? You know she will be afeart of me. I do not want a marriage like that, mind. I want not to force my own wife each time I wish to bed her." Blessed St. Michael, he could feel himself becoming aroused just over the thought of bedding her.

"Then go back up yon stairs and do it right this time, you dolt." When Grant looked at Warwick with surprise, his friend advised, "Go back and woo the lass.

"Och, aye, in light of what happened, she may be afeart at first," came Warwick's admission when he saw Grant's unconvinced look.

He steepled his fingers and studied his young chief. "That is understandable. What you did had to hurt, so go slow this time. Make her body crave yours as much as you want hers." He added with a rueful glance, "Och, son, do what you should have done to begin with. Do it right this time."

With a wolfish grin, Warwick couldn't resist teasing Grant, "I have no doubt you can do it if you really want her to love you. Take your time with her. If we dinnae see you for a few days, never fear, we will send food up to you."

"I doubt she will let me anywhere near her," Grant groaned and shook his head.

"At first, nay, she probably will not," the wise old man conceded, making a mental note that Grant hadn't denied wanting Victoria to love him. "'Twill be up to you to make her change her mind. Make her body change it for her."

His men nodded their agreement. When they began to make lewd comments about helping, the time had come to return to his solar. Aye, he'd mucked this up and he had to be the one to straighten it out.

He opened his chamber door and noticed his lovely bride wore his bedrobe. On her it looked large indeed, but the shapeless garment did nothing to conceal her loveliness. Grant shook his head. When had she become so beautiful?

He saw fear return to her face in a rush when she saw him. He didn't fancy that. He didn't want his lady wife being afraid of him – for any reason.

He'd brought wine and two goblets with him. If she didn't break them over his head, Grant thought that would be an auspicious beginning. Setting the wine on a small table, he poured two goblets and took one to Tory. She looked at him warily.

"'Tis all right, lass. You are safe. I have no wish to harm you." Her red eyes confirmed she'd been crying while he'd been downstairs.

Grant felt like a monster.

"I am sorry, Tory. Truly. All I can do is ask your forgiveness. I never would have acted so thoughtlessly had I known you were a maiden still. I should have believed you, and for that I apologize. "To be honest, Sweeting, I felt jealous."

Tory grunted in disbelief.

"I know you will not believe me, but I felt jealous of other men I thought you had been with. I thought you did not want me."

Tory refused to meet his gaze and didn't look the least bit inclined to forgive him. Grant tried a different tact, "I promise 'twill never hurt again, Sweeting. It only hurts the first time, and that is behind us now. I acted like a fumbling, jealous lad of but ten summers trying to get his first grope."

"The next time?" she strangled out. She looked horrified as her eyes finally flew to meet his. "You plan to do that again?"

Grant felt miserable at the turmoil he saw in her eyes. He'd put that fear there and he alone could take it away. He also noticed his oversized robe slowly loosening, but had no thoughts of bringing that to her attention.

"Aye, lady mine, I plan on us doing *that* quite often," Grant ruefully smiled at her use of terminology. She couldn't bring herself to call it making love, let alone consider doing it. But then, she had nothing to relate to but the one incident, and she wouldn't consider that making love. Holy Mother, Grant thought grimly, neither could he. It had been painful, pure and simple. He couldn't have eliminated the pain completely, but he should have made it easier.

He shook his head in dismay and wondered how he'd change her mind.

Tory paced as she contemplated his words, and had no idea his bedrobe now gaped almost to her waist, affording Grant an ample view of the cleft between her full breasts.

"But why?" she swallowed hard, and her voice rose in panic. "You did what you wanted. You c..c..consummate the marriage. Wh...why would you want to do that again?"

"Because, making love is beautiful – or should be," Grant added affectionately. He saw doubt spring to her face and tried to reassure her, "Remember how you felt when we rode in the glen?" When he saw a blush come to her cheeks, Grant pressed his point, "That is just the beginning, *Mo Chridhe*. I want to make love with you. Not be impatient like afore. I cannot stress that enough. I assure you that will never happen again. And we did not consummate the marriage."

Seeing Tory didn't understand, Grant clarified, "When I realized what I'd done and the pain I caused, I pulled out afore I spilled my seed."

"I do not understand," she said with a quizzical look and sick dread in her stomach.

"I know you do not, Sweeting," Grant explained and gazed into her beguiling brown eyes. "That is part of the reason I love you so much. You are an innocent still, and I know 'twill be me teaching you how to make love. I cannot to tell you how it thrilled my heart to realize no other man had ever touched you.

"You are completely mine," Grant smiled while giving her hand an affectionate squeeze. He didn't realize he told her he loved her.

Tory hesitated.

"Please, my lady, let me show you what I should have done afore. Let me make you my wife the right way. I will not rush this time, mind. Let us sit afore the fire and relax. Come have some wine."

Tory saw the desire in Grant's eyes. She didn't want to repeat the former pain, but she wouldn't mind feeling what she had other times he kissed her. Her emotions were so conflicted.

If only she wasn't such a coward.

Mayhap if they just kissed. They'd done that before and it had felt wonderful – and he said they'd just sit together. Suddenly she didn't want to be alone.

As she looked at him with uncertainty, Grant walked to her and gathered her tenderly into his arms. Tory buried her face in the crook of his neck and he brushed kisses on the top of her head. He felt her shaking all over. Pulsating with desire, his arousal would be obvious, even to someone as skittish as she. He breathed deeply, and reminded himself to go slowly.

Very, very slowly.

Grant took Tory's hand and led her to the hearth. He sat in a chair she recently placed there and pulled her down onto his lap. He sat and held her closely, not moving. Nervously she gulped her wine. She rarely drank, so to do so without comment showed her nervousness. He felt her slowly relax, and poured more wine into her goblet. He thought one more cup wouldn't harm anything and he wanted her more relaxed.

When Tory did finally relax, Grant rubbed his hand up and down her arm. Lightly he brushed the tips of his fingers against the edge of her breast while he rained kisses on the back of her neck and down her shoulder blade. She closed her eyes and sighed, her nipples hardening of their own accord. Tory flushed and thought she'd die of embarrassment.

Turning her to face him, Grant kissed her in earnest. While his ardor built and her body flooded with feelings she hadn't known she possessed, Grant deepened his kiss. Soon his hands roamed her entire body, and Tory breathed deeply with her first flicker of response. He'd skillfully removed her robe without her being aware of it. She had nothing on now but his roving hands, and her skin felt exquisite. When she kissed him with as much feeling as he kissed her, Grant stood and moved her towards the bed. He removed the empty goblet from her hand and considered giving her more wine, but decided against it. He wanted her relaxed, but not drunk or passed out, and knew she had little experience drinking.

He reached the edge of the bed and Grant felt Tory tense. "Relax, Sweeting," he told her softly and moaned in spite of himself. He rained kisses on her face. First her forehead, then her cheeks. Then he kissed the tip of her nose and her chin. With the touch of a butterfly, Grant lightly brushed his lips over hers.

She hesitantly parted her lips in response to the sensual caress of his fingertips and Grant thought he'd die with need. *Slowly,* he reminded himself. Slowly.

When he lowered her onto the bed, Grant inhaled sharply at the sight of her lying naked.

Since he only wore his plaide downstairs when he stormed from the room, he easily slipped out of it now. Soon he lay naked beside Tory on the bed.

Feeling her tense again, he pressed his lips to her brow, then leaned over and claimed her mouth. She opened to him and Grant deepened his kiss. When she relaxed, he released her mouth and trailed kisses again on her face and down her neck.

Grant's hand closed softly over Tory's bare breast and caressed it, teasing her nipple until it puckered on its own and her breaths became ragged. Slowly he trailed kisses on her arms and over to her breast where his hand had been working its magic. Her eyebrows raised in surprised pleasure.

After he laved her breast with his tongue, Grant suckled her nipple, causing her breath to intake sharply.

"Grant?" she moaned uncertainly and let out a shaky breath.

"Shh, *Mo Chridhe,*" Grant whispered tenderly while he tried to calm her fears. "Relax and enjoy."

"B...but, I know not what to do," Tory said tremulously. "And...I...I am scared."

"Do naught, Sweeting. Naught but relax and enjoy. I'll do everything this time. Later I'll show you more. This time is for you. Relax. You have a lifetime to learn all I plan to teach you."

Grant's mouth once again lowered to claim hers.

Slowly Grant built Tory's passion and she stirred and whimpered beneath his ministrations. Yet when his hand slid to the private junction between her thighs, she tensed. "Relax, Sweeting," Grant said reassuringly, while his heart hammered in his chest. "It will not hurt. I already promised you that. I'll never hurt you again."

Tory tried to relax, but couldn't, even though the things Grant did felt wonderful. In truth, she felt stunned by all he made her feel, but she feared it would hurt again. And now she was afraid she'd disappoint him. Surely she had before. Hadn't he stormed from the room? It mattered not that she ordered him out. If he hadn't been upset he wouldn't have left, would he? Tory feared if she did something wrong, Grant would never return.

She suddenly knew she wanted him to stay.

Tory's attention temporarily diverted, he slid his finger inside her while his thumb began to massage. She couldn't believe all she felt and inhaled sharply. Unconsciously her hips thrust up to meet his hand.

Grant rolled over on the bed and brought Tory with him, making her lie on top of him. Slowly and methodically he ground his hips into hers, which caused his raging manhood to lightly caress her.

Grant swiftly switched positions, not giving her time to think about what happened. He wrapped Tory's legs around his thighs, and moved cautiously as she tensed. When he finally entered her, he stopped to see if she felt any pain, and his mouth covered hers in a long passionate kiss that let her know how much he needed her.

Knowing she wanted something, but having no idea what, Tory shifted position. Her movements caused Grant to move deeper. The sensation caused her to widen her eyes in surprise and amazement. Hesitating no longer, Grant plunged into her welcoming depths, thoroughly filling her until they both spiraled over the magical edge. His seed filled her to her core, and Grant collapsed on top of her. He remained still for quite some time.

Finally he felt her stir beneath him. "Are you all right?"

"Aye," she said bashfully, unable to make eye contact, "but I do not think I can breathe."

Grant laughed and rolled onto his back, carrying her with him.

"Better?" Grant asked with a smug smile.

"Better," she whispered back, a look of awe on her face.

161

"I am glad of that, wife." Holding her tightly, Grant added with a wicked gleam in his eyes, "Now might you consider doing *that* whenever and as often as I want?"

"Aye," she responded bashfully, running her fingertips lightly over his lower lip and blushing clear down to her neck. "I believe you may do that anytime you wish."

"Good," Grant said, a satisfied look on his face. "Then that is your wedding night, my lady wife. I would consider it an honor if you pray would forget the other. I acted like a jealous fool and will never forgive myself."

Tory rewarded Grant with a look of happiness and delight he'd never forget. Shyly she said, "Aye, my lord husband, 'tis a wonderful wedding night after all. I never imagined I could feel this way." She bit her upper lip and asked, "Will it always be like that – and never like...that first time?"

Grant lightly rubbed his thumb over her cheek and smiled, "Hopefully, it will only get better and better."

Tory's soft brown eyes looked at him with doubt. "Sleep now, *a leannan*. I know you wore me out. I believe I did the same to you. Good night, *ma gey lassie*," Grant whispered.

She hesitated and asked, "You said you were jealous. Why?"

Grant had the grace to blush. "Because I thought you did not want me in your bed. I did not know you were afeart. I thought you were thinking of another man." He looked shamefaced as he awaited her reaction.

"And that mattered to you?" she questioned in astonishment.

Without hesitation Grant answered, "Och, aye, very much."

Tory smiled and rested her head on his chest. Grant closed his arms tighter as she continued lying on top of him and promptly fell sound asleep.

In the pre-dawn hours of morning, Grant awoke to find Tory snuggled up beside him, her smooth, soft body half-sprawled over his. She felt marvelous. He gazed over her body through the dark shadows and immediately felt his loins responding. The light breeze from the windows carried her scent of roses to his nostrils. Dare he love her again? Would she be too sore? Grant considered the idea carefully and knew he should leave her alone and let her sleep, particularly after his first fumbling attempt. Unfortunately for his firm resolutions, his hand wandered of its own accord and rubbed gentle circles on her back.

As he lightly caressed her breast, Tory stirred and peered at him through slumberous eyes. Slowing turning her head, rekindled desire hazed her eyes with nary a hint of fear. When she didn't pull away, Grant began a slow seduction. He told himself this would be the last time. He'd love her one more time and then let her rest. He had, after all, an entire lifetime in which to make love to her.

And, he thought smugly, he planned to do just that.

Tory responded with an easy crooked smile. Grant didn't know if she'd awoken completely, but knew she would be soon. No one could sleep through his lovemaking.

After he rained kisses over her face and neck, Grant moved down to her breasts. Suddenly he knew she'd awoken completely. He lightly brushed wisps of hair from her temples. Gazing at her with longing, he slowly brought her to the peak of passion. She opened herself to him, and Grant nudged her thighs further apart and settled himself between them. He entered her, and they joined together in the rhythm as old as time.

Sated, Grant rolled off and pulled her close to his side. They both fell asleep again before the smile faded from his lips.

Chapter Nineteen

Tory awoke to the feel of Grant's arms wrapped around her. "Good morrow, *Mo Chridhe*," he said and brushed his lips lightly over the nape of her neck.

Turning slightly, she glanced at Grant and questioned, "What does that mean? That *mo* whatever you say sometimes?"

Grant smiled softly. "Dearling. It means dearling."

Satisfied, she turned away and leaned against him. She felt so safe in his arms. Tory thought she could grow to fancy this wife thing quite well. She snuggled closer to Grant's hard, warm body, wiggling her bottom slightly as she maneuvered to get more comfortable.

"Do that any more, wife," Grant teased while lightly kissing the back of her neck, "and I'll be making love to you again afore we even break our fast this day."

Tory turned to look into his dark, intense eyes and teased, "You mean you were going to feed me, too?" Her breasts were firmly pressed against his chest as his arms wrapped around her.

"Aye, lady wife," Grant teased right back, "but if you continue with your wanton ways, food will be the last thing on my mind. I could feast on you and forget food." That said, he leaned over and nibbled on her earlobe.

Panicking, Tory pulled away and wrapped the bed covering over her. "Grant," she exclaimed in shock, a blush staining her cheeks, "'tis daylight! We cannot make love now."

Grant realized she wasn't jesting. She really meant it. Not able to stop himself, he burst out laughing. "Sweeting, we can make love any time – day or night, and I plan to do just that."

"B...b...," she sputtered in unbelief, seemingly at a loss for words, "but, you can *see* me!"

"Aye, I can," Grant answered, a wicked leer on his face, "and I fancy what I see." He reached for her playfully and pulled the covers from her grasp. He soon forgot his resolve to leave her alone the remainder of the day and once again brought her to a fevered pitch. He covered her body with his, and brought them both to the apex of pleasure.

Later Grant smiled and lightly kissed her blushing nose. "See, wife," he smiled to himself as he thought of how thoroughly he'd possessed her body, "daylight can be as wonderful as the dark of night." He jumped out of bed and walked to the door.

"However, this time I believe we really should break our fast or we will both be too weak to do anything else." Forestalling further conversation, he strode the remaining distance to the heavy wooden door, flung it open, and bent to retrieve something from the floor. Tory heard him briefly speak to the guard outside their door. Returning, he closed it behind him with his foot.

The man stood stark naked!

In his hands he carried a tray of food. "See, Cook prepared a glorious assortment of food for us to break our fast." Grant set the tray on the table and returned to the bed to grasp her hands. Pulling her up, he propelled her toward the table. He sat and pulled her onto his lap, but Tory abruptly pulled away and ran back to the fireplace. She grabbed Grant's robe, and wrapped it around herself.

She donned it and tied the rope belt before she walked back and lowered herself into his waiting arms, where he shared food from his trencher. Grant smiled over her display of modesty. After everything they did together over the past several hours, the woman still worried about him seeing her.

He'd change that in time.

Grant had given her a few bites of fruit when a knock sounded at the door.

"Enter," he boomed.

Tory blushed as Dallas, their young chambermaid, entered the room and eyed them significantly. Tory felt extremely glad she'd donned Grant's robe. The knowing smile the girl flashed had been embarrassing enough. Grant didn't look the least bit nervous about being caught naked in his bedchamber.

Dallas smiled broadly at Grant, then mentioned she needed to change the bed linens and would quickly be out of their way. Grant continued to feed Tory while Dallas walked around the room. He paid no attention to the young woman, nor did he try to hide his nakedness.

When she finished her task, Dallas looked at her chief and lady and asked if she could fetch them anything. Without looking up, Grant shook his head and thanked Dallas for her services. His eyes never left Tory. As the young woman left the room with a knowing smile, Tory commented she thought it odd Dallas had come that morning.

"I would have sworn the sheets were changed yestermorn." She also mentioned she thought Dallas had looked at Grant overlong.

"That is possible, lady wife," Grant whispered into her ear and ignored her last comment, "but do you not think it nice she thought of us?" Smiling, he didn't tell her the real reason their bed linens had been changed. He felt quite certain before they finished eating everyone in the castle would have seen the sheets and known his beautiful wife had indeed been a maiden when he bedded her the night before.

For some reason he couldn't explain, that thought pleased him immensely.

Grant felt as full as Tory when they completed breaking their fast. They ate everything Cook sent. The hot porridge with fresh cream had been steamy and delicious, and the bannocks, served with butter and quince marmalade hit the spot. He had mutton as well, but Tory pulled a face at having fish or mutton for breakfast.

While they ate, Tory suddenly asked, "How did you know food would be outside our door?"

With teasing eyes and what he thought would b a wicked grin, he told her, "We'll probably have food delivered for the next several days."

"Why?" she asked in amazement.

"Because I do not plan to leave this room for several days," Grant replied with a lusty gleam in his eye.

Tory frowned. "And Cook knows this?"

Grant couldn't contain himself and burst into laughter. "Aye, Sweeting, everyone knows."

His true meaning sank in and Tory blushed deep crimson. "And they know why?"

"'Deed they do, wife. I do not plan to leave this room 'til I feel certain I've planted my bairn in your belly." With that, Grant pulled her close and kissed all the places that were blushing – and a few more for good measure. Words were soon forgotten.

The next few days flew quickly by. Grant only went downstairs for emergencies, and he forbade Tory to leave the room. He didn't feel ready for her to go back to her everyday life yet, albeit this precious time couldn't last forever. Soon they'd both have to return to their duties.

Once they rejoined the world to his men's lusty comments, Grant called together his closest advisors. Tory tried to return to her daily routine, which changed once she and the castle's chief were wed. She found herself in charge of running the day-to-day castle activities and though some people didn't greet the change happily, most were not overtly rude.

Weeks passed, and Grant determined he needed to leave. He wouldn't tell her why, just that they must leave in two days and would be gone about a fortnight. Tory hated that he'd be gone. Their situation still felt too new for her to wish him to leave.

Teasing her unmercifully about her wanting him to stay, he reminded her, "In past you couldn't wait for me to ride off and leave you alone."

As the morning of his departure loomed large, he gently stroked her body. He didn't really want to leave, but felt he needed to do this. Before departing, he determined to love her one last time.

Tory sleepily rolled into Grant's embrace. Soon, she awoke and responded passionately to his ministrations. Her lips were parted and tingling with passion and her hips moved restlessly. Waves of pleasure coursed through her body and with a groan Grant lowered his head and kissed her, taking them both to the brink of total exultation – and well over the edge. When they finally headed downstairs to break their fast, he held her hand. Men seated at tables saw them and broke into grins and teased them as they neared the head table.

Tory blushed at the lewd comments, but refused to release Grant's hand. She wanted him to remain close before he left.

Too soon the parting they dreaded was upon them and Grant prepared to leave. He mounted his horse, bent down, and kissed Tory. She still felt self-conscious in front of his men, but wouldn't let him ride off without a farewell kiss. They could tease her all they wanted.

Grant and twelve clansmen departed and headed south. They'd been riding about an hour when he raised his hand to stop. Something felt wrong. Unable to explain it, premonitions of danger beat within his pulse. He couldn't shake the feeling that something felt dreadfully wrong – and his concerns centered on Tory.

Though not able to put his fear into words, Grant felt something amiss and knew he needed to return home. "Something is wrong, men. I'll leave it up to you to decide if you return with me or wait here for me."

To a man, they trusted Grant's instincts and decided to turn back. They spurred their horses forward and rode as hard as they could back to Drummond Castle.

Tory turned and entered the keep after the men rode from view. Grant had just left, and she missed him already. *This is ridiculous*, she chided herself. A few weeks in the man's arms and she acted like a lovesick kitten. His actions meant nothing. He certainly didn't love her. He just fancied bedding her.

The thought quickly flashed through her mind, *but you're in love with him.*

Rubbish! Where had such a ridiculous thought come from? Setting such thoughts aside, she headed to the garden, thinking today a good day for solitude. She planned to spend many hours of Grant's absence in total tranquility. After pulling weeds, she decided to rest a spell.

Though she didn't understand why she tired so easily, Tory leaned against the tall stately copper beech tree and promptly dozed.

She awoke with a start. Something had startled her, but she had no idea what. She glanced furtively around, and recognition jolted through her. Taken aback, she saw Michael sitting on the stone bench just a few feet away from her.

Tory couldn't believe her eyes. Surprised to see Michael, she couldn't speak. She couldn't remotely imagine what he might be doing in Scotland. And why had he come to Grant's castle? He should have been at her old home in England.

"Michael," she began hesitantly and peered at him with brows furrowed. "How...how good to see you again. Indeed, what are you doing here?" Her voice sounded strange and unnatural, even to herself.

Michael's eyes flickered over her coldly as she greeted him.

"I came to take you home, Victoria," he began in disapproval as his lips tightened, "where you belong." He eyed her dispassionately. "The house has not run properly since you left, and you are needed to return and resume your duties."

Tory looked at him in stupefaction. "Resume my duties?"

Michael nodded as if she should have perfectly understood his intent. His eyes were empty and cold.

"Of course," he retorted, and rage swiftly appeared in his eyes. "It strikes me you cannot possibly wish to remain in this heathen country."

168

"But I cannot leave," Victoria told him as she stood, astonished he could so easily walk back into her life and assume nothing had changed. "I am wed now."

"Married?" The tall Englishman laughed bitterly, and his hard, cruel eyes flickered over her, lingering on her breasts. "You jest. You would take the word of a priest from this country? I misdoubt they even worship the same God in this godforsaken area. They are naught but heathens." He spat into the dirt, clearly to show his disdain.

"W...well, actually," Tory stammered and wished she could take back her words, "we were not quite wed in a kirk." At Michael's frown, she paused and began to wring her hands in the folds of her shift. "He kind of claimed me."

Michael loomed over her without saying a word. Silence continued and a cruel smile formed around the edges of his mouth. Seemingly unable to contain his mirth, he burst into laughter, unable to stop. Yet his eyes shot daggers.

"Claimed you? He claimed you?"

Tory bit her lips painfully. The cruelty in Michael's eyes began to frighten her and caused a ripple of unease to course through her veins.

"Claim you?" he ground out again as he arched a brow. "You mean he made you his whore."

With a sharp intake of breath, Tory angrily sputtered, "I am not a—"

"Do not waste your breath, wench," he spat out, a hard cruel line to his mouth. "'Tis too funny. You who always fought us off because you thought you were too good for the likes of us have become the whore to a bloody Scot."

Tory continued to shake her head. She felt starkly alone in the garden, uncertain how she'd escape this large man. Fear and tumult overtook her as Michael's angry eyes bore into her. Somehow she must get inside the Hall. Grant's men wouldn't check on her in the garden. Not after she repeatedly nagged him to have them stop watching her every move. There had been a time when she felt she couldn't breathe without someone being present.

Now she wished she hadn't raised such a fuss. She looked furtively about and saw Michael had firmly ensconced himself between her and the keep's entrance. Fear began to claw through her, but so did anger.

"I am *not* a whore," she yelled with growing indignation, "and I am tired of people calling me that!"

Slowly, she wended her way around him. Her subtle movements didn't escape his notice and proved futile. "Nay, Victoria," he ground out menacingly. "You are going nowhere except with me."

Eyes widened in fright, she stammered, "But, M...Michael, I really cannot leave. I promised—"

"You promised?" came his mocking tone. "You promised a filthy Scot you would be his whore and you think I'll leave you here? I think not." He ended his tirade by knocking her to the ground with a powerful fist to her cheek. Tory saw the blow coming, but couldn't react quickly enough to avoid it.

She rose from the fall, then backed away as the taste of blood filled her mouth. Sore from the blow, she started to get downright cross. She'd not tolerate this abuse.

She flung herself at Michael and pummeled his chest. "How did you find me?"

Michael laughed, but all humor was gone from his eyes. Grabbing her hands in his, he backed her up against the copper beech she sat by earlier and lowered his head to kiss her.

It wasn't a gentle kiss and Tory jerked her head away.

"Do not touch me!" Fear and anger clawed through her as she freed a hand and swiped the back of it over her mouth.

"You'll not get away from me this time," he thundered. "You really believe you can lay with that heathen and ignore me? Rubbish."

Michael held her hands above her head with his left hand and struggled with the fastenings of her bodice. He lost his patience, grabbed its neckline, and pulled. It tore with little effort.

With a sneer, he moved closer and lowered his head to kiss her.

In panic, Tory raised her knee and with a quick thrust kicked him in the most vulnerable of places. With a howl of pain, Michael released her and doubled over. She took advantage of that distraction and ran.

Michael regained his bearings enough to rage after her and grabbed her before she made it to the entrance. He spat with a sneer, "Nay, wench. I already told you that you'd not get away from me. You will never get away again. You will return to England and do exactly what I tell you from now on. You will be *my* whore and I'll hear no word of complaint. Now do not struggle so."

A backhanded blow with his clenched fist drove Tory to the ground. This time Michael didn't give her time to get back up. He kicked her...over...and over...and over!

A scream of terror lodged in her throat and tears of pain leapt to her eyes. She couldn't escape! Dear merciful heavens, would she die?

Michael's anger over never bedding her clearly festered within him and erupted in violence. He kicked her, heedless of where his boots landed. From her head to her feet, he continued to batter her. Tory attempted to crawl away and tried to escape his brutal kicks, but Michael stopped her by grabbing her and stomping down on her leg with the full impact of his brute strength.

Tory heard the horrible sound of bone cracking as pain shot though her body. While she'd still stood, she tried to fend him off. After her leg broke and she could no longer stand, she quit fighting and curled her body into a ball. She tried to protect herself with her arms against the never-ending brutality Michael rained upon her in his rare fury.

Chapter Twenty

"Help!" Graeme shouted and ran headlong into the courtyard. "Lady Tory needs you!"

Several men chuckled as Graeme yelled. Everyone knew the children had fallen under Tory's spell. What did the lad think their young mistress needed help with? Weeding the garden? Was this plea naught more than a bit of whimsy?

"Cannot you hear me?" Graeme called in frustration when no one moved. Jumping up and down, he stomped his foot like he'd once seen his father do. "She is hurt."

That set men moving. "What speak you about, Graeme?"

"Some big man I never saw afore is out there with Lady Tory," Graeme gasped. "Hurry." Suddenly he saw Grant ride under the portcullis. Without thought to being trampled by incoming horses, Graeme ran toward his chief and breathlessly called, "Laird Grant, the bad man is hurting Lady Tory."

Reining in, Grant gracefully slid off his mount and looked to his men to decipher the small boy's words.

"We know not, m' lord," one man said and shrugged his broad shoulders. "Graeme just ran out and we thought he jested. We were going to find your lady when you rode in."

"Graeme?" Grant glanced at the small blond-haired boy. This had been what his instincts were telling him.

"She is in the garden, Laird Grant," the small boy said breathlessly, causing Grant to turn in that direction. While he tried to keep up with his laird's long strides, Graeme ran alongside him. "I went to see if she would tell us a story, and I saw this man. He is really big." Spreading his arms wide as he tried to demonstrate the man's size, he added, "This big. Bigger even than Archie." He said this with a hint of awe. With all the importance a six-year-old could muster, Graeme voiced the words that set all the men running.

"And he is hitting Lady Tory. She sent me to get help." He said this to Grant's back, since his small legs could no longer keep up with his chieftain, who'd increased his speed as the import of the boy's words hit him.

Running full out, Grant dashed into the garden, followed closely by several men. What he saw cut him to the core of his being. Someone was beating his lady wife senseless! Rage and fear overwhelmed him, and Grant released a furious bellow that tore from the depths of his soul.

This woman belonged to him!

As he leapt through the air to reach the stranger, Grant heard Tory's anguished shrieks. Using every ounce of strength he possessed, he grabbed the unknown man and yanked him off her, and freed her from the man's grasp as she released a blood-chilling scream. The stranger sent a ferocious kick to her arm.

Grant barely spared a glance at her before he swung at the lowlife, but he saw the fright in her eyes. Unsheathing his sword from its scabbard, he saw Tory crumpled in a heap on the ground. Over his shoulder he ground out, "Get her out of here!" His voice as harsh as his fury, Grant swung around to give full attention to his opponent, sword at the ready.

Grant heard Tory call out, but couldn't understand her words.

The Englishman proved a formidable foe. Grant would give him that. Regardless, the stranger would die this day for what he'd done to his woman. No one dared touch her. No one! Her home should have been a haven for her. This behemoth violated her safety and he wouldn't tolerate that. He swung instinctively to attack and the clash of swords soon rang out loudly in the garden.

The intruder fought with a vengeance, and Grant had no chance to collect his breath. The stranger's weapon sliced the air with deadly intent, but Grant slowly wore him down, his rage providing added strength. Sword pointed at the stranger's chest, he breathed heavily, "Who are you, and what are you doing in my keep?"

Sprawled on the ground, the other man spat at him, hate glistening in his eyes. Grant placed the tip of his sword into the man's throat and drew blood.

"Who are you?"

"Who I am is none of your concern, Scotsman," the Englishman shouted acidly. His voice permeated with sarcasm while he jerked his head toward where Warwick cradled Tory. Archibald stood over them both glowering. "She is supposed to be mine. You have no right to her."

Working to control his blinding rage, Grant grabbed Michael and jerked him to his feet. "There you are wrong, stranger," he said

173

testily. "She is my lady wife and she is my only concern right now. You will die this day for what you did to her."

The Englishman's steely grey eyes glared with contempt. "She is mine, I tell you – or should have been. You had no right to take her. Why should she be your whore when she'd let none of us touch her?"

He laughed menacingly. "She tells me she is your lady wife. Not bloody likely! We should have tried that tactic, too."

With a sneer of contempt, Michael taunted, "Tell me, Scotsman, does she spread her legs willingly, or must you force her like we tried to do?"

With the tip of the sword lessening at Grant's angry intake of breath, the intruder's eyes blazed as he twisted away and tried to slash Grant with his drawn knife. His mouth twisted in scorn.

Attention focused on the demented man challenging him, Grant instinctively swung his sword toward Michael, slashing the man's throat with a swift, clean death stroke.

The intruder soon lay in a pool of his own blood.

Face dark with outrage, Grant ground out, "Get rid of this whoreson. Check inside and outside the gates. If he had accomplices, question them. I want to know how he got in and what traitor helped."

Grant walked to Wick, who held an almost lifeless Tory. He breathed raggedly, and hunkered beside the old man, who transferred her easily into her husband's engulfing arms.

Carrying Tory to their bedchamber, Grant lowered her tenderly to their bed. She shook from the memory of her recent experience. He poured water from the ewer into the washbasin and got clean cloths, then returned and lowered himself beside her. Without saying a word, he gently washed the tears and blood from her face. Placing the cloths and water on the floor, he leaned over and kissed her gently, then removed her torn clothing.

"Wh...what are you doing?" a barely conscious Tory asked tremulously.

Grant smoothed her hair from her face to quiet her, and leaned over and placed a feathery kiss on her swollen lips. "I must check your injuries. I wish not to frighten you, but I will know what damage that monster did."

Tears welled in Tory's eyes.

Gazing at her tenderly, he hesitated before asking softly, "Did he...ravish you, wife?"

Grant hated to utter those words, but had to know. God help him, the thought of another man touching her proved more than he could bear. Why it mattered so much he still didn't understand, but matter it did.

Tory shook her head, and Grant released the breath he hadn't realized he'd been holding.

"Are...you...certain?"

"'Twould be some...something I would know," she stammered faintly. She started to tremble and couldn't stop, her body finally reacting to the terror she'd been through.

Grant moved to cradle her in his arms and caught the flash of pain in her eyes.

Lips quivering, yet firmly clenched, Tory drew him close. She wanted him to hold her, make her feel safe.

"I think he planned on it," she continued in a strangled voice, "but then he became too cross when I told him about you and he started to beat me instead."

"Angry? About me?"

Tory looked at him in despair and shook her head.

"Why?" Grant asked in amazement, his worried eyes searching hers. "He does not even know me."

She blushed. "Because you bedded me and he never did."

The import of her statement struck Grant full force coupled with what the stranger said while fighting. The blackguard wanted to bed his lady wife.

Of a sudden, she paused. "Grant, I thought you were gone." She shook her head slowly, trying not to lapse into unconsciousness. "How is it you came to be back here?"

"I know not, lady mine," he responded honestly. He saw her eyes glaze with pain. The thought of how close he almost came to losing her shook him more than he cared to admit. When had this woman so ensconced herself in his life?

"I headed out earlier, but a niggling started in the back of my mind. Something told me to turn around." Looking grave, he bent and kissed her forehead. "Now I know you were calling out to me." At Tory's questioning look, he smiled tenderly. "I heard you in my heart, wife."

After he examined her carefully, he confirmed her brutal beating. The bloody Englishman spared little. Tory's face already looked swollen and bruised. Grant feared her left arm and leg might both be broken. Her entire body began to discolor, showing where she'd been slapped and kicked.

Feeling extremely clumsy, Grant's heart raced. He felt all thumbs and brute strength and could do nothing right. After all, he was a warrior, not a goodwoman nor a healer. What did he know of treating a woman tenderly? And he felt far too shaken with her close brush with death.

"Wick," he bellowed in frustration, knowing his men no doubt waited outside his chamber door, "to me. I need your help. I think the bloody Sassunach broke my lady's bones." He watched her with a pained expression and didn't relish what would come.

Warwick hurried to where Tory laid still and silent on the bed. She thought she saw genuine concern written on his face. Had pain affected her senses? They all must hate her. Some still disliked her just for being English and it couldn't be denied Michael had come because of her. Yet, Warwick didn't look like he hated her right now.

Warwick gently held her arm. "This will hurt, lass, but I'll try to be as gentle as possible." She winced in pain as he probed her arm, and Wick nodded his assent to Grant. "'Tis broken. It must be reset." He then felt Tory's leg, seemingly feeling awkward touching his chief's lady wife. He grimaced when he felt that break, too. Looking up, Wick sighed and nodded, unable to voice the words.

Grant responded with a muttered string of expletives as his anger ebbed and anxiety flooded through him.

The gentle old man muttered as he turned to face Tory. "This will hurt somethin' fierce, lass, but I know you will be able to handle it. You are a Drummond now, mind."

His remark took Tory aback.

"Might you fancy a dram of whisky to dull your pain?" Being the first thing he personally would have reached for, he obviously assumed she'd want it, too.

"Nay," Tory answered tremulously, a soft whimper escaping her bruised lips. "I cannot take whisky right now." She didn't elaborate. "Please... do what you must." The muscles in her arm already throbbed. Albeit, so did the rest of her body. How would she ever bear more pain?

Heavy of heart, warmth tinged his eyes as the elderly man commiserated. "We must hold you down, lass. We will need more men for that. I apologize, but it will help so we can set your wee arm. Bear up now," he told her gently. "Will you tell us which of your wee herbs and potions we should use?"

Tory nodded and her breath caught as her heart filled with trepidation at the knowledge of pain yet to come. "Aye, fetch me my basket and I'll set them aside for you. I doubt I'll be much help afterward." She smiled wanly and ineffectually tried to rise. Failing, she wryly told them, "You must cleanse my arm with the solution I told you how to make." She drew in her breath. "Then will come the painful part. You'll need to set the bones. You'll need to make a cast of birch bark. 'Twill dry stiff and hard and hold my bones in place." Warily she added, "If I do not have enough birch bark, you can use setwort in its stead."

She told them, "You must do everything quickly, since my arm will soon start to swell and then the cast cannot be used." She saw they didn't understand. "If a cast is placed on an injury while swollen, it becomes too loose once the swelling abates and does not properly support the bones."

Realizing that meant they had to work doubly fast, since they needed to set her leg as well, they swore softly.

Grant, Warwick, Archie, and Ian diligently worked on her arm, as well as the multiple cuts and bruises. She tried to be brave, but when the pain grew too intense, she fainted. More than likely, the men attending her were grateful, since it gave them more freedom to work on her without worrying how badly she hurt.

The entire time they tended her injuries, young Graeme continued to relay everything he saw and heard in the garden. The wee lad certainly championed his lady's cause. He crept into the room when the others entered, and refused to leave even when Tory screamed in pain before she passed out.

"I am not leaving my lady," he insisted. "She needs me. I'm the one who saved her."

While they tended her injuries Graeme informed them, "You should have seen how the bad man beat her. She told me to run so I'd not get hurt. She told him this is her home now and her men would be coming to protect her."

He frowned and shook his head sadly. "I do not understand why she did not protect herself more and fight back. Once she fell to the ground, she curled up and kept her arms and hands in front of her belly." He proudly stated, "You might think me only a lad, but I can fight better than she did!"

Grant also thought it odd his feisty, young wife would quit fighting.

When Tory regained consciousness, her arm was casted and had carefully been placed in a sling. Her leg had been encased in her herbal medicaments and Grant paced like a caged wolf in front of the fireplace. As soon as he saw she'd regained consciousness, he moved closer and drew up a chair.

"How are you feeling?"

Tory tried to ignore the sharp stabs of pain caused by her movements. "Fine, except for being a trifle sore." Her face paled with pain and belied her attempt at casualness. Grant frowned and she admitted, "All right, I ache everywhere." She looked at her arm and acknowledged, "It looks like you followed my directions well." Seeing his curt nod, she looked around the room and saw men milling about.

Here it comes. This is where they tell me to get out. The moment she dreaded had finally arrived.

The thought should have pleased her, since she'd told them that was what she wanted since her arrival, but truth be told, she didn't think she wanted that anymore. She'd begun to think of this as her home. *Oh, I'm so confused.*

Of a sudden her stomach roiled.

Nay, she thought in despair, *I cannot give in to the sickness I've had these past days.*

"Why are these people in our bedchamber, Grant?" Her arm throbbed violently as she pulled the bed linens higher to cover herself more. When Grant didn't answer, but just stared, Tory nervously cleared her throat and tried to sound calmer than she felt. "I suppose you wish to know his name?"

"Aye, wife," he said, clearly trying to contain his turmoil of emotions. "That we do. And this time, we will have all of it."

"Wh...what mean you?" Tory asked hesitantly and shifted in discomfort.

Eyes hard, he reproached, "We wish to know everything. All the things you conveniently withheld these months past."

Looking back with eyes full of despair, Tory gulped. "I...I know not what..."

"Aye, woman, you do," her frustrated husband cut in and tried to keep his temper in check, his eyes never wavering from hers. "Everything this time."

Tory could scarcely breathe. She couldn't do this. She also knew Grant wouldn't give her a choice. She couldn't blame him, though, after all that happened. Still, she stalled.

He lost his temper. "Now, woman!"

Tory turned bleak eyes on him. "H...his name is Michael. Michael Singleton. He grew up in our m...manor house and train...trained with my father."

As she hesitated again, the men in the room said nothing, just stared with hard, unflinching eyes. "He...he came here to take me back to Blackstone Manor," Tory agonized.

Unable to continue, she felt as if their eyes bored into her. And she still had that terrible feeling in the pit of her belly she'd experienced the past few days.

"And?" he prodded and tried to keep his voice calm.

"Michael is an odious man and I told him I'd not go back. There is naught else to it. Truly. He became upset and took his anger out on me." In a bid to stall, she said in a voice barely above a whisper, "I think I would fancy resting now, please. I need a bit of a lie down." She chewed on her lower lip. "I really am quite tired."

Tory leaned back and gave what she hoped appeared to be a look of dismissal.

Her stubborn husband shook his head. "Nay, wife. There have been months for you to tell us all. You conveniently chose not to. Now you will."

"Grant, please..." Tory pleaded and frantically shook her head, guilt and fear in her eyes.

"Nay, Tory. Too much happened this day. My men fought his for you and could have been killed. They have the right to know all."

With a groan of resignation, Tory collapsed against the blue bolstering pillow she'd recently made. "What do you wish to know? I told you why he came here. There is naught else to tell." Her voice quavered as she spoke.

"Woman, why did he think you would return with him?" he questioned stubbornly. His exasperation quickly became evident.

Tory had to take several deep breaths before she could answer. After glancing around the room, she closed her eyes to gather her courage.

"Michael wanted things he could not have and expected them handed to him on a shiny platter. He wished to be in charge of Blackstone Manor. He felt he deserved it. He told me he needed me to run the manor. Said things were not as they should be since I left."

Grant could see he'd have to drag everything out of her. He arched a brow and asked, "And why would that be? What were you to Blackstone Manor?"

Tory visibly blanched and her breathing quickened. She looked at him and covered her mouth. "Grant, please, I am going to be sick. Please leave."

Grant didn't budge.

What could she do? Merciful heavens, with her leg in a cast, she couldn't flee the room. As her stomach continued to roil and full-blown nausea assailed her, Tory did the only thing she could. She rolled to the side of the bed and became violently ill.

Grant jumped back quickly this time!

"I did not know you meant really *sick!*" With a shout over his shoulder, he yelled, "Get a wet cloth." When one of his men handed it to him, Grant helped her sit and gently cleaned her face.

"I am sorry, lady wife," he began apologetically and studied her closely. "I knew not you meant that kind of sick. I thought you meant you were upset." A frown furrowed his brow. "Think you the beating upset your belly?"

Ignoring his question, Tory straightened her shoulders and held her head high. "Please leave me alone!" When he refused to leave, she spoke as if the words she had yet to utter pained her. "You really are not going to leave, are you?"

When Grant shook his head, Tory inhaled deeply, glowered up at him, and angrily flung the words he waited to hear, "You win! I'll tell you whatever you wish...and then, I vow, sir, I'll never speak to you again."

Stopping to take a breath, or to gather strength – Grant never felt quite certain which – Tory blurted, "My name is Victoria Elizabeth Catherine...Blackstone. My father was the man you went to kill that night in Berwick."

In afterthought, she sheepishly admitted, "My grandmum... and sister are the only people who call me Tory."

Chapter Twenty-one

Surprised when Grant merely nodded, Tory thought he'd would explode at this information.

"What were you really doing the night we found you?"

Tory glowered. "You mean the night you kidnapped me? Exactly what I said – run away. You didn't believe me then, and I doubt you'll believe me now, but 'tis the truth. I tried to run away from there."

"Why?" his tone sharpened. He didn't smile.

Growing agitated, her gaze flew to his face. "Because my father betrothed me to someone I detested. I refused to wed him and knew the only way to avoid it would be to run away. I'd not planned on being kidnapped by the likes of a vile creature such as you instead."

Her hands clasped nervously into fists as she grumbled the last.

"Women often marry men they do not fancy." Grant shrugged nonchalantly and thought this a daft explanation. "'Tis the way of the world. Why think you this should be different?"

"You do not understand—"

"Nay, wife, we do not. Nor will we if you do not explain. Saints toes, woman, do so," Grant exploded, exasperated he couldn't get his own lady wife to tell him the truth. His jaw set in fierce determination.

Tory bit her lower lip and Grant feared she'd chew it raw before she told them what they wanted to hear. They knew much already from the auld peddler, but Tory didn't know that. He had to know for once she'd trust him enough to tell him the whole truth.

"'Twas not just that I did not love him." She let out what sounded like a frightened whimper, "I...I knew if I wedded him he would kill me." At Grant's frown, she continued warily, "He killed his first two wives, and I knew I would be next."

"What are you speaking about?" Grant looked at Tory as if she were daft. He wanted facts and she spoke of silly things like love. Everyone knew love only existed in women's minds. It didn't really exist.

She looked so fragile as tears ran down her smooth cheeks, Grant almost lost his resolve to make her continue. He wanted to gather her in his arms and hold her close. He felt like a brute, but stood firm.

"Some things cannot be proved," she said in a barely audible voice. "'Tis just known. He wanted sons and got none, so he beat his wives. In the process he found he enjoyed doing that."

Continuing, she lowered her eyes and blushed profusely, "Old and vile, the man made my flesh crawl. I could not bear the thought of him touching me...like that...*like you do*. You know...there." She tentatively looked up to see how he'd react to that news and blushed all the more when she remembered other people were in the room. "I knew I would soon anger him and that he would beat me worse than my father had."

She closed her eyes and dragged in deep breaths of air. Her voice caught. "I am certain 'tis the only reason Father agreed to let me wed. He finally found someone he thought would torture me more than he had."

"All fathers discipline their children." Grant leaned forward and looked at her closely. "Why would you expect yours to do less?"

Tory shook her head. She couldn't bring herself to answer. Drained, she felt an aching grief having to remember all the things she'd tried so hard to forget. If she told them all, everything she'd learned to love here would be lost.

And for some reason she couldn't fathom, she suddenly knew for a fact she no longer wished to leave. This had become her home—the first true home she'd ever had. Once the children accepted her, adults slowly came around. Most of them anyway. But, after what happened this day with Michael, it didn't matter anymore. Everything crashed down on her in the split second of a heartbeat.

"Answer me, Tory," Grant pressed, his grey eyes flashing. "I have told you myself I would not hesitate to discipline you if I felt the need. That is not only a father and husband's right, 'tis his responsibility."

Profoundly upset, she could speak no longer and released the flood of grief that threatened to choke her. Grant watched her, saw the truth he sought, and pulled her within the safe confines of his arms. He sat beside her on the bed and held her tenderly while she sobbed inconsolably.

"Tell me, Tory. Say the words—just once. You will never overcome your fears nor get rid of your nightmares if you cannot admit it," Grant soothed.

Seeing the sadness in her eyes, he ached to take her pain away.

Overcome by emotion, tears streamed down Tory's face. She looked at Grant as though he were the only other person in the room. "I have told you, over and over. You just do not believe me. He beat me. My whole life my father beat me." She buried her face in the hollow of Grant's neck and sobbed. "The only good thing about my childhood... is that...I survived it."

"Why, Tory? Why did he beat you? What did you do to anger him?"

Desperate now, Tory gathered strength and pulled away from Grant. "He hated me. Not being the son he wanted, he never forgave me for it. He told me that oft enough."

Turning inward, she dredged up feelings she'd buried long ago.

"I tried to make him love me. Truly. I tried to excel at everything so he'd be proud of me, but instead he grew angrier. No matter what I did, 'twas never enough."

Grant already heard much of this from Gofraidh, the peddler. Unable to believe the awful words before, he doubted 'twould be any easier now, but he needed to hear it from Tory. He knew about the time she proudly announced she could read like the boys in her manor. Instead of rejoicing as most fathers would, the blackguard took away her beloved horse. It had been the only thing Tory had told him about herself, and she hadn't done so willingly.

Then there'd been the time she thought her father would be pleased if she helped him with household accounts and told him she learned to cipher. The scoundrel had hobbled her outside in the rain during a horrible storm like an animal. The peddler'd said her father refused to let anyone release her, even though Tory's screams echoed through the manor. As jagged lightning flashed, the man sat inside and drank himself senseless, laughing all the while. Thanks to the children in his keep, Grant knew to this day Tory feared thunderstorms. The we'ans always worried about her when it stormed and made it a point to gather around her. She seemed to well-come their presence even though they never told her why they did it.

"Tell me, wife."

With Grant's arms safely encompassing her, Tory spilled out a lifetime of horrors.

"He...he did cruel things. Not just beatings. Sometimes he locked me in small rooms, like the laundry room here, and made me stay for hours." She chewed her lower lip nervously. "One night he got so drunk he forgot me and left me there overnight. I told you that already. I felt truly terrified. Dark and tiny, I thought the room would smother me."

Tory whimpered softly as she remembered the horror of it.

"Other times he hit or kicked me." When she couldn't continue, she sagged against Grant's chest, felt the strength radiating from him.

Her entire body hurt, but the pain in her heart hurt more. She felt without a doubt this would be the last time Grant's arms would be a safe haven for her. He'd set her aside after this. 'Tis what she should expect since she'd hid the truth from him. And now she'd placed them all in danger. Grant could have been killed fighting Michael and now he knew her father's name. Never could he forgive her for being Blackstone's daughter.

Grant started to release her, but Tory held onto him fiercely. She wanted the feel of his body against hers a little longer. She wanted to memorize the scent of him.

"Please, Grant, hold me. Just one last time."

Grant didn't understand what she meant by that request, but hold her he did. She tired and what he had to say would upset her even more. "The men saw your back, Tory."

She reflexively jerked away, her eyes wide in terror as a knot of fear lodged in her stomach.

"Nay!"

"They couldn't help it. Your shift tore afore we got out to the garden. Tell us what happened." Grant made his voice sound calmer, so as not to frighten her even more. Other than the time she'd been unconscious, not once had he asked her about the scars. He'd patiently waited for her to volunteer the information. That time had never come.

Tory stiffened against his hold and gathered strength to pull away, but he refused to release her.

"Nay! Not that," she shouted hysterically and fought threatening tears. "Never that! *Let me go!*" She struggled to no avail. Grant saw how painful this revelation would be.

"Nay, Tory. Not this time. Who gave you the lashes?" Grant made no attempt to hide his annoyance, yet understood her pain.

"Do not make me tell you," she sobbed and visibly flinched. "Leave me some dignity."

Grant said nothing, but his eyes held an abundance of questions. Somehow he knew how much it would cost her to tell him, and knew he couldn't make her continue. He'd pushed her as far as he could this day. She'd been through enough torment. From the pained look on her face, he could see she'd revealed more horrors that befell her than she ever planned. Time for questions had ended. Her emotional well-being appeared far too fragile.

Tory pulled away, and this time he didn't stop her. Wracked with sobs, her shoulders slumped. She looked visibly sick and her voice quavered. "Grant, pray forgive me for not telling you this before, but I could not speak of it. Actually, I never planned to mention it, but I never meant to shame you either. I ask your pardon and that of your men. I'll gather my things and leave now, unless...you choose to kill me." She faltered. "I would not fault you that choice, but, if you allow me to leave, I promise I'll not take much. Nothing, if that is your will. Since we were never wed in a kirk, you will have no problem setting me aside. You will be free to wed with someone you can love."

She never thought saying those words would hurt so much. She no longer wanted him with anyone else. She wanted to stay with him forever.

"Pray grant me permission to stay until the morrow. I verily do not believe I could move this night."

Grant sat speechless. Sweet merciful heaven, he couldn't believe all he heard. He stared in shock as she turned her pleading face up to his. No one in the room made a sound.

Of a sudden the last part of her speech broke through his consciousness. *Leave him*? What the deuce did she mean? Saints alive, had she finally cracked a screw, as he'd heard the English say?

Anger evident in his voice, Grant shot to his feet. "I told you months ago I would never let you leave. Naught has changed." He softened his voice. "Must I know one more thing, *a leannan*." Although he felt he already knew what her answer would be, he prompted, "When you say your da beat you, do you really mean similar to what this *foosty scunner* did this day? Once and for all, I must know the truth."

Pain speared her heart as she shook her head. "He did not beat me to the extent Michael did today, but he often came close. I am quite certain 'tis why Michael did not hesitate to do so. 'Tis

185

what he'd seen, what all the men in my house saw Father do."

Tory shrugged as if it didn't matter and bit her lip. "Why, milord, is that what you plan to do now? If so, I ask you have done with it quickly."

She'd gotten good at concealing her feelings, but she failed miserably at the effort now.

Grant saw how much courage it took for her to ask such a question, but nevertheless it angered him. He clenched his jaw and gritted out, "Woman, you shame both of us by asking such a question. I would never hit a woman thusly. I told you afore and I'll tell you but one last time, if you need correction, I will not hesitate to do so. That is a husband's right and responsibility."

Taking her wet face between his hands, he tilted it up to look at him. "But I promise you, Sweeting, you will never be beaten like this again. 'Tis also a husband's responsibility to protect his wife. I failed you this day, but this will never happen again. You have my vow."

When she looked dubious, he asked, "Do you wish me to kiss my blade?"

Tory didn't understand his question. She spoke of honor and leaving and he now stood there talking about kissing a knife? She didn't want to hurt his feelings, but...

Seeing confusion written on her face, Grant explained as if speaking to a child, "I meant what I said. I give you my solemn vow. In the Highlands, when we give a pledge, we seal it by kissing our dirk. Should I ever break my word or dishonor my vow, I know the blade I kiss will be the one you may use to take my life. I do not give vows lightly."

The unspoken plea in Tory's eyes wrenched his heart. He could see how much she wanted to believe him, yet confusion and disbelief were also present. Too many years of painful abuse had taken their toll.

"You really meant what you said?" she stammered.

Grant nodded.

She shook her head slowly as she contemplated his words. "I appreciate what you said. More than you will ever know. I'll treasure your words always, but you must let me go. I cannot stay here with your men knowing what happened. 'Twould bring shame to you. Not to mention danger."

"Twice have you spoken of shaming me. How can what your perverted da did shame me? You had no control over his actions. Mayhap you were not most wise to have provoked him, but in

186

truth he just looked for excuses." Grant shook his head in frustration at the thought of pain her father had inflicted. He could see vestiges of emotional pain she endured as well as the physical pain.

If Grant hadn't known the man was already dead, and more than likely burning in Hell, he'd have sworn to avenge her now.

Tory's lips quivered with the effort of trying to stay her tears. She looked like she didn't believe him, yet a spark of hope appeared in her eyes.

"*Mo Chridhe*," Grant's tone of voice was resolute, unyielding, "the past's shame belongs to your da. Have you naught to be ashamed of."

Tory shook her head as Grant gently pulled her close and rubbed her back. She sighed ruefully and looked away, embarrassed. "I could never face our men again, Grant. I am a coward. I admit that. But 'tis too dangerous for all of you."

"You are one of the bravest women I know," Grant told her honestly, "but you keep saying 'twill be dangerous." He looked bewildered. "What do you speak of?"

"Michael knows where I am now," Tory implored. Her shoulders shook with silent sobs and alarm sounded in her voice. "I know not how he found me. Even though I worried about my grandmum and sister, I swear by all that is holy I sent no missives. Please believe me. I did not ask him to come here, but now that he found me, he will return."

She looked at Grant with the saddest eyes he'd ever seen.

A frown appeared on Grant's face and she rushed on, "Then there will be more fighting. I know your sense of honor, Grant Drummond, and you will fight because you will think 'tis the right thing to do, even though you really do not want to."

As his frown deepened, she added, "You will be hurt and I could not bear that. I would be responsible."

Grant exploded. "You think that worthless scum will injure me?"

She felt frightened at Grant's quick display of anger, but nodded nevertheless. "I...I have seen him fight. That is what I tried to tell Archibald earlier – that Michael fights really well."

"And I do not?" Grant bellowed as his powerful body shook with anger. "Did your beating addlepate you, woman?"

When Tory didn't immediately answer, Grant spun toward his men and began a tirade the likes of which they hadn't seen from him before.

"Did you hear her?" He didn't wait for a response. "This... woman thinks I cannot fight!"

Grant paced and ranted. He spun around and fixed Tory with an angry gaze. "By all that is holy, she thinks that worthless Sassenach fights better than me."

"I do not think she meant quite that," Wick began while trying to calm him.

Grant ignored the interruption and continued to pace. A muscle in his cheek began to tic.

"She thinks I cannot fight well enough to protect her." Grant mumbled things no one could hear before he turned to face Tory and ranted, "All right, so I did not do such a good job of that this day. But I came back, did I not?"

Grant's men quickly nodded assent.

"And I killed the bloody pervert for hurting her, did I not?" Again his men affirmed his statement.

Tory said nothing. She sat on the bed and stared at her husband. She'd never seen him so upset. His arms were folded over his massive chest.

"But does that matter? Nay! This woman thinks I cannot fight." Grant slammed his fist on the nearest table. "Am I not the best warrior in these parts?"

His men unanimously murmured their assent, but by now smiles crept onto their faces. Clearly Grant was upset about Tory's lack of awe regarding his fighting capabilities. The wee lass had quite flustered their young chief.

Grant's mentor tried to placate him. "I dinnae believe Lady Tory has ever seen you fight, Grant. You always forbid her being anywhere near the lists and she is little acquainted with your fighting skills."

Grant heard Wick, but ignored him and waved his hand as if to discount that theory.

"But is being the best good enough for my lady wife?" Grant ranted as if no one had interrupted. "Nay.

"Wives are supposed to be devoted," he shot a sideways glare at Tory. "They are supposed to support and honor their husbands. They are supposed to love and *obey* them."

At that Wick could no longer contain himself. "I thought none of that mattered, Grant." A touch of sarcasm tinged his words.

The look of menace Grant shot Wick quickly silenced the elderly man's comments, but couldn't contain his laughter.

Again ignoring the interruption, Grant inquired, "Does my lady wife do any of those things? Nay! She would much rather malign my fighting abilities..."

Of a sudden Tory realized what Grant yelled earlier and blurted, "Did you say you killed Michael?"

Grant spun back to face her and looked ready to explode. He marched over to the bed and stormed, "Did I not already say that, woman? Did your beating destroy your hearing as well as addlepate your brain?"

Before Tory could open her mouth to respond, Grant spun and paced again. "Do not think I take your beating lightly, but there are a few things we will get clear."

"But..."

"Silence!" Grant bellowed, his eyes boring into hers. "Do not interrupt when I am yelling!"

Grant glared at Tory, silencing her quite effectively.

"Let me clarify one thing." Grant walked back to the bed and placed his face in front of Tory's wide eyes. "Your name is Victoria Elizabeth Catherine... Drummond!" Grant narrowed his eyes as he continued, "And do not ever forget that."

It didn't matter one whit to him that women usually kept their maiden names. His wife wouldn't, period!

Nodding his head as if he'd scored a major coup, Grant straightened and continued to pace. Tory sat with mouth agape, far too shocked to speak. Every time Grant thought of another point, he glared.

"Second, you will never leave my house. This is *our* home and here you will stay – forever. I will not tell you that again." His face held a triumphant look as he delivered his command.

"Third, for the anger you caused this night, you will do whatever I tell you, whenever I tell you." When Tory opened her mouth to say something, he gave her such a ferocious glare she wisely withheld her comments.

"'Tis quite certain I am there is a fourth, fifth, sixth, etc., but I am too aggravated to think of them. We will discuss them later." He nodded firmly, as if to confirm the matter.

Aggravated with her? Tory thought that an understatement. She'd never seen him this cross. She drew her head up and looked at him with eyes filled with trepidation. "If you think to beat me now, sir, I would rather it not be in front of our men." Her lower lip quivered as she looked up at him. "I think I have been shamed enough this day without having to endure more."

"Beat you for what happened this day? Do not spout such foolishness." Grant suddenly calmed and smiled. At that moment he could think of no one braver than she, but he didn't know how to convince her.

Inspired, he said, "Let our men make the decision." Seeing her look of fear, he whispered, "your men, lady mine. Wee Graeme told us he heard you tell that English braggart your men would protect you." He gently turned her so she faced the men in their chamber while Tory frantically shook her head.

She only wanted to bury her face in his chest and never face their men again. What must they think? She took a quick peek out of one eye to see their reaction to Grant's proclamation.

To her surprise, she saw no hatred on their faces.

As he tightened his protective hold, Grant addressed the men in his chamber. "Men, it seems my lady wife has a wee concern you might not want her here anymore. I told her that is nonsense, but I believe she must hear it from you. What say you?"

To a man they couldn't bring themselves to torment their chief's lady wife, but not the first man spoke. The look in Grant's eyes indicated in no uncertain terms he'd brook no arguments from them, and he expected them to do no less than make her feel comfortable.

Warwick approached first. "My lady, we dinnae wish you to leave." Tory looked at him in disbelief. "'Tis true." With a wave of his hand he encompassed everyone in the room. "We all feel that way."

Tory looked like she doubted every word he said. With a scowl on his face, Archibald grumbled and moved forward. "You will not be leaving." He said no more as he turned and exited the room, but he suddenly knew with horrifying clarity that Grant was truly going to keep this woman.

Tory stood speechless.

Suddenly Grant looked around the room. "What the deuce are you all doing in my bedchamber? Get out! 'Tis not seemly for you to be here! Out!"

Unable to contain their laughter, his men left the room. *My, how the mighty have fallen,* Wick thought. One wee slip of a lass had turned their chieftain into a jiggling mass of jam. Never before had they heard Grant take such offense at a single comment someone made, let alone one made by a mere lass.

The fact that it truly mattered to him how he appeared in Tory's eyes proved extremely telling. Their great chief had fallen head over heels in love – but all knew him well enough to know he'd never admit it.

Chapter Twenty-two

The next day, Grant fed Tory dinner in bed, since he refused to let her go downstairs to eat. The stubborn man seemed determined she rest for several days after her trying ordeal.

He passed her his tankard of ale, but she declined.

"Would you rather have mead, Sweeting? Or some sherry? You need something to help you relax so you can sleep. I'll not have you disturbed by pain or nightdreams."

"Thank you, milord," she smiled, "but goat's milk is fine. Perhaps later I'll see if I can move around enough to mix some herbs together. They should help me sleep fine."

"Tell me what to use and I'll mix it. You cannot get out of bed." Grant patiently rubbed the backs of his fingers over her lower lip.

A shiver ran through Tory as he slowly lowered his head and his lips feathered hers. He kissed her gently since he could see her lips were far too bruised for true passion. He really wanted to make wild, passionate love to her all night to ensure himself she hadn't been injured even worse—and that she belonged to him. He didn't understand why that should be so important, but it was. He ruefully admitted he'd almost been undone by the thought of losing her.

Instead, he pulled away and again asked about herbs. He mixed together spearmint, rose leaves, and orris root, and took great care to get the draft correct. He brought the drink to Victoria and held her gently while he waited for the potion to work.

When he felt her relax, he lowered her to their bed. He covered her with furs and lightly kissed her lips before he left the room.

Bright and early the next day Tory stirred sleepily in Grant's arms. She opened her eyes and tried to stretch, but grimaced as pain shot sharply through her body.

"Feel you up to coming down the stairs to break your fast, or wish you to remain abed?"

"I definitely wish to bide in bed, but I promise I shall eat soon. You needn't worry about me milord. Pretend I'm not here and go about your normal routine. You need not look after me every moment."

"Aye, I do." He kissed her forehead, jumped out of bed, and headed downstairs to break his fast then work outside with his men in the lists.

Pretend she wasn't there? He could no longer imagine his life without Tory in it. She'd become far too important to him.

After he broke his fast, he realized he'd forgotten his sword and shook his head at the oversight. He never forgot his sword. A man wasn't considered dressed without it, and a warrior always had to be ready to protect himself and those around him.

How could he have been so careless? The lass made him forget. He'd been too worried about her.

Heading to his chamber, Grant chanced upon Triona when she approached the room. When she saw him, she appeared to panic.

"My lord," she began nervously, "what are you doing here? You should be outside this time of day."

Grant laughed at her and thought that a foolish thing to say. "'Tis my room, and I forgot something."

Triona tried unsuccessfully to block the door. "Nay, milord, you cannot enter. Tell me what you forgot and I shall get it."

Telling Grant not to enter his own chamber certainly wasn't the right thing to do. Suddenly he feared the worst. He pushed the young maid aside in his haste, flung open the door, and strode inside. He stopped in his tracks.

Tory'd gotten out of bed, knelt on the floor, and leaned over the chamber pot. Grant silently faced Triona, a question in his eyes, but the young woman merely handed him a wetted cloth and quietly left the room.

She feared her lady was for it now!

Grant frowned, thoughts swirling in his mind. How had the maid known Tory felt ill? She hadn't even been in his room yet. Did Tory's belly still bother her from her beating? Mayhap he should find a physician to attend her. Something could be seriously wrong.

Quietly approaching Tory, Grant hunkered down without saying a word and handed the cloth around her. Something definitely seemed amiss.

"Thank you, Triona. You are such a blessing. I know not how I could bear this without you. I must find some bistort to calm this nausea or Lord Grant will become suspicious of my not breaking my fast with him. Perhaps we could find some ginger root, although I do not fancy that nearly as well. I certainly cannot avoid him every morning." She raised her head slightly and wiped the perspiration from her face.

"Have the men headed out to the lists?"

Grant furrowed his brows. "The men have gone outside, but your husband has not, wife. Tell me what is going on that you wish me gone, and what will I get suspicious about? Why can you not break fast with me?"

Tory froze at the sound of his voice. When she didn't respond, he turned her around to face him. She looked white as a ghost.

"Tory?"

Tory stared at Grant's chest, her breathing ragged, and she chewed on the inside of her cheek. He gently tilted her chin up.

"You've been ailing?" Grant asked. "Triona acted as if she knew you were ill. Is this from your beating? Needs I find a physician?"

Tory turned, a blatant attempt to hide her face, but Grant gently turned it back. She could tell from the spark in his eyes that he expected an answer.

"Aye," she admitted stubbornly and knit her brows together. "I have been ill about a fortnight."

"A fortnight?" came Grant's surprised question. "Why did you not tell me? Is it some woman's ailment? 'Tis not from the beating if you ailed afore."

"'Tis nothing you need worry yourself about, milord. Naught is wrong."

"Then what? Is your wame curdled?" Grant stormed as he jumped to his feet and paced the room, worry evident in his voice. "Answer me."

He refused to let the incident drop.

She breathed deeply to calm herself, not knowing how he'd react to her news. Unconsciously she raised her hand to her throat. "Nay, my stomach is not upset. Not in the way you mean."

Grant frowned.

"I believe I am with child." She held her breath and waited for what she thought would be an angry explosion. "*Your child.*"

Grant stopped pacing and spun around to face her. His eyes held his surprise. "A bairn?" he repeated softly. "You are going to have my bairn?"

Tory bit her lower lip and prepared herself for an argument. She nodded and didn't release her breath until she saw a smug grin settle over his face.

Grant asked with mounting excitement.

Grant asked with mounting excitement, "Have you been late in your courses?"

She nodded.

Grant walked over to her and pulled her to her feet, wrapped his arms around her, holding her tenderly. Releasing his hold, he kept his hands lightly on her shoulders so she couldn't wriggle from his grasp. This definitely wasn't the reaction she'd expected.

Cupping her chin with his hands, he kissed her lightly on her still bruised lips. Before she could utter a sound, he swept her into his arms and carried her downstairs to shout his news to everyone in his castle.

As always, he totally ignored her threats to put her down.

A few nights later Grant glanced at Tory with an odd expression on his face. They sat silently before the crackling hearth in his chamber. She thought he meant to speak, but at the last moment obviously changed his mind.

"Grant," she questioned in an effort to try to get him to tell her what bothered him, "is aught wrong? You look odd – almost troubled."

"Nay, wife," Grant began after a short pause. "I am not troubled. I am blessed. I hesitate to say this, but I thank you for having my child. Were I honest, I must admit the thought crossed my mind that with your knowledge of herbs you might prevent yourself from having my bairn."

Tory's eyes registered astonishment and Grant hastened to continue. "I am not talking about you goin' to an angel-maker or finding an auld crone with a stick to rout it out..."

"I would hope not!" she interrupted, aghast. "I would never do something so horrible. Kill my own babe? Never!"

She glared at him, ready for an argument.

"I know that now, Sweeting," Grant interjected, trying to calm her, "but I did think you might take some of your herbs so you'd not have my bairn at all." His words trailed off as he glanced at her sheepishly.

Tory raised her hand to touch his face and console him, but hesitated at the last minute, being uncertain how he'd react to that intimacy. Instead, she assured him, "I would never do that, Grant. If God wishes me to have your babe, that is what I'll do. Having a baby is one of God's most special miracles. I would never stop that.

"Howbeit, since we are being honest, I must admit I did not think you wanted me to have your babe. You once told me you did not, and I thought you might want to wait."

"Wait for what?"

"Until you could wed with someone you love, of course," she answered as if he should have already known the answer.

Shaking his head, Grant pulled her close and sighed deeply. "You are my lady wife, lassie – this day, on the morrow, and for always. I have told you this afore. You just do not believe me. 'Tis a great flaw of yours, that."

Suddenly he set her aside enough to look into her face. "Woman, is there anything else you should have told me that you have not?"

She smiled and assured him there wasn't.

Two days later Grant determined she felt well enough to remain downstairs, unlike the day he rushed her down to announce their great news and promptly carried her back to their bedchamber. He'd been adamant she still needed to rest.

"Grant, I feel fine. I am just sore." Her protestations fell on deaf ears.

"Are you certain I do not look too horrible?" Tory questioned hesitantly a few days later. "I quite imagine I must look a fright." Based on how the bruises on the rest of her body looked, she feared her face couldn't be much better.

"You could never look ughsome to me, lady mine," Grant answered honestly. Concern over how she looked from her beating weighed heavily on her. She feared it too great a reminder to everyone of her being the reason Englishmen invaded their home. "You are *aluinn*."

When Tory frowned, Grant clarified, "You are beautiful, Sweeting." He ruined it by adding, "I'll admit you are a few shades that are not on a rainbow, but that is to be expected."

Tory frowned and Grant tried for a bit more levity. "At least you are not black and blue anymore." He continued in a rush, "Now you are purple, green, and yellow!"

She threw a pillow at his head. "Ooh, that makes me feel so much better." She sat back down on the bed. "I am not leaving this room."

Laughing, Grant scooped her into his arms and carried her to the door. "Aye, lady wife, you are."

With that proclamation, he headed out the door and down to the Great Hall.

Grant noticed one of his men about to make a teasing comment and imperceptibly shook his head. His men knew him exceedingly well, and caught on immediately. Their chief felt Lady Tory not quite ready for a spot of teasing.

Cook made a special effort to have Tory's favorite foods, since he was pleased to have her back in their midst. He found he missed having her daily input. She challenged his creativity in ways that brought out the best in him.

On top of that, she was a true joy to be around.

A young serving woman brought food to the table when she caught sight of Tory. 'Twas the first time she'd seen her lady since the accident, although she heard about it as had everyone else. Inhaling sharply, the lass screamed, dropped the tray of food, and ran back to the kitchen.

Everyone sat dumbstruck.

Soon Cook exited the kitchen. Upset, he motioned Grant to join him. Without a word Grant rose and followed, as did several men.

They found the serving lass, Fionnan, sobbing in the kitchen and wringing her hands.

"What goes?" Grant questioned.

Eyes flying between Cook and Grant, the sobbing woman cried, "'Twas me, Laird Grant. I let the English in that day."

Grant's look darkened and she tremulously continued. "My sister lives outside the village, my laird. One day she told me there were men at her house that wished to see Lady Tory."

Unable to continue, Fionnan worried her hands in the folds of her kirtle.

"What did you do, woman?" Grant ground out.

"The next day my sister appeared at our castle with an Englishman," she stammered, looking into Grant's angry face. "I could tell she'd been crying. The man threatened her and said if she did not fetch him to me he would kill her bairn."

Grant didn't look the least bit swayed by this bit of information.

She rushed on in a flurry, "He said he wanted to talk with Lady Tory a few minutes and then he would leave. When I told him I couldn't let him in the keep, he threatened my sister's family."

Tears streamed down her face . "I am sorry, Laird Grant. I never imagined he would hurt her. Och, I never should have let him in here. I know that now, but I feared for my family."

Grant glared at her, his lips pursed in a thin line.

"I heard the lady had been hurt, but I realized not how badly until I saw her. I never dreamed he would do something like that. I swear before God he said he wished to speak with her."

Looking into Grant's eyes for the first time, she sobbed, "I am sorry, Laird Grant. I would never hurt Lady Tory apurpose. I think the world of her."

"Get off my lands," Grant shouted in fury.

"But I have nowhere to go."

"Leave now," Grant exploded, "before I decide that is not enough and punish you elsewise as well."

A quiet voice sounded behind them. "Grant, please let her stay."

Grant spun to see Tory standing in the doorway.

"Nay," he said quietly, knowing his eyes revealing his steely resolve. "You could be dead because of her."

Walking over slowly to touch his arm, she looked squarely into the young girl's face. "I heard not your story. Only yelling." She asked the sobbing young woman, "Why did you do it?"

The devastated woman repeated her story as Grant glowered. Tory merely nodded.

"Grant," she said and turned to her husband, "she protected her family. I understand that. Please let her stay."

Grant pulled her to the side and tried to reason with his young, generous wife. "Woman, I would have a word with you." When he made no headway, in frustration he finally returned to Fionnan. "My lady wife insists I not banish you fom my home. However, I cannot allow you to remain here after what happened. My lady could have died because of what you did. Had you trusted me enough to care for you and your family, this would not have happened. But you did not, so I must take action. My lady has suggested, and I'll reluctantly agree, letting you remain on my lands with your family. You will no longer work in my house. I cannot allow that."

Sobbing, the young woman thanked him and Tory. She could have been banned for life. Had Grant so chosen, he could have seen her dead for her actions. She turned her wet eyes to Tory. "Thank you, milady. Truly I meant you no harm." Her lips trembled as she said the words.

198

Tory returned her smile and nodded.

Grant looked at the young woman in frustration. "Next time you need help, I would suggest you trust your chieftain, or the men I leave in my stead. I'll not be this lenient again."

He turned and headed back to the Great Hall. His lady wife again had been far too generous.

After things settled back down and they had eaten, Tory looked at Grant and asked if he'd help her out to the garden. She thought to spend some time resting there.

The reality of what she said struck her immediately. "Oh, nay, Grant, I cannot. What could I have been thinking? I cannot face being out there yet."

She immediately burst into tears. "I am sorry. I thought I could do this, but fear I cannot. Please forgive me."

"There is naught to forgive, *Mo Chridhe*," Grant told her while he held her close. "Right now the garden still holds bad memories. I understand that. As much as you love it, though, I hope you will be able to go back out there soon."

Lifting her into his arms he headed to the courtyard. "Today it matters not, for I already have your day planned."

She looked through tear drenched lashes and asked, "What are we going to do?"

"Be patient, Sweeting." He chuckled, knowing patience had never been one of his wife's better virtues.

Soon he had Tory bundled up on a chair near the training lists.

She couldn't believe Grant had brought her out here – and had planned it in advance. The chair and blankets had been set out for her.

Grant told her, "I think it will be good for you to get some sun and fresh air."

As if she could get much of either with all these blankets bundled about her!

Grant left her and went about his daily routine in the lists. Tory glanced in amazement at the amount of activity that occurred out here. She'd witnessed training in her father's household, but that held nowhere near the precision Grant demanded from his men.

Soon she saw Grant unsheath his sword and begin to train. Tory watched him and smiled. Clearly he was the handsomest man around, and he moved with the grace of a cat. She felt surprised at how well everyone fought, although she supposed she shouldn't have been. Her husband was exacting in all things, so why did she think he'd expect anything less of himself or his men.

Grant defeated each man in turn. Seeing him wield his sword with precision, Tory watched in amazement. His men were extremely skilled warriors, but not one could best Grant. Were they allowing their chieftain to win apurpose? From their looks of exhaustion leaving the field, she doubted it.

Could Grant really be this good? She'd never seen anyone fight this well before. He fought man after man and didn't allow himself a chance to rest. Tory tired watching him.

Now she knew why he brought her out here today, she thought with a smile. He must still be upset about her comments the other day. She realized now why it had been such a blow to his ego. But she'd seen Michael fight before. She'd never witnessed such a display.

Warwick shouted, "Enough, Grant. 'Tis time we rested. We have all trained enough this day." He turned to Tory. "And your lady wife is getting tired. She has been out here a long time."

Finally Grant allowed himself to stop. Breathing deeply from his exertions he approached Tory and knelt beside her chair. "Is that aright, wife? Are you weary?"

She smiled and as she nodded her affirmation, Grant stood and told his men they could stop training. Grant faced Tory and waited like an expectant child, but said nothing.

"Do you and your men train like this every day?"

Grant nodded. "A man can lose his skills quickly if he does not keep them well honed. I will not allow that to happen."

"You were magnificent, Grant," she beamed. "Thank you for fetching me out here. I never imagined anyone could fight so well."

Those were the words Grant had been waiting to hear. With a roar, he smiled broadly. "Now that is the response I expect from my lady wife! Did you hear her, men?" He spun to face his kinsmen. "She admits I am magnificent."

Everyone burst out laughing at the unexpectedly childlike response from the massive warrior.

"Aye, Grant," Archibald, said, slapping him soundly on the back. "We heard. And if we hadn't, you'd make certain we knew what she said."

Laughing together, they all stumbled inside the keep and headed toward the ale keg in the Great Hall. After training, they'd worked up quite a thirst.

200

Grant carried Tory inside. "Fancy you something to drink afore I take you back up the stairs?" She looked to be in pain again.

Tory shook her head. "Nay, I cannot have anything to drink."

Grant didn't understand her reasoning, since a good Scot never passed up any excuse for a drink. He thought mayhap it would interact with herbs she'd taken for her pain.

Seeing his look of perplexity, Tory finally explained, "A woman who visited my home as a child told Grandmother she believed any type of alcohol might injure an unborn child. Such thinking is quite prevalent in Eastern countries. I'm not certain whether 'tis true or not, but I wish to take no chances that might harm my babe." She didn't particularly fancy alcohol anyhow, so she didn't feel she was giving up much.

As Grant had quickly discovered, she drank so little it didn't take much to make her drunk. He seemed to enjoy teasing her about it.

And that suited Tory. Other than a bit of mead or Sherry, she didn't like to drink, and she definitely didn't like the horrible feeling she'd had the one time Grant allowed her to drink too much.

She swore 'twould never happen again!

The men, on the other hand, rarely considered themselves drunk. If they could still stand, they thought themselves just fine!

Grant had a walking stick made for Tory so she could get around without him carrying her every place. She had to walk slowly, but that suited him fine. He didn't want her to rush around and fall and hurt herself or their bairn. One thing he'd noticed about his young wife had been that while she was exceedingly graceful in many ways, she rushed around much too quickly, often putting herself at risk for injuries. She often plunged in to do a task heedless of whether she could be injured.

Since the messenger's arrival the day before, he could no longer put off leaving. He must head south to meet with William Wallace to do some planning. It appeared Edward seemed determined to continue wrecking havoc in Scotland.

The man simply had to be stopped.

Grant hated the thought of leaving, and he thought that disconcerting, not being accustomed to the protective feelings he had about Tory. What if something happened to her again? The thought that scared him the most, however, seemed to be why it mattered so much. Never before had a woman meant so much to him. Not even when he'd been young and thought himself in love with Maeri. He learned quickly that what he felt for her had been naught but a case of calf's love.

What he felt then in no way came close to what he now felt for Tory.

Grant collected his thoughts and finally told Tory he had to leave. As expected, she didn't take the news well. Particularly when he told her he'd be meeting with Will.

"William Wallace!"

When Grant nodded, she looked plaintively into his eyes. "You cannot!"

Grant looked stunned. "Why not?"

"Because the man is a murderer!"

"That is nonsense. He is no more a murderer than I."

"He is. Father told me—"

"I do not wish to hear anything your da said," Grant cut in roughly. "I can only imagine the vicious lies he filled your head with."

"But Grant—"

"Nay, Tory, William is not the villianous murderer you heard about. He is a man who's had many injustices done to him. Through it all, he's only continued to fight for a free Scotland. I cannot fault him for that. And he's a good friend of mine," Grant stated adamantly.

She saw she wouldn't change Grant's mind, so she grumpily said, "You do not take no for an answer often, do you?"

"Not often," he teased and ruffled her hair.

"Then tell me about him," she pouted.

Sitting in a chair before the bedchamber hearth, Grant motioned Tory to come to him. He pulled her onto his lap and wrapped his arms around her, one hand lightly rubbing circles on her belly.

"Where should I begin? I am certain much of what you heard was not true. So much has been blown out of proportion." He shifted to make himself comfortable.

"Will is mayhap five years younger than me, around four and twenty. His two brothers were Malcome and John. His da was Sir Alan of Elderslie." He lowered his brows in thought. "John is now Will's most trusted comrade-in-arms.

"His mam taught the boys to read, then sent Will to be educated by Paisley Abbey's monks." He grinned at Tory's wide-eyed surprise. "See, Will is not quite the heathen you thought him."

Tory quirked a brow.

"Not being the eldest, he knew he'd not receive his father's lands, so he opted for the kirk. His best friend, John Blair, is a Benedictine monk and is now his chaplain."

Grant gently massaged Tory's back. "Will's da and brother, Malcome, fled north to avoid penalties imposed when they'd not swear allegiance to Edward. That same year, his da was killed by a knight. Will curses his name like an oath—Fenwick. It took Will a long time to avenge his da's death, but when he did, they declared him an outlaw. He did what he thought necessary. 'Tis no different than my actions."

He turned Tory's face upwards to see her reaction to that comment. After all, it had been her father he'd killed while avenging his own father's death.

She surprised him by nodding. Grant still couldn't reconcile himself to the despicable things the man did to his daughter.

"Another time Will aided a servant being bullied. He killed the man in self-defense when he lunged with a hunting knife. When soldiers caught him, they threw him into a dungeon, gave him only water and rotten herring, then left him to perish in his cell."

He shuddered at the remembrance.

"The day of Will's trial, the gaoler thought him dead. That *foosty scunner* threw Will's body over the wall into a dungheap." Though trying to temper it, his voice conveyed his anger at his friend's foul treatment.

"Will's former nanny went to the gaoler and asked for Will's body to give him a Christian burial. Reluctantly the man agreed, caring naught if Will received any burial. Imagine the auld woman's shock when she found Will still alive! He'd lapsed into a coma from lack of food and his inhumane treatment. Blame you him for his feelings?"

Tory didn't answer. She looked up at Grant with eyes wide. Clearly she wanted to believe him, but he knew if she did, it meant everything she heard about Wallace before had been lies.

"Will fights not for himself, but for a free and independent Scotland. He and his brother lead men out of Selkirk Forest. Sometimes they use barbaric tactics to win their battles, as do I when I fight with him. Am I an outlaw as well?"

Grant waited with baited breath until Tory answered. Though he hated to admit it, what she thought mattered very much.

"Nay, husband, I think not of you as outlaw. I warrant you fight for what you believe in, but most Englishmen fight for the same reason. 'Tis King Edward that plays with mens' minds and emotions. He wants what will benefit himself. It appears he wants too much. Living here now, I wish he'd leave Scotland alone. Unfortunately, I believe Edward is far too greedy to let that happen."

Pausing, Grant implored, "Can you possibly understand why Will fights?"

She nodded, bumping his chin with the top of her head.

"I can," she affirmed with a wistful voice. "I just wish there were no fighting. I want no one on either side to be hurt. Does that sound childish?"

Smiling, Grant tilted her head for a kiss. "Childish, nay. Simplistic, aye. Unless England agrees to let us have our independence, there can be no peace." He smiled and thought his wife truly wore her feelings on her sleeve as the women of his keep were wont to say.

Chapter Twenty-three

At dinner that eve, Grant launched into a lengthy list of things Tory couldn't do in his absence. "My men will be watching you closely – whether you like it or not."

He had no doubt she wouldn't.

"You will not ride a horse until after you give birth." At Victoria's scowl, he tapped her gently on the nose with his forefinger. "Heed me well, my lady."

Though softly given, his command had an edge of finality that brooked no argument.

To her chagrin, he also ordered she do no climbing or lifting.

When Grant repeated everything after walking hand-in-glove with her up to their bedchamber, Tory hit him with a pillow.

Startled, he turned and gave her a strange look. "Why did you that?"

"Because you are treating me like an invalid," Tory responded peevishly, "and I am not."

At Grant's look of disbelief, Tory shook her head. "Aye, husband, I am still sore. Other than that, I fare fine. You have given repeated orders to the men you leave behind until you drive them as daft as you are me."

Of a sudden a thought crossed her mind. "Why is Archibald remaining? He hates me. I thought he would use any excuse to leave."

Grant looked at her sagely. "You really wish to know the reason?"

At Tory's nod, he continued, "I noticed Archie's attitude seemed changed. I questioned him, and his answer surprised me."

Grant ignored her furrowed brows. "After I turned you over to Archie the day that blackguard beat you, you screamed. I heard you yell, but couldn't'e hear what you said."

He closed the few steps it took to reach her, then took her in his arms and tipped her face up to meet his. "Archie said you kept yelling for him to leave you and go protect *him*. To please not let him get hurt. At first that angered Archie. He thought you meant the Englishman. You changed his mind quickly when you grabbed his hand and pleaded, 'Archibald, please protect Grant. Pray, dinnae let him be injured.' Then you passed out from pain."

Blushing and embarrassed from the compliment he'd given her, Tory said the first thing that sprang to mind. "I never said dinnae."

Her husband chuckled and kissed the tip of her nose. "Nay, my heart, I am quite certain you *dinnae* say that, mind."

"And because of that he likes me?" Tory questioned incredulously. "I would not think—"

"That is not the only reason."

"Well?"

"Wee Graeme championed you whilst you were unconscious. He told us everything that happened in the garden."

"I do not understand."

Grant looked at her intently. "The wee lad told us how you did not protect yourself. How you laid there and let that blackguard beat you whilst the only part of your body you protected was your belly."

Tory raised her eyes as Grant added lovingly, "You endangered yourself to protect my bairn."

When she didn't respond and lowered her eyes, Grant persisted. "Is that correct, Tory? Is that why you protected only your belly? You knew you carried my bairn?"

Tory looked at him a long time before she nodded.

"My men know it as well, wife. After what you did to protect my child, any of them would now give their life for you."

"'Tis my baby, too," she said in amazement. "Of course I would protect it."

"Not everyone would." He scowled at the way she always discounted her actions.

Tory tried to change the subject, feeling awkward having him praise her.

"You are leaving on the morrow, husband," she reminded him. "Is there not anything else you'd rather do this night than repeatedly give me orders?"

"Aye, Sweeting," Grant leered seductively and pulled her to his firm body. "There definitely is something else I would rather do, but I do not think you are ready for what I am thinking."

Smiling sweetly, Tory moved closer to her husband and wrapped her arm around his neck. "Ah, but husband, mayhap I am willing to try. You would need to be a wee bit creative – given the casts on my arm and leg, but," she kissed him lightly on the mouth, "I am quite certain you will figure out something. I have confidence in your creativity."

'Twas the first time she'd initiated their lovemaking. Grant didn't need a second invitation.

Parliament convened at Berwick and two thousand Scottish landowners were summoned to appear with a signed and sealed document prescribing their homage to Edward.

One of the first to sign the Ragman Roll was Robert the Bruce. Not everyone signed the Roll, though. Grant departed the next morning, wishing he didn't have to leave. He received word Will headed north to Perth and not south to Berwick to sign the Roll. This could prove a difficult battle and thought Will might need assistance. He decided not to sign his name in support of Edward even knowing the ramifications such an action could pose.

Joining Will's forces, Grant was surprised when siege engines were used during battle. 'Twas the first time they'd done so, and they proved quite effective. Their use emphatically won Perth back for the Scots.

With the exhilaration of battle fueling them on, Will talked Grant into remaining. "Stay. Fight with me."

Duncan's men joined them the next day and all forged toward Aberdeen. As they headed north, they stopped at Dunnottar Castle in Stonehaven, family home of Clan Keith. About four thousand English troops were killed, trying to escape.

Will laughed in the face of a plea for leniency from the Bishop of Dunkeld, after he surveyed the carnage inflicted on the area. "Not bloody likely. When have English forces granted Scots any leniency?"

The men chose to rest for the night at Dunnottar. They entered the massive keep through the great door set within a nine meter-high curtain wall. With the English gone, the area's peacefulness was once again ensured – for a while. The stately castle stood on a flat-topped rocky promontory overlooking the sea and its view proved breathtaking. Sheer cliffs on three sides of the castle jutted out into the North Sea and the massive rock the castle sat atop attached to the mainland only by a narrow strip of land.

The only sounds to be heard in the center courtyard were birds that swept down from surrounding cliffs that provided secure nesting places, and the sea lapping gently against the shore below.

The peaceful sound of waves soothed everyone's minds after the day's tumultuous events.

Duncan reflected, "This is probably the same spot men stood and watched Vikings approach fifty and two hundred years ago."

Enroute to the chapel, Grant reflected, "As with other battles, it is not how our men died this day that makes them heroes, but how they lived."

Tory hated that Annie, a tiny orphan, had no place to call home. She spoke with Grant several times before he left about fetching the small girl into the castle, and finally convinced him to move the child into a vacant room near their own chamber.

Now she wondered if there might be somewhere in this huge castle with extra furniture she could move into the small room. She felt determined to make it comfortable for the waif. She'd moved furniture from other vacant rooms into Grant's solar and he hadn't complained overly much.

He often teased, "I never know what I'll see in any given room in my castle anymore."

Walking down a hallway, Tory stopped before a closed door. The room belonged to Grant's mother, and no one entered it except to clean it. She'd heard Grant's father turned it into a shrine, his grieving so fierce after her death.

She should turn away. She'd expressly been forbidden to enter this chamber, but the temptation proved too great.

Eyes shifting in both directions, Tory saw no one. Surely it wouldn't hurt to glance inside. No harm could come from that.

Cautiously she approached the locked door. She had keys to every room, she rationalized, so mayhap...

Tory quickly found the correct key and slipped in silently. She closed the door behind her and gazed in wide-eyed fascination at the lovely room. Grant's mother had exquisite taste. Her possessions were as lovely as the kirtles Grant lent her when Duncan came to visit. Unable to stay her curiosity, Tory moved further inside.

She walked around the room and examined everything. Obviously someone lovingly maintained everything, since not a speck of dust could be found. The woman truly must have been treasured to have people painstakingly care for her possessions so long after her death.

Tory mused that her own grandmother seemed much the same. She lovingly kept many of her husband's gifts. She sighed. If only she could have found someone to love her that way. Grant was certainly kind, but he'd never love her. He didn't believe in love.

Entranced by the lovely items, she visualized furniture being used in other rooms, knowing full well it would never happen. She could never tell Grant she'd seen them.

Of a sudden she thought she heard a sound outside the door, causing her to start. She spun to face the door and accidentally bumped the maple table beside her.

What happened next threw her into absolute panic. Noticing an intricate Chinese vase on a table wobbling precariously, Tory instinctively reached for it. Unfortunately, her swift movements caused the vase to fall to the floor with a resounding crash, splintering into hundreds of pieces.

Tory clasped her hands to her mouth to smother her cry of anguish and stood transfixed. Grant would kill her! Merciful saints, what could she to do?

Eyes frantically scanning the room, without further thought, she fled without securing the door behind her.

She had to escape!

Glancing neither right nor left, she raced downstairs, her feet barely touching the steps. She didn't respond to anyone's comments as she raced through the Great Hall and out the front door. She ran headlong through the courtyard, and stopped for no one.

Although surprised to see their lady running in her condition, no one approached or stopped her. She ran out the front gate unchallenged as guards looked at her with mouths agape. By the time they realized something truly must be amiss, Tory had disappeared far beyond the tree line which obstructed their vision.

Men groaned as they spurred themselves to action. Grant wouldn't be pleased to hear this. Blessed St. Ninian, how would they tell him! As they considered having to break the news to their young chieftain, a guard shouted from the ramparts that Grant approached the castle. They knew someone needed to apprise him of the situation.

No one rushed to volunteer.

Ian met him on the hill overlooking the castle and quickly informed him of damage found in his mother's chamber. The look which darkened Grant's face didn't bode well for telling him the lady under discussion had just vanished.

Returning to the keep only long enough to tend their weary mounts, men mounted fresh chargers and left the keep. They headed in the direction Tory had last been seen running. The sound of horses' hooves pounding the earth seemed the only sound to be heard, and the stormy look on Grant's face hadn't abated for an instant. Not only aimed at his wee wife, everyone knew too well he meant the stormy look for them as well since they let Tory escape.

After an extensive search, Tory couldn't be found. This only heightened Grant's black mood. "She couldn't have gone far," he bellowed in anger. "The fool woman is afoot."

There remained no doubt in his mind he'd kill her when he found her.

A further search revealed nothing. It suddenly occurred to Grant that the strange woman Tory visited sometimes lived nearby. Most people thought her odd and feared her, yet Tory had befriended Agnes ever since the auld woman saved her life when Elfrieda poisoned her. In itself, that hadn't surprised Grant. His young wife tended to befriend everyone.

Grant instructed, "Turn your horses, men, and head for that crone's house. The one hidden within the woods. I have a feeling Tory may be there."

Please God, he thought anxiously, *let her be safe.*

Straightaway they reached the hut and dismounted. Grant approached and pounded on the door, then called out for the old woman. No one answered. He quickly grew impatient. "Open this door, auld woman. Now! I know you are there."

Finally the door opened a crack. "What might I do for you, Laird Drummond? You appear at my door just as I am ready to bed down for the night." She raised her bony hand to pat her mouth, as if to stifle a yawn.

"Open the door, auld woman," Grant said curtly. "I look for my lady wife and believe she is here."

The door didn't budge. "Nay, m'laird," Agnes said and shook her head forvently while looking pointedly into Grant's eyes. "I cannot let you inside. I told you already I am bedding down now."

Something in the old woman's eyes revealed she didn't speak the truth. Grant started to force the door open, but the wiry woman held fast. "Nay, Laird Drummond, you cannot enter."

"This is my land, woman," Grant snarled. "Open this door immediately or pack your belongings and be gone from my property."

His harsh tone of voice told her he meant it.

Reluctantly she opened the door, but before he could enter, she blocked his passage. Saying nothing, she shook her head slowly and then turned her head. Grant followed her gaze and inhaled sharply.

Tory crouched huddled in the corner.

His beautiful young wife looked like a small, frightened child. As he entered and approached cautiously, Tory stared at Grant with eyes wide with fright. When he held his hand out to help her rise, she made small mewling sounds and tried to press herself farther into the corner.

Grant's brows furrowed together and he turned to question Agnes. "What happened?"

"She has been like that since she arrived," the auld crone muttered. "She barely said an intelligible word. Said she did somethin' she shouldn't and her da would murder her." She shook her head sadly. "She asked me to hide her."

When Grant glared, she raised an eyebrow in response and queried sarcastically, "And would you rather I let the wee lass wander alone in the woods in her condition?"

Grant muttered something unintelligible and headed back to Tory. "Come, wife, 'tis time to go home." When she didn't rise on her own, but continued to stare like she didn't recognize him, Grant pulled her up. Shaking her head wildly, Tory screamed and started to become hysterical.

"Nay, Father, please," she begged in a broken voice. "Pl...please do not beat me. I am sorry I disobeyed. Please! I promise I'll be good." She seemed to regress to her childhood.

The pitch of her voice rose with every word, causing men outside to rush to the door and peer inside. Their startled looks brought Grant back to the present.

"Tory, 'tis me," Grant soothed gently. "'Tis not your da, lass. Your da is dead."

Agnes looked surprised at that revelation.

Tory continued to shake her head and moaned uncontrollably. When Grant reached for her, she screamed, "Nay! Please do not kill me! I am sorry!"

At the look of terror in her eyes Grant vowed never to see such fear in her eyes again. He swore he'd do something to never have the likes of this happen again. He didn't want her o fear him.

Spinning on the old woman, Grant beseeched, "Agnes, have you aught you can give m'lady wife to calm her?"

"Aye," she nodded while she peered sadly at her young chieftain. He seemed quite rattled over the lassie's condition. He'd never before called her by her given name, always calling her *woman*. "I can give her a draught that will calm her. More than likely, 'twill make the wee lassie sleep."

"Good," Grant mumbled in worry. "Do it quickly. Give it to her afore she hurts herself." He felt incompetent being unable to comfort his own wife, used to being in charge and in control of everything.

Leave it to his wee lady to make him feel inadequate.

While Agnes prepared the draught of mint and lavender, Grant left Tory alone, but his eyes remained fixed on her. Finally turning to Agnes, he questioned, "Said she aught else?"

Agnes shook her head.

"Said she aught about me?"

Again Agnes shook her head, causing her wispy grey hair to shift from side to side.

"Nay," she mumbled. "I already told you that. She said naught about you, just mumbled her da would kill her. She dinnae tell me what she supposedly did." Agnes hoped Grant would share that information with her. He pointedly ignored her.

She pursed her lips and tried again. "The poor wee bairn is out of her head right now. Something mighty fierce scared her, mind."

Grant didn't fancy that thought. He regarded it as his bounden duty to keep her safe and secure. How could he do that if he couldn't rid her of ghosts from her past?

Agnes mixed the draught and added a few drops of poppy syrup to ensure Tory would sleep. She felt her lady needed rest more than anything else right now. Grant let her approach Tory, although he stood to one side and watched every move. As she had when she cared for Tory earlier, the auld woman proved exceedingly gentle. Crooning in a low voice, she encouraged her lady to drink the warm liquid. At first Tory neither moved nor responded, but as Agnes continued to talk in a mellow voice, she looked up into the auld woman's caring eyes. At Agnes' urging, she took the cup, downing the drink slowly. Within a short time, she fought to keep her eyes open. Agnes moved closer and placed her arm around the young woman's shoulders. Tory didn't pull away, nor shake her off, but stared as if she didn't recognize Agnes.

Grant approached when Tory finally leaned against Agnes and appeared to be asleep. He cradled her limp body in his arms, and lifted her carefully.

Agnes said nothing, but silently moved away while he gently wrapped his red and green plaide around his wife.

When he reached the door, Grant stopped and turned back to Agnes. "I know you thought you were helping m'lady this eve, auld woman, but do not ever lie to me again. Under the circumstances, I'll forgive you this time, but I will not excuse such in future. I abhor lies."

He looked down at Tory and hugged her closer to his body. "For now you have my deepest thanks for protecting my lady wife." At her brusk nod, Grant turned and stepped out the door into a blast of cold air. He mounted his steed with little effort and reined the horse in the direction of his castle.

Since the door to the hut had been open during Grant's exchange, men outside heard the majority of it. They followed Grant back to their keep with little conversation between them.

Riding under his portcullis to his courtyard, Grant dismounted and proceeded to the Great Hall, stopping to answer no one. He entertained thoughts of heading up to their bedchamber, but thought better of it and headed to the chairs Tory had placed before his hearth. She loved to sit there. Without a word to anyone, he sat and shifted Tory so he cradled her in his arms.

He remained like that all night.

Chapter Twenty-four

Whispers surrounded Grant and questions were answered by men who'd accompanied him to the old crone's hut. No one approached or bothered him, but simply watched as their young chief rocked his body gently and tried to soothe his young wife. Only the tired lines around his eyes bespoke his inner turmoil.

As the fire slowly waned, Tory stirred in Grant's arms. Leaning down, he whispered in her ear. His lips gently feathered the top of her head as he brushed hair from her forehead. She immediately calmed and relaxed in his arms.

They remained like that, unmoving.

When Tory finally awoke the next morning, Grant let her speak first. "Good morn, milord." She glanced around the room and looked at him in surprise. "Why are we downstairs? Why did you not wake me so we could go upstairs?"

She shifted positions and started to rise, but Grant stopped her. Puzzled, she commented, "Your arm must be painfully sore, husband." She furrowed her brows in thought. "Actually...I do not remember sitting before the fire last eve."

Frowning, she tried to concentrate. Suddenly her eyes widened and Grant knew she had, indeed, remembered. He just didn't know how much.

Jumping from his lap, Tory's hand flew to her mouth. "The vase! Grant, I am sorry."

She backed away, fear clouding her eyes. He rose and halted her movements. "Nay, Tory. This time you will not get away from me."

When she looked at him with eyes wide with fear, Grant asked, "Remember you what happened yestereve?"

Tory caught her lower lip between her teeth and nodded. "Aye." She didn't elaborate.

Grant prodded, "What do you remember?"

She took deep breaths and whispered, "I went into your mother's room – and broke her vase." Looking frightened, she quickly added, "I did not mean to break anything! I swear it. I know I should not have gone in there, but I just wanted to look around. I did not think it would hurt anything."

"What did you do after the vase broke?" Grant tried to remain patient.

Tory gnawed on her lower lip. Grant could see she tried to assimilate previous day's events, but was having problems doing so. When she said nothing, just stared wide-eyed, Grant prompted, "Where did you go after the vase broke?"

"I...I went nowhere," she answered softly, thinking quickly. "I left the room, but I cannot remember coming downstairs." She frowned at her inability to remember and rubbed her hand over the back of her neck. "Did you bring me downstairs? Nay, you were not home."

The uncertainty in her eyes upset Grant. After the condition he'd seen her in last night, and now seeing she remembered nothing, he knew he must do something to prevent a recurrence.

"What did you think when the vase broke?" he asked, forcing himself to sound gruff. Although he didn't want to scare her, he needed to impress the situation's seriousness upon her. She'd consciously disobeyed his orders.

"I...I do not remember," she carefully avoided his gaze. "I know I felt scared. I never thought I would damage anything." She blushed as she looked at Grant. He could tell by the look on her face she specifically remembered being told not to enter the room. "Truly."

"You disobeyed me, wife," Grant affirmed quietly.

Looking quite woebegone, she nodded slowly. "I know." She backed away and added, "And now you are going to beat me."

Although a question, she stated the last as a foregone conclusion.

Grant pondered her words a long time before he answered. "Aye, I am."

A collective gasp filled the room. No one expected that response after what they'd been through yestereve.

Grant clarified for her and for everyone else, "'Tis time you learned the difference atween discipline I told you about over and over and the beatings your da gave you. In your heart I think you do not wish me to be as cruel as your da, so you blocked me out and substituted him in my stead."

Grant held Tory's gaze. "I do not wish to ever be blocked out of your mind and heart again, wife. You will know the difference atween your da and me from this day forth."

When Tory didn't answer, Grant rose and strode to her. "I have told you time and time again I am not your da and will never treat you in such a horrendous fashion. No matter how many times I told you that, you never believe me. You always think I'll act as he did. That will stop this day."

She said nothing, but looked at him with wounded eyes.

"Why, woman? Why will you not believe me?"

Tory refused to answer. She shook her head and bit her lips as tears freely streamed down her face.

"Tell me, Tory."

She worried the fabric of her kirtle, but no answer proved forthcoming. Grant ordered with frustration, "Tell me."

Grant could contain his anger no longer. He placed his face in front of hers and yelled, "*Tell me!*"

Between quavering lips, she whispered, "Because you are a man."

Grant looked as if she'd slapped him.

"What?" he roared.

"Because you are a man," she repeated softly, as tears glistened in her eyes. "That is what men do. They beat women."

She looked like she lost her only friend.

Anger clouded his eyes and Grant grasped Tory's hand. He pulled her firmly toward the chair where he sat and cradled her the night before.

Tory tried to dig her feet into the ground to halt her progress, but could gain no purchase with the rushes underneath. He sat and pulled her over his lap, being careful how he placed her belly.

"Woman," came Grant's roar of frustration, "it pains me to do this, but I should have done this a long time ago!" With that he slammed his hand down upon her bottom.

Tory shrieked.

Grant's hand fell – again and again.

Tory jerked from side to side, trying to escape his punishing hand to no avail. Finally his hand stopped and rested lightly on her bottom. Tory thought she must be dreaming. Surely he couldn't be through. Her father would just be starting his torture.

To her surprise, Grant set her aside and stood to face her. He placed his hands on her shoulders and looked into her tear filled eyes. "Now, wife, you know the difference atween my beating and your da's. I assure you, I'll do that again if you disobey me in future or cause danger to yourself or my men." She started to say something, but he gently placed his fingertips over her lips. "But that is the only kind of beating you will ever get from me.

"That is my solemn promise, lady mine."

Tears ran down her face from the pain of her spanking, but a glimmer of hope shone in her eyes. "That is the only kind of beating a man should ever give a woman. Taking advantage of someone because they are smaller and weaker only proves that person is naught but a weakling themself. No man who is truly a man would ever beat a woman."

Extending his hand, he held his breath until she tentatively placed hers within his.

"Come, Sweeting, let us go up the stairs. I did some thinking myself during the night and have something I wish to show you."

Tory followed quietly until Grant stopped before his mother's room. Frightened, she began to pull away, but he held her firmly. "Nay, Sweeting, we must go inside. That is where I wish to show you something, aye. I pondered it a long while last eve whilst you rested in my arms."

"Grant, please," she searched futilely for words, "I said I was sorry. Please do not make me go in there."

Grant ignored her pleas. He opened the door and pulled her behind him. He observed she took small, quick breaths as she reluctantly followed. Reaching the center of the room, he stepped behind her and wrapped his arms around her, which gave her a strange feeling of safety. She tried to crane her neck to peer up at him.

"Your actions yestereve were wrong, Tory," Grant said solemnly. "You disobeyed my orders, and I admit I felt quite cross when I first heard you had been in here."

Looking around the room, Grant fell silent a long time. "I have not had time to come here afore now to see what happened." He tried to lighten the tense mood by adding, "I was too busy looking for my wayward wee lady wife." Tory didn't smile, so he continued, "It has been so long since I saw this room, I'd forgotten everything Mam collected."

He paused. "After I calmed, it occurred I'd been wrong as well. You made me realize 'tis a waste to keep everything Mam loved closed up where no one can enjoy them. 'Tis not what she would have wanted. She would have shared everything."

Grant squeezed her lightly. "She would have loved you, Tory, and would have joyfully shared her belongings with you."

Tory craned her head and looked at him in disbelief.

"So," he turned her to face him and pressed his lips to her brow, "everything in here is now yours."

Eyes wide with amazement, Tory opened her mouth to speak, but no sound emerged. Grant threw back his head and roared with laughter. "If I knew that would be all it took to silence you, I'd have done it a long time ago! The look on your face is priceless." Unable to stop himself, he continued to laugh.

Tory glowered and pulled away. "Do not jest with me, milord."

"I am not jesting, love," Grant affirmed. "Nor do I tell falsehoods. You should know that by now. Look around the room and see if there is aught you fancy moving elsewhere." At her look of uncertainty, he added, "What about wee Annie's room? Is there naught you would fancy moving into her room? You said you wish to decorate it."

With a grin Grant teased, "Why should this room be any different? You moved things from every other room in my keep."

Taking no offense at his teasing, she breathlessly asked, "You really mean it? Ooh Grant, can I really use these lovely items?" She spread her arms to reflect the oom's interior.

"Woman," Grant growled, "I am tired of you always questioning what I say. I said it did I not?"

Tory nodded in excitement.

"Then I meant it! Quit second-guessing everything. I do not fancy that one bit." Grant glowered and reiterated, "If I said it, 'tis the truth. Period. End of discussion!"

Tory joyfully rushed about the room and pointed out items she thought perfect for Annie's room. Suddenly she stopped. "Are you certain, Grant? You really will not change your mind?"

With a deeply inhaled breath, Grant roared, "Woman! Did I not say so? Have you a problem with your ears?"

Before he could change his mind, Tory quickly shook her head. Grant pulled her close and bent his head to kiss her. "I believe we should open this room up again."

At Tory's amazed look, Grant smiled. "Would you fancy using it? 'Tis right next to my chamber you know."

To Grant's surprise, the light went out of Tory's eyes. She said nothing, but nodded slowly in agreement before she turned away. He puzzled over her response.

'Tis what I should expect, she thought. *Of course he'd want me out of his room after what I did yestereve.*

"Tory?" Grant frowned with impatience at her inattention. "Did you hear me?"

Startled by his words, she turned. She'd had her head in the clouds again and hadn't heard his approach. When she spun around, she turned into his chest. She stepped back to look up at him. "I did not hear you, Grant. I am sorry. I fear I was woolgathering. What did you say?"

Grant frowned at her lack of attention. Not used to people ignoring him, he'd thought she'd be thrilled to open the room and convert it into a nursery. He shook his head and wondered if he'd ever completely understand this woman.

"Do not you think that a good idea?" Grant looked totally perplexed at her lack of enthusiasm.

"Of course, milord," she answered falsely. The last thing she wanted to do was move out of his room. "I think 'twould be a good idea. I shall start to move my things out later today."

He could tell something bothered her.

Reaching up, Grant scratched his head and looked at her like she'd grown two heads. "What are you speaking about? You had no things in here. These were my mam's."

"I know that," she answered in exasperation. "I meant my things from your room. I could move them later today. I know I have cramped your style by moving things into your room that I fancied. I should have asked, of course, but everything seemed to fit so perfectly after I placed them in there--"

"*Wheesht!*" Grant yelled and cut off her rambling. "By all that is holy, woman, what are you speaking about now? I am talking about moving everything out and you are prattling on about moving things in. What does one have to do with the other?" he sounded as if he were losing patience.

As Tory started to answer, Grant growled ferociously, "What do you mean you're going to move your things out of *my* room?" He paced and his eyes narrowed. "Woman, I would suggest you choose your words carefully and cease goading my temper."

He glowered, daring her to give him an answer he didn't fancy.

"You said you wanted me to move into this room," she looked at him sadly, "so today would be as good a day as any to move my things." She feigned a lightness she didn't feel and turned away. "Why put off 'til the morrow what you can do today, you know. My grandmum always said that."

"You ramble again, wife," Grant said, a slow grin spreading over his face as he turned her back to face him. "Now, I fancy knowing how you get from me wantin' to open up this room to me saying you are to move out of my chamber."

He couldn't wait to hear whatever illogical answer she'd come up with.

Arms on hips, he stood and waited.

"Well," she began shyly, "you are cross with me for disobeying you, so you decided you wanted me out of your room. I can understand that, you know. I'd not fancy me either if I did something wrong all the time."

Grant threw back his head and roared. He held his stomach to contain his laughter and gasped, "You are the most exasperating woman. You hear only what you think I'll say rather than what I say."

When she started to protest, Grant cut her off. "I did not say I wanted you out of my bed. That will never happen, wife." He rubbed his thumb lightly over her soft swollen lip. "I said I thought of opening this room up again. Since 'tis right next to *our* room, I thought 'twould make an excellent nursery for our bairns!"

Tory stood transfixed. Drawing in a deep breath, without another thought she flung herself into Grant's arms. Her kiss of joy soon turned to something much, much deeper.

Tory felt that now familiar stirring in the pit of her belly and felt herself being moved backward. Grant pushed her down on the bed and followed right behind her. "Grant..." she murmured. He silenced her with his lips, and her mouth surrendered completely.

Soon he had her breathless, and she had no thought to try and stop him or to tell him this probably wasn't proper since this had been his mother's room. He knew that as well as she, and obviously didn't care. The only thing that concerned him right now seemed to be removing her clothes, and that he did quite expediciously.

His followed just as quickly.

He once again brushed her lips, and trailed kisses down the length of her body. Moving back to reclaim her lips, he positioned himself above her and with one quick thrust sheathed himself in the luxuriousness of her body. He closed his eyes with sheer delight. This was right. Their life should always be like this. Grant made a mental note to ensure it always stayed this way.

Then his mind thought no more as he lost himself in the wonder of her.

Having gotten no sleep the evening before, Grant fell fast asleep, arms wrapped firmly around Tory. When he woke, she still lay within his arms. She too had fallen asleep. He smiled and leaned forward to kiss the nape of her neck. She stirred sleepily. Tory turned to face him and smiled sweetly.

Grant raised himself up onto one arm, and leaned his head on his hand as he watched her closely. He hated mentioning the subject again, but knew he must. "Remember you aught of what happened after you left the keep yestereve?"

Frowning, she shook her head and whispered, "Nay, I remember naught from the time I ran out of this room until I woke in your arms before the fire." She told him honestly, "'Tis like I lost a part of myself. Tell me what happened." She pressed her lips together and frowned. "Did I do anything I should not have?"

Her look of embarrassment told Grant she wouldn't have been surprised if she had.

Not wanting to overly frighten her, Grant told her only the barest of essentials. "You ran from the keep to that crone's hut and told her your da chased you. When I arrived to fetch you home, you were fair panicked. I tried to talk to you, but even though you looked at me, you did not see me.

"You looked right through me," Grant added. "I have never been so scared in my entire life as seein' the look of fear in your eyes, lass. I never again wish to see such a look on your face.

"That is why I spanked you this morn." When Tory frowned at that reminder, Grant continued. "Nay, m'lady, do not frown at me. Other than your da and men from your auld house, you had naught to compare to and obviously thought all men ruthless. I couldn't let you keep thinkin' that of me. You needed to know I would never beat you. I'll punish you, mind," he quickly added when he saw her start to say something, "but there is a huge difference atween beatin' to hurt someone and punishing someone to teach a lesson. I hope I showed you that this day. A real man does not feel the need to hurt a woman."

Grant received a missive that William was near Crieff and wanted to know if he could safely visit Drummond Castle. He quickly returned a message stating Will could, indeed, come and bide awhile.

Shouts soon rang out that riders approached. Thinking Will couldn't have arrived so quickly, Grant dashed up to the ramparts to watch the horses' approach. Soon they were close enough to ascertain Will had, indeed, already arrived. He'd obviously been close to hand when he'd sent his missive.

Grant rushed down the stone steps to find Tory, anxious for her to meet Will for the first time.

Watching her visitors, Tory stood dumbstruck. The man was huge. Grant and Duncan were large, but Wallace towered over them both. He stood even taller than Archibald! Unaware of her discomfort, which had nothing to do with the day's brisk wind, Will greeted his guests.

Finally Grant pulled Tory forward to meet Will. When he glanced down at his wife, sunshine glinted off her hair. Thinking back to comments Duncan made during every visit, Grant agreed she looked beautiful. He couldn't have been more proud.

Smiling shakily, Tory unconsciously clung to Grant as she graciously well-comed Will and his companions to their home. When William turned to look at her, she saw he had piercing blue eyes and a great mane of brown hair.

Will bowed in greeting, yet appeared coldly polite. Tory saw a guarded look of mistrust in his eyes as he looked at her.

"Come inside and bide awhile after your journey," Grant told them as he moved Tory towards the entrance to the Hall. "What brings you to our home?"

He seemed oblivious to Will's aloofness.

The men entered the Great Hall after sheltering their steeds and supplies and headed for the whisky. Everyone at Drummond Castle had already had their nooning meal, but Tory quickly ordered leftovers brought back out for their guests. Effortlessly she consulted with Cook and made minor changes to the evening meal. She felt she had to prove herself to Will and determined the evening meal would be bountiful.

Tory eyed Will warily and tried to maintain her distance. She'd rather they not discuss war, but the subject seemed uppermost in everyone's minds. After all, it was what brought Will to Crieff.

While she walked through the Great Hall, Tory heard Will talking about the army he formed which skirmished across southwestern and central Scotland. "I do not fight mass battles since my forces are not yet strong enough to withstand their contingent. They are too well armed since they have heavy cavalry and archers."

He went into a tirade of what he thought of Englishmen and their despicable practices. Mentioning the English, he unconsciously stole a glance around the room to ascertain Tory's whereabouts.

222

Grant saw Will's cursory sweep of the room. "We have had this discussion afore, William. Aye, my lady wife came from England. You knew that afore you arrived. Now whilst I agree she is one of the most difficult women I ever met..." he teased for Tory's benefit.

The lady in question shot a glare in his direction.

"She is my lady wife and would never betray me."

Will arched his brows in question. His ingrained hatred made him sarcastically ask, "Are you certain, Drummond? Have you asked the wench where her loyalties lie?"

Grant grew so angry he almost punched his friend.

Fortunately, Warwick interrupted. "Grant tells the truth, William," he interjected with a note of impatience. "Our lady is just that – *our lady*. We dinnae need ask such a question and every man in this keep would give his life to protect her."

Men nodded in agreement. Will looked at Grant and saw the unbending, angry look on his host's face. From the corner of his eye he saw Tory. Standing still, she held a platter to her breast that she'd been carrying to the kitchen.

She faced Will with courage and dignity, her chin slightly trembling.

Tory held her breath as she awaited Will's response. This is what she feared from the moment Grant told her of knowing William. Everyone in the Hall fell silent. When William didn't respond immediately, having too many years of hatred to overcome in a mere instant, the steel platter clattered to the ground. Mindful of all eyes watching her, she ran through the Hall and out the door.

Grant derisively shot Will a glare as he stormed after his wife and left the men in his wake to become embroiled in a heated debate over Will's actions.

"Hold, wife!" Grant shouted. When she neither responded nor turned around, Grant thundered after her and caught up with her out in the windy courtyard, arms wrapped around her in an effort to keep warm.

He spun her around to face him. The sight of her tear stained face proved more than he could bear and Grant let out a frustrated groan.

"Och, I told you to halt, wife. Did you not hear me?" Her teardrops glistened in the moonlight and she tried to flash an apologetic smile. Grant said nothing, just opened his arms to his distraught lady. When she rushed into them and clung to him

223

closely, he wrapped his plaide around her for warmth and gently caressed her cheeks with his knuckles.

"'Tis hard for William to trust any English after what they did to his wife, Sweeting," he began softly and held her safely within the comfort of his arms. "But he is wrong and I'll not allow him or anyone else to hurt you. He will leave when we return inside."

Tory quickly shook her head, bumping it against his firm chest. "Nay, Grant, pray do not do that." When she looked up into his eyes he saw sadness reflected in hers. "He would not have come if he'd not thought it important. You need discuss battle information with him, and he should not have to leave because of me. He has the right to hate me if he so chooses. I should be used to it because of my father, but it hurts just the same."

"Nay, my heart, no one will ever make you feel that way again – and certainly not in your own home." Sweeping her off her feet, he held her closely and carried her back into the warmth of his Hall.

He rubbed his fingers lightly up and down her arms. When he set her back down she said nothing, but forced a smile and headed to retrieve the dropped serving platter.

The glare Grant shot William spoke volumes.

Tory whirled and headed toward the kitchen, but William sternly called after her. "Turn about, Lady."

Tory stopped, but didn't turn.

Making a decision he didn't make lightly, Will nodded to Grant and conceded the eyeball-to-eyeball confrontation. "You are right. 'Tis your home and I apologize – to you and your lady. I allow I know you well enough to know you would never invite me to share your home only to place my life in peril."

He walked to Tory and turned her to face him.

Tory backed away slightly as Will's hand rose. His eyes holding hers, she stilled and held her ground. Will broke the silence that permeated the entire Hall. "I acted boorishly, Lady, and I apologize."

He rubbed the pad of his thumb lightly over her cheek and wiped away a tear. "I cannot abide tears, Lady. 'Tis sorry I am I made you cry. 'Twill never happen again."

When Tory realized William only meant to wipe away her tears and not to strike her, she released the breath she'd been holding.

Grant saw her reaction, realized instantly his beautiful wife had been afraid Will would strike her. Would she never forget the torment of her past?

He lengthened his stride at the same time Will told Tory, "I shall leave if you wish."

"I already told her you would be leaving," Grant chimed in, still glowering as he watched the tense, heated scene in his Great Hall. He'd by now joined Tory and latched onto her arm in a protective manner. Pulling her close, he stood behind her and wrapped his arms around her. She made no move to escape his comforting embrace. She leaned against him and drew strength from him as she continued to face William, her eyes never wavering from the man's stony face. Grant didn't look at Tory. He focused his entire attention on William, and the tone of his voice made the atmosphere inside the Great Hall almost as frigid as the windy temperature outside. "But my lady wife will not hear of that. I have repeatedly said she is far too generous and softhearted. She said you are our guest and that you shall remain."

Will ignored the anger evident in Grant's voice and focused his attention on Tory. "Lady? Will you forgive an obnoxious fool?"

This time Will held his breath while he waited for Grant's lovely lady to answer.

Tory nodded graciously.

Chapter Twenty-five

Unbeknownst to her, Grant planned a special evening of entertainment. Tales were told, songs were sung, and everyone had a marvelous time as they joined in festivities. Grant never held with the mindset nobility should only associate with nobility. Were that the case, Will wouldn't be present since his father was only a small landowner.

During a lull in entertainment, Tory turned to Will. "I am sorry about your wife. I wish you had a home you could safely go to like Grant and I do."

Will's eye's flared in anger. He grew silent, but said nothing. Tory saw him unconsciously fist his hands. She looked at Grant to see what she'd done wrong.

Grant pulled her closer to him on the bench and faced Will. "I am sorry, friend. My lady wife is not aware you never speak of Marion. She meant no harm."

Before Tory could say anything, Grant shook his head to silence her.

An awkward silence followed as Will rose from his bench and paced, his shoulders fraught with tension. Tory looked up at Grant. She managed a distraught smile and mouthed the words, "I am sorry." He nodded and squeezed her waist, assuring her he wasn't cross with her. She made an honest mistake and there was no need to belabour the point.

Will returned and sat, saying nothing.

Grant raised two fingers and entertainment quickly resumed in an effort to cover the awkward lull in conversation. Soon all seemed forgotten and everyone once again enjoyed themselves. Tory breathed a silent sigh of relief.

As festivities wound down, everyone headed to their respective sleeping quarters. While Tory prepared for bed, she remembered her gaff and how ill at ease everyone became. She rushed to Grant and spread her hands. "I am sorry, milord. Truly. I did not know I should not mention Marion. I am sorry I upset him."

Grant pulled her close and placed a kiss atop her head. "I know, Sweeting, and no one is cross with you. I should have told you this afore. I did not think to mention it. 'Tis the one thing Will is adamant about. He will not speak of Marion."

"Tell me about her." Tory patted the bed and pulled him down beside her. "In the wake of what happened, I need to know more about Will."

Grant nodded his assent.

"Will and his wife, Marion Braidfute, secretly wed in St. Kentigern's kirk in Lanark. Knowing the English hunted him, he visited her by stealth, thinking it unsafe to visit her openly."

Grant shook his head sadly. "One eve after kirk a patrol accosted him. He fought his way clear, but made the mistake of rushing to Marion's. Although he escaped out the back, they followed him to her house.

"Furious Will had eluded him, William Hesilrig, the English sheriff, ordered Marion's house burned and all within put to the sword." Breathing deeply, he finally said, "Marion and her brother were murdered."

Tory's eyes widened in alarm.

"Will never speaks of whether they had a daughter, although I believe 'tis why they finally wed. Although if he has a bairnie, even I know not where she is. From then on, Will vowed undying vengeance against everything English."

Looking into Tory's anguished eyes he saw his gentle wife hurt over what she'd heard. She always took everything to heart. He gently touched her shoulder.

"Accepting you as my wife is a great sacrifice for him. I should have thought of that afore I invited him. I am happy he bent that wee bit, although I meant it when I said I'd have him leave. Your happiness is what matters."

Grant scooted up to the head of their bed and pulled Tory between his spread legs. Cradling her against him, he ran his hand lightly over her belly.

"Will went to Hesilrig's home. Breaking down the front door, he found the man in bed. With a single stroke of his sword, he cleaved Hesilrig's head and neck in two from his forehead to his collarbone."

Tory shuddered and shifted her head from where it rested on Grant's shoulder.

Grant kept tight hold on her when he felt her stiffen. "Do not judge him too harshly, lass. Remember, I killed someone who tried to harm you after we wed. If someone hurt you now, I'd not be responsible for my actions."

He lightly placed kisses on the back of her neck.

Tory spent the next days looking around the castle. She always seemed to be rearranging something.

He teased, "I never know what my home will look like when I return from trips."

She didn't think he really minded.

While exploring the castle's upper floors, she found another unexplored room. Curious as to how she'd missed it, she tried every key on her ring. A rusty one finally opened the lock.

When she opened the door, she had to brush aside numerous cobwebs. Obviously no one ever came into this room. Certainly not to clean it! It seemed to have been completely forgotten. Yet as she looked around, Tory's eyes widened with delight. The entire room contained children's furniture.

Why had Grant not mentioned this room? Had he forgotten it? The furniture would be perfect in their nursery, and Annie could use it as well. The young girl seemed so proud of her small room and few possessions. She'd never had anything of her own and Tory delighted in helping her decorate.

Relentlessly questioning people in the keep, she finally learned Annie's parents had both been brutally murdered. The tiny young girl had been the only survivor.

Suddenly Tory spotted a lovely wooden cradle hidden in a corner. Its carvings were extremely intricate. Not quite able to make out the design, she decided it must be a family crest. She thought it strange the cradle hadn't been placed neatly in the room like all the other furniture, but looked as if it had been tossed into the corner as an afterthought.

Tory couldn't wait to tell Grant. This had to be his childhood furniture.

She decided to surprise him when he returned. That thought uppermost in her mind, Tory climbed the stairs to clean the room every day over the next weeks. With Grant gone, she devoted hours cleaning it and the tiny furniture.

Measuring the cradle, Tory sewed blankets, linens, and a downy pillow for the babe. When finished, she placed everything inside the cradle so Grant could see how everything looked. Now all those sewing lessons her grandmother gave her paid off. She couldn't wait to show Grant. Everything would be perfect and ready to move to their nursery. She'd have moved the furniture herself, but she'd promised Grant she wouldn't lift anything.

Finally Grant arrived home. Tory wanted to rush him up to the room, but he had other ideas for his first hours back. Heading from the courtyard to their chamber, Grant soon made her forget all about her surprise. She thought of nothing but the wonderful things he made her feel.

The next day, however, she felt the timing perfect. After they broke their fast, she made him close his eyes and marched him upstairs while she held his hand.

Knowing her as he did, he repeatedly asked, "What are you up to now, wife?"

She didn't answer.

Opening the heavy oaken door she stepped to the side and proudly said, "You can open your eyes now." Tory held her breath while she waited to see the look of delight on his face.

What she saw could never be construed as delight.

Grant looked around the room and his eyes darkened with anger. "You had no right to enter this room!" Pulling her roughly, he jerked her from the room and locked the door behind him. He grabbed her keys and removed the rusty key that opened the offensive door before he flung the remaining keys back at her.

Taken aback, Tory remembered the items she'd sewn for the baby. Not understanding his attitude, she told him, "I must go back and get some things from the room."

He yelled furiously and refused. She tried to reason with him, but he growled, "There is naught in that room I'll ever want."

As he dragged her behind him heedless of her condition, Tory tried to tell him about the lovely furniture, particularly the cradle.

"No child of yours will ever touch anything in that room. Do you hear me, woman? Do not let me ever hear you entered that room again."

Tory thought her heart would break. When they reached their chamber, she pulled away and rushed inside.

Grant didn't follow, but stormed down to the Great Hall.

In a flood of tears, she threw herself across the bed and cradled her head in her hands. How could she have been so blind? She thought he wanted their child. Now she realized he felt her baby not even good enough to use his old cradle.

That hurt. If that was how he really felt, why didn't he send them away?

Several hours later, spent and exhausted from crying, Tory went downstairs. Everyone acted as if her world hadn't come crashing down upon her. She assumed to them it made no difference. They'd probably known all along.

Days passed, and Tory performed her everyday duties, but inwardly she withdrew from everyone. It seemed so much easier that way. Then she wouldn't get hurt. The only problem with that was that she already cared for these people, and she hurt already. She remained devastated by Grant's reaction, but mentioned it to no one.

She thought about having to resew everything, but couldn't do it. Night after night her sewing basket sat idle at her feet. Everyone wondered why she'd suddenly lost interest in sewing. They knew something bothered her, but knew not what.

Tory discussed it with no one. Not even Triona.

Grant noticed she seemed more reserved, but though her behavior bewildered him, he attributed it to her growing belly. He'd heard women often acted strangely while they were breeding. Tory was obviously no different. Even in bed she seemed subdued. He thought mayhap she feared their nocturnal activities might injure the bairn.

Over the next weeks Tory remained quiet. Not understanding her mood, Grant didn't pay a great deal of attention to it as he busily made plans to attend the market faire in a nearby southern town. The weather should be beautiful for traveling, and several men's wives were excited about attending. They looked forward to it every year, although he never understood the excitement the faire caused. He thought it merely a place one went to buy needed items and return home. He looked forward to that the most – coming home. He hated being away. This year seemed worse than others. After traveling and fighting for so many years, he now hated being away from home since he didn't want to be separated from Tory.

He didn't understand how one stubborn woman could mean so much to him, but he no longer had any doubt in his mind that she did. When away from her, his thoughts always drifted back to her.

This year he looked forward to attending the faire since he had several items he planned to purchase. There were several things he wanted to buy their bairn, and others he wished to surprise Tory with. She seemed far too downhearted lately and she wouldn't discuss it. Even the cradle he'd had his carpenter make for their bairn hadn't made her happy. She'd burst into tears when he gave it to her. That certainly wasn't the reaction he'd expected. He thought the carpenter captured his design perfectly.

Warwick continuously reminded him, "Dinnae forget, son, breeding women often act strangely. It has something to do with changes within their body."

Grant had no idea what that meant!

When he went up to his bedchamber one afternoon before his scheduled trip, he found Tory bustling about. *Finally,* he thought. She'd ended her brooding. Then he saw a small packed bag. *She couldn't be thinking of leaving him,* he thought with a frown. *Surely such thoughts were behind them.*

Grant looked at her curiously. "What are you doing, Sweeting?"

Tory happily turned at the sound of his voice. Grant stood in the doorway. Actually, he didn't just stand in it, he filled the entire doorway.

"Cassandra told me today about our trip to the market faire!" she fairly gushed. "I cannot believe you've not mentioned it yet, Grant, but 'tis a wonderful surprise. I cannot wait to go." She quickly added, "Can Annie go, too? She has never been before either."

Grant looked at her in amazement. "I did not tell you about the trip, lady wife, because you are not going." His eyebrows furrowed over her misconception.

Tory stood stock-still. "Not going?"

Her voice trailed away as disappointment sharply gripped her.

"Aye."

"You are going to market and taking everyone else," Tory began in an injured voice, "but you're not taking me?"

Again Grant nodded. "You are breeding, wife. I would not take you to such a place in your condition. It will be owercrowded and you shouldn't be riding a horse. And it is later in the year than we normally go. Even though 'tis fine right now, I wish not to take the chance of running into bad weather."

"I see," she said quietly. *Too quietly.* She looked at Grant long and hard, but said nothing. A sad, wistful expression crossed her face, but she quickly veiled it. Turning back to the bed, she slowly removed items she'd only moments before happily packed.

Tory didn't come downstairs later, nor did she go down the next day, saying she didn't feel well. Though the truth, of sorts, she didn't tell Grant he'd broken her heart. For his part, considering her physical condition, he thought nothing unusual about it.

Soon the morn of the awaited trip arrived. The weather proved gorgeous, and perfect for travel. The morning sky looked bright and sunny and the air held but a faint hint of chill that had been in the air the evening before.

Everyone going on the trip assembled in the main courtyard and Grant observed sharp glares from nearby women. He had no idea what they were upset about. He could have understood the glares had he been taking their husbands to battle, but they were merely accompanying him to the faire this time, and he had agreed to let the women come, too. He knew how much they looked forward to the yearly trip. Why then did they seem so angered?

Grant looked for Tory so he could tell her farewell, but saw her nowhere. She must still be in their chamber. He thought perhaps her belly bothered her again since he noticed her trying to stay tears the night before. He hated she felt so badly and hoped these feelings wouldn't last too long after their bairn's birth.

Were women always this sad while breeding? Odd he hadn't noticed it in others before.

While he made final preparations, one wife walked by and grumbled, "I hope you are proud of yourself for making Lady Tory miserable." Head held high and shoulders pulled back, she strode toward her horse without stopping.

What the deuce had that been about, he wondered and looked at her retreating back.

A few minutes later another woman made a similar comment, then another.

Soon it became apparent all the women were cross with him. Grant wondered what he'd done to deserve their ire. They'd all referenced Tory. It appeared his wee lady wife could cause quite a stir even when not present.

Aggravated, he mounted his steed and headed to the fore of the group. He began to think the more space he placed between himself and these infernal women the better.

Of a sudden he remembered he hadn't kissed Tory farewell. He couldn't leave without seeing her. He quickly dismounted and dashed back up the curved staircase. Opening his chamber door, he found her standing at their window gazing on the bustle of activity below.

Grant approached her silently and stood behind her. He turned her gently.

She didn't look upset this morning, just sad.

"What is wrong, Sweeting? I already told you I'd not be gone long." He assumed her sadness was caused over his leaving.

When she said nothing, but looked at him with soft doe eyes, he bent to kiss her. "You will hardly have time to miss me, my heart. I promise."

Tory tried to smile, but it didn't make it to her lips. With great difficulty she tried to keep her voice from breaking. "I shall await your return, milord."

From the doorway a small voice piped up, "She has never been to a faire."

Grant spun around to see Graeme. Ah, his lady's wee champion. "What nonsense do you speak, wee Graeme?" he asked, humoring him. "Of course, Lady Tory has not been to our faire. This is the first one since she arrived here. But I already told her we will be back afore any of you can miss us and 'tis no different than any other faire."

The lad sauntered into the room looking at Tory adoringly, and Grant tousled the small boy's hair. He continued to hold Tory with his other arm. Graeme, however, would have none of it and evaded Grant's hand. He shook his head at Grant emphatically, and persisted with a glare. "She has never been to any faire. Her da never took her, and now you went and hurt her feelings because you'll not take her either." His eyes narrowed as he glared up at Grant.

Grant looked perplexed. Frowning as he looked from the small freckle-faced boy to Tory, he queried, "What does the lad speak about, lady mine? What means he you've never been to a market faire? Rubbish. Everyone goes to faires."

At first Tory didn't respond, but when Grant persisted, she proudly held her head high. "Nay, milord, not everyone. You forget my father hated me. If something seemed of great import, he ensured such things never happened. Graeme is correct. I have never attended a faire." She tried not to let him see how much this hurt.

"But I understand why you do not wish me around at such a time." She looked into Grant's confused eyes. "You would not want anyone to see me while I am in this condition and misunderstand our relationship."

"I do not want anyone to..." Grant roared, his voice lowering to a feral growl similar to that of an angry animal. "Woman! Where do you get such ridiculous ideas?" Not proud of how she looked? He fair burst with pride. His bairn was growing in her belly.

"'Tis not ridiculous," she responded as she tried to keep her emotions in tact. "You made it abundantly clear the other day—"

"You have until the sun lowers one notch on the sundial to pack your bag, woman," Grant roared his command, veins bulging in his neck from anger. He suddenly found himself in a foul mood. "Were I you, I'd not waste any of those minutes arguing. If not packed after that time, you will go with naught save clothes on your back."

He turned and stormed out the door.

Within the allotted time, Tory and Annie appeared at the large front door. Huge belly aside, she found she could move quite quickly when necessary.

Grant paced angrily in the courtyard. When he saw Annie also had a tiny bag, he eyed her with a speculative look then glared at his wife. "Woman, I did not say you could fetch anyone. I said you could pack – not anyone else."

Holding his gaze firmly, Tory let him rant. "I spent my entire childhood wanting to attend such events. I never got to do so. My father made certain of that. I missed out on everything everyone else got to do." She put a protective arm around Annie. "I'll not let that happen to Annie just because she has no one to speak for her."

She bit her lip. "If I must make a choice between myself and Annie, I'll stay behind and let her go in my stead." Grant lowered his head and glared into his stubborn wife's face. Her confrontational stance told him she stood braced and ready for battle.

"Woman—"

"Nay, Grant," she firmly held her ground. "Pray do not be cross with me, but I mean it. I would give anything to go on this holiday, but Annie is but a child. As much as I desire to go, she needs this more. I am used to being ignored. It has been done my entire life and 'tis not a feeling I wish her to experience firsthand."

Mumbling a curse beneath his breath, Grant grabbed Tory and dragged her to his horse and swept her up on the glorious steed before she had a chance to voice her refusal. Pointing to Murdoch, he told him curtly, "Fetch the child." He hoped the man's cheery face would comfort her, since the lassie was as skittish as a newborn colt.

Determined to put an end to this folly, Grant spurred his horse forward.

Chapter Twenty-six

Tory and Annie rejoiced in looking at extravagantly decorated booths dotted throughout town.

"My lady," a merchant shouted, beckoning Tory to approach. "Fish here! Come see the fresh fish for yourself."

Tory smiled, but shook her head and kept walking.

Just a few steps later, the cheese merchant tried to tempt her. "Cheese. Come taste, my lady. You've never had any better."

Tory laughed in sheer delight as men and women touted their many offerings. "Oh," she said, smiling up at Grant, her eyes brimming with happiness, "this is wonderful. Thank your for bringing me. "Oh, do smell that heavenly aroma. I vow, sir, I could eat everything!"

Grant laughed. "I am pleased you're enjoying yourself. Be forewarned, though, vendors will try to entice you to approach their booth. Each will vow whatever they're selling is better than whatever their neighbor has."

Catherine giggled like a child as they walked the path, each person doing exactly what Grant had said.

Laughing, Grant was unable to tell who acted more the bairn on this outing – Tory or Annie.

An exciting experience, both clearly delighted in the sights and sounds of their adventure. For two days they gleefully absorbed everything around them.

Crowded booths created an illusion of one long building offering everything imaginable. Hawking vendors continued to extol the virtues of their wares, ensuring Tory she would be foolish to pass them by. When she seldom believed them, Grant found her a frugal shopper.

She saw fruits, vegetables, fish, meats galore, silver chalices, ornate looking glasses, and much, much more. Anything a person could possibly want seemed to be offered.

Scarcely able to contain her glee, Tory behaved like a child with a new toy at Hogmanay. Not wanting to miss a thing, Grant watched her look around with the unrestrained curiosity of a child.

He felt amazed Tory didn't buy everything that took her fancy. Though thrilled by much, she bought little, and most purchases seemed to be for Annie. His young wife delighted in ensuring the holiday proved a journey of a lifetime for the youngster.

She bought several ribbons for the lassie with the money he provided her with upon entry into town. He couldn't contain his smile over Annie's reaction when she saw a rag doll. The young girl's eyes widened in awe, and as Tory perused everything in the booth, Annie's remained glued on the small doll. When Tory took her hand to advance to the next booth, the little girl made no sound, but one huge tear rolled down her smooth freckled cheek.

Just as he was about to comment, Tory noticed as well.

Kneeling to comfort the little girl, Tory asked, "What is wrong, Sweetheart?"

Annie refused to tell her, seemingly feeling she had no right to ask for something. Had the child never owned something as precious as her own doll?

"Did you see something at the last booth you wanted, Sweetheart?" Tory prodded.

Annie worried her upper lip and nodded – first yes, then no as if in afterthought.

"Will you take me back and show me what you liked?" Tory asked gently, her arm draped protectively around the girl.

Grant never ceased to be amazed at how gentle she could be with the children. He knew his eyes filled with admiration while he watched her interaction with the child.

Annie slowly shook her head no. Unable to stop herself, she wrung her hands and tried to keep her tears from falling.

Tory rose and gently moved the young girl back to the booth. 'Twas apparent it must have been special for Annie to react as she had.

Used to holding her feelings inside, the small girl rarely expressed her emotions or desires. Annie tried to keep her eyes averted from the beloved doll, but failed and they went back longingly.

Ascertaining the item in question, Tory watched the moppet closely for a few heartbeats. Then she bent her head and counted her remaining coin. 'Twould take almost everything she had, but she didn't care. Annie had never responded with so much enthusiasm, and Tory refused to deny the child now.

Instead of paying the merchant herself, Tory handed the coin to Annie. "You pay the man, dear."

The small girl's eyes widened in anticipation as she paid the burly merchant and he handed her the treasured doll. The look on

Annie's face as she glanced from Tory to Grant made the expenditure worthwhile to Tory's way of thinking. Grant smiled down at the child, so Tory thought he couldn't be too upset with her decision.

Cradling her doll to her heart, Annie's face glowed with delight. 'Twas the most magnificent doll she'd ever seen.

"Let me give you more coin so you can buy additional items."

"I thank you, but no. I made my purchasing decisions and shall stick with them. I can't ask you for more money just because I spent what you've given me. I'm just happy I got to come on the holiday."

Grant was amazed at his wife's selflessness. Several of his men were purchasing items Tory had delighted in, but hadn't purchased for herself. He chuckled at the actions of his hardened warriors. His lady wife slowly, but most assuredly, had wrapped them all around her graceful finger. Ever since the day of her horrible beating, his men had bent over backwards to protect her.

Grant found great satisfaction in this knowledge.

Laughing inwardly at the sheer delight on Tory's face as she embraced the surrounding sights and sounds, he'd sent several men back himself to purchase items she'd exclaimed over.

She'd 'ooohed' over some of the cloths. "Oh my, they are exquisite," she'd sighed.

He watched her and decided he wanted her to have kirtles from them. Since she seemed not to expect anything, he truly enjoyed buying things for her. Many women would have demanded everything they saw.

In late morn, Grant reluctantly left the group to join a meeting with representatives from various clans. Once again Scotland needed to band together against Edward and plans had to swiftly be made.

"I'll not be overlong," Grant said, issuing last minute instruction to his men. "Closely guard Tory and Annie. There are too many people in town now, and anything could happen. Be vigilant at all times."

He headed to the meeting with Warwick and Ian.

"Aye, Edward finally crossed back to England—and not a moment too soon if you ask me. And an innkeep overheard him proudly proclaim, 'It is a good job a man does, to be shot of such shite.'"

A furor arose and the McPherson growled, "Get rid of Scotland? That will never happen, but we will get rid of him, aye!"

Called the *Hammer of the Scots*, Edward truly proved to be the most implacable foe Scotland had ever seen.

While Tory and Annie sampled a meat pastie that tasted as good as promised, Tory observed some men she thought stared at her. Though they were too far away to confirm, she found it disconcerting nonetheless. Surely she must be imagining it. She knew no one in town save Grant's men.

Ansley and Barrie stayed close to hand.

Grant had already noted the young men seemed to have a case of calf's love for his young wife. He laughed, remembering Tory had told him both young men's names meant bold. Though certain she hadn't meant that at the time, the foolish pups were certainly bold in trying to win his wife's favor. Grant thought they'd soon outgrow it, but if not, he'd speak to them.

He'd gone through enough problems with men coveting his lady wife without his doing so as well.

The boisterous group rounded a corner of the cheese shop to sounds of laughter, and Tory suddenly stood face to face with Percival Bothington. Her eyes widened in shock, but Bothington looked unsurprised. It became clear the men she'd thought staring had been Bothington's.

Fighting growing panic, Tory tried to retreat from whence she came, but Ansley's huge bulk stood behind her and she was unable to maneuver around him. Reaching down, she took Annie's hand firmly within her own and tried to smile nonchalantly.

"Ansley, I believe I have changed my mind and prefer to return the way we just came. Do you mind? I wish to revisit a shop we saw earlier."

Before she could retreat, Bothington grabbed her arm with his bony hand.

His voice dripped with sarcasm. "Is that the way you treat your betrothed, Victoria, my dear?"

Looking into his face, Tory saw no friendship, no warmth. This vile man meant to torment her. His touch upon her arm felt as foul as she remembered.

"Kindly take your leave, sir," she began, sounding calmer than she felt and trying to maintain an air of control. "I fear I am busy with other acquaintances."

"I think not," the evil man smirked, both brows rising in condescention.

Smiling in an effort not to frighten the child, Tory calmly turned to Annie. "Take Ansley's hand, dear." She carefully placed it within the man's meaty hand as he frowned at her actions.

She assured the two men, "I shall be quite all right. Please feel free to walk about whilst I chat with a former acquaintance."

She tried her best to give them a convincing smile, but didn't think she succeeded.

Although not feeling comfortable doing so, Ansley and Barrie backed away as their lady requested, but not far enough for her to be in danger to her person. They were painfully aware Grant wouldn't be pleased. When the two men saw Tory's agitation rising and the old man's belligerence increase, Ansley turned to Barrie. "Get assistance and to send someone to fetch Grant." He looked back toward Tory. "Hurry man, I'm feeling a premonition of impending danger."

"You and your fey senses."

"Aye, but I am usually right. Hellsfire, our lady is a joy to be around, but a veritable nightmare to protect." Shaking his head, he bade, "Go fetch Grant."

Bothington's men felt confident they could easily overpower Tory's bodyguards. When Barrie left with the child, leaving only Ansley remaining, they closed ranks.

Bothington loudly threw slurs at Tory. Feeling a wave of fear rush over her, she tried to back away, but Bothington roughly grabbed her arm and refused to let her leave. She instinctively felt a presence behind her and knew without turning Grant had arrived. A feeling of both relief and fear surged through her. Relief he'd come to protect her, and fear of what Bothington might reveal.

A murmur of anticipation swept through the crowd with the force of a storm. No good Scot ever passed up an opportunity to witness a fight!

Bothington also surmised the powerful figure's identity behind Tory. With a sneer he spat, "You must be the unfortunate man saddled with this slut."

Tory felt Grant stiffen behind her and her blood ran cold. What must he think of her?

"You are correct in your assumption. I am her husband, and you will apologize this instant for your words to my lady." Grant's

239

tone indicated he'd accept no less than a public apology and held an unmistakable threat if one didn't come quickly. His hand tightened into a fist at his side and moved closer to his sword.

He felt an immediate urge to plant his fist in the old man's sneering face.

"A young pup like you thinks to upstage me? Not bloody likely."

Grant saw the smug look on the old man's face as he uttered, "One need not apologize for the truth, sir. Has your wife told you we were betrothed when she ran away from her devoted father and tricked you into marrying her? Or did you not bother to wed the strumpet and just keep her around as your leman? 'Tis all she is good for. But then, 'tis common knowledge you mount the wench more than you mount your horse."

Grant felt Tory inhale sharply at Bothington's crude remark. His usually verbal wife was obviously too shocked to utter a retort.

The old man continued to taunt, "Truly, sir, I do feel sorry for you, but I feel most blessed you took the wench off my hands." A leer curved the corners of his mouth. "She is naught but used goods, you know. Her father told me, you know. Someone of my esteemed elevation would never have accepted one already so blemished, and I'd had many a discussion on the subject with her saintly father, although he tried to convince me otherwise."

His belittling look made Tory wish she could climb under the nearest rock and disappear.

"Her father, God rest his soul, tried so hard to keep the stubborn wench in line, but alas," Bothington continued with a derisive sigh, "'tis said she whored herself to almost every man in his keep." He waved his hand palm outward, as if indicating his men, too, had all known Tory intimately. "And who knows how many other clans the wench serviced. I feel quite certain by now you have provided her to your men for their enjoyment as well." With a mock sigh of sorrow he added, "There is, after all, naught else one can do with a wench so debased."

Her dread contined to increase, and Tory couldn't stop herself from shaking. Grant drew his sword and stepped in front of his wife to address Bothington's scathing remarks, but Bothington moved closer and forcefully jerked Tory's neckline, causing it to tear.

Livid, Grant reacted swiftly and roared out his wrath. "You miserable whoreson, you will apologize to my wife immediately – or this will be the last night of your sorry life."

Bothington's sneer proved his only answer until he boasted loudly, "Have you not wondered why the wench bears lash marks on her back? Look." An evil grin crossed his face as he tipped his head towards Tory's torn kirtle. "The marks do not lie."

In a blind rage Grant pushed Tory farther behind him.

His men formed a human barrier around her. A cape miraculously appeared and someone wrapped it protectively around her shoulders.

She choked back a sob.

"Draw your sword, sir," Grant said with resolute calm.

With a look of scorn the old man angrily hissed, "Are you threatening me, you impertinent upstart?"

"I do not threaten, auld man," Grant growled in response. "I act."

Noting Bothington's men drawing their swords, Grant spun around. "This fight is atween your laird and me. Keep out of it and you may live. Intervene and you shall die."

Grant spun back on Bothington just as the elderly man tried to put his own sword in Grant's back, his face mottled with fury. "Och, a man of honor, I see," Grant mocked the man's evil intent.

"Do you intend to kill us all, young man," the evil man baited.

"Nay, auld man," Grant replied as their swords clashed. "Just you!"

To Grant's surprise, Bothington fought well for his age and the clash of swords rang out in the small town. But youth and strength won out and the vile man soon lay dead.

Grant turned to Bothington's men. "Remove this scum and let me never see the likes of you again. Depart Scotland and return to your bloody English soil where dogs like you belong. Or," he continued with a low, steely voice, "you will receive the same fate as your worthless laird."

With his men surrounding him, Grant advanced on Tory. Still and silent, she watched his approach. When she moved gratefully into the comfort of his arms, he placed his arms securely around her and rushed her through the gathering throng of people.

Chapter Twenty-seven

He remained quiet enroute to their small building. Once inside he seated Tory carefully on a mat. "Are you all right, wife?"

Looking up at him with glazed eyes, Tory nodded, still unable to speak. Unease welled within her as she anticipated the confrontation. Trying to compose herself, she said, "Grant, please allow someone to take Annie away for awhile."

Eyes wide, the tiny girl looked terrified and clutched Tory's arm. Her other arm held her beloved doll close to her chest.

Grant ensured the lass, "Sweeting, would you do me a favor? Can you help Barrie fetch Lady Tory something to eat? 'Twould be a big help. No one else knows her as well as you do, so you are the only person who would know what to buy."

Annie looked unwilling to move, so Grant urged, "Will you do that, Sweeting?"

Still uncertain, Annie's eyes shot to Tory. Only when she nodded her agreement did the little girl allow Barrie to escort her from the building. Reaching the door, she again held back. She clutched her small doll tightly and glanced apprehensively at Tory, her lower lip quivering. With a final nod of assurance from her lady, Annie reluctantly acquiesced.

Assured Annie had depared, Grant turned to Tory. "Well, wife, wish you to tell me what happened?" Frustrated, he blurted out before she could begin, "Damnation, woman, can I never leave you alone without some strange man from your past accosting you?"

His lips tightened with evident displeasure.

Gulping, Tory's composure dwindled as she looked around the room. No one would leave until she answered. Once again she'd placed them in danger, causing them to fight for her. Grant's voice indicated his anger, yet she could see by the lines of his body and the twitch in his cheek he held himself tightly in check. She feared it wouldn't take much for him to explode.

Mentally cringing, she rose and paced.

"I knew not Percival would be at the faire, my lord," she began in a rush. "Only after you left did I begin to think someone might be watching me."

"And which of my men did you report this to? I wouldst speak with them about letting their guard grow lax after you mentioned your fears."

Tory squirmed. "I told no one. 'Twas merely a f...feeling I had. Pray do not be cross with our men. They did naught wrong." Her voice trailed off, and a sense of discomfort rose with each question her husband voiced.

"Finally you speak the truth," he admonished. The look on his face revealed his growing annoyance. "I do not misdoubt the only thing my men could have done differently was to keep you locked in this building!" he lashed out in frustration. "Truth be told, wife, you attract trouble wherever you go."

He grabbed her arms to shake her, but restrained his actions at the last minute. He took a deep breath and calmed himself as his fury rose. How could one woman get into so much trouble? Why wouldn't she do as he bid so he could protect her? Didn't she yet realize how much she meant to him? She was a danger not only to herself, but to others.

Tory sagged at his words. She felt as if Grant had just slapped her. Had she stayed home as he wanted, none of this would have happened.

"Now, wife," he glared through narrowed eyes, "once and for all you will tell us what happened to your back. 'Tis frustrating a man you profess to hate knows more about your past than me. I'll tolerate that no longer."

It rankled she didn't trust him enough to reveal everything.

"No more stalling," he affirmed. "We will have the truth, woman, and we will have it now." His eyes locked with hers and didn't release them. He saw the flash of pain in hers, yet his tone remained emphatic.

"Who lashed you?" Grant yelled when she didn't immediately supply him with the information he wanted.

Knowing she had no choice this time, but angered just the same, Tory spat through clenched teeth, "My father! Damn you, Grant Drummond, my father lashed me."

She vainly struggled to loose herself from his grip, but Grant held her firmly.

Tears burned at the back of her eyes, but she refused to let them fall, too stubborn to let him see how much she cared. This would drive the final wedge between them. Grant would never forgive her after this.

The shock of her words left Grant momentarily speechless and he tried not to let his astonishment show. He never expected that answer, and of a certainty he knew she'd finally told him the full truth.

Questions flashed through his mind like bolts of lightning. Saints alive, should he stop questioning her? Would it be too difficult for her to continue? Would her nightmares ever end if she didn't face the truth? Could he stop now, short of discovering answers to everything?

The look of shock reflected on his mens' faces clearly mirrored his own. Even Archibald gaped. Things had come too far to turn back. This time they'd know all.

He stared a long time, finally said, "Tell me, Tory. Tell me – without your wee bit of profanity this time." Though he tried to keep his voice casual to not frighten her, his arched brow reminded her she knew better than to speak thusly, frustrated or not.

The tears filling Tory's eyes and her defeated posture indicated he'd won. She bowed her head until her long, brown hair shrouded the tears that appeared on her cheeks. Deep in his belly Grant felt uncertain whether he really wanted to hear.

With resigned voice, she raised remorse filled eyes. "All my life I tried to please Father. Everything I did only angered him more, but foolishly I kept trying. I thought I could make him proud, if he would but let me."

A sob escaped her, but she forced herself to speak.

Grant felt the tension in her body and patiently tried to calm her.

"Every year we held a race for young men at our manor. Even though Father forbade me to ride Galahad, I secretly did so whenever I got the chance – whenever he and his men were away from home. I considered entering the race, thought I could beat everyone else.

"I had to," she affirmed softly, her eyes intense. "Father would never give me permission to participate, so I disguised myself and joined the young men at the starting line."

She paused to take a few shattered breaths, and Grant grimaced at the thought of his young wife yet again in breeches and all they probably revealed.

"I raced like my life depended on it, and won. Oh, Grant," she proudly, but sadly began the story of that fateful day. "I cannot tell you how happy I felt. I foolishly thought Father would acknowledge I was just as good as any son since I could ride like one. I'd accomplished a feat of skill this time rather than the book learning he so disdained."

He watched as she collected her thoughts.

"I never could have prepared myself for the anger I encountered instead. He railed like a madman, slapped me across my face, and spat at me. I thought I couldn't have been more embarrassed." She gave a small laugh and her body shook.

Grant feared his wife might become hysterical.

"I couldn't have been more wrong. I pushed him too far and naught I said calmed him. His face held a horrific sneer and I feared for my life. He seemed in the grip of an icy rage. Looking back, that might have been much kinder than what happened," she said in a soft, broken voice. Tears coursed down her cheeks. Emotions she'd clearly kept inside for years finally snapped. Her glance shifted around the room and back to Grant.

His attention remained focused on her.

"He dragged me toward our center courtyard. I tried to pull away, but couldn't escape him. He proved too strong. In all my years I had never heard his voice so cruel – far past the point of hatred. He yelled that if I truly wished to be treated like a man, I would also be punished like one." Grant noticed Tory's breathing quickened, and agony and despair echoed in her voice.

"I found out soon enough what he meant."

She shuddered, and Grant guessed she replayed the scene in her mind's eye.

"He dragged me to the whipping post in the center court. Father always took great pleasure awarding that punishment. He usually meted it out to vassals himself since it delighted him so."

She laughed harshly with the memory.

"He...he fastened my hands with cords at the top of the post." She inhaled deeply and shuddered.

Grant's eyes widened in surprise and he braced himself, unable to believe what hed'd heard. Could a father be that cruel?

A deafening silence filled the room.

"Though shocked, I believed not he'd do something so vicious. True, he'd made it plain enough over the years how much he hated me, but I was still his daughter. Too soon I discovered the answer." She shuddered in remembrance.

"He walked behind me where I could no longer see him. I thought he fastened me to humiliate me and planned to leave me hang there. I honestly thought he'd walked away."

Tory faltered in the telling and stared down at her hands as a sob escaped. Silence filled the room.

"Next I knew, I heard a *whoosh* and felt a sting across my back." Grant stiffened and his hands clenched. "I would like to say I bore it well and remained brave, but I fear that happened not. I screamed. Twice more I felt that vicious whip." Raw pain filled her eyes as she focused on the horrible memory. "I proved naught but a weakling after all."

Grant slanted a glance at his men to judge their reaction. They looked as shocked as he felt.

"I knew not how much more pain I could stand. Suddenly Father stopped his beating. I thought him finished when he walked in front of me, and I breathed a sigh of relief."

Her knees buckled and Grant caught her. Her chest rose and fell heavily as she looked up at him, agitation apparent in her eyes. "The pain was so horrible I thought I would pass out, but at least he was finished."

She met Grant's gaze squarely. "Evil emanated from his eyes such as I'd never seen before. I cannot explain the hatred I saw. I thought him mad. He looked me in the eyes and with an evil laugh said, 'Nay, *daughter*, this is not right. You wished to be treated as a *man*, but this is not how a man would be punished.' Before I knew his intentions, he grabbed my collar and pulled, tearing my kirtle completely down to m...my w...waist." Her voice collapsed on a sob. "S...similar to what Bothington did this day. I felt so ashamed."

The rest of what she said came so low Grant had to lean forward to hear. "Grant, he bared me to all...our...men. He laughed and said after that day no decent man would ever want me. That I'd be no better than the manor's whore. That mayhap that is what he would make me."

Tory's eyes glazed over, and Grant could see her reliving her pain.

They weren't happy memories.

Grant's touch gentled as he watched her and smoothed hair from her face. He affirmed silently that somehow he'd break her free from her father's dark influence. She'd suffered far too much pain.

His tenderness almost her undoing, she continued on as if Grant hadn't touched her. "Then he stepped behind me and continued to hit me with that detestable whip." A sob choked her throat. "I fear I passed out after the next lash. He only stopped because someone rushed inside the manor to tell my grandmum. They told me she burst outside and tried to wrench the whip from Father. Since she was weak and aging, Father pushed her aside as though naught more than a bothersome midge.

"She never spoke of it with me, but I heard she placed herself between me and Father's whip." She breathed deeply and released it with an audible sigh. "Grandmother apparently yelled that if he meant to strike someone, 'twould be her."

A cheerless chuckle caught on a breath. "He didn't, of course. He meant to torment me, not his mother. Tis said he turned to leave and ordered his men to remove her from the courtyard."

Breathing deeply, she tried to gather inner strength. "I know not how long I hung there afterward or who cut me down. No one ever told me. 'Tis said Grandmum forbade it. When I awoke, she tended my back with goose grease and charcoal and spoke naught of it. She never once mentioned what she did for me that day," came the whispered shudder. "She rarely left her bedchamber because she is so weak, yet she chose to sacrifice herself to save me if the need arose. I have no idea how she got the strength to come downstairs and outside the manor." She fought to hold back her emotions, but they flooded over her.

Anguish shown on her face as she clearly remembered her father's reign of terror on her life. "From that day on, Father made my life more miserable than before. The culmination became the betrothal to Bothington. Father knew that would ultimately lead to my death. 'Tis obvious 'tis what he wanted, but he could in all honesty say it had not been done at his own hand."

Tory pulled away from Grant, and this time he didn't stop her. He felt like he'd been struck by a thunderbolt. It dawned on him he'd heard this, but hadn't recognized it for truth at the time. When she'd talked in her sleep while fevered, he'd asked about her back. She'd mumbled about her father. At the time he thought her comments mere fever ramblings. Now he knew she spoke the truth!

Suddenly he realized Tory was still speaking. Her body wracked with sobs, she looked at him earnestly. "I am sorry, Grant. You tried to make me tell you before, but I could not. I never spoke of this before and truth be told, I wished you never to know."

Touched by her sincerity, Grant watched her force herself to draw and exhale deep breaths. "Though I tried to pretend otherwise, what you thought of me mattered. I no longer wished to leave. I foolishly thought of it as my home, too. I know now that is pure folly. I'll never have a home."

Tory bravely tried to talk as tears of humiliation burned her eyes. Her lower lip quivered with such intensity she almost bit through it to still it.

"Grant, pray believe me. I never meant to shame you thusly." Confusion and fear flashed in her eyes. "And now I did so in front of an entire town. I never should have allowed you to wed me – although you really did not ask, you know.

"I should have told you Father's name and what he'd done immediately. He spoke the truth. You wouldn't have wanted me. No decent man would, and you deserve so much better. I beseeched you before to let me leave and you did not allow it. Now you have no choice." Her head shook sadly.

Grant frowned. Not want her? Was she daft?

"You can take solace in the thought that since you wedded me not wed in kirk," she rushed on, "you will have no problem setting me aside. And since you want not my babe, this is the perfect solution for that, too."

Grant thought Tory through speaking when she began again, her voice quavering and her red-rimmed eyes filled with pain and a look of apology. "You called me whore when you brought me into your life, Lord Drummond. Now the whole world knows the truth. Forgive me."

Pressing her hand to her lips, she sobbed raggedly.

With that she fell silent. Jumping up, she looked around the room wildly, as panic blinded her, then dashed from the building. Grant's men were in such a state of shock no one moved to stop her.

Grant surged to his feet. Forgive her? She'd done naught to be forgiven for! She was the innocent in this.

Finally, as if one, everyone ran after her, but the daft woman disappeared. Grant's anger escalated to outrage that the wee lass had again run from from him. He'd thought her through with such nonsense.

He'd fetch her back immediately and set her straight on that issue.

He couldn't have been more wrong.

Grant reached the frantic stage by nightfall when Tory hadn't been found.

And what was this nonsense about not wanting her child?

"Turn the town inside out to find her. *We must find her!*"

She was his wife, after all. Blessed St. Michael—*she was his life!* That thought scared him to death. When had that happened?

Chapter Twenty-eight

Gathering back at the hut, no one had news of Tory's whereabouts. Adults were worried, but Annie proved inconsolable. Though many tried, she couldn't be calmed.

Women tried to get her to leave the hut, but Annie refused, holding fast to a nearby table leg as she clutched her doll. The look on her anguished face told everyone she wouldn't leave until Tory returned.

Grant, Warwick, and Ian again searched for Tory with no better luck. They returned near the witching hour with only angst and darkness surrounding them. Grant's eyes were etched with worry.

Shortly, a knock sounded at the door. Angus answered and quickly pulled small man into the room after conversing briefly. Escorting him to Grant, the man repeated his information.

With Warwick, Ian, and Alexander accompanying him, Grant followed the wizened man with renewed vigor to a tumbled down barn, the moon lighting their way. Once inside, Grant gazed at a sleeping Tory. Curled under straw in the makeshift stable, a large piece of cloth hid most of her. Apparently in the throes of a nightmare, she thrashed about.

The shopkeep said, "She seems in midst of a bad night dream. 'Tis probably why the cloth shifted, allowing me to discover her when I tended my animals before turning in for the night."

"I thank you for your assistance, my friend." As Warwick handed the man a bag of coin, Grant bent and picked up his sleeping wife. He felt so relieved at her safety, he had trouble getting his legs to move. Only his friends' knowing gazes finally propelled him forward.

She belonged to him, and he'd protect her forever.

He'd kill her when she woke!

Exhausted, Tory remained asleep until noises inside the building woke her when Grant placed her on the straw sleeping mat. Rousing herself and looking around, she instantly remembered what happened. Crying out, she jumped up to run out the door.

Her expanding belly prohibited her from moving quickly,

and this time, Grant expected as much. "Nay, woman!" He grabbed her arm and caught her before she fled. "You are going nowhere. You ran us a merry chase yestereve and we are in no mood for your antics."

He mumbled a fierce expletive and berated, "Here is where you belong, lady mine, and here is where you will stay."

He turned to his men. "We shall leave the city shortly. Make plans accordingly." He cared not one whit that it was the wee hours of morn. With all that happened, they'd certainly not sleep.

He hunkered down to her level, and his eyes bored into Tory's. The fear he felt in her absence quickly turned to anger now assured of her safety.

He vowed such an incident wouldn't happen again. She meant too much to him. Grant had no idea when that happened.

"You have run away for the last time, lady wife. If you try doing so again, you will seriously pay the consequences. Mark me on that. Do not tempt me, or I may do you violence right here in front of our men."

She stiffened and jerked away.

"Och, wife," Grant mumbled, "what am I to do with you?" He felt truly amazed she provoked such feelings of caring in him. He'd thought his heart dead.

"I knew you would be angered," she answered, avoiding his eyes, "and I did not blame you. 'Twas wrong of me not to tell you what Father did. You had the right to know I am no better than the town whore," she tremulously confessed.

Biting her lip, Tory's voice filled with raw emotion. "But I did not wish to die, husband." Seeing Grant's look of shock and perplexity, she continued in a flurry of words. "I thought you angered enough to kill me. Father would have, and you have every right to be cross after I shamed you before everyone. But," stopping, she rose to her knees as she rushed on with dread, "I could not let you do that in anger. Though you probably feel I deserve it, I had to protect our babe. Even if you do not want it, I could not let it die because of my stupidity."

She blinked frantically to stay back tears and looked at Grant expectantly.

A collective gasp filled the room.

Grant boomed, "Kill you? Saints preserve me, woman, what sort of monster do you think me?"

His eyes looked pained that she could think thusly of him.

While Grant stomped around the room, his voice rose in anger. "We just spent an entire day and eve looking for you! We knew not what daft thing you might do!"

"But—" she began and cast a startled look.

"Nay, woman," Grant stormed, his face rigid with control. Holding up his hand to silence her, he shook his head to gather his wits about himself.

This woman infuriated him!

"You spoke enough this day. Now 'tis my turn." The tone of his voice sounded unyielding. Sitting in a chair in effort to calm himself, he leaned forward and pulled Tory closer. "Listen to me well, wife, for I'll only say this once." His voice sounded low, intimidating.

Fearing the worst, she clasped her hands together to stop them from trembling.

"What you told us this day will not soon be forgotten." He collected his thoughts and gathered Tory's trembling hands into his. "It explains why you are afeart of many things, or why you constantly fear we will hit you, even though I've told you time and again we will not."

Grant's brow furrowed as he pulled her closer. "But to think I would harm you or my bairn. Woman, how can you think that?"

He knew his pain was reflected in his eyes.

"I know you heard me tell you this in the past, but do you never truly listen?" He shook his head in exasperation.

"I told you repeatedly that you are my wife." He gathered her tightly in his arms and rocked her. His voice ragged with concern, he added more to himself than to Tory, "Granted, the way we wed was not romantic, nor did I behave especial kind when I first brought you here, but I never hurt you, did I?"

At Tory's headshake, Grant rushed on. "You told us you thought of my home as yours. It *is* your home. Och, woman, you wormed your way into our hearts whether we wanted you there or not – and most of us did not," he ruefully admitted. "Think you now to depart and leave our hearts with a hole in them?"

She opened her mouth to speak, but Grant halted her.

He spoke with so much emotion, his words revealed more than he realized.

"You want us to love you, but not once have you said that to anyone except the bairns. Them you shower with unconditional love. Can you not do the same to the adults?" he finished in exasperation, not realizing he'd raised his voice.

Words failed her as she tried to speak. Tears spilled freely down her face and she didn't bother to brush them away. Could Grant really be asking what she thought? Would he *want* her to love him? Nay, that couldn't be possible. *Could it?*

A flicker of doubt crossed her mind, yet deciding to take a chance, she rose to her knees. She placed her hands on either side of Grant's face and looked at him a long time before she spoke. "I do love you, Grant Drummond. God help me, I did not want to, but I do."

Hearing Grant's sharp intake of breath, she feared she misjudged his comments. Unable to retract her words, she continued, "I have for a long time, but knew you could never love me back, so I feared telling you. It gives you too much power."

Grant seemingly frowned at her choice of words.

"But do you not see?" she implored and her shoulders sagged. "'Tis why I must leave."

Grant started to respond, bewilderment obvious in his eyes, but she stopped him when her hand gently caressed his cheek. "My lord husband, I love you with everything I am, but I cannot stay here. Not after everything that has been revealed. No matter what our men may say, I know they will always remember what happened yestereve. 'Tis confirmation of their worst thoughts of me."

Grant's brows drew together in a frown.

"I must leave, and pray you will allow me to keep our unborn child. I cannot see you should mind, since we both know you do not want my child. Yet I'll always have a part of you with me. As much as I do not wish to admit it, I could not bear if I had naught left of you. And once I leave you will have many other children with whomever you wed...next...out of love."

She had trouble saying those words. She didn't want him wed to anyone else. She wanted to stay with Grant forever.

"'Tis for the best, you know. I never should have allowed myself to wish for more. I should have known better then to nurture such a fantasy."

She started to remove her hands from his face, but Grant grasped them within his own and looked into her distraught face. "You...you love me?" he stammered, barely able to get the words out.

He found himself unable to assimilate anything past those words.

At her barely noticeable nod of assent, Grant's scowl deepened. "And you must leave me because you love me?"

"Aye."

"And you want to leave me?"

"Of course not, but--"

"Then 'tis because of what your da did that you must leave?" Grant frowned at her logic.

"Aye. Oh, Grant, do you not understand? It confirmed everyone's worst thoughts of me," came her ragged sob. "I am sorry. Truly. But you deserve much better than that in your wife. You deserve someone you can be proud of, not someone who brings shame upon you."

Lowering her head, she tried to pull her hands away, only to have Grant grasp them firmly and chuckle.

She jerked her head up and glowered. Her eyes lost their pain and were now as cold as ice. "I find naught amusing. If your plans are to humiliate me further, I would rather you just let me walk out that door."

"Wife, I am not laughing at you," then stopping himself briefly, Grant added in after thought, "well, aye, in a way I am, but you do not understand..."

From the glower on Tory's face, this admission did nothing to endear him to her. Grant looked around and tried to contain his laughter. "Men, would you tell her you know this is not true?"

His fearless men said not a word.

"Wick?" Grant smiled. Now that his fear had fled, he seemed unable to stop his laughter. He imagined it a reaction based on relief.

At this, Tory's anger grew. "You are enjoying this, are you not?" she shot at him, her voice low and husky. When she tried to jerk her hands away, Grant wrapped his arm around her waist and scooped her into his lap.

Her belly got in the way.

"Nay, wife," Grant chortled and tried to cover his smile, "'tis not a matter of enjoying this."

When no one said a word as she glowered, Grant beseeched, "Ian? Archie? Saints knees men, save me here." Tory sat rigidly in his embrace.

An embarrassed silence followed.

Ian looked uncomfortable. "Grant, 'tis not something we can speak of with your lady wife."

Grant shook his head, bewildered. "You would rather she left?" Seeing he'd get no help from his burly clansmen, he pursed his lips thoughtfully. "*Mo Chridhe*, my men all know you are not—nor never were—a whore. As a matter of fact, everyone knows you were a maiden when you came to us."

When he stopped to take a breath, she glared and asked sarcastically, "And how, pray tell, would everyone know such a thing? Certainly not from my repeatedly telling them. Lest you forget, no one believed a word I said when you so rudely kidnapped me."

Tory grew angrier by the moment.

Having come this far, Grant could think of no other way to say this besides revealing the entire truth. "Because they all saw our bedclothes from the first night I bedded you."

Looking around with a frown and narrowed eyes that told each of his men he'd pay them back later, Grant saw most turning red. Never would he have believed it. His men were battle hardened warriors, not delicate maidens.

Tory interrupted his thoughts of revenge when she yelled, "They what?"

Pushing away from him with sheer determination, she spun and glared at everyone.

"Aye, wife," Grant said smugly, remembering their wedding night and the wonderful hours they shared making love.

"Think back, Sweeting. Remember when our young maid, Dallas, came up after I fetched food to break our fast that morn?" When Tory nodded agreement, he recounted, "Whilst we ate, she changed our bedclothes. Remember? You even commented you thought that unusual since she just changed them the day afore."

Turning one of her stories around on her, he said, "Well, the young lass—and do not forget you told me her name means gentle and tenderhearted—took our marriage sheet down the stairs and showed it to everyone."

"She what?" Anger and embarrassment crept slowly up her face.

He added with a reassuring smile, "'Tis common practice, Sweeting, and my men were quite pleased with the knowledge."

Tory pulled her hand free and hit him. Not able to contain himself any longer, he burst into gales of laughter.

Seeing the look on her face, Grant sobered quickly and tried to ease her discomfort. "Sweeting, you got upset for naught yestereve. Had you stayed and discussed this, I could have told you we knew Bothington spewed naught but lies from his filthy mouth. And truth be told, I care not what others think, so it matters not what he shouted. I know the truth and naught else matters."

Grant still felt perilously close to losing her. He refused to let that happen.

Before Tory could say anything, Archibald stepped closer and impaled her with a glare. His body towered over hers. "Lady," he began gruffly, eyes flashing and gaze offering no quarter. "'Tis no secret how I felt about you when you first came." Tory rose and stepped back to escape the dark look on Archibald's face. His roar stopped her and she stood rooted to the ground. "There have been a lot of things I have not fancied about you in past, but I never thought you a coward. I should have suspected as much, your being English!"

Tory's head shot up. No one had ever called her a coward.

"I...I am not—"

"Are you not?" came Archibald's scornful sneer. "Then prove it. Why are you running away? You had no control over your da's actions. Plan you on running like a dog with its tail tucked between its legs the rest of your days?"

When Tory didn't immediately respond, but stood with her mouth open, Archibald challenged, "That is what you will do, mind. Once you start running, you will never stop." He sneered. "Now if you wish to prove me correct in my original thoughts, then run." Glaring, he continued to provoke, "I have about reached the end of my tether on this needless discussion, lady. Should you wish to prove me wrong, I suggest you retrieve your backbone and return to be the lady of our keep."

Tory glanced at Grant and then at men nodding agreement. Her eyes shifted back to Archie's.

"Well, lady," the stubborn man questioned with a derisive snort, "are you going to turn tail and run, or are you going to go home where you belong?"

He received his answer when she shot him a look of disdain. Poking him firmly in the chest with a long, graceful finger, she answered, "How dare you speak to me thusly? I am not a coward!"

Turning on her heel, Tory strode to the far side of the hut, murmuring under her breath.

Not looking back, she didn't see Archibald's amused smirk. Following her with his eyes, he inclined his head towards Grant and asked in a voice only Grant could hear, "Well?"

"I owe you, Archie."

That you do." He strode from the hall while Grant stood with a smug smile.

Fingers pressed to his lips, Grant stood in thought. "Well, wife," he turned and walked to Tory.

People milled about and gathered items for departure.

Leaning his tall frame against the wall, Grant spoke as if he had no care in the world. "I'll leave the final decision up to you. Will you return home this day to where you belong, or will you stay in this strange town where you know no one and begin this new life you spoke of? If my thoughts matter, I would prefer you came home."

Grant's men stopped in their tracks as he searched his lady's face for a hint of an answer.

What could their young chieftain be thinking?

After everything they'd done to find her and fetch her back, and after Archibald's successful attempt to anger her to make her return, Grant was now giving her a choice? Had the day's stress finally become too much for him?

Had he gone daft from worry?

Without warning Grant removed his linen shirt. His body trembled with suppressed anger. "I did not know my body disgusted you so." A hint of disillusionment sounded in his voice.

Tory's mouth opened in amazement. Disgust her? She'd never seen a man so handsome.

"What are you talking about?" she stammered when she could finally voice her thoughts. His comment caught her so off guard she could hardly think straight. "Of course you do not—"

"Do I not?" he questioned mockingly. "Look at me closely, wife. Do my battle scars not sicken you? That is what this is really about, is it not? 'Tis not that you are worried what I think of a few lashes on your wee back, 'tis that you cannot stand the sight of *my* flaws."

"Nay!" she yelled in horror. How could Grant think something so trivial could matter to her? He earned every scar he had. 'Tis what made him the man he'd become.

"Och," Grant retorted and noted with concealed delight that his lovely wife had started to squirm. "So 'tis not that I sicken you, 'tis that you think you are so much better than I."

Tory's voice failed as his cruel words taunted her.

"You say you can overlook the multitude of scars on my body, but you think me so shallow I cannot ignore a few marks on your back." Grant snorted in disgust as he turned away.

Still in shock that he should think such a horrid thing, Tory could neither move nor say anything. She just stared with imploring eyes. Merciful heavens, he'd cut to the heart of the matter. She never thought he could accept her with the marks on her body, so she hadn't given him the chance to make the decision.

Ignoring her, Grant rose to his feet, pulled his shirt and plaide back on and casually collected his belongings.

Please let that have worked, he silently prayed.

He walked to the door, gathering up Annie, who cried so hard her small body shook. Grant had to pry her tiny fingers from a table leg.

As he started to walk out the hut's large door pulling her firmly behind him, Annie vehemently shook her head and yelled, "Nay!"

Her innocent gaze never left Tory's face, and the soul-wrenching sound of her plea reverberated throughout the room.

All activity ceased. *Annie had never spoken!*

Pulling her hand out of Grant's, Annie raced back to Tory, her beloved doll dragging on the floor in her wake. Sobbing, she threw her arms around Tory's legs. "P...pray come with us, Lady Tory. P...pray do not leave me alone!" Her unused voice sounded strained as she tried to form the sounds so new to her.

Stunned, Tory collapsed to the ground and wrapped her arms tightly around the small waif. Both sobbed hysterically. Her eyes encompassing the entire room, Tory saw tears in everyone's eyes.

Truly, they'd witnessed a miracle.

Annie pulled away slightly, and once again spoke as agony and despair echoed in her small voice. "Please, Lady Tory. Come home with us. I need you there. I love you. Do not m...make me be alone again."

Her small lower lip quivered. "I was alone so long afore you came."

Extending her hand, Annie proudly waited for Tory to choose. "You told me you loved me, Lady Tory. No one ever told me that afore. Did you not mean it?"

The small girl's pale blue eyes filled with tears as she waited for an answer. Rising to her knees, Tory wrapped her arms around the waif and hugged her close to her chest, their tears mingling. "Oh, Annie. Aye. I meant every word I ever told you. I do love you. I love you very, very much."

"Then did you not mean what you told Laird Grant afore? Do you not love him after all?" An edge of uncertainty tinged the child's voice as she looked expectantly at Tory.

Tory looked at Grant, their eyes meeting above Annie's head. Merciful God in Heaven, had she really been foolish enough to blurt that out to him? Well, 'twas too late to take the words back. Turning back to Annie, she hesitated but finally acknowledged, "Aye, Sweeting, I love Lord Grant, too."

"Good." Everyone saw Annie nod her small head in affirmation, as if that settled everything. "Then we should all go home." Delight settled on her small cherubic face. Clearly, in her young mind there was naught else to settle.

When Tory still hesitated and gazed at Grant, Annie backed away and once more held out her small hand.

Glancing toward Grant, Tory saw him make the identical gesture. He held his hand out as he implored, "Wife?"

The remainder of his unspoken plea tugged at Tory's heart. She still had many unanswered questions, but making a decision she hoped was correct for the rest of her life, Tory placed her hand around Annie's. They both rose and walked to Grant, tears of joy streaming down their faces.

Grant said nothing as they approached, afraid to break the spell.

Watching her, Grant finally asked, "Are you certain, wife?" At Tory's nod, he smiled broadly and clasped her tightly to his side. "Then let us be off home."

Without another word, the three walked out the door. Grant's arms were wrapped firmly around them both.

Truly, he'd never let this woman out of his sight again!

Giving the signal to ride, he spurred his horse forward. He refused to look back at the town that caused them so much anguish.

Later that day, Tory relaxed against him. She felt the breeze touch her cheeks while horses traveled at a sedate pace due to her condition. She looked up into Grant's eyes and asked the question many wanted answered. "Would you really have let me stay? If that had been my decision, would you have let me stay?"

With a wide grin splitting his face, and winking at the men around him, Grant chortled as he leaned down and kissed the top of her head. "Nay, my heart. Never in a thousand lifetimes. I hoped you'd not make a stramash of the situation and would make the

259

right decision. If not, I would have thrown you over my shoulder like a sack of wheat."

Grant chuckled and teased, "In your delicate condition I do not think you would be comfortable that way!"

He looked quite pleased with himself.

"Grant," she stammered, afraid to ask her next question. "'Tis not just that Father lashed my back, you know." Grant started to interrupt, but she placed her fingertips to his lips. "Nay, please let me say this. I have to get everything out once and for all."

Grant nodded for her to continue.

"'Tis true I thought you'd not want me because of my back," she admitted. At Grant's frown she rushed on. "Everyone saw me, Grant. Father meant to humiliate me and truly did. Can you really live with the knowledge everyone in our courtyard that day saw me bared from the waist up?"

Grant considered his words carefully. "I am not pleased with that thought, Sweeting, but what happened is in no way your fault. Your da was a twisted man, his mind festering inward. As Warwick once told me, if he'd not known the man already dead and burning in Hell, I would kill him myself now. We will never again discuss this, Tory. That subject is closed."

He looked at his beautiful young wife. "Did you really mean what you said? Do you...really love me?"

He was afraid to say the words.

Hesitating briefly before answering, she rubbed her hand lightly over his cheek. "Aye, husband." She seemed oblivious to men riding around them watching. "I truly meant it."

"But why say you it gives me too much power over you?" He'd pondered that question all day. Of course he had authority over her. He had command over all his people.

She paused to collect her thoughts, indecisive about how much to say. "Because when you really love someone you give them all of yourself. Not just day-to-day routine things a husband and wife do, but the deep recesses of your being."

Tears pooled lightly in her eyes. "The only person to ever love me that completely is my grandmum. The kindest, sweetest person I know, she taught me what real love is. 'Tis what she had with my grandfather and 'tis something I always wanted, but never thought I would be fortunate enough to find. I knew I would never have that in my father's house, but I found it in yours."

She laughed ruefully. "The last place I ever thought it possible."

Facing forward, she settled back against Grant's chest. The full impact of her words hit him like the force of a battering ram against one of his castle doors. Could it be possible? Could she really mean what she said? After a moment's silence, he said softly, "Thank you, *Mo Chridhe*. You have made this a special day for me."

Tory turned to gaze up at him. Her eyes held a multitude of questions, but she only asked one. "Why does my being afraid to love you make today special?"

Grant smiled and pulled her closer. "Not that you are afraid, Sweeting, but that you love me. I hate to admit it, but deep inside there is a part that always thought no one would ever truly love me but my mother."

Seeing the frown forming on Tory's face, Grant tried to interject a bit of levity. "She had to you know, being my mother and all."

Without thinking, Tory turned as best she could on the horse's back and threw her arms around his neck and her mouth immediately opened to him, kissing him soundly. Grant felt totally taken aback. His men were there. Tory never showed affection when his men were around. He always went to her first. Upon reflection, it dawned on him she never pulled away after getting over her initial shyness.

Her breasts pressed to his chest, he felt that ever-present stirring in his loins. Blessed St. Michael, no longer a stirring, he was already painfully hard and aching. Just like he always seemed to be when around her.

Of a sudden Tory realized what she'd done. Turning away, her face burned with embarrassment as she moaned her distress.

Grant smiled to himself as she rested against his chest.

Chapter Twenty-nine

After being home a sennight, Grant reflected on the past several weeks. The thought that Tory loved him proved humbling. He was pleased she was back where she belonged, yet something still seemed amiss. Although unable to put his finger on it, something niggled at the back of his mind. She'd been pleased to return home, yet at the sight of their nursery, sadness returned.

As he returned to the Great Hall with Warwick, Grant voiced his concerns.

To his surprise, Warwick readily agreed.

"Know you something I should, Wick?" Grant asked, eyeing him closely.

"Nay, but I wish I did," came the old man's sad response. He rushed to assure Grant, "Dinnae get me wrong, son. She seems happy to be home, yet something still bothers your lovely lady. The light that normally shines in her eyes is not there."

Warwick decided to broach a subject he previously hesitated to mention. "What happened atween you when you returned from fighting with Wallace the last time?"

Grant narrowed his eyes. "I refuse to speak of that day." He'd tried to forget the shock at seeing Tory in his old nursery. Too quick to deny anything happened, Warwick knew him too well.

"I dinnae believe you, son," he said wisely as he braved his young chieftain's ire. "Whilst you were gone your lady wife brimmed with happiness. She sewed things every spare moment she had."

Grant showed surprise at the news.

"She made beautiful things for the bairn. The women commented on her stitchery. She's done none of that lately, mind. Nor have I seen anything she made afore."

Grant frowned and thought that odd. Tory had shown him nothing.

"Then you came home and everything changed," Grant's mentor said sadly. "The lassie is downhearted and subdued and has yet to pick up a needle again. And," he continued emphatically, "if I remember correctly, you stormed down the stairs after she said she had something special she wished to show you."

When Grant didn't respond, Wick prodded, "What happened that day? Whether you wish to speak of it or not, 'tis still hanging over your head, mind. Whatever happened, 'tis not resolved, and that is when the problem started."

Grant walked silently beside Wick. Finally he said, "Walk with me afore we go into the Hall. I must speak with you in private."

When Grant finished telling Wick about his volcanic reaction to Tory finding his childhood furniture, Wick shook his head remorsefully.

"You were wrong, lad." When Grant protested, Warwick stopped him. "Nay, son, dinnae try to justify to me. The secrets you try to keep are not worth the pain they are causing. I believe your young wife would handle your news well if you told her the truth. As it stands, you hurt her feelings with a reaction she cannot understand. What did you say?"

Running his fingers through his hair, Grant groaned as he frowned in thought. "I know not, Wick. I remember naught but the shock of seeing it again. I did not mean to be so abrupt, but I just wanted to be out of that room. I couldn't face it."

"You must speak with her about it."

"Nay!" Grant yelled as the implication of Wick's comment hit him full force. "I'll never tell that horrible truth."

"Och, man, you must speak with her. If you can do it without revealing all, then do so, but I dinnae know how you will manage that," he concluded.

" Wick," Grant groaned, "what am I to do?"

"The only thing you can. Speak with your wee wife. 'Tis not fair to leave things so unsettled. She thinks she did something wrong and you cannot let her continue to feel that way. 'Tis not right."

Grant nodded. "You are correct, of course, but it makes what I have to do next no easier."

From the sun's placement, he knew Tory would be resting, as she tired easily nowadays.

Opening the heavy door to their chamber, he held it ajar with his foot and maneuvered a cradle inside. He'd had it made for Tory and their bairn.

As the door creaked, Tory stirred. She stiffened when she saw Grant carrying a cradle – *that cradle*.

What did he have in mind now?

Grant edged his way to his massive bed and set the tiny cradle beside it before he lowered himself next to Tory. "Lady wife, we must speak." He cleared his throat in a bid to stall for time.

A mask settled over Tory's face. When he saw her steeling herself for the conversation, Grant felt painfully aware of the rift between them. He didn't fancy she thought she needed to conceal her feelings. He wanted her to feel safe and comfortable.

"What must we speak about?" she began frostily. "Indeed, I have naught to say. You made yourself quite clear that this is the cradle you intend to use." She turned away. "I do not need it in our room. Please take it to the nursery."

"Tory," he began, not knowing how to start. "I made a mistake that day...in my auld nursery. I ask you to forgive me, and—"

"I am tired, Grant," she interrupted in a weary voice. She fought an impulse to throw herself into his arms and have him comfort her. "I really fancy resting if you do not mind." Although it hadn't been her intent, her voice turned cold.

When she refused to face him, Grant reluctantly rose and carried the cradle through the adjoining door to their nursery. *Och, I made a muckle fine mess of things.* He didn't know how to undo the damage he'd caused.

Tory knew the instant Grant returned, but refused to acknowledge his presence. If she faced him, she'd burst into tears, and she had no intention of doing that.

Grant sighed and left without a word. He proceeded down to the Great Hall, but instead of stopping, he headed into the courtyard's bright sunlight and to the stables. Mayhap a brisk ride would stem his feelings of dread.

Warwick watched his chief depart the keep's front door. Based on the dark look on his face when he bolted through the Hall, Wick knew naught had been resolved.

Hoping not to regret his actions, he headed upstairs and knocked on Tory's door.

"Go away," came the muffled sounds from beyond the heavy wooden door.

He didn't think it an auspicious beginning.

He knocked again. When no answer proved forthcoming, he did something he'd never done before – entered his chief's chamber without an invitation. He only hoped Grant wouldn't beat him senseless when he found out.

Lying in bed, Tory had the covers pulled to her chin. Despite her resolve not to cry, she found herself unable to stop. Her emotions had a mind of their own nowadays. Hearing someone enter, she rolled over to face him, glaring all the while.

She looked totally taken aback when she saw Warwick standing there and not her husband.

Sitting up quickly, she clutched the covers around her tightly. "Wick!" she exclaimed, panic crossing her features. "Is Grant all right? Is someone injured?"

"I believe you are, my lady," Wick began, hoping he did the right thing. Though a tenuous situation, he felt he had no choice.

Stubbornly she told him, "I do not wish to talk, Wick." Instinctively she guessed what subject he planned to discuss.

"Then let me do the talking," Wick interjected quickly. "Something happened to you, my lady, and you've not yet recovered from it, yet speak of it to no one."

Tory tried to attain the same mask she wore for Grant, but in one unguarded moment Wick saw the pain she tried so hard to conceal.

"Nay lady," he quietly said. "Dinnae block me out. That may work with your young husband, but I'll not leave until we have spoken."

The censure in the kind man's tone surprised Tory.

Pursing her lips together, she tried to keep her voice level. "I have no idea what you're talking about, Wick. Naught is wrong. I am just tired."

Wick raised his eyebrows. "Och, 'tis glad I am to hear there is naught wrong." Grabbing her by the hand, he pulled her out of bed. "Then let us look at the cradle your husband just brought up here."

Tory tried to pull her hand away, but Wick held firm.

"I saw the cradle, Wick. I need not look at it again."

"I believe you do, lass." He tried to add a bit of levity. "I may be auld and ugly, but I am not witless." Sobering, he reluctantly added, "There are things you dinnae understand, and unfortunately I cannot speak of them. That is up to your husband. But, he dinnae purposely hurt you. There are things in his life that scarred him so badly he cannot speak of them."

"Then you tell me," she sulked.

This time Wick did chuckle. "Lady, you know us well enough by now to know we are feisty and opinionated." Tory rolled her eyes to agree with him and Wick continued, "But we are also loyal to each other, mind. You know I cannot tell you something your husband does not wish talked about."

"He made me tell him things I did not want to discuss," she grumbled in complaint.

"Och, aye, he did," Warwick assented and clasped her hand in reassurance. "And I agree he probably shouldn't have done so since he has secrets of his own. But he did, and there is naught I can do about that."

Tory pulled a face and thought it a losing battle to try and get this loyal, stubborn old man to tell her anything he didn't want to say. "You really wish to help me?" she shot at him.

"Aye."

"Then leave. Go out that door and leave me alone."

At the stubborn look on her face, Wick threw back his head and roared. Looking into her sad eyes, with a resigned sigh Wick stroked his chin and prodded gently, "Lass, do you really wish to hurt Grant?"

That angered Tory enough to make her sit on the bed's edge. "Hurt *him*? You must be jesting. I did naught to hurt him."

"Did you not?" Wick questioned, hoping she'd tell him what happened without having to actually ask.

"Nay. I only showed him some old furniture I wanted to use. Little did I know he thought so little of my baby he thought it not worthy enough to use his precious childhood furniture!" A sob escaped her lips.

"That's not what happened, lassie," Wick began, eyes wide as perception dawned.

"Do not tell me what did and did not happen," she yelled as the dam finally broke, releasing her emotions. "You were not there. I was, and I'll never forget it."

"Then tell me," Warwick urged in a calm, patient voice. "Tell me exactly what happened." He felt so close to discovering the truth.

Clenching her lips together, she almost bit through her top lip before she finally conceded.

"He yelled at me. I spent weeks cleaning that tiny furniture." She stopped and looked at Wick closely when he showed no reaction. She sounded calm, but looked shaken. "Ah, I see you know exactly which room I am talking about. I assume everyone knew about it except me?"

She asked the last as a question, but Wick chose not to answer.

"I sewed things to go with that lovely, little furniture. I foolishly thought Grant would be pleased to have his child use it. If anyone had cared enough about me to keep my baby things, I would have loved my child to use them, but I was not that fortunate. My father destroyed all my childhood items. Since I turned out to be such a big a mistake being a female, he did not want it to happen again." She strangled a sob.

"But was Grant pleased?" she yelled, unable to control her emotions. "Nay! He yelled and dragged me from the room. I am surprised he did not pull my arm from its socket," she added, and bitterly glowered at Wick.

Tears rolling down her cheeks, she slumped against the head of the bed. "He fancied naught. Not that I'd cleaned up his old furniture, nor that I made things to go with them. He refused to even let me return to get them."

Wick thought she'd say no more when she suddenly began again. "But the worst part..." she tried to say it, but couldn't continue. Her voice sounded flat, like she'd lost all hope.

Shaking her head, she turned away. "Never mind. It matters not. I do not wish to speak of it any more. 'Tis too painful. Please leave."

"Nay, lassie. Tell me what you think Grant said." Wick's voice sounded paternal. Placing his hand gently on her shoulder, he frowned with concern. Tory wished with all her heart she could throw herself in this gentle man's arms and weep.

She again tried to turn away, but Wick caught her chin and turned her to face him. "Now, lassie. Tell me." His voice sounded kind.

Soft whimpers emanated from the back of her throat and she looked helplessly at Wick. "He said no child of mine would ever use that furniture!"

When Warwick didn't react in the way she thought, her shoulders sagged. "Ah, so you already knew he did not want my babe." Her lips quivered in anguish.

Though shaken, she tried to keep her voice even. "Did everyone know but me? I am such a fool."

"Not want your bairn? Dinnae spout such nonsense," Warwick said sharply. "Och, lassie, of course Grant wants your bairn. That is not what he meant."

Firmly drawing her from the bed against her muffled protestations, Warwick pulled her toward the nursery. Lancelot plodded behind her, barking at her heels to get her attention. Too drained to protest further, she followed Warwick weakly. Kneeling by the cradle, Wick took her arm and brought Tory down next to him. He gently ran his battle hardened hands over the tiny bed's smooth wood.

"Look closely, lassie," Warwick insisted. "Really look at it."

When she refused, Warwick fixed her with a meaningful stare. "See the headboard's design? 'Tis the Drummond crest." His big, calloused hand enveloped hers.

"I figured it must be something like that," she said grudgingly.

"Would Grant put his crest on the cradle if he dinnae want your bairn?"

Tory shrugged her shoulders.

Wick thought she looked confused and broken. His heart went out to her and his hand stretched out to comfort her.

"Notice you the interlocking hearts weaving their way through the crest?"

Tory glanced at him to see what he meant.

Wick didn't watch her, but knew instinctively when she turned her head. He lovingly traced the two hearts. Intrigued, Tory watched his movements.

Aye, she could see the hearts. She hadn't noticed them before.

"These hearts represent you and Grant – the wee bairnie's parents. Did you know your husband designed this cradle?"

Tory shook her head.

"He sat up several nights drawing the pattern exactly the way he wanted it. Then took it to our carpenter to see if it would be difficult to make. He wanted it exactly like he sketched it, with no changes unless he approved them first." Slanting a glance at her he saw she'd turned to look at the bed.

Wick pressed his advantage.

"Och, lassie, if he really dinnae want your child, why go to so much trouble designing a cradle for your wee bairnie?"

Tory couldn't answer the question. She honestly didn't know. Glancing from Wick to the cradle and back again, she appeared totally confused.

"I know you have questions, lass," Wick began patiently as he watched the raw emotion that crossed her face, "but lest you allow your husband the chance to explain, you will never have answers.

"I assure you, our young chief wants your bairn. I cannot begin to tell you how excited he is. Och, you should hear him talking about plans he has for the future." Seeing the look of confusion on Tory's face, Warwick said, "I'll leave you alone to think things through. I suggest you not toss your husband out the next time he tries to talk with you."

Grant returned from his ride to find Warwick pacing back and forth waiting to meet him. Joining him enroute to the Great Hall, Warwick suggested, "Head back to your solar to speak with Lady Tory." Without admitting what he'd done, Warwick intimated, "She might listen now."

"What did you after I left, Wick?" When he received no immediate answer, irritation surged through Grant. "I told you I'd not tell her everything. Did you--?"

"Nay, I revealed naught," came the quick assurance, "but I did interfere a bit." The embarrassed smile on Wick's face did nothing to reassure Grant.

"Go up the stairs, son. Talk with her and be as honest as you can." When Grant looked unconvinced, the wise old man continued, "The lassie needs you. She thinks you dinnae want her bairn."

"Of course I want my bairn!"

Wick sadly nodded. "*I* know that. You dinnae have to convince me, but you do need to convince your lady. But before you leave, listen closely to what I said."

When Grant looked like he didn't understand, his mentor repeated, "The lassie thinks you dinnae want *her* bairn. Think closely on what you said the day she grew upset and you will have your answer."

Grant frowned, not comprehending what Wick meant, but knew he had the right of it. Rapidly mounting the steps, he needed to speak with Tory.

Slowly opening the door, he poked his head inside his chamber and looked around. No projectiles flew at his head. *Och, 'tis a promising start.*

"Sweeting," Grant began, and advanced a single step into the room, "are you feeling any better?"

"I feel fine," she said in a defeated voice. "Just tired."

Tired of these thoughts, she thought inwardly. *If only I could believe whatever Wick tried to tell me earlier.*

When she sat up and started to rise, Grant strode over and

stopped her progress. Though he firmly held her arm, his touch remained gentle. "Stay where you are, Sweeting. We must talk."

She sighed and her face paled with the strain of trying to keep her emotions in tact. "We have talked, and I really do not want to do so anymore. 'Twill accomplish naught."

The disillusionment her voice conveyed tore at Grant's heart.

"Let us go downstairs," she said dejectedly.

"Nay, Sweeting," Grant said stubbornly. He wanted to settle things once and for all. "This is important. I did a lot of thinking this day and I must know why you do not fancy the cradle I had made."

Tory eyed him warily. Dare she answer truthfully?

Deciding on honesty, she plunged ahead with her answer. "'Tis beautiful, Grant. Truly, but I do not understand why you'd not let me use your childhood cradle."

She lowered her eyes to look at her hands. She couldn't face him as she asked the most important question. "And...and if you really do not want my baby, why keep me here? Why did you not let me remain at the market faire?"

Swallowing slowly, Grant took her hands tenderly within his own. "My heart, this will not be an easy discussion. Pray listen closely – and pay attention this time. Do not do what you usually do and hear what you think I am saying rather than what I am."

"I do not—" she started as her eyes rose abruptly to meet his.

"Aye, Sweeting, you do. I cannot tell you everything. I simply cannot." She frowned at his words, but he proceeded nevertheless. "There is more involved here than me. I needs ask you to trust me."

When Tory scowled, Grant continued, "Och, Sweeting, take that dismal look off your face. 'Tis more than I can bear. I do not want you in that room because I do not want *anyone* in there again – ever. It had naught to do with you. I should have burned that furniture long ago, but I...have not. I avoided it."

"But why—"

"Nay, my heart, that is part of what I cannot tell you. I am sorry."

"You made me tell you everything," she retorted, hurt apparent in her eyes.

"Och, aye, I did." Grant smiled and met her gaze levelly. "I knew you'd get around to that comparison."

He'd always been sure of himself, but the pain he caused her now made him begin to doubt himself. He didn't like that feeling.

"I made the cradle especial for you, Sweeting. I hoped you would fancy it for our bairn." Gazing at her dejectedly, he added, "But you do not."

He paused and waited for her to say something.

Looking at him with a curious expression, she suddenly blurted what she'd kept pent inside for so long. "You said my baby was not good enough to use your old cradle!"

Stunned, Grant moved closer. "I never said such a thing!"

"You did," she affirmed as tears welled in her eyes.

Taken aback and trying to keep the edge from his voice, Grant levelly asked, "Exactly what do you think I said?"

Her lower lip quivering, she responded with resignation. "I do not *think* you said it. I know you did. You dragged me from the room and told me no child of mine would ever use any of that furniture."

Grant's eyes widened with clear understanding of her misperception.

In agitation she rushed on, "And you locked the door! I spent weeks making things for our baby and had everything in that room for you to see. I thought you would like them, but when I tried to go back to fetchthem, you said you wanted naught in that room."

She lost control and tears finally fell, her voice rising dismally. "I do not understand you, Grant Drummond! One minute you act like you want my baby and the next you turn around and tell me 'tis not good enough to even use your old furniture."

Grant pulled her into his arms. His eyes warm with love, he soothed her as her tears fell. "*Mo Chridhe*, I am sorry I hurt your feelings. That may be what I said, but 'tis not what I meant. I never would have said something to hurt you so."

He could tell she didn't believe a word he said.

"I meant your bairn – our bairn – is so special I would not allow it to use that auld furniture. That is because of my personal feelings about the furniture. I never meant our bairn was not good enough." Grant ached with the knowledge he'd hurt her.

"Blessed Saint Michael, Sweeting, I am thrilled you are having my bairn. I would never have purposefully hurt you. I swear." Grant tilted her face up so he could look into her wet eyes. "I designed the new cradle, myself, Sweeting. I wanted it to be special for you – for *our bairn*." He rained kisses lightly on her forehead while feeling annoyed at not having figured out what bothered her. All the pain she endured could have been avoided.

Before she could say anything, Grant swept her into his arms and held her.

"No wonder you've been so sad. Saints knees, woman, you really thought I do not want our bairn?"

She nodded against his chest.

"I am sorry, lady mine. I never imagined you took my words that way," he mumbled against her hair. "Och, my heart, pray forgive me?" He held his breath until she answered.

She smiled wanly. "Truly, Grant? You really want my baby?"

Grant grimaced and shook his head that she continued to doubt him. He told her repeatedly when he said something he meant it, but she couldn't seem to believe that. Under the circumstances, he wouldn't fuss overmuch this time. In her fragile condition, she needed his assurances, not chastisements.

"Aye, my heart," he lovingly stroked her back and bent to kiss the nape of her neck. "I want this bairn." He moved her away and placed his hand gently on her belly, then pressed her palm to his mouth.

The look of trust in her large brown eyes took his breath away. He didn't deserve this woman.

Grant led her into the nursery and explained the cradle's intricate design. Tory reached to rock it and Grant instinctively stopped her. Seeing her startled look, he explained, "A cradle should never be rocked whilst empty – before or after birth. Highlanders believe 'twill bring bad luck if rocked without the bairn in it."

After all the weeks of tortured emotions, a feeling of deep contentment settled over Tory. It felt wonderful.

She peered closely at Grant's handsome, tanned face. "I am sorry I jumped to conclusions, Grant. 'Tis that…I am so used to not being wanted. 'Tis difficult to let go of memories."

Grant pulled her gently into his arms and said with great tenderness, "Mayhap we needs make new memories for you, my heart. And we will do that – starting now. The past is gone. No more looking back." He lowered his head to kiss her.

She pulled back from his embrace and gazed into his eyes. It seemed as though she tried to read the truth there. If she did, she seemed well pleased with what she saw. She threw her arms around his neck and kissed him soundly.

"Thank you, Grant. Thank you for that."

With a smile that stopped his heart, Tory timidly told him, "Hopefully some day you will feel you can trust me enough to tell me everything."

"I do trust you, lady wife. Truly. But there are things I speak of to no one."

Tory nodded and snuggled beside him while he nuzzled her neck. His hands soothed her back as he moved them in a caressing motion. Mollified for the present, she determined to let the subject drop. Someday she'd get him to tell all. She knew that for a certainty.

Soon she fell asleep, cuddled against him.

Chapter Thirty

Tory could scarcely stand the thought of it. Her first Yuletide in her own home! She had such delightful plans in store for decorating. She always enjoyed this time of year because her grandmum made it special for her, but this year would be extra special.

As she paced before the hearth, she waited impatiently for Grant to return from his trip outside. In her excitement she gave up waiting, bundled up in her heavy cape, and went outside to cut ferns. She wanted to decorate the entire castle, not just the Great Hall. She wanted the entire place to be festive.

The winds were fierce, but they always were in the Highlands, she thought with a chuckle. 'Twas one of many things she'd had to adjust to.

Tory headed toward the tall, snow-covered mountains and gazed in wonder at the white expanse ahead of her. She saw Ben Chonzie to the north and Ben Vorlich to the west. Both mountains rose majestically toward the heavens. She was glad Grant finally started to teach her names of nearby mountains, since she wanted to know everything about her new home. She wished her grandmum and sister could see the breathtaking mountains.

Finally deciding she had all the ferns she could carry, she trudged through the snow back to the keep. The temperature plunged rapidly and she fought to suppress a shiver. She'd had to adjust to the freezing temperatures in the Highlands, too. Although cold in England, it never seemed to get quite this cold! In an effort to quicken her pace to return to the keep's warmth, she lost her footing and sprawled in the snow. Fortunately she found it soft and fluffy and it cushioned most of the blow, so she felt certain she hadn't hurt herself or the baby. Grant would lecture her about being outside on her own in her condition. He did seem to worry overmuch. She just needed to be more careful when outside. Her belly was beginning to grow now, and she didn't seem to be as graceful as usual since becoming with child. Mayhap she'd be lucky enough to return before Grant and he wouldn't see her covered with snow. In case he did, she brushed off as much snow as possible.

Pushing open the heavy door, Tory saw she wouldn't be that fortunate since the bloody man stood before the great stone hearth warming his body.

When he saw her enter the Hall, he immediately strode over and divested her of the branches.

"Woman," he boomed loudly, "what have you been up to now?" He dropped the branches on the floor and turned her around to look at her. Her eyelashes were tipped with flakes of snow and her cheeks were ruddy from the cold. She looked beautiful. "You fell again." His arched brow indicated she best answer truthfully.

"I just slipped a wee bit in the snow," she said, trying to make light of the situation by using one of his favorite Scottish words to divert his attention. It didn't work. He ignored her attempt at humor and glared.

Tory frowned at her unsuccessful attempt. Why did he have to be so stubborn and set in his ideas?

She shook the snow from her heavy winter cape and proceeded to hang it on a peg beside the door. 'Twas the one her grandmum had given her last Christmas, and Grant brought it when he returned with her beloved horse. Grandmum had remembered to send it with him. Ever thoughtful, Tory knew it was only one of many reasons she loved her grandmother so much.

Swinging around to face him, she bubbled, "Grant I have the most wonderful idea. The Germans have this marvelous tradition of decorating their homes with trees during Christmastide."

He probably wouldn't fancy the remainder of what she had to say. Knowing his lovely wife, he had no doubt it involved work!

When he didn't comment, she rushed on, "Could we cut down one of our trees and place it in our Hall? Oh Grant please, 'twould look divine."

She looked so excited and childlike, Grant didn't have the heart to tell her he saw no purpose in cutting a perfectly good tree. However, his curiosity got the best of him. "And why would you think a tree would look good *inside* our Hall? God meant trees to grow outside."

"We would not grow it inside, you dolt," she giggled. "We'd go outside and pick out the most perfect tree and cut it down." When Grant quirked his brows, she quickly added, "And then we would fetch it inside to decoratc."

"Decorate?" Grant choked out. In his mind's eye he had visions of faeries prancing around his Hall.

"You will not have to do any decorating. The children and I will do it all. I promise."

Waving his arm to the pile of branches on the floor, Grant queried, "Would not this be enough to decorate? We need not go overboard, you know. Christmas is not special in the Highlands, and I vow I cannot imagine the purpose of having a tree inside my home."

"Oh," she said in a subdued voice, the excited light fading from her eyes, "of course. I'll make it be enough. I am sorry I mentioned it."

She walked to the hearth to warm up and struggled to contain her disappointment.

Grant felt like a heel. He couldn't deprive her of something so simple as a tree, although for the life of him he couldn't imagine what she planned to do with it. She'd finally blossomed in his home, and he had no intention of letting her remember her unhappy days as a child. She appeared as a gentle flower blossoming into full bloom. It had been a joy watching this transformation, and he didn't plan to let her wither now over so simple a request. Following her to the hearth and wrapping his arms around her, he pulled her close. "You really want a *tree*?"

As he lightly brushed her face with the backs of his fingers, she said, "Nay, husband, 'twas a daft idea. I just thought we could do something my grandmum did after Grandpapa saw such a tree in Germany. After he told her about it, we had one every year. I never saw one any place besides our home. But dinnae fash yourself about it. I'll decorate with other items – mayhap branches and berries." Disappointment flooded her face although she tried to conceal her true feelings.

Grant flung back his head and roared. "Woman, realize you what you said?" At Tory's blank expression he informed her, "You said, 'dinnae fash yourself.' I knew we'd make a Scotswoman out of you in time!"

He placed his arms around her swelling body, picked her up, and swung her around. She no longer grumbled about him picking her up like she had when they first met. Since he always ignored her mumblings, she saw no purpose in dissenting.

"For that," Grant teased lovingly, "you'll get your bloody tree and anything else you want." He lowered her gently and placed a tender kiss on the tip of her blushing nose.

Bright and early the next day Tory paced impatiently in the Hall, her face flushed with excitement. After they broke their fast,

Grant promised they'd search for a tree right after the morning post, should a courier arrive. One by one, children began to arrive in the Hall, bundled up for freezing weather. She'd promised they could all help select the tree. They were as excited as she, even though they had no idea what she had in mind. When Grant entered the Hall, he stomped his boots to dislodge the snow.

"Saints feet, woman, 'tis cold out there," Grant greeted. "Are you positive you wish to go outside? I do not believe you should do so in your condition."

"Grant," she said in exasperation, "women have had babies for centuries, and I am quite certain their husbands did not make them remain inside. I'll be fine." She gave him a brilliant smile and said cheerfully, "Now let us go, while the sun is out a spell. You know how early it grows dark."

Glancing around at the mass of gathered children, Grant questioned in amazement, "And all these we'ans are going on our trek?"

Tory nodded, her happiness this morn radiating from within. "Of course. You'd not want the momentous decision of selecting the perfect tree to fall on one person, would you?"

Grant shook his head even though he had no earthly idea what his wee wife meant. Of course one person could decide on a tree. A tree was, after all, just that – a tree. Nevertheless, he enfolded her gloved hand in his and led the procession out the door. By the time they reached an area Tory deemed satisfactory for a brief respite, several men had also joined them. As he scanned the snow-covered hillside, several women trailed behind their husbands.

Blessed St. Columba, would everybody be joining them? How many people had his lady wife told of this tradition? From the looks of it, his entire keep would soon be present. Passing by leafless trees, they trudged through snow for what felt like hours. It just seemed like forever since it was so bloody cold.

The air felt crisp and clean as they tramped through the woods.

Unable to find a tree she seemed pleased with, Tory gathered nuts and berries en-route. Grant assumed they were for his evening meal. When he decided Tory should return to the Hall's warmth, she burst out, "There 'tis. That is the one. Oh, Grant, 'tis perfect. Can we have that one?"

By then Grant would have willingly chopped down any tree, scrawny or large, to return to his hearth's warmth. As he approached it, Tory stayed his arm. He frowned. "What is wrong? I though you said that is the bonny tree you want."

"Because the tree will belong to everyone, husband. Quit frowning. I believe we all must agree on it, and I failed to ask anyone what they thought before I blurted that out." She faced the children and asked, "What think you? Do you fancy this one?" They all jumped up and down and circled the tree. *Oohs* and *aahs* were heard from many tiny voices. Since all agreed the tree looked pretty, Tory turned to the women. "And you? Do you fancy this tree, or should we find a different one?"

The women seemed taken aback that their lady would even deign to ask them. No one ever asked their opinion about something as simple as decorations before. Amazed, they all murmured 'twould be perfect. They also admitted silently they had no idea what the perfect tree looked like, but no one thought to point that out to Tory.

"Then we will all have the most wonderful time decorating it. You will see, Grant," she beamed, unable to contain herself any longer, "'twill be the loveliest tree ever."

"May we begin cutting now, wife?" Grant feigned exasperation, yet smiled and shook his head. Not even his dear sweet mother, God rest her soul, had been this concerned about what people living in her keep thought of something as simple as decorations. He could see Tory's concern pleased his people well.

Tory nodded her agreement.

"Then all you women and bairns need move out of the way," Grant said firmly. "Head over there." He pointed to an area well away from where the chosen tree would land.

It didn't take long to fell the tree with several men taking turns chopping. Soon the entire group trudged back to the keep, laughing and singing as sunlight shimmered off the snow. Grant couldn't remember the last time he'd had so much fun doing nothing productive. He hoped Tory wouldn't be too disappointed if her great tree didn't turn out as she envisioned.

On the way back, Tory stopped to gather holly, since she wanted to place it around the keep. Grant walked with his arm firmly around her waist and looked into the basket she carried on her arm.

"Sweeting," Grant said suddenly, as if an important thought had struck him, "you are bringing a few new traditions into our home." Tory looked up quickly with a hint of doubt in her eyes, but

Grant assured her, "That is fine, but would you also fancy learning some of our traditions?"

"I would love to," she quickly assured and wove her arm through the crook in his.

"Good. Our bairnies should learn from both of us." Reaching into her basket, he pulled out a sprig of holly. "Do you know about holly?"

"Of course," she assured with a smile. "The red berries signify the blood of Christ."

"Aye, 'tis so, but one tradition we do keep is to place holly leaves and branches around our homes. 'Tis done in a kindly and hospitable fashion, that." He elaborated when he saw she didn't understand. "So the wee fairies that live in our forest can come inside our homes and use the holly for shelter against the cold."

"Ooooh, 'tis delightful. I'll gladly continue that tradition."

"Of course," Grant continued and tried to keep a serious look on his face while laughter danced in his eyes, "in some of our homes women hang holly to ward off mischievous fairies."

Tory tried to conceal her smile.

"Druids thought holly's evergreen nature made it special," Grant continued thoughtfully.

"Why?" she questioned and lost her balance as she misstepped in the deep snow.

"For protection." Grant quickly caught her and brought her body close. He stroked her back through her cape as they trudged back through the snow, not commenting on her near fall. "They used it to decorate their windows and doors in hopes 'twould stop evil spirits from entering their homes."

"Will we use it for that, too?" she questioned, a smile on her face.

"Well," Grant said, almost shamefacedly, "there is no harm in using any extra help we can get."

Shrugging lightly, she looked pensive. "Then I believe we shall need to make several more trips to gather holly. This wee basket could not possibly hold enough for all those uses." She smiled and placed her gloved hand within his as they headed home.

The solitude she felt her whole life seemed to be dropping away, as if a weight had been lifted from her shoulders. Loneliness no longer seemed such a burdensome weight around her.

For the first time in her life she felt content, and Grant saw it on her face.

Tory stuck her tongue out to capture snowflakes. The bolt of lust that shot through Grant made him nearly stumble. He wanted more than the taste of snowflakes right then. He wanted all of her.

By the time they got back to the keep, 'twas well past the nooning meal. Everyone quickly ate, and although Tory wanted to put the tree up immediately, Grant thought her too tired.

"Nay, I insist you take a wee kip. You have plenty of time to decorate, lady mine. You need not do it all in one day. Rest." Brooking no argument, he scooped her up, stepped over her sleeping pup, and purposefully headed upstairs to their chamber with her nestling in the comfort of his strong arms.

Tory hated that she tired so easily, but the other women told her it a perfectly natural side effect of breeding.

Since he still harbored thoughts of bedding her, Grant left the room so she could rest. He closed the door quietly behind him. More exhausted than she'd thought, Tory didn't rise until almost time for the evening meal.

While she dressed, Grant walked into the room. "A messenger has arrived. If you do not mind, I fancy inviting William Wallace to spend Yuletide with us."

Since his wife's murder, Will was a hunted man, and rarely had a place to rest his head. After the problems during Will's last visit, Grant wished to make certain 'twould be all right to invite him. He didn't want anything to spoil this special time for Tory.

Shaking her fears aside, she assured him, "'Twill be fine."

"I also fancy sending an invitation to Duncan."

"I would be delighted to have Duncan for as long as he can stay." Her eyes lit up in delight.

Smiling, he walked over, gave her a hug and patted her vastly expanding belly. "Just think, Sweeting, this time next year we will have a bairnie getting into all your Christmastide decorations. Then you shall truly have your hands full." He smiled and realized such a thought pleased him immensely. He chuckled as he headed to send dispatches to two of the people closest to his heart.

Tory thought it odd Grant wanted to invite Duncan for the holidays. She'd assumed the handsome young man would spend the time with his family, but since she enjoyed his company so much she made no comment about it to Grant.

Over the next days everyone busily helped Tory decorate the castle. Grant felt certain at the rate she was going she'd soon decide to decorate everything—including the guarderobe! The activity level in his keep seemed at an all time high, yet no one seemed to mind. It seemed it had become everyone's personal goal to ensure their lady had a wonderful Christmastide.

And the tree! Grant couldn't believe how well it was turning out. Never in his mind's eye could he have envisioned what it would look like. In all his travels, he'd never seen such a tree. He was glad his wee wife had heard of the custom. Marveling at all she'd done, he decided 'twas one tradition he rather fancied.

Or at least he thought so until he paused at the threshold to the Great Hall and saw his breeding wife attempting to climb atop a table to decorate the top portion of the tree!

He angrily strode inside his Hall. With one strong swoop of his arm, he caught her around her expanding belly and swung her off the table.

Tory shrieked.

"Heaven forfend, wife, if ever I see you climbing on anything again, I'll warm your tempting bum." She started to protest, but he interrupted. "Nay, wife, do not try telling me you were fine on yon table. You are not the most graceful person even when you do not have a growing belly to throw you off balance."

He shuddered at the thought of her being injured.

"But, milord..." she protested sharply, inhaling his familiar masculine scent as he held her close. How dare he call her ungraceful? She grumbled and thought she just tended to be a little accident-prone right now.

"But 'm'lord' naught, and quit scowling," Grant fussed. "You will do no more climbing, and that is the end of it." He glanced towards the offending tree and saw the problem. The bottom half where the children had helped looked lovely, yet the top was totally empty. Grant scratched his chin and tried to cover his mouth so Tory wouldn't see his grin. He didn't want to hurt her feelings. "Need you a bit of help with the tree, Sweeting?"

He pulled her into his arms and gently rubbed his hands up and down her back as she nodded. Feeling his laughter, she pulled away and shot him an aggrieved look. "Aye, but I told you we would decorate it by ourselves."

"But if I offer, 'tis not the same as having to help," Grant affirmed. "I think myself and a few other men could finish it quickly. Considering several wives are breeding, I misdoubt too many men would want them climbing. We will place your decorations and you can do the directing. Does that sound satisfactory?"

Tory's eyes glistened with joy as she looked at the tree and nodded her thanks. Going on tiptoe, she brought his head down so she could kiss him and show how much his offer meant.

Within the hour the tree was fully decorated. Grant hadn't expected so many women to take such pleasure in directing their husbands on exactly where this berry or that nut should be placed. Women were certainly peculiar. He decided they took this directing entirely too personally since they happily yelled directions from every angle.

With the mood in his keep lighthearted, he wouldn't change a thing. He glanced around and decided he couldn't tell which woman had the biggest smile on her face. And the children glowed. He couldn't remember the last time his people looked this happy.

And he attributed it all to Tory.

The next day, Grant thought everything that possibly could be decorated had been, when Tory asked, "Can we get the Yule log soon?"

"I cannot believe I forgot it. Da and I always got it for Mam. She, too, loved the Yule log celebration. She always kept remains from the last year's log safely wrapped for use with the new one."

Duncan arrived before the nooning hour, pleasing Grant that he'd arrived early. Grant grabbed Tory's hand as she walked past him and pulled her toward the bustling courtyard. "Come, Sweeting. Let us greet our guests together."

As always when she'd been in the kitchen too long, Tory had flour on the tip of her nose. Grant smiled as he lightly brushed it off. She'd been there most of the morn helping Cook prepare for Duncan's visit.

The afternoon remained bright and clear – and very, very cold. Grant grabbed the cape her grandmother had given her from the peg beside the door and wrapped it tightly around Tory before they stepped outside.

Grant hailed Duncan as he and his companions dismounted. "Well-come, Duncan. We are pleased to have you visit. As always, your rooms are ready. Come inside and warm yourself by the hearth. I am sure you must be fair frozen after your journey." He and Duncan clapped their arms around each other.

Rather than his full escort, Tory saw he only had three men with him. She'd had scant time to prepare for his visit and wondered if she could handle a full keep of guests. She noticed with pleasure that Erwin wasn't among the three companions.

Duncan turned and bowed formally to Tory. A fine dusting of snow fell on the hood of her cape as well as the tips of her eyelashes. She looked as lovely as he remembered.

"Good day, my lady. I hope your auld reprobate of a husband is taking good care of you." Eyes as blue as the sky traveled down to her expanding belly. He chuckled, "I see he is taking good care of himself!" Slapping his hand on Grant's back, Duncan grinned and his eyes danced in merriment. "Congratulations."

Turning back to Tory while they walked into the keep, he queried, "When will the bairn be born?"

Although he knew about the babe from Grant, he couldn't believe how long it had been since his last visit. To him Drummond Castle seemed like home.

"Around April, I believe," she answered, clearly flushed both by the cold and the attention Duncan paid her belly. The subtle play of sunlight glancing off the snow enhanced the glow on her face.

Duncan thought Grant indeed the luckiest of men.

Duncan again slapped Grant. "Good job. Planted your seed right after the night you claimed the lass, eh?"

Tory blushed clear to her toes at his forthright discussion, and Grant pulled her close in an attempt to buffer her from Duncan's good-natured ribbing.

They walked into the Hall, and Grant denied, "I never claimed Tory."

Duncan waved his hand and cut off Grant's efforts. "Nay, do not waste your breath. I knew that night the lass had not been your wife afore you claimed her in yon Hall."

"Then why--?" Grant's brow furrowed.

"Because I knew for you to make such a claim, you wanted the lassie yourself." He looked affectionately at Tory and continued with a wolfish grin, "Whilst I would dearly have loved the wee thing in my own bed that night, for you to make such a statement after cutting yourself off from everyone after what happened to Maeri, I knew I had to back off."

"But--"

"Nay, you great lummox. Do not apologize nor attempt to give me some cockamamie story. I knew she was not your wife, and that is the end of it."

Grant quickly grew annoyed. "How?"

"Forget you we all saw this lovely lassie bustling about trying to clean and set everything in order when we first arrived?" At

Grant's upraised eyebrows, he continued, "Now whilst I agree most good chatelaines would do that, most would not do it dressed in the most hideous kirtle I have ever seen!"

Duncan couldn't contain his laughter.

"Nor would any man of our ranking have his own wife dressed as a serving lass to play a joke on a guest." At this point Grant had the grace to blush, his eyes quickly shifting to Tory to see how she took this news.

She frowned at him.

Seeing the look on Tory's face and Grant's consternation, Duncan chuckled. "Looks like you're in need of some help here, friend."

"Help?" Grant retorted with a huff. "You have been in my home less than a notche on the sundial and already everything is turned tapsal-teerie. Pray do not help me anymore or my lady wife may turn violent on me."

To Grant's vast relief, Cook informed them the nooning meal could now be served. Grant escorted Tory to the table and seated her between himself and his guest.

Duncan looked at Tory a long time before he commented. "You look happy, my lady. I am pleased to see that. I have but one question, although I hesitate to bring up a sore subject."

Tory smiled. "Indeed, I am happy. You may ask anything you want."

The depth of feeling Duncan saw in her eyes confirmed she meant it. He grinned his most endearing smile. "The night my good friend claimed you, did you know then you were wed to the rogue after he did that?"

Though he tried to keep his tone of voice light, Tory heard the undercurrent of concern. Her face flushed with the memory, she lowered her eyes and shook her head, wishing to quickly allay his concerns. "Nay, I thought we pretended. It came as quite a shock when I discovered the truth. And nay, I did not fancy the idea at the time. I am sorry we deceived you."

"But that changed?"

Tory smiled. "Aye, it has. I am quite happy." She glimpsed at Grant. "I am glad my husband had the foresight to *claim* me." She jabbed her elbow in Grant's side and caused him to choke on his food.

Duncan laughed heartily, and the meal continued in pleasant rapport. While they ate, he glanced around the Hall, and suddenly noticed the decorated tree. Looking at Tory, he cocked a brow.

Grant interjected after he saw where the man's eyes wandered, "Aye, there have been many changes. The tree is the least of them. My lady has quite impacted our home."

Again directing his attention to Tory, Duncan asked, "Is that one of those German trees I heard of in my travels?"

"Aye, 'tis a tannenbaum. A Christmas tree," she clarified.

"'Tis lovely. The whole castle is lovely, but not as much as the lady of the keep." Duncan simply couldn't stop himself from flirting. He saw Grant's immediate frown. "I am not making a move on your wife, but you must admit she is charming. And the bloom of her breeding only makes her more so. I envy you."

Grant believed the praise most sincere. After their meal Grant and Duncan wandered around the keep and reminisced.

Chapter Thirty-one

While the two men gathered the Yule log with help from Lindsay and Adam, Tory headed upstairs to rest per her stubborn husband's insistence.

Grant soon spotted mistletoe on a nearby Oak tree. His wee wife hadn't mentioned this. He certainly didn't plan to let the celebration pass without mistletoe in his Hall – not when he had a lovely young wife to use it on. Hadn't she had it growing up? If not, he planned to make certain she knew of the ritual now.

Duncan teased, "Do you really need mistletoe as an excuse to kiss the wee lass?"

Grant shot him a glare, and Duncan chuckled good-naturedly. "It seems you already kiss her whenever you get the chance."

Stomping their boots as they returned to the Hall's warmth, they carried the log to the hearth. The four men struggled beneath its weight, and Grant was glad he and Duncan had taken their two strapping companions with them. Grant never understood why the log always had to be from the largest trees. He headed back to the doorway and pegged up a bunch of the mistletoe.

Tory descended the stairs at the same time the men arrived and hurried over to Grant to kiss his cheek.

"Och, aye, so you do know the story," he smiled and pulled her close to return her kiss.

Tory looked at him like he'd gone daft.

"What are you talking about? I am happy you are back with the decorations."

"Och," Grant sighed happily, "in that case, come here." He pulled her fully into his arms and kissed her soundly under the mistletoe. He couldn't resist casting a teasing glance at Duncan over her head.

Pulling him with her toward the hearth, Tory thanked him for fetching in the Yule log. "'Tis perfect," she exclaimed happily. "Let us—"

"Let us sit and rest," Grant cut in, smiling at his exuberant wife. "You may have rested whilst we gathered your Yule decorations, but we were outside working our fingers to the bone and freezing our bums." He playfully pulled Tory toward the chairs before the great hearth. He pulled her into his lap and kissed her again. Looking up, she saw he held a plant over her head. He pulled a berry off it and popped it in his mouth.

She quickly grabbed them out of his hands. "What are these? The white berries are edible?"

Grant quickly pulled the plant away before she had the chance to pluck one and place it in her mouth. "'Tis mistletoe. Did you not have it in your home?" He frowned when she shook her head, thinking that strange. He thought everyone had heard of mistletoe. "In Celtic, mistletoe means All Heal."

"What does it do? Should I stock it in my herbary?" Her eyes grew wide with excitement. Here was a plant she didn't know about.

"Mistletoe dates back to the Druids. They claimed it had all sorts of healing properties. And, aye, my mam kept it in her herbary. She, as well as the Druids, believed it held power for healing many diseases. They also used it for banning evil spirits. I believe Agnes used dried mistletoe on you when you were poisoned."

"A plant that can do everything?" Tory chuckled, doubt evident in her voice.

"Druids believed that. Now 'tis used more for good luck and blessings. And as long as there are berries on the plant, I may kiss you as oft as I want." When she crinkled her brows, his eyes twinkled. "For each kiss I steal I must pluck a berry from the plant. I can kiss you as long as berries remain."

"And when they run out?"

"Och, then I fetch another plant, of course," Grant teased right back, hugging her and drawing her closer for another kiss.

When he finished kissing her, he plucked another berry. "In aulden days, mistletoe was believed so sacred that if enemies chanced upon each other under it in the forest, they'd lay down their arms, exchange greetings, and keep a truce until the following day." Laughing ruefully, he added, "Can you see Edward doing that?"

Tory grinned and shook her head. "Do you still believe that?"

"I've learned not to discount auld ways. Whilst I do not use mistletoe merely for luck and blessings – and to be able to kiss beautiful women under it," he added as he playfully kissed the tip of her nose, "we do keep some auld customs – one in particular."

"Which is?"

"You cannot laugh," Grant growled and pretended to look fierce.

Tory looked up at him tenderly. "I would never ridicule your beliefs, Grant. I may not agree with them all, but I would never make fun of them. Tell me." He heard the love in her voice.

He nodded. "We give a sprig of mistletoe to the first calf born after Hogmanay every year – the New Year. We believe this will protect our entire herd throughout the year." Regardless of what she'd said earlier, Grant expected her to laugh.

She didn't. Instead, she snuggled in his arms and leaned against him. "'Tis a wonderful story. You must share that with our children as they're growing up." She wanted them to learn things from both of them and rejoiced Grant let her bring a few of her own traditions. She'd been afraid he wouldn't.

She saw they were creating their own memories. Grant let her have the tree, even though he had no idea what she'd been talking about at first mention. He'd finally admitted his doubt one night after they'd made love. That meant so much to her she couldn't begin to explain her feelings. Looking at the tree now, she knew she'd have one every Christmastide. She realized she felt happier than she'd ever been in her life. If only her grandmum and sister could be here.

After dinner, everyone gathered around the hearth. The room's fragrance combined the scent of peat and pine. Tory bent to retrieve a branch and extended it into the fire, then turned and handed it to Grant to light the Yule log.

"Nay!" came a collective gasp.

Looking at horrified faces, Tory glanced at Grant to find out what she'd done wrong. "Do you not light the log? I assumed 'twould be the lord's honor."

Grant quickly moved to his wife's side, removed the burning branch from her hands and threw it back into the hearth. He turned her to face him. "This is one of those traditions I've not told you about yet, Sweeting, but it holds a special place in our hearts. One reason Yule logs are burnt is to keep demons away from our homes, and every home in the Highlands will light them in the same fashion this night to ensure that."

"Demons?"

"Aye. Cinders from the log protect our homes from lightning and Satan's malevolent powers."

"How can you light the log if you do not use fire?"

Grant smiled at her innocence. "We do use fire, but we do it the same way every year. We light it on the eve of the Winter Solstice. That is this night, mind, but we must light it with the remains of last year's log. 'Twill bring us good luck."

He continued patiently, "Since the log must burn for half a day, someone will stay up all night to ensure it does not burn out. Then, when this season is over, we will wrap up a part of this year's log to use next year. We've done this my entire life."

Grant looked around the room. "We all have." Everyone nodded their affirmation. "The tradition started with the Vikings."

"I knew that," she responded, "but how does that relate to-?"

"Vikings held a festival to celebrate their beliefs in their many gods' powers. They burned the log to honor them and have good luck during the coming year."

Tory nodded her understanding.

"The father of Norse gods is Odin, or Thor as they sometimes call him. He's also the Yule Father, since Yule refers to the sun. The first Yule log ceremony celebrated the sun during the Winter Solstice, which is why we celebrate it this day instead of when the English do. I think *they* switched their celebration to the eve of Christmas around two hundred or so years ago." Grant said this with a hint of disgust over such a sacred event being changed.

Tory looked amazed. "I thought the log was just for decoration." Of a sudden a thought sprang to her mind. "And you know where last year's log is?"

"Of course," Grant nodded sagely. "'Tis not something we would forget." He left the room and returned, unwrapping the remnant. Kneeling, he bent to place holly beneath the log. He looked back over his shoulder. "This will kindle the fire."

As he stood, Grant sprinkled the tree trunk with oil, salt, and mulled wine which Warwick handed to him. Solemnly Grant asked God's blessings upon his house and all those within his care for the upcoming year.

When the ceremony ended, he took the remnant and set it ablaze. He used it to light the new log, and a raucous cheer resounded around the room.

He took Tory's hand, pulled her close, and handed her a sprig of holly. "Toss it into the fire."

"Why?"

"We do that to burn up the past year's troubles."

At first she eyed him warily. Then, thinking of all the sad events in her life, she willingly threw the sprig into the blaze.

Others moved forward to toss their holly into the fire as well.

Warwick added, "And 'twill keep our homes safe from burning down next year, aye."

Settling into comfortable silence, everyone wandered in different directions while Grant and Duncan relaxed in chairs before the hearth, their legs comfortably stretched in front of them.

Tory walked over to the door and held it ajar. A rush of frigid air swirled around her ankles, causing her light green kirtle to billow. She considered going outside into the peacefulness of the night, but thought it too cold. Before she closed the heavy wooden door, she noticed the moon glowing through the falling snow cast an eerie yet beautiful glare around the center courtyard. Everything looked lovely and peaceful.

Although she tried to demure upon nearing the hearth, Grant insisted Tory sit beside him and propped her swollen ankles in front of her.

Duncan broke the silence and reminisced about when he left for school and some of the daft things he'd done. He looked at Tory and smiled. "I tried to get your lackbrain of a husband to come with me, but he'd not leave Crieff."

Tory turned to Grant. "Why did you not go to school with Duncan? I would think going to a different country would be fascinating. You would have been an excellent student."

Grant glared at Duncan and tried to discern some way to answer without hurting him. He thought of none. "Because Da saw no reason to send his son away." Glancing at Duncan he mumbled, "I am sorry, friend."

"No offense taken. 'Tis but the truth. MacThomaidh used any excuse he could to rid himself of me." Though he tried to hide it, Tory saw the hurt in his eyes as he spoke those words.

Grant continued, "Da felt he could teach me everything I needed. He did not even foster me out like most families do." He stopped, watching her closely. "Why, wife, are you ashamed of how I speak?"

"Of course not," she rushed to assure him. She'd grown so used to his speech she hardly heard the differences anymore. "I would never be ashamed of you. I wondered why someone so intelligent hadn't taken advantage of that opportunity." She teased Duncan, "I imagine people where you studied should be glad, though. Had the two of you gone together you'd have turned the place upside down with your antics."

Leanne Burroughs

The two men smiled indulgently.

Being allowed to stay up late for this special occasion, the children soon clamored for a story. Her eyes settling on the lovely tree as she glanced around the Hall, Tory asked, "Do you fancy hearing about the first Christmas tree?" The children all bobbed their heads in agreement and smiled from ear to ear. "Give me a moment to recollect the tale. It's been quite awhile since I heard that particular story." Soon she nodded and began with a smile.

"The story I heard took place a long time ago – around the early 700s. A monk named St. Boniface traveled all the way to a country called Germany. Though not understanding why, he felt God wanted him to share the great Nativity story with Germany's Druids. He wound up in a tiny town called Geismer." She looked at each child in turn. "People who lived back then believed oak trees were sacred. Trying to show them the oak was no more special than any other tree, Boniface approached a particularly large oak and felled it on the spot. The huge tree toppled and crushed every tree and shrub in its path—except for one tiny fir sapling." She glanced around the room and smiled as she saw the children's eyes growing wide with excitement.

"He interpreted the small fir's survival as a miracle. 'Tis reported he told them, 'Let this be called the tree of the Christ Child.' After that, Christmases in Germany have always been celebrated by planting fir saplings."

Content with her tale, the children wandered away and headed off to their beds, anxious for the day ahead. Since Tory seemed so excited, all knew it would be special.

Grant pulled her into his lap, "Where learned you all these tales?"

She met his tender gaze. "From my grandmum. Father gave her no coin, so she told me her tales were the only legacy she could give me. I treasured the time we spent together while she shared them with me." Growing quiet, she sniffed. "I miss her so much."

She tried to rise, but Grant held her tightly. Although she again tried to demure so the two men could have private time together, Grant insisted Tory remain. She soon curled up on his lap and fell asleep from the hearth's lulling warmth and the comfort of his strong arms.

He looked around the room and smiled, feeling content and happy. He soon felt Warwick's presence behind him. "Even your mam dinnae decorate the keep like this. I believe your wee lassie must be a bit of a faery sprite herself. We needs make this a special

291

Yuletide for her, to make up for the ones she dinnae have as a child. Whilst we've not made a big occasion out of Yuletide afore, I have a feeling everyone on Drummond land will in future."

Duncan smiled at Warwick's words and nodded agreement. He felt pleased to see Grant looked peaceful. It had been a long time since he'd seen such a look on his face. His friend had been tormented too long. While Grant may not have realized it—and certainly would never admit it – the lassie seemed to be good for him. They complemented each other, and she brought something to Grant's life that had been missing far too long. Peace. Duncan found himself jealous of his friend's happiness.

It turned out to be a beautiful day. Mist dissipated, the sun shone, and the weather felt wonderful. Although cold, Grant thought it pleasant. He chuckled, knowing Tory would think it freezing, but he wouldn't trade living in the Highlands for anything. He loved it.

Being the eve of Christmas, he knew Will would arrive soon. When he finally heard they approached, he went in search of his wife and found her once more in the kitchen. Not only did she help, she spent the entire morning learning more of her new family's customs.

To her surprise, unmarried women came into the kitchen throughout the morn to have their fortunes told by dropping eggs into a tankard. She thought the practice strange. "What are they doing?"

Cook informed her, "Unmarried women do this every year on the eve of Christmas. The egg's shape signifies the occupation of their future spouse."

Loath to waste so many eggs, she thought a moment, then smiled. "Let us mix them with oatmeal to make Christmas bannocks."

Women frowned, despite her exhuberance. "If the cakes split while baking, we might have bad luck in the upcoming year."

Tory thought about that awhile. "Then we must make quite certain we mix them well so that does not happen. We want only good luck around here."

After hours of baking, she felt ready for a break and looked happy when Grant came for her. Although still not knowing Will's true feelings about her, she wasn't quite as hesitant to meet him this time.

Grant well-comed the men to their home. "Come inside out of the cold." Snowflakes fell lightly as they made their way inside.

Earlier in the day Tory helped Cook prepare Mugga, which he served to everyone before the main meal. She'd given him her grandmother's receipt. Cook glanced at her strangely throughout its preparation.

"Hopefully it tastes better than it sounds, m'lady," he muttered with a grimace. A wheaten porridge, he sweetened it with honey. The men thought it strange when they heard its name, but they seemed to enjoy it when Cook served it at the nooning meal. Either that or Grant ordered them to try a bit of everything she prepared in order to not hurt her feelings.

Later that afternoon Tory busily placed candles around the castle.

Grant had told her of a sweet tradition while they broke their fast that morn.

"Every home on Drummond land will place candles in their home to light the way for the Holy Family. This eve is the Night of Candles, or *Oidche Choinnle*."

When he'd purchased the Yule candles at the faire, he'd been given the traditional greeting received each year – 'Fire to warm you by and a light to guide you.'

The meal Tory planned sounded scrumptous. She asked Cook to prepare quail, roast pork, and neeps in cream sauce. The aroma wafted through the Great Hall.

Grant couldn't imagine how she planned to top it for Christmas day, but she promised a meal he wouldn't forget. He hoped she meant that in a good way! He tried to explain, "Sweeting, Scots do not particularly celebrate Christmas. Hogmanay is our big celebration."

She'd hear none of that.

She wanted to celebrate Christmas, so that's what they'd do. There was nothing wrong with starting new traditions at Drummond Castle, Grant assured himself with a smile.

After the hearty meal, men gathered round the hearth to talk. Fetching her warm cape from the peg by the door, Tory stepped outside for a few minutes to gaze at the night's beauty.

The children followed. "Have you ever heard the animals speak, Lady Tory?"

She looked at them and thought they'd all lost their minds. "What do you speak about? Animals cannot talk." She tried to hold back a smile. Were they teasing?

"Of course they can, Lady Tory. They talk at midnight on the eve of Christmas. Everyone knows that. Have you ever heard them?" a small lad named Elfric queried anxiously. The freckled, red haired boy had just begun joining her storytelling group. It seemed more and more children came every day. She wondered where they all came from.

The small boy's remark taking her aback, Tory shook her head warily. "Nay, Elfric, I am afraid I have not." She didn't know if that would be a good or bad admission.

"Och, thank the Blessed Virgin," the small boy sighed with obvious relief, his face revealing his dimples. "We all try to stay away from them near midnight since 'tis unlucky to hear them talk. I am glad you've not heard them. We'd not want you to have bad luck."

He said this with such sincerity Tory didn't have the heart to tell him she imagined 'twas just a tale.

Growing chilled, they returned to the Hall, the fragrance of evergreens wafting in the warmth as they opened the door.

Tory tried to slip away after her sojourn outside to give the three men a chance to talk. She felt Will still didn't feel comfortable talking in her presence, but Grant had other ideas.

He seemed determined she enjoy all activities. He'd planned an evening of entertainment. Tales were told and songs were sung and a marvelous time had by all, with everyone joining in the festivities.

The midnight hour approached. Soon it would be Christmas day. To her surprise, the men all started to scramble in different directions. Laughing, they threw open the doors.

Heaving a sigh, Tory closed her eyes and shook her head. "Have you all lost your minds? Why are you letting in the freezing cold, when all evening we've tried to keep the Hall warm?"

When Grant and Duncan came back smiling, she cocked her head and arched her eyebrows.

Grant laughed. "'Tis a time-honored tradition to fling our doors open wide to let out trapped evil spirits." Looking at her with a half grin, he glanced sidewise at Duncan. "You'd not want any evil spirits in here this night wouldst you, my lady?"

"Of course not," she answered sarcastically, as if his explanation made all the sense in the world. "I should have known your actions would be as logical as something like that." She rolled her eyes heavenward. How many more customs did these people have that she hadn't heard about?

She started to say something, then thought better of it and simply closed her mouth, dumbfounded.

Grant could no longer contain his laughter. Throwing back his head, he laughed a deep belly laugh. His wife's reactions were such a delight. He couldn't remember the last time he'd enjoyed a quiet day so much.

"The look on your face is priceless, lady mine." Seeing her frown, he added, "'Tis a time-honored tradition, aye."

When she started to say something else, Grant silenced her with a kiss, then placed his hand at the small of her back and urged her toward the stairs. "No more talking this night. I have other things in mind. I want you to go to sleep with happy thoughts. Your first Yuletide here must be perfect."

Stepping inside their chamber, he smiled as he kissed her and lowered her to their bed. Tory trembled when she felt his fingers slide between her legs. Without another word, save a few moans of pleasure, Grant proceeded to make her last waking hours just that – absolutely perfect!

Bright and early Christmas morn Tory rushed to the kitchen to make final preparations for the meal. "Cook, I've decided we must add Christmas Pudding to the menu."

"Now? We have plenty of other food, my lady."

She was adamant, and she informed each person who entered the kitchen, "You have to make a wish and stir the mixture three times so you can see the pot's bottom."

When some women refused, thinking her quite daft, she simply mumbled behind their backs, "Well, do not say I told you so later. Unmarried women who chose not to stir the concoction simply will not find a husband next year." She felt quite certain of that.

She quickly dropped a silver coin, a thimble, and a ring into the pudding.

Cook tried to stop her. "My lady, *what* are you doing?"

She animatedly told him, "Oh, Cook. I cannot wait to see who finds them." Rushing on before he could interrupt, she said, "After all, the person who finds the coin will receive luck throughout the year, the person who gets the thimble will be ensured of prosperity, and the lucky person finding the ring will hasten a wedding for someone in their family." She had a wonderful time trying to envision the reaction to the three tokens.

As they did every day, children gathered around Tory after she broke her fast, and begged her to tell them a story. Clearly, they adored her.

Gathering them closely around her, she began, "Let me tell you of our Lord Jesus' birth. After all, this is what the day is all about—His birthday." The children sat cross-legged on the rushes and listened in rapt attention to Mary and Joseph's frustrating attempt to find lodging in the crowded town where they had to go to pay their taxes. They wrinkled their noses when told how the stable would have smelled when Joseph settled his lovely wife, Mary, there. Tory finished the tale with, "And can you imagine? What a place to give birth to a tiny, blessed child!" She lowered her voice to a conspiratorial whisper. "The angels must have thought it perfect though, since the heavenly host soon began to sing with beautiful voices."

When they clamored for yet another story, she sighed. "Oh my, another story? How about if I tell you of Father Christmas?"

As one, the children all nodded their heads.

"When Vikings landed on our shores, they brought their god, Odin, with them. He chose a different personality each month of the year. In the twelfth month they called him Jul. 'Tis why we call this special season Jultid—or Yuletide.

"Did you know Vikings believed Odin would come to earth riding his lovely horse, Sleipnir?" she asked the children with a twinkle in her eye. They all shook their heads. "When he came, he disguised himself in a long, blue hooded cloak. Everywhere he went, he carried a satchel which contained loaves of bread. He also had his staff and a raven with him."

Men walking by smiled as they glanced at the little ones who sat in rapt attention. Tory continued her saga with remarkable patience. "Odin often sat with people just like you and me around their hearths, so he could learn if they needed anything, or if they were satisfied with their lives. Depending upon what he heard, sometimes he left them a gift of bread."

When her tale ended Tory got up to tend to a few chores. "Now do not forget, the twelve days of Christmas starts this day," she reminded the children. She arched her aching back, massaging a bothersome spot.

Grant saw her movement and frowned. She'd done too much these past days, but since she seemed so excited, he hated to temper her activities.

Soon 'twas time to head off to the small room she'd set aside as a chapel. Grant thought about having one built inside the keep. Tory seemed pleased the priest accompanying Will agreed to perform the blessed service.

She'd told him, "I cannot imagine Christmas day without the message of Christ's birth and a holy blessing."

When she returned to the kitchen following John Blair's inspiring service, she worried about the meal. Entering, she saw the room astir with activity and teeming with people. Earlier she'd given Cook another of her grandmother's receipts – this time for mince pie. She'd tried to honor their Scottish traditions and felt glad they were letting her include a few of her own.

Tory had nothing to fear. As she hoped, the meal turned out to be a gala affair and a tremendous success. She planned goose with orange sauce, pork in an herbed cream sauce with a touch of cheese, carrots, and parsnips. Soon 'twas time for pudding. She smiled, thinking everyone would love the desserts she'd planned.

While Cook brought the pies out, Tory announced, "You all must make a wish, since they're the first of the season." With a smile, she informed them, "We'll have mince pie with every meal for the next twelve days." Chuckling, she said, "This will ensure us of good fortune throughout the year—and I think you'll fancy them, since they contain a goodly amount of brandy."

Next year she'd have to start her preparations about three months in advance, so the pies would have more of a chance to mature. Grandpapa had told her they always tasted better that way.

Tory also had Cook make plum puddings, and these she topped with a brandy sauce. She asked Cook, "Think you we should served them with brandy poured atop them, then light the puddings, causing the alcohol to burst into flames?" At his look of horror, she added, "Mayhap not. That might be too flamboyant for my first holiday meal."

Choruses of surprise arose as the three items were found inside the Christmas pudding, bringing a smile to her lips. Everyone seemed pleased with the introduction of the novel dessert. She'd set a separate batch aside for the servants as well, and was pleased when Triona found the ring.

After everyone enjoyed dessert, Cook served cheese and biscuits prior to men dissembling.

Choruses of "I am stuffed" echoed throughout the Hall.

Grant assured her, "Your menu indeed surpassed our expectations."

He surprised her with entertainment and mulled wine he'd had delivered so she'd have something festive to drink along with everyone else. Duncan had brought it with him, and they'd kept it hidden.

Duncan also brought a lovely scarf which he presented to Tory.

"Duncan, I cannot possibly...oh 'tis lovely. Thank you so much!"

Warwick came forward and handed her a small wrapped package. Eyes wide, she opened it and gasped. "I saw these at the market faire!"

Trying to stay the tears of happiness which threatened to fall, Tory quickly went up to her chamber and brought down a small package she'd done her best to keep hidden. She'd made Grant a white linen shirt to wear with his formal plaide. Her stitching was perfect.

"Thank you, my lady. I did not expect to receive anything from you." He eyed the shirt carefully. "You did this yourself?" At her nod, he seemed pleased. "Your stitches are most perfect."

To her surprise, Grant drew out a small pouch and handed it to her. Opening it, she found a silver band engraved with the Drummond family crest.

"Our smithy crafted it for you," Grant told her.

"'Tis beautiful." Surely it couldn't be what she thought, but she eyed Grant expectantly nevertheless.

Seeing the question in her eyes, Grant smiled and nodded. "Aye, Sweeting, 'tis time you had a wedding band." He took it from her shaking hand and gently slipped it on her finger, as tears of happiness slid down her cheeks.

It fit perfectly.

Behind them, Duncan smiled smugly as Tory impulsively touched Grant's face with shaking fingertips. Soon the hour grew late, and everyone drifted off to bed. Grant rose to escort her to their bedchamber. "Good eve, everyone. I hope your Yuletide has been special."

Firmly closing the door to their chamber, Grant trailed warm kisses down Tory's neck. She sighed happily as she thought about their day. It had been wonderful – her best Christmas ever.

Before she knew what he planned, her kirtle dropped to the floor and his hands greedily roamed her body. Tory smiled in contentment. Suddenly Grant tumbled her to the bed and laughingly fell atop her. He braced his weight with his arms and looked at her lovingly before lowering his head to kiss her.

Ah, she thought with a smug smile. Not only had it been a wonderful day, 'twould be a wonderful night, too.

Chapter Thirty-two

Back in the eighth century the church opened its alms boxes to the poor. In England people of noble birth gave filled boxes to people who worked for them the day after Christmas. Tory and her grandmother did that and she'd enjoyed the tradition. She knew it as Boxing Day. She didn't know, however, if Scottish lairds followed this same practice. She hoped they did, since she wanted to do something especially nice for everyone. They'd given her such a wonderful Christmastide. She hesitated to ask Grant about it lest the idea anger him if they didn't follow the practice, but one afternoon about a sennight before Christmas she finally asked him, "Know you of Boxing Day?"

"Aye, many in Scotland follow the practice. Wish you to give gifts?"

Smiling, she bobbed her head up and down.

"Then of course you may do so. I believe our clansmen will be quite pleased."

Tory busily spent the week preparing boxes for everyone who served them in the keep.

Grant teased, "Woman, you shall bankrupt me with as many items as you place in each box."

Knowing he only teased, she merrily went on preparing her boxes with Annie's assistance. Giggling over everything and nothing, the two had a marvelous time.

Now that Boxing Day arrived, she felt bashful about distributing the boxes. She approached Grant. "My lord, would you do me the honor of handing out these boxes to our people?"

He shook his head. "Nay, wife. I shall accompany you and carry them while you deliver them if you wish, but you need to hand them out. You're the one who spent so much time preparing each one."

Although nervous about their response, to her delight, everyone seemed pleased with their gifts, and thanked both she and Grant profusely.

Grant made certain to tell everyone, "'Tis all my lady wife's doing. She chose everything that went into each box, although I did at least watch her make some of them. She made each box specifically for every person here. Why, in addition to fruit and nuts, she's placed one item of significance for each of you--even making a point to include something for your children."

The children squealed with delight as they tore into the boxes, and everyone seemed pleased with their lady's thoughtfulness.

She was exhausted, but pleasantly surprised with the day's outcome. Grant once again made her head upstairs to rest.

During Christmastide Will, Duncan, and Grant were nearly inseparable. The three plotted how they planned to free Andrew deMoray from Chester Castle where he was now being held prisoner. He'd been moved there after the Dragon of Challon urged Edward toward leniency.

"We can do naught until the snow melts, but I am determined to have a plan in place so we can move as soon as possible, probably around March," Grant told them.

A few days past, Grant explained the tradition of First Footing to Tory. She thought it sounded quite sweet even though they had nothing similar in England. So, she busily placed candles around the Great Hall again, like she had on the eve of Christmas. Only this time they were there to light the way for the First Footer for Hogmanay.

Grant told her, "First Footers carry coal, black bun, and whisky to the homes they visit in order to share them with the hosts. They carry coal to symbolize there be warmth in the home for the entire year."

"That sounds like a nice tradition."

"For the First Footer to bring us luck for the upcoming year, he must be a tall, dark haired man."

Tory quirked a brow. "Whyever would the color of a person's hair matter?"

None of their answers satisfied her. "You really believe someone will show up at our door at midnight? A storm rages outside. Surely no one would be foolhardy enough to brave this weather." Nevertheless, she busied herself with preparations for her first Hogmanay.

She hated that Duncan had chosen this day to leave for his own home. She'd tried to make him stay longer. "Duncan, the weather is far too dangerous for you to be out traveling." However, she'd learned long ago he was as stubborn as Grant, and she had no chance of changing his mind.

301

True to form, the stubborn man had ignored her completely.

She already had her menu for the next day set out with Cook. She planned to serve venison stew, mashed tatties and neeps, Black Bun, and shortbread. Humming to herself as she walked to the kitchen, she opened the door and told Cook, "I believe we should serve Clootie Dumpling this day. Everyone seemed to fancy it the last time we had it." She'd tried it, too, but couldn't seem to acquire a taste for it. Thinking back on her experience, she added, "Ooh, and make sure we have plenty of warm cream to put atop it."

As midnight approached, Tory looked at Grant nervously. Did he truly believe his clan's luck hinged on the appearance of a single midnight guest? Based on many other things he believed, she assumed he probably did. She hoped he wouldn't be too disappointed when no one appeared in this blinding snowstorm.

He seemed unconcerned about the weather, though. As he leaned back comfortably in his chair before the hearth, his legs were comfortably stretched in front of him and he had a chalice of wine in his hand.

Soon a pounding sounded at their door. Tory started. She really hadn't expected anyone to arrive in this horrible weather. Downing the last of his wine and grabbing her hand, Grant pulled her up from her chair. Placing his hand at the small of her back, he propelled her toward their heavy front door.

Everyone else had been given specific instructions not to open it. They all anxiously awaited Tory's response.

Grant motioned for her to open the door. He wanted this honor to be hers for her first Hogmanay in the Highlands. Moving slowly, Tory opened it and came face to face with an impishly grinning Duncan. She stepped back and looked at him in astonishment.

"Woman," he grumbled pushing past her as he hastened toward the warm hearth, "it took you long enough to open that door! Planned you on freezing me on yon doorstep?"

In his hands he carried the necessary items for a proper First Footer. "Here, my friend," he told Grant. "Coal to ensure warmth in your home throughout the year." He turned to face Tory, a wide smile crossing his face. "My lady, please accept this Black Bun for the meal later this day." The whisky he gave to Grant with instructions "to open it quickly, man."

Tory stared in astonishment. "But Duncan, you left early this morn. Why would you leave if you knew you were going to come back?"

Everyone smiled conspiratorially.

"I did not go far, lady." At her questioning look he finally admitted, "I have been out in your men's quarters gaming and dicing with them. We planned all along for me to be your First Footer. I told Grant I wanted to be the one to do the honors and he agreed wholeheartedly."

Turning to look at Duncan, she asked, "Why did you want to be our First Footer?"

"Because it is a time honored tradition that the First Footer gets to kiss all the lasses." With that, he cocked a sardonic eyebrow at Grant and pulled Tory into his arms.

His wicked smile right before he soundly planted a kiss on her lips made Grant want to smash his fist in the bloody man's face. He said naught, since 'twas indeed tradition, but he glared until Duncan released his wife.

Blast it, he'd forgotten about that part of the tradition. Leave it to Duncan to remember.

As Duncan concluded the kiss, Grant quickly jerked Tory away. The glare he shot Duncan let him know he treaded on thin ice.

With a mocking smile Duncan bowed to Tory and chose to ignore Grant's glare.

Blushing clear to her toes, Tory glared at Grant. "You made this poor man stay outside in the cold all day? How could you?"

Grant rolled his eyes at his wife's upset. "Sweeting, if I know my friend – and I do indeed – the only time he felt cold today is when he stood waiting for you to open yon door. He already told you he spent the day with our men. And it would not surprise me if at least one of our lasses helped warm a bed with him this day."

"Grant!" she squealed in dismay. "Duncan would not have..." She got no further with her outburst when she saw the guilty look on the man's face. "Duncan!"

When they finished their whisky, Grant took his flustered young wife in his arms and informed her, "Speaking of bed, everyone will be turning in soon, we they all have a busy day ahead of us. The children will go from place to place asking for gifts." He knew without doubt they'd all come to his tender-hearted wife.

Grant locked the door behind him when they entered their chamber, and pulled Tory into his arms. The moon entered the room through the long arrow slits.

She gave him an inquisitive look. "Grant? I thought you said we—"

"Were turning in to our room," Grant completed. "At no time did I say we'd be sleeping." The mischievous smile on his face and the firm, thick muscularity of his thighs pressing against hers told her exactly what he had on his mind. She could feel he was already swollen, hard with desire for her. With a playful look on her face and eyes flashing with mischief, Tory unfastened her brooch, and let her shift fall to the floor. Her lips were already parted in passion.

Grant stepped back and looked at her in frank admiration. Aye, she swelled with his child, but he thought her the most beautiful woman he'd ever seen. He'd always thought her pretty, but when had she become so beautiful? She took his breath away.

Still marveling, he picked her up and carried her to the fur in front of their hearth. Soon his knee parted her thighs and Tory assumed he'd make love to her immediately.

Grant had other ideas. He planned to draw this out as long as he could. He pressed a kiss on her brow and slowly, teasingly began a seductive descent down her body. Transfixed by the look of passion on her face, he could sense her desire for him building. Raising himself back up to her face, his lips came down on hers.

His fingers were well practiced, and she moaned softly in spite of herself. When she thought she could stand it no longer, Grant made the two of them one and everything else about the night was forgotten.

When they awoke later that morning, Grant's arms were firmly locked around his wife. They hadn't moved from the fur after their lovemaking and had fallen asleep right where they were in front of the hearth. Looking at her, he wanted to love her again. That would make this the best Hogmanay he'd ever had.

He didn't have to think about it twice.

When they finally headed downstairs to break their fast, he lightly patted his sporran. Her Hogmanay gift was in there and had been chosen with careful deliberation. Grant smiled to himself. This was by far the happiest Hogmanay he'd ever experienced. He never thought a wee wisp of a woman could make him so happy.

Tory thought it strange gifts were exchanged on the first of January as well as Christmas, but she wouldn't put a damper on everyone else's excitement, especially the children's. She hadn't expected another gift from Grant, so she remained speechless when he presented her with a beautiful new brooch.

He told her, "Use this to fasten the Drummond plaide around your kirtle." He leaned forward to nuzzle her ear, then whispered so only she could hear him. "You are mine, lass, and I want everyone to know it. Wear my plaide."

While Tory headed to the kitchen to help Cook with the special meal preparations, Grant told her, "I must go to the village for the annual New Year's ceremony."

"What is that?"

"'Tis called the Creaming of the Well." He patiently explained, "The *cream* is the first water drawn from the village well on Hogmanay. Since water can only be drawn from the well once, all women who participate race to it to be the first to draw the water."

Duncan chimed in,"Possession of the first water drawn supposedly guarantees marriage within the year. You can be sure most unmarried women gleefully participate in the race."

Grant smiled. "For it to work, the woman somehow has to get 'her intended' to drink from the prized water before day's end. Thank goodness, most find that easier said than done."

Tory smiled and asked, "Have you been to many celebrations in the past?"

His smile suddenly left his face. "Nay, Sweeting. 'Tis the chieftain's responsibility to preside over this ceremony. In the past my da always went. And," he added as his smile returned, "I always stayed as far away from the celebration as possible. I want no lasses trying to get me to drink the *cream*."

Turning, he chuckled and asked Duncan, "Wish you to attend the celebration?"

Duncan threw his head back in laughter. "I would rather be hobbled to a snake than attend the annual ceremony. Why think you I make it a point to stay away from my own home in Rhiedorrach on Hogmanay? I am not taking any chances. Unlike you, I've not found the one woman I wish to spend the rest of my life leg shackled to."

Duncan stayed until Twelfth Night, the sixth of January before heading back to his own home. Castle MacThomas awaited him, but he certainly didn't look forward to returning there. He simply didn't understand how his father could support the King. There were other reasons as well, but he didn't want to dwell on them.

The Feast of Epiphany concluded the period of Christmas festivities. "I have stayed here long enough. 'Tis time to head home."

Will had departed the day after Christmas.

Grant and Tory were sad to see Duncan leave. He promised, "I shall return as soon as I can. I certainly look forward to seeing my new godson after his birth."

Tory looked at him with mock indignation. "Are you so certain 'tis a boy, sir?"

He ruffled her hair before he turned to mount his horse. "Och, aye, sweet lady. I am that certain." With a tip of his bonnet, he and his entourage were off. With a knowing look to Grant he added as he rode away, "Inform me when you need help with Andrew."

Grant shook his head in understanding.

Grant glanced around his center courtyard and noticed the children running around more than usual. They kept up a steady stream of chatter. He chuckled to himself and knew they were up to something. And knowing them as well as he did, he'd bet his favorite sword it had something to do with his Tory.

That afternoon he noticed Tory walking about with early blooming flowers in her hair, her small dog racing along beside her. When he finished training in the lists, he walked into the Great Hall and noticed a floral bouquet on the great table.

His curiosity finally got the best of him. Pulling, Annie off to one side, he asked, "Why have you children given Lady Tory flowers all day?"

"Because today is her natal day," Annie exclaimed happily and flashed him an endearing smile. Looking at the small child now, one would never have known she'd spent most of her life not speaking. The change Tory had wrought in her amazed everyone.

"We want to make it special for her since her da never did nothing whilst she lived at her auld home." She said this last in a conspiratorial tone, her small mouth making a distasteful moue.

"I did not know 'twas Lady Tory's natal day," Grant said, his brows dipping in a frown.

Annie wrinkled her freckled nose and muttered with the barest hint of censure, "Because you never bothered to ask her the date." Her expression showed she clearly felt this Grant's fault.

"Are you certain 'tis her natal day?"

"Aye," Annie announced, raising herself as tall as a five year old could muster and bobbing her head up and down. "She told me a long, long time ago, and I 'membered." She added the last with obvious pride as her smile widened. Clearly, Annie thought it quite momentous to remember something so important.

Grant laughed indulgently and patted Annie's head. "I am proud of you for remembering, Annie. Be a good lassie now and run along. I have a few things I needs take care of."

She nodded and skipped away smiling, her eyes twinkling with pleasure.

She felt quite certain her chief would now take care of Tory's natality personally. The day would be so much fun—and Lady Tory would be so surprised.

Grant rushed to the kitchen. He peered inside to make certain Tory wasn't around, then strode inside. "Did Lady Tory plan anything special for our meals this day?"

Cook shook his head and went about his work.

"Did she mention anything about today being her natal day?"

That stopped Cook cold. Turning slowly, he again shook his head. "Well," Grant said earnestly, "Annie told me 'tis Tory's natal day. I think we should do something special. What think you?"

"Och, aye, of course we should," Cook stated, bustling about the room. "And I know just the thing. Leave preparations to me." He shot an accusatory glare at Grant for not knowing this information before now. "It would have been better had I known this in the morn, but I can change things quickly enough." His face wreathed in a smile as his mind whirled with plans. "I shall make her a feast."

He added conspiratorially, "You needs keep her out of kitchen, mind."

Grant assured him he would and quickly left the kitchen. Hunting Tory down, he found her upstairs resting.

Making one excuse after another, Grant occupied her for the remainder of the day, and soon Cook served the evening meal.

Cook brought in different courses, and Tory murmured to Grant, "This is not what I planned for this night's meal. I wonder why Cook changed the menu."

Trying not to smile, Grant queried, "Did you not fancy it?"

307

"Oh aye," she quickly affirmed, "'tis delicious. As a matter of fact, 'tis one of my favorite meals." She shrugged her shoulders. "I wonder what made him change his mind."

Grant mumbled as though he thought it unimportant and quickly turned to Warwick to avoid the subject.

When the meal almost ended, Cook could contain himself no longer. Coming from the kitchen with a smile almost a furlong wide, he cheered, "Happy Natal Day, my lady! We hope you enjoyed your special meal."

Tory was stunned. Glancing around the Hall, all the men suddenly wished her a happy natality.

Grant reached below his chair and handed her a present. "Happy Natality, Sweeting. I hope you fancy it. I did not have much time to plan. I did not realize today was your natal day since I never bothered to ask. Annie pointed that out to me quite emphatically. I do apologize for that lapse and will never make such an oversight again." He grimaced at his thoughtlessness. "The we'ans told us it was your special day."

Dumbfounded, Tory unwrapped a looking glass Grant bought for her while at the faire. He also handed her a new comb and brush set. Tory looked at him in amazement. "Other than my grandparents and little sister," she started, "no one ever gave me a gift before. Except for the flowers the children gave me today, of course. Thank you, Grant. These are wonderful. I never expected..." She became too overcome by emotion to finish her sentence.

"I have one other present for you, wife," Grant told her tenderly. "I hope you fancy it as well. 'Tis a family heirloom. It belonged to my granddam and she passed it to my mother." He handed her a necklace consisting of a leather thong with a polished silver cross on it. "If my mam were still alive, she would have wanted you to have this."

To his amazement, Tory didn't take it.

She looked somberly at the necklace and worried the fabric of her sleeve. Stammering, she shook her head and sputtered, "Nay, I cannot. Excuse me I must..."

She bolted from her chair and ran upstairs.

Everyone looked after her in shock.

Warwick finally broke the moment of silence. "'Tis probably best if you go after the lass to see what is wrong, son. Dinnae leave her alone now."

Nodding, Grant rose in one fluid movement and took the steps two at a time. He opened his bedchamber door and found Tory sprawled across the bed with her head buried in a pillow.

What could she be upset about?

Striding toward her, he stood over the bed. He'd been cut to the quick when she hadn't fancied his gift. It meant a great deal to him.

"You were not pleased with my present?" he questioned sarcastically. "I realize you were used to finer jewelry, but I thought you might like it. However, if you think it not good enough, I could go into my mother's jewels and find something you consider more appropriate."

The sound of Grant's bitterness caused Tory to sit upright on the bed.

"You do not understand!" she cried in torment. "I do not want jewels from you. I do not want...anything from you." *Except you*, she thought silently.

When he frowned, she rushed on. "Grant, the necklace is beautiful. 'Tis not that I do not want it. I would dearly love owning something like that, but that necklace belongs in your family. You need to save it and give it to someone else."

"And why would I give this to someone else?" Grant said in exasperation, turning his palm upright to once again show her the delicate cross. "My granddam gave it to my mother. Had she been alive to meet you, Mother would have given it to you herself. She wanted to keep it in our family. That is what I am doing."

Shaking her head, she emphatically said, "Nay, Grant. You will never know how much your kindness means to me, but you should keep it and--"

"Give it to my wife," Grant exploded, interrupting her before she could infuriate him more. "Gorblimey, you are one exasperating woman! I told you, that is what I am doing. Now, for the last time, do you fancy the necklace or do you not?"

"Of course. 'Tis gorgeous, but--" she started with a tremor of nervousness that sounded barely distinguishable in her voice.

"But naught," Grant interrupted, wanting to wring her neck and kiss her at the same time. Why couldn't she accept she was the only woman he wanted?

"This necklace belongs to my wife – you. I do not wish to hear one more word of argument." He leaned forward and fastened the thong around her neck. Then kissed her gently.

"Now, wife, unless you want to hurt Cook's feelings, you'd best head back down the stairs. He still has pudding for you."

"Grant, are you certain...?" She sniffed in an attempt to keep her tears from falling as she gingerly touched the intricate cross.

"Aye, I am. And in future, I would rather you did not question gifts I give. If I give them to you, 'tis because I want you to have them. 'Tis not polite to refuse a gift."

Eyebrows arched in amusement, he teased, "And you are the one who always tells me what is polite and what is not."

With that declaration, he pulled her from the bed. Wrapping her in his arms and kissing her soundly one last time, he propelled her toward the door. When they reached the great table, Cook already had her cake on the table!

Cook smiled and nodded when he saw the necklace around his lady's neck.

"Cook!" she exclaimed with delight, spinning to face him. "Where did you get chocolate?"

"'Twas not easy," came Cook's chortle of delight, "but when I realized how much you fancied it, I knew I must find some. Laird Grant had some merchants look for it and had it shipped in for you. After it arrived, 'twas quite a trick to keep it hidden. Now cut the cake, lassie. The men are eager to taste chocolate, having heard you rave about your grandfather bringing it to you. If you plan to share it with them, mind."

"Of course I shall." Tory smiled and cut the precious cake into small pieces. "I cannot believe you found chocolate for me. 'Tis almost impossible to come by." Taking a bite, she inhaled deeply and purred, "Oh, Cook, 'tis delightful."

Looking around the room she teased, "Help yourselves, men, or I may change my mind and eat the entire cake myself."

Grant chuckled and reached in front of her to get a slice. "She probably would, men. Best you grab a bite while you can. As difficult as this was to fetch, we will probably never have more again."

Later in their bedchamber, Tory sat on their bed and brushed her hair. She used her looking glass time and again to admire her necklace. She couldn't believe the intricate detail on the tiny cross – or the fact Grant wanted her to have it.

Coming up behind her, Grant kissed her gently on the nape of her neck. With a teasing gleam in his eye, he told her, "I have decided I still have one more thing to give you."

She glanced at him in question.

310

A wicked smile crossing his face, he said, "I mean to deliver it myself." When she smiled, he pushed her on her back and lowered himself atop her. Sighing with contentment, he sensuously delivered that last promised gift.

Chapter Thirty-three

Finally returning home after releasing Andrew from prison, Grant strode into his Great Hall and saw Tory having problems descending the steps to well-come him home. By now her belly had become so swollen she had difficulty keeping her balance. She'd soon have to give in to her woman's confinement.

He knew the thought terrified her.

Grant rushed to her so she didn't have to descend all the way, and held her lovingly. "I missed you, Sweeting," he whispered into her ear as he lowered his head to kiss her. Heavy with his child, he thought her beautiful. He considered himself the luckiest of men.

"Grant, are you all right?" she breathlessly questioned. He'd been gone a fortnight and she missed him dreadfully. "Truly sir, I worried so while you were gone. Were you able to free your friend?"

Grant chuckled at her concern and lightly rubbed the backs of his fingers over her cheek. "Aye, and aye."

When she frowned over his terse answer, Grant released a guttural laugh. "Aye, I am fine and aye, we released Andrew from Chester Castle. 'Tis a disgusting place. Unfortunately, his da and uncle were already moved to London's Tower, so we couldn't free them."

Smiling tenderly, he added, "Though anxious to get home, he wished to meet you. I hope you do not mind I brought him home." Canting his head, he indicated a man who stood in their Great Hall.

Tory panicked and overreacted. "Grant! I look a fright. You cannot bring strange men home when I look like this!"

Grant chuckled and gave her a quick, exuberant hug. "Och, Sweeting. You do not look a fright. A beached whale mayhap, but not a fright."

'Twas the wrong thing to say.

Turning on her heel, Tory burst into tears and started upstairs. While away rescuing Andrew, Grant had forgotten how easily she got distressed. He glanced at Andrew, motioned he'd be right back, then took off after his wife. It didn't take long to catch her, since she hadn't gotten far.

Turning her into the circle of his embrace, Grant gently rubbed his hands up and down her back, while he assured her he'd only been teasing.

"Help me upstairs, so I can change clothes and repair my hair. I vow, sir, I cannot let a strange man see me like this."

On the stairs behind him, Grant heard Andrew's approach. "My lady, if you keep calling me strange, I mayhap will believe you and think something is terribly wrong with me. After being locked in that horrible prison for what seems forever, I can only imagine how badly I look. Conditions were deplorable. Forget whatever you heard about nobility being treated better in English gaols. I misdoubt they treated me any better than the common serf. So, lady, believe me when I say, to me you look as beautiful as Grant told me you are – all the way back here I might add."

As Tory peeked around Grant to see who spoke, Andrew flashed a smile warm enough to melt butter. She dried her eyes and glanced at Grant.

"You are fine, Sweeting," Grant assured her tenderly. "Just as you are. Do not fash yourself about it."

Drawing herself up to her full height, she untangled herself from Grant's embrace and walked slowly down the few steps to Andrew. "Pray forgive me, milord. I did not mean to bruise your ego. I did not mean *strange* in that sense. I only meant I knew you not."

"I knew what you meant, lady," he teased. "And 'tis delighted I am to meet you after having repeatedly heard how *wonderful* you are."

She giggled and flashed a smile. "I doubt that, my lord. Knowing my husband, he probably spoke only of the ongoing war, with me as a mere afterthought."

"You know your husband well, lady. Aye, we spoke often of strategies we will employ within coming months. However, I assure you that you were far from an afterthought."

"Sweeting, I think we should allow Andrew time to freshen up," Grant smoothly interrupted the conversation. He didn't know if he wanted Tory knowing how much he thought about her when they weren't together. He didn't want her to take him for granted.

"Might you have a room he could use? He will only be here this day, mind, since he is anxious to return to his own wife and son. But," Grant cautioned, "I do not want you climbing the stairs too often in your condition. I'll help ready the room if everyone else is busy." He rubbed his hand lightly over her swelling belly.

313

Suddenly Grant asked with concern, "Are you certain 'tis not time for your confinement?"

She shook her head emphatically. "Everyone says 'tis, but I wish not to be shut away by myself. And I hoped you'd arrive soon. You promised you would be here when our babe is born."

Grant grimaced. His wife would hold him to that promise. Some men were lucky enough to have their wives give birth while they were away from home. He certainly didn't relish the thought of pacing the Great Hall while she lay in pain.

He helped her upstairs while she escorted Andrew to his room, and wasn't the least surprised to find it immaculate and ready for any surprise guest. Grant shook his head in amazement. Even in her present condition she ensured everything remained perfect.

While Andrew freshened up, Grant found clothes for him to wear on his journey home. Conditions for prisoners at Chester Castle had been less than sanitary. They'd be too large for Andrew now, since he'd lost so much weight due to his cruel treatment, but at least they were clean.

Tory wanted to head to the kitchen to make new arrangements for their evening meal, but Grant had other plans and pulled her behind him into their bedchamber. Although her condition was far too advanced for lovemaking, he could certainly hold her. He needed that right now, having been away too long. These next months would be draining for their country and he'd have to fight. That meant he'd have to leave repeatedly. For now he wanted to hold her and know all would be right with his world.

Grant needed assurance of saneness and peace, and only with Tory did he feel that anymore. He could relax with her.

Tory was only too happy to be held. The thrill of awareness she felt whenever around Grant never ceased to amaze her. She'd missed him terribly while he'd been gone and had prayed daily for his safe return. Tilting her head up to kiss him, she wrapped her arms around his neck and murmured, "I missed you."

Those words were music to his ears. With the close proximity of their bodies, Grant shifted uncomfortably. "I missed you, too, Sweeting, but we'd best head back down the stairs after all. I do not think I can do this holding thing like I planned. I have been away much too long."

Tory moved as suggestively as she thought a *beached whale* could.

"Tory!" Grant groaned and tried to break their lustful embrace. "You are killing me here, my love. You know we cannot-"

"I know *I* cannot, milord. That does not mean you cannot."

"Wife, what are you talking about? Stop that!" Grant groaned as she showed him what she meant rather than telling him. Within moments, he no longer wished to stop anything she did.

They headed downstairs later, and found men gathered in the Great Hall. Most had lascivious grins on their faces as Grant and Tory approached. Their mutual disappearance hadn't escaped anyone's attention. Although looking quite guilty, they both tried to ignore the knowing glances. Tory quickly headed off to the kitchen, and Grant settled in for a chat with Andrew.

During dinner, Tory learned William and Duncan were both headed home – Duncan north to his family home and Will south to Selkirk forest.

"I am pleased to hear they are both well." She adored Duncan and had grown to respect Will during his visits.

Tory took the time to observe Andrew and thought him handsome in his own way. Not as tall or handsome as Grant, of course, but her feelings were slightly biased on that account. Though leaner than most men, that was to be expected after his long confinement. With blue eyes and sandy brown hair, his appearance looked quite pleasant.

He spent most of the meal telling her about his wife, John Comyn's daughter, and their son, also named Andrew.

"I cannot wait to see them both again. I lost a lot of time in their lives because of my imprisonment. I cannot wait to see how my son has grown. I know I missed so much."

Sheepishly he told her, "I hope my wife was with child when last I saw her. If so – and I think I noticed a few telltale signs – I'll have a new son or daughter awaiting me!" He laughed. "My wife already had names selected for their next child – William if a lad, and Katrine if a lassie."

He told her about his home at Avoch Castle, where he planned to head next. No stops. No detours. "I mean to raise my standard over the castle and do whatever is necessary in order to raise men and fight the English."

Unlike William, Andrew made no reference to her being English. In his mind he'd already transitioned that she was now Scottish since she and Grant were wed. No question of her loyalty remained whatsoever.

With a gathering of men, someone inevitably mentioned Edward and talk turned to his horrible act of removing their beloved Stone of Destiny from Scotland. The audacity of having himself crowned king on it had been the ultimate slap in the face to the Scots. Tory hoped no one would mention fighting, but knew such a wish probably futile. She asked, "Why is the stone so special?"

Grant told her, "Angus probably knows the stone's history best." Deferring to his friend, he let him explain.

"The stone dates back to Old Testament times. According to legend, Jacob was in Bethel when he used our great stone as a pillow when he dreamt he saw a ladder rising to heaven. Angels came down the ladder and prophesied to Jacob. When he awoke, he used that same stone to build a pillar to worship God, and anointed it with oil."

Tory looked confused. "Near Israel?" When they nodded, she queried, "How did it get all the way to Scotland?"

Angus continued, "I dinnae know names, but a Phoenician left the Holy Land for Spain and took it with him." He saw Tory again about to interrupt, so he quickly interjected, "Later he sent people to colonize Ireland and sent the stone with them. From there it arrived in Scotland with a man who took it to Argyleshire. Later 'twas moved to Scone and affixed to our royal chair."

Angus sadly recounted, "From then until when Edward stole it, all Scottish kings have been inaugurated there."

From the side of the room, someone said, "'Tis not our real stone he has—but we'll not be telling him that!"

After hearing Angus' tale, Tory understood why it meant so much. If the tale was true, they considered the stone blessed. "Edward had no right to remove it. I hope some day it will be returned."

Bright and early the next day Grant saw Andrew on his way to Glenrogha with his friend, Hadrian. Andrew planned to hole up in Glenrogha's Pict broch until he gathered men to his standard and could return safely to his lady wife. "Godspeed. I shall see you soon."

When Andrew and an escort rode under the portcullis, Grant dashed back into the castle. He'd refused to let Tory come downstairs this morn, since she'd awakened with severe back pains.

As he rushed inside, Triona ran down the stairs, eyes wide. "She is havin' the bairnie! Someone fetch the midwife. I told her 'twas time for her lying-in, but she would not listen!"

Grant took the steps two at a time.

Tory smiled, but her pale face revealed her pain was already quite severe.

Grant bent to kiss her. "Sweeting, this probably is not the best time to tell you this, but my women will likely do a few things you are not familiar with in childbirth."

"Actually, I have never done this before, remember," she tried to smile through gritted teeth. "So I am not really familiar with anything. I ran our home, but never assisted with birthings." She paused as a pain gripped her.

"I know that," Grant assured and smoothed stray wisps of hair from her forehead, "but I meant some practices we use in the Highlands may be different than what you may have seen or heard afore."

"Indeed, sir, do I really want to know?" She rolled her eyes.

"Probably not." Grant smiled, chuckling to himself. "Let them do as they wish."

Tory tried smiling again, but another pain gripped her.

Grant frowned. "I did not think pains were supposed to start this early. I thought it took hours to reach this point."

Grimacing, she admitted, "Actually, it has already been several hours. The pains started during the night, but you were so tired from your journey I did not wish to disturb you."

Grant growled his frustration.

Several women entered the chamber. They turned to Grant. "You may leavenow and start walking."

A frown creased Tory's brow as she eyed Triona, who reentered the room when other women arrived.

"Walking?"

The young maid nodded. "Aye, lady. Laird Grant must walk around the keep seven times sunwise."

Trying to grin, but having a pain hit at the same time, Tory groaned through gritted teeth. "Why?"

Triona looked like she thought her lady daft. "To keep fairies away, of course." She frowned in thought. "Why else would he do it?"

Tory did laugh then. "I have no idea, Triona. I never heard of the custom."

"Oh," came her maid's response. She didn't elaborate.

Changing the subject, Triona sat next to Tory and tried to distract her from the pains. Soon several women rolled Tory on her side, pulling on her back to do so. As she grimaced in pain, she asked, "Why must I roll over? 'Tis extremely uncomfortable."

"Putting a knife here, lady," the midwife's assistant, Isobel, said gruffly.

"A knife!" Tory panicked. After all she'd been through, now they planned to kill her? Grant! She must get him back here. "Triona, go get Grant. Hurry!"

The maid looked confused. "Why, my lady? We can do this ourselves. We do not need Laird Grant. In fact, the knife is already under your bedding." With that, they slowly rolled Tory onto her back.

"Under the bedding? You're putting the knife *under* the bedding?"

Triona nodded her confirmation.

"You do not plan to kill me?"

"What?" everyone yelled in unison.

Elbethal, the elderly midwife, grumbled under her breath,"Och, our chieftain's wife truly must be daft."

"What are you speaking about, lady?" Tory's maid asked. She sat beside Tory and gently picked up one of her hands, concern showing in her eyes.

Tory's lower lip quivered. "I thought you were going to stick a knife in my back."

She heard the young woman's chuckle. "Not in your back, *under* your bedding. It helps cut the pain." She pulled a face, desperately trying to contain her laughter. Though sweet, her lady certainly had some strange notions.

Embarrassed, Tory mumbled under her breath, "Well 'tis not helping."

Tory frowned as she glanced around the room.

"What is wrong, lady?" came the question as her maid noticed she lady looked upset.

"I need the cradle moved in here. 'Tis still in the nursery next door."

A gasp filled the room and all eyes riveted to her. Tory shook her head and knew she'd pulled another gaff. "My baby cannot have a place to sleep? I suppose there is a perfectly good explanation for that?"

"Och, of course," the gruff Elbethal said while she rolled her eyes in frustration. She'd been the Drummond midwife ever since she could remember and felt far too old for such nonsense. Especially on days like this. It would be quite trying if she had to listen to her chieftain's wife make daft comments all day. Shaking her head in exasperation, she looked forward to turning the duties over to someone else soon. She'd done this for over one and thirty years now.

"And that might be?" Tory questioned, returning Elbethal to the logic – or illogic – of her statement. Aye, the midwife reaffirmed, this would be one long day if she had to put up with the lass' pain and daffin ideas to boot.

Simultaneously, Tory thought it would be a long day if she had to deal with pain and trying to second-guess everything these women did.

Why hadn't Grant told her some of these superstitions?

"Because you must use a borrowed cradle for the wee bairnie when 'tis born. Everyone knows that," the auld woman muttered in disgust. Did this Englishwoman know nothing?

"Why?"

"Och, to keep faeries away, of course," came Elbethal's grumble as she let out a frustrated sigh. "Are you not listening at all?"

"I am trying, Elbethal. I really am. But you do things slightly different than what I am used to." After a pause, Tory questioned before her next contraction hit, "Is there anything else unusual I should know about?"

Everyone appeared to be thinking. "Unusual? Nay," the young, plump woman who always assisted with births finally answered. One day soon Isobel knew she'd take over when Elbethal felt too old to continue with birthings. She looked forward to doing it herself, since at times she thought Elbethal too brusque.

Hours passed and Tory's pains increased. Triona sat beside her and wiped her face with a cool, wet cloth.

As soon as Tory started having full pains, Grant sent someone to get the priest. He told Warwick, "I want to have the bairn's christening as soon as possible. Not knowing when I must leave to fight King Edward, I want to make certain I shall be around for my child's christening."

Throughout the night Grant poked his head into his chamber to see how his wife fared.

"Be gone with you," Elbethal screamed belligerently. "'Tis not seemly for a man to be in the birthing room." She remained cross that he continued to return despite repeated threats to leave and not return.

After breaking his fast the next morn, Grant could stand it no longer. Tory's screams hadn't abated. "Something must be wrong!" Heading up the circular stone staircase to his bedchamber, he walked in without knocking and headed to the bed, ignoring Elbethal's graphic threats.

Tory looked as white as a ghost.

Spinning to look at the midwife, Grant grabbed Elbethal's arm and pulled her from the room. "Something is wrong, woman. What is it?"

The auld woman refused to look into his eyes. "The bairnie is turned wrong. 'Tis either sideways or breech."

Grant frowned. "Sideways I understand. What does the other mean?"

"The bairnie could be trying to come out bum first," she explained in a tone she'd use if speaking to a child. Men, she thought! They dinnae know a thing about bairnies except how to make them.

"Can you do naught about it?" Grant appealed in exasperation. Elbethal shook her head. "Can you not stop her pains?" Again the wiry woman shook her head.

"Is she no closer to having the bairnie than when she started yestermorn?" Grant questioned in shock.

Sighing heavily, the midwife shook her head.

Spewing a string of expletives, Grant turned back toward his room. Elbethal tried to stop him. "Nay, woman," Grant growled in frustration. "You overstep your bounds. This is my home and my bedchamber. I'll go where I wish. I care not what has been done in past. I make the rules and if I wish to be with my lady wife, neither you nor anyone else will stop me."

He headed to his bed and sat beside Tory, reaching for her hand. "Good morn, Sweeting."

When her next pain hit, Tory squeezed his hand. Hard. He hadn't known she was that strong. When she released her grip, Grant stared at his hand. The wee lass left marks on it. He wouldn't tell her that, of course, nor did he pull his hand away. If she could handle the pain she was feeling, he could handle the pain in a mere hand.

After her next contraction, Grant didn't know if he still believed that.

He sat beside her for hours, held her hand, and cooled her face with a damp cloth. Still no progress.

Tory paled with each passing moment and Grant knew without asking that she steadily grew weaker. He didn't have a good feeling about this. He rose and headed to the door, motioning Elbethal to follow.

"Tell me the truth, auld woman," Grant eyed her gravely. "Is she going to live?"

Elbethal shook her head ruefully. "Nay, Laird Drummond. She will not make it. She is too weak, and it has been too long." Seeing the look of anguish on her young chieftain's face, she reached a bony hand out to comfort him. "I am sorry. All we can hope for is the bairnie to be born alive."

"Nay!" Grant yelled as his heart sank.

Staring at her, Grant asked, "Is my bairn still turned wrong?"

Elbethal nodded.

"Turn it."

"M'lord, I cannot do that!" She looked shocked at such a suggestion. "'Twould go against nature."

Frustrated beyond reasoning, Grant roared, "How goes it against nature? We do it with animals."

"Your lady wife is not an animal," the auld woman said, outraged at his suggestion. "English or not, she is still a child of God. The kirk would not condone such an act."

Muttering, she thought surely this must be one reason why men were banned from the birthing room.

"The kirk would not condone saving a woman's life? Rubbish!" Rage and grief pushed Grant to the limit of his patience.

"Not like that. 'Twould be sinful."

Grant stared angrily, and Elbethal saw his long, powerful legs braced apart. She glared right back, but he dismissed her. "Good woman, I thank you for all the work you did for our people as midwife. You served my family well these many years. Pray do not take me wrong about that. I appreciate your efforts. I think, however, time has come for you to step down as head midwife in my keep. I believe I need someone willing to use whatever means are necessary to save a child – and the child's mother.

"I will not allow my lady wife to die. Do you hear me?"

His voice rose louder than he intended.

When she glared and turned back toward his room, Grant grabbed her arm. "Nay, woman. Leave now. You will not return to my chamber."

Shouting unladylike curses, she spun on her heels and rushed downstairs. "'Tis all the fault of the English. She did naught right about this birth. Refused to go to her lying-in room, she did, and now she's in the chief's own bed having his bairn. Disgraceful."

Not wishing to hear any more of the old woman's tirade, Grant turned and headed back into his room. He sat on the bed and told Tory what he planned to do.

She shook her head wanly.

"Nay, my love." Another pain gripped her and she grabbed for his hand. She waited until it passed before she spoke again. "I appreciate the thought you have given it, but 'twill never work." Reaching up to gently stroke his cheek, she turned serious. "I know I am dying. I realized that a long time ago. I only pray God will allow our son to be born safely and grant me a few precious minutes to hold him just once."

"Son?" Grant frowned.

"It must be a son," she smiled through her tears, making an effort to tease him. She could see the worry on his face and hated to be the cause of it. "No daughter of mine would ever be this stubborn. Only a son of yours would choose to be so pig-headed." Once again a pain gripped her body, weakened it with each pain.

Tory tried to smile, but the effort proved too difficult.

She sighed.

"I love you, Grant Drummond, but I'll not be here to care for our child. Promise me you will love him."

"Of course I'll love him," Grant stormed, standing up. "What kind of monster—"

"And if by...some wry twist of fate it should turn out to be a daughter...promise me you will...love her, too," she interrupted his tirade as if he said nothing. She hesitated a moment, then added, "Promise me you'll not do to her what...my father did to me."

It felt like a knife twisted in Grant's heart. He knew how much it cost her to ask him that. "Of course I promise, but," he amended as he sat, and smiled with a reassurance he didn't feel, "I promise I'll love all our children. That means you must live so we can have other bairns. I want a whole houseful if that is agreeable with you."

Tory grimaced at the thought, but shook her head sadly. "Nay, my love, I'll not be around to give you other children. This is the one and only, I fear." She looked at him lovingly. "Any other children you desire, you will have to have with your next wife."

"Damnation, woman." Grant stood again and railed, "I'll not listen to such rubbish. I have told you repeatedly you are the only wife I will ever have." He added, "I'll hear no more on the subject."

Frustrated, he turned and asked the women in the room, "Can you perform the procedure I speak of?"

Clearly scared beyond reason, they all shook their heads.

Grant contemplated the procedure. "My hands are too large. I might kill Tory just trying and will not take that risk."

His face clouding, he stormed, "Nay! I will not allow it. Do you hear me, wife? I forbid you to die."

He stormed from the room and down the stairs. He started to shout for his men, but realized most were already gathered at the bottom of the staircase. Apparently his shouting had caused quite a stir.

"Warwick," he ordered, "take men and our fastest mounts and fetch back that auld crone. Tell her she is needed to save my lady wife's life. If she will not come willingly, throw her over a horse. I care not how you do it, just get her! Ride like your life depends on it."

Sadly he added, "My lady's does."

Grant didn't wait for Warwick's assent. He turned and bolted back to his chamber, striding for his bed and placing Tory's hand within his.

"I sent Wick to fetch Agnes, lady mine. Hold on now and she will be here soon. She will know how to help you," Grant assured with far more conviction than he felt. A feeling of deep anxiety washed over him as he watched her slowly fade away from him.

Tory sighed, barely able to hold her head up any longer. Merciful Father in Heaven, she didn't want to die. She finally found someone to love and didn't want to leave him now. She'd been happier here than she'd been in her entire life. Why did her time with Grant have to be so short? She'd dared to hope her life would finally be happy. Why had God given her Grant only to take her away from him so soon?

Tory decided that would be one of the hundreds of questions she planned to ask God when she met Him. Her list was quite long, since she'd started it as a child. Her priest in Berwick hadn't believed God would waste His time talking to her since she was a mere woman, but Tory didn't believe that for a moment. God would be the kind Father she never had on earth.

Time passed and the lifeblood seemed to fade from Tory's eyes. Grant never left her side. He cared not what gossip women of his keep started. This was his home and he made the rules. Banning the husband from the birthing room seemed sheer nonsense. To his frame of mind, pacing at the bottom of the stairs, hearing Tory's screams and not knowing what was happening could certainly be no better than being with her and hearing her screams. At least here he felt slightly more productive.

He could hold her hand.

Of course, he doubted he'd ever be able to use it again after the way she squeezed it. *'Twould likely be totally useless. Well*, he mused, *I learned to fight with my right hand, now I shall learn to fight with the left.*

Finally Agnes walked into the room. She approached Tory and assessed the situation. "The bairn is turned wrong," she told him with a worried look in her eyes.

"Och, I know, woman," Grant yelled in exasperation, checking the impulse to shake her. "I knew that hours ago. 'Tis why I sent for you! I need you to turn the bairn so it will come out."

Agnes' eyes grew huge. "You want me to what?"

"Turn my bairn."

"I do not think it can be done, Laird Drummond. I never heard of it afore."

Grant watched Agnes' surprised reaction. Clearly she though his grief over possibly losing his wife caused him to go daft. Well, it hadn't—and he'd not give up now.

"I do not care that it has never been done afore. There must be a first time for everything. That is what Da always said."

When Agnes looked down at Tory, Grant roared huskily, "She is your friend, auld woman. Probably the only one you have in this world. Do not let her die."

Agnes looked at him awhile, then beckoned him outside the room. "Why do you want the lassie to live? What if I just save the bairn?"

"Nay!" Grant yelled and shook his head emphatically. "Both must live."

"Why?"

"Why, what?" Grant groaned in exasperation. He couldn't fathom why this woman wasted time asking questions when his wife's life hung by a sheer thread.

"Why do you want her to live? Give me a good reason and mayhap I'll try what you ask." Agnes stared up at him. She met him eye-to-eye and didn't flinch once when he tried to stare her down.

"Because I said so," Grant said, standing straighter and towering over the wizened, auld woman.

Agnes refused to budge an inch, and shook her head. "Not good enough."

After another scream resounded from inside his bedchamber, Grant's gaze strayed to the bed where Tory lay in agony. He broke down and looked at Agnes pleadingly, hoping the true depth of his feelings reflected in his eyes.

"Agnes, please! Do not let her die. I...I...*need her*."

That was all he could admit right now, but please, God, let Agnes know what he really meant.

Agnes nodded.

Walking inside the room, she headed straight to the basin. While she thoroughly cleansed her hands and arms, she asked, "How do you turn your animals?"

Grant described the process in minute detail as he brushed a tendril of hair from Tory's sweat soaked brow.

Waiting until the next pain had passed, Agnes worked her hand carefully inside her lady. "I never thought I'd be doing something like this!"

The other women in the room stood with eyes wide, while Triona went to a corner to pray, unable to watch anymore.

When Tory had her next pain and clamped down on Agnes' arm, Agnes let out a screech almost as loud as Tory's. The pain was awful! She'd be surprised if her arm hadn't broken.

Not wanting to experience such pain again, as soon as Tory's pains passed, Agnes made a grand effort to turn the babe before the next contraction began.

She met with no success.

When Tory's contraction subsided, Agnes yelled at Grant, "Push hard on her belly. Mayhap by placing pressure on the baby's buttock, it might help me turn the child." She let out an exuberant yell when the wee body rotated – and pulled her arm out quickly.

Just in time, too, for with her next breath, her lady let out another yell. Only this time Agnes could see the top of the bairn's head.

"Lady, push with every ounce of strength you have left."

Tory bore down.

With only three more pushes, Laird Grant and Lady Tory had a braw wee son!

As soon as they cleaned the babe, Isobel handed him to Grant. "Your son, Laird Drummond."

Grant was elated, probably grinned like a lack-witted fool. He smiled down into his son's wrinkled, red face. He tried without success to look nonchalant about the situation now that things were back under control. Never had he seen anything so beautiful – or so small.

Grant glanced up and saw Agnes' frown. "What is wrong?"

"Och," she admitted, "the poor lassie hemorrhages. Just what she didn't need. She needs every bit of blood she has left to help her mend after the lengthy ordeal she's been through."

Grant choked out, "But you can help her, right?"

Agnes nodded her head in determination. "Och, aye. Both son and mother shall make it through the night. After the last hour's miraculous events, I refuse to lose my lady now."

Grant took his son to Tory and placed him on her chest so she could see him. The love he saw shining in her eyes brought him close to tears. Nay, this woman couldn't die. God simply wouldn't give him such a rare gift only to take her away from him so soon. In his heart, Grant knew it. Agnes would do whatever she must to save his wife.

Tory hallucinated for the remainder of the night.

Agnes shouted, "Bring clean cloths. I need them to pack Lady Tory in an effort to staunch the bleeding." While waiting, she deeply massaged Tory's belly.

Tory cried out.

"You hurt her," Grant remonstrated.

"Aye, I've heard it hurts, but for the massage to do any good, it must be deep." She continued this process throughout the night and well into the next day.

Grant was torn between wanting to take his son outside to show him to everyone and letting the poor laddie sleep. It had, after all, been traumatic for him, too. Grant finally opted to let him sleep. He placed him in the borrowed cradle, and moved it beside the bed so Tory could see the babe should she awaken.

She didn't.

Sometime during the endless hours of waiting and pacing, Agnes cast a sympathetic glance at him. "Your lady wife is in God's hands, m'lord. 'Tis the best place she can be."

After breaking his fast, Grant remained concerned. His son needed to nurse, and Tory still hadn't wakened. Pacing before his hearth, he decided he'd introduce his son to his men, and then find a milk mother.

He headed upstairs and heard his son's lusty cry as he entered the chamber. Agnes walked him to and fro in an effort to quiet him. Clearly pleased to see him, she handed the babe to him upon his entry.

The babe quieted immediately and Grant couldn't stop a smile from spreading across his face. "He knows me!" That *must* be why he stopped crying. Heading upstairs to the ramparts, Grant called down to everyone, "I have a son!" Those milling around in the courtyard cheered. Then Grant felt foolish. They'd already known that, of course. They'd known since the minute the laddie had been born.

Grant descended to the Great Hall, where his men waited. 'Twas amazing how one tiny person had so many grown men talking gibberish.

Not wanting to keep his bairn away from Tory overlong, he headed upstairs. Now if only she'd awaken. He walked into his bedchamber and was surprised to see her awake and smiling. He quickly turned to Agnes. "How fares she?"

Agnes smiled. "She is fair weak, but I believe she is safe now." She offered a feeble smile. "She was not too pleased with me awhilst ago when I tried to get her bleedin' to stop. I know 'tis painful having her belly pushed, but 'tis necessary."

At that his son let out a howl and Grant took him to his mother. "Feel you up to nursing our wee laddie, Sweeting, or should I find a milk mother?"

Tory raised her arms weakly and smiled as Grant placed her babe beside her. "I already told you I wanted to nurse him myself. I know you said laird's wives usually do not nurse their own babies, but I care not. He's my son, and I want to care for him. I want not to give him to a milk mother. If I live, I want him to depend on me." She adjusted her nightrail and carefully placed her tiny son to her breast. After a few howls of frustration from the babe at not getting what he wanted, Tory finally adjusted him so he latched on properly.

Grant smiled at the sight of Tory nursing his son and his heart swelled with the love he was so afraid to express. The bairn's tiny fist curled tightly against Tory's breast as he suckled. Blessed St. Michael, he'd never seen a sight so beautiful. He never thought he could feel this proud—or this protective. Nothing would ever harm these two people. *I vow I'll do my best to keep that promise.*

While Tory fed his very hungry son, Grant went to the nursery to fetch in their cradle. Now that his bairn had slept in the borrowed cradle, he could return it to his ghillie and they could begin to use theirs. He really liked the tiny version of his coat of arms his carpenter chiseled in the corner.

Tory remained upset about not being able to use the cradle she found, but he couldn't allow that. He hoped she'd eventually appreciate his having the new one built.

Carrying the cradle into their chamber, Agnes helped him set it up on Tory's side of the bed. He reached under Tory's bedding. She watched him as her tiny son continued to suckle.

"What are you doing?" she asked while he fumbled beneath the bedding.

"Trying to find the knife they placed under here." Looking up quickly, he asked, "They did do that, did they not? Och, mayhap that is why it hurt so badly. Did they forget?"

She rolled her eyes. "Nay, my love, they did not forget, but it certainly didn't help. 'Twas one of those many things you forgot to tell me, right?"

He nodded shamefacedly.

"I thought they were trying to kill me!"

Grant burst out laughing. "You did not tell them that, I hope."

"Oh, aye, I did. Elbethal kept looking at me as though she thought I was daft. You could have warned me, you know." She glared up at him. "If you were closer, I would hit you, sir."

Grant grinned. "Then I am glad I'm far enough away so you cannot cause me bodily harm." He found the knife and turned toward the cradle. When he bent over it, Tory ordered, "Do not put that anywhere near our son's cradle, Grant Drummond! What are you thinking?"

Grant straightened and turned to Agnes in appeal.

Clearing her throat, the crone walked slowly to Tory and sat on the bed. "Now lassie, your young man does naught but what we've done for years."

Tory sighed with resignation. "Another tradition?"

"Aye," Agnes responded, smiling. "Putting a knife in the cradle, keeps away faeries who might switch your bonny child for a sickly faery child."

"Faeries?" Tory questioned in disbelief as Agnes and Grant nodded their heads. What were they talking about? How could these people be so intelligent, yet so superstitious?

"And faeries want my child?" Biting her lip, she tried to keep from laughing.

"Och aye," Agnes nodded without hesitation, "'tis a *changeling*."

Tory had no doubt Agnes believed every detail. "A changeling?"

Grant and Agnes solemnly nodded. Not wanting to hurt their feelings, she didn't laugh, although it took great effort. How had she wound up in the middle of such superstitious people? Moreover, how hadn't she realized how ingrained these old beliefs were?

"I see. Well then, of course, you must do whatever you can to protect him." She nodded agreement for Grant to place the knife in the cradle as she looked down at her son's beautiful face and tiny lashes. "But it doesn't have to stay there long, does it? I'd not want him to injure himself moving around."

Nodding, both assured her that wouldn't happen.

Tory handed the babe to Grant and patted the bed, indicating Grant should sit. "Have I missed any other unusual customs?"

In unison, Agnes and Grant both assured her nothing untoward had happened.

Seeing her tiring, Grant insisted, "You must rest before our babe wakes and wishes to nurse again. He's a strong lad, will have a healthy appetite."

Though insisting she wasn't tired, Tory quickly lost that battle when she had difficulty keeping her eyes open. She hated going back to sleep, knowing there must be so many things Grant and Agnes still had to tell her. She really wanted to know some of their customs before they happened instead of always after they occurred. The fact they considered none of these things odd seemed amazing, but before she could ask any more questions, she fell fast asleep.

Smiling, Grant leaned down and brushed a kiss on her forehead before he exited the room.

Chapter Thirty-four

Grant hated he had to leave so soon, but Andrew sent word he wished to meet with Wallace. Friend to both, it seemed logical he act as liaison. If the need arose—and he had no doubt it would—a possible joining of forces could only benefit Scotland.

He rejoiced that the priest made it to the castle in time to hold the christening ceremony before his departure. Being present for his son's christening was of great import to him and had been the reason he'd sent for the priest as soon as Tory's pains began.

Now he walked about his keep, ensuring everything remained on schedule and in place.

When he explained their christening practices to Tory, she insisted, "Agnes must be returned to the castle. I want the woman who saved both of our lives to be the person who carries him to the blessed ceremony. I owe her that honor."

Although dubious over her selection, he finally agreed and quickly told Warwick, "Have someone return Agnes to the castle."

To his surprise, the auld woman seemed overwhelmed at her lady's request.

Warwick reported, "She turned female on me and blubbered when told of our lady's request."

"I thought the crotchety auld woman would refuse my lady wife's offer. How like her to know a person's true heart better than I do. 'Tis only one of many things I admire about her."

Now Agnes held his precious son. Being unwed, she qualified for the honor of carrying the young lordling to his christening. While she carefully held his bairn, he handed her a small parcel to carry downstairs.

Tory hoped no one saw her smile about the bread and cheese. She'd never mention they would do no such thing in English christening ceremonies. Agnes was to present these offerings to the first man she met on her way to the ceremony, regardless of what position he held in Grant's keep.

To Tory's delight, it wound up being Warwick—since the man determinedly waited at the foot of the staircase. With proper formality he accepted the proffered bread and cheese.

Before they left the room, Grant told her, "I must find a small bit of parchment so I can write our son's name on it. 'Tis not to be spoken aloud until the priest officially announces it at the christening cermony." Although he hadn't attended many christenings, his mam ensured he knew all the particulars for the day when he had children of his own. Never planning on giving his heart to anyone, he never thought that day would come.

Thinking of how proud his mother would be, Grant smiled. She'd wanted grandchildren so much. He hoped she rested with angels now.

When the group proceeded into the Hall, he noted its appearance with pride. Women had outdone themselves decorating for this blessed event.

Again the thought flashed through his mind that he should build a chapel inside the keep. He'd not thought of it often, but now wondered if he should consider it seriously. After all, this wouldn't be the only christening ceremony. He hoped he and Tory would have many children together – assuming she ever let him touch her again after the ordeal she'd just been through! And his men needed a place for their christening and wedding ceremonies, as well. *Aye*, he thought to himself, *a chapel that can be used by all.*

He'd mention it to Tory and see what she thought, although he betted his lady wife would love the idea. Since she worried they didn't have their own priest, Grant thought the least he could do was give her a proper place to pray. The tiny room she'd set aside before Christmas day showed him how much her faith meant to her, as it had his mother.

Soon the small group stood before Father McLeod. Though still weak from the birthing, Tory had been adamant. "Do not even think about keeping me away from my son's christening, my lord."

Seeing the resolute gleam in her eyes, Grant hadn't even tried to talk her out of it. Knowing how important the ceremony was to him, he knew it would be as important to her. So now he carefully supported her from their chamber to the Great Hall, one arm tightly around her waist. Looking down, he smiled warmly into her eyes and saw his slow sexy smile sent a shiver of pleasure through her.

Father McLeod began the blessed event, smiling at the child presented before God. "Och, Laird Drummond, what a bonny braw laddie he is."

Tory frowned at the priest. Didn't he plan to say anything to her? She'd been a major factor in this *bonny braw laddie's* birth! Some things never changed. 'Twas a man's world, and always would be. Tory determined she'd somehow make a difference in it.

After intoning God's blessings, Father McLeod turned to Grant. "And the child's name?"

Following proper tradition, Grant handed the neatly folded sheaf of paper to the priest.

Father McLeod opened the parchment and smiled when he saw the name. "Lord, I humbly ask your blessings on this wee bairn." He turned to all gathered in the Hall. "I introduce to you, Master James Duncan Malcolm Grant Drummond."

The tiny, wee bairn had big shoes to fill. He'd been named after his da, his grandda, and his da's best friend. Not to mention a former king. 'Twas a perfect name for a perfect bairn.

Tory giggled softly. "Aye, and after all that pomp and circumstance, we'll simply call him Jamie."

Grant left the next morn as the rising sun burned off the heavy mist. He'd left Tory and Jamie snuggled beneath their bed covers. Tory finished nursing Jamie when Grant forced himself to rise and leave. He insisted, "Stay abed, my love. No need for you to accompany him me to the courtyard. You still look weak and wan." Besides, he'd thought to himself, he'd be unable to leave if he saw her standing in his Hall's doorway right now.

"Grant, please do not leave," she said, trying one last time to talk him out of leaving, but knew what his response would be before she even started. Not willing to admit defeat, she stubbornly told him, "If you die, sir, be assured I shall not cry for you one whit."

Grant feathered kisses on her forehead and gently drew her closer. "Aye, wife, you would, and you know it." When she tried to turn her face so he wouldn't see the tears which threatened to fall, he held her fast. "But you will not need do so. I will return, my heart. That is my solemn promise."

Holding held her tightly, he nuzzled his lips against her neck. *Please God, let that be the truth.*

Knowing his actions would benefit Scotland in the long run didn't ease the ache in his belly. Although the danger posed by Edward couldn't be ignored, he never thought it would hurt so much to leave. Sighing in resignation, he spurred his steed forward and headed for the distant mountains.

Having traveled north, Grant met with Andrew. Days later, Will joined them.

Grant asked, "What news of the war?"

Will approached and shook hands. "At Wisehart's request, we marched to Scone and surprised them."

Soon they headed north to meet Andrew. Although their fighting styles were vastly different, many of their ideas were the same, and their mutual goal was their desire to free Scotland from Edward's heavy-handed rule. They realized the danger he posed had to be confronted head on.

For days they tossed around ideas, then Will headed south to Lanark and Grant returned to Crief.

Andrew returned to Avoch Castle, where he'd raised his Standard. While pondering his future whilst in gaol, he'd decided the great stone fortress would be the base where he and his forces would gather. Its formidable stone curtain walls and entrance towers kept most strangers at bay, and he relished fostering that appearance. And the English *would* pay for his treatment in gaol.

Knowing his chosen path would be demanding, Andrew started his campaign in the north, confident Will did the same in the south.

Not long after beginning his northern revolt, Andrew received word Sir William Fitzwarine, Urquhart Castle's constable, intended to travel to Inverness Castle. Fitzwarine's men were unprepared for battle, but regrouped quickly. To Andrew's consternation, the man escaped. Despite that, many hastily abandoned their sworn allegiance to Edward and united with him under Scotland's banner of freedom.

Andrew vowed, "Fitzwarine will not elude me again." He proceeded to Urquhart to capture the man and his castle.

Boxed in by Andrew's forces, things looked bleak for Fitzwarine.

"We need only sit tight and outwait those inside the fort. They'll either capitulate," Andrew told his men, "or they'll starve."

He felt confident of the outcome.

"Damnation," Andrew roared upon discovering the Countess of Ross sent her son with goods to provision Urquhart Castle. "'Her actions are a betrayal of trust."

He paced and fumed. "She shall pay for this. Siding with the opposition isn't the way to obtain her husband's release. Had it not been for the bloody English, he wouldn't be a prisoner in the first place."

Andrew quickly had his revenge. With a defiant shout, sounds of battle resounded when his men stormed Balconie Castle and seized her family castle. He soon split his forces and utilized both strongholds—Avoch and Balconie.

Alarmed by the crisis sweeping Scotland, Edward was determined to end the rebellion. He summoned leading Scots to an Eyre-court in Ayr.

"Meet at the Barns," he said.

Everyone had been told, "The Eyre-court will be held in the Barns."

All knew its location, and Edward felt certain Scots would attend. He'd summoned them after all, and who dared naysay him?

Contrary to Edward's belief, many nobles couldn't bring themselves to attend. Shouts of "I want naught to do with the Sassunach king" were heard all around the Highlands.

Someone was overheard saying, "I do not wish to listen to anything that murderer has to say. 'Twill be naught but lies."

Days later, men gathered with Wallace in Leglen Wood.

"What incenses me," Will said as he looked at those gathered, "is the underhanded way bloody barstards massacred our fellow countrymen."

"Here, here," men chorused, waving tankards of ale.

"I did not fancy some of those nobles, but none deserved to die like they did." For the benefit of Grant, who'd recently arrived, he explained, "They must have been restrained as soon as they were herded in, single file. The lot were gagged and nooses placed 'round their necks. Then they were strung up from the rafters. Edward's *meeting* was naught but a trap!"

"Curse Edward's damnable hide," Grant stormed.

Sending scouts before them, the rebels stealthily entered town a few days later. In the middle of the night, Will ordered, "Take fifty men to Ayr Castle. Keep it under surveillance. Remaining men, follow me." They approached The Barns and found the doors their scouts had marked.

They found the English judge inside, along with a contingent of soldiers, obviously sleeping off the effects of a heavy night of drinking. Will motioned for the door to be barricaded and brush placed around the building.

Determined the vile atrocities be repaid in kind, they doused the building liberally with oil.

Will gave the silent signal to torch the building, setting it ablaze and trapping its occupants inside.

Satisfied justice had been dealt, Grant turned his men homeward. Thinking of home instantly brought Tory to mind. She represented the peace and love he equated with home. It had taken him a long time to find such peace.

He quickened his efforts to return.

Back home after endless fighting, Grant rejoiced in holding Tory. Leaning her against him as he held her after having made slow, passionate love to her, he was surprised when she asked, "Tell me about your family. How came they to Scotland?"

With a teasing smile, he nuzzled her neck. "Och, so you wish to know all my family secrets?"

Jabbing him with her elbow, she teased right back. "Family secrets? Nay, my lord husband, I want to know where all your coin is!" The radiant smile on her face made Grant draw her closer as he accepted her teasing, nibbling on her ear as he did so.

"I suppose you should know something of the family you wed into. I only know it back about two hundred years, mind."

"That sounds like a faery tale," Tory teased.

"Och, aye, you are right. All of the faery tales Mam told me as a boy began with the words, *it happened about two hundred years ago.*"

She batted her lashes playfully.

He shifted on the bed to make himself more comfortable. "Let me see. After the Norman invasion, Edgar the Atheling fled from William the Conqueror. He and his mam set sail for Hungary to escape men invading their homelands. His sisters, Margaret and Isabella, accompanied them."

"Where were they fleeing from?" she asked, curious to know all she could about the man she now freely admitted loving.

"England."

She drew in a surprised breath. "Your ancestors came from *England*?" She turned to glare at him. "You made derogatory comments about my being English and *your* forbearers came from England just as mine did?"

"That was a long time ago, wife. I'm a Scot, and that's that." His eyes dared her to contradict him, although the stunned expression in her eyes almost made him laugh.

"But..."

His glare effectively silenced her, although she huffed in indignation.

"The ship's captain they sailed with was grandson of Hungary's King Andrew. Suffice it to say I am descended from him. We will not go into the *how* or *why* of that," Grant chuckled.

When Tory again opened her mouth to ask a question, Grant interrupted. "If I go back far enough, I am also related to Attila the Hun." At the look of wonder on her face, he teased, "That must be why you think me a barbarian."

Tory rolled her eyes at his observation.

"Actually, if you combine this with marriages to Scottish Stuart kings, I've a link to almost every royal house in Europe."

"Bragging, my lord husband?"

Grant ignored her comment. "The King of Scotland well-comed my family. He wed Edgar's sister, Margaret, who was later made a saint."

She muttered under her breath. "Spare me your arrogance, sir. 'Tis a good thing someone in your family is a saint. You certainly are not."

Lips twitching, Grant ignored her derogatory comment. "The King of Scotland made the man who brought my family over on his ship the thane of Lennox. 'Tis a title Drummond chieftains still hold. Part of the lands given were those of Dryman, on Loch Lomond's eastern shores. 'Tis where the name Drummond comes from, mind."

Tory giggled. "This, sir, is pure folly."

Grant leaned around her, and with a mock stern look enquired, "Wish you I continue, wife?" Before she could answer, he said, "Because if you do, I suggest you do not laugh. Especial," he muttered and gave her an impatient scowl, "when I tell you how great I am."

Looking like she tried to stifle a smile, she dutifully nodded agreement.

Grant tried to frown, but couldn't contain his own mirth.

"My grandda loved my granddam very much and started our garden for her. Da was named after him. Though he believed it his responsibility to swear fealty to England's monarch, he remained a fervent supporter of Scottish independence. 'Tis partly why I fight for it. I do it for him, as well as everyone who depends on me."

Tory twisted in Grant's arms.

"What?" Grant asked at her continued stare. From the pensive look on her face he doubted he'd like her question.

"Your grandfather loved your grandmother, and your father loved your mother. Yet you do not believe in love. Why?"

Grant gazed at her a long time. Leave it to his lassie to think of that! She was far too astute. He answered with a long sigh. "Too many things have happened in my life." He tried to change tactics. "Mayhap they did not actually love their wives. Mayhap they *cared very deeply.*"

"Think you could ever care deeply for someone?"

Knowing exactly what she asked, he measured his words carefully. "Once I would have said nay."

"And now?" she prodded.

Locking his gaze with hers, Grant carefully responded. "Och, aye, now I believe I could care for someone very much." He pulled her closer and nuzzled her neck. "Very much indeed."

Feeling safe and content in his arms, she changed the subject. "Tell me about your mother."

"She was the kindest woman I ever knew. Da loved—cared for—her very much. Even more than my grandda loved—cared for—my granddam." A far away look entered his eyes. "She fit in here from the moment Da brought her home. She loved our garden as much as my granddam did. That's why Da enhanced it. She spent hours out there. Said it calmed her spirit."

Grant added with a heavy heart, "Mam would have loved you, wife. In many ways you are quite like her."

"I wish I'd known her." She shifted on the bed so she could tilt her head to kiss him. "I would like to thank her for the wonderful son she raised."

Grant beamed with thankfulness as he pulled her into his arms. His kisses silenced the rest of her questions.

In August, William heard Warenne and his men were headed to Stirling. Will headed there as well, sending out a call to arms to Andrew, Grant, and Duncan.

In what now seemed a common occurrence, Grant's men headed to fight for their freedom. *Och, I feel old*, he thought. *All I want to do is stay with Tory, but I cannot shun my duties to my country.*

That didn't stop him from thinking of his lady wife, though. He loved watching her with Jamie.

She carried the lad everywhere and told him all she knew about everyone they came in contact with. Grant always laughed when he saw her speaking to the boy, just like he understood every word.

She always had him outside while regaling the children with stories. Little ones often ran around yelling, or made funny faces at the tyke in an effort to make him laugh. Tory laughed at their antics.

A remembrance of his son trying to push himself up or roll over made him laugh out loud. Jamie's bottom would push up in the air as he drew his knees beneath him. As he tried to move one tiny hand forward, he'd flop on his face—only to start the entire process over again. A happy child, Jamie always smiled and cooed. To listen to Tory, one would think her son the most talented child in the world.

What Grant thought more amusing, was he completely agreed.

When home, he'd practice in the lists, then rush to take his son from his lady wife's arms and walk him around the keep. He loved holding the miniature version of himself.

I'm blessed, he thought. *I never thought I could feel so much love for such a tiny being – or that person's mother.*

Not after what happened in the past.

And now he had to leave them both again. As agreed the past moon's passing, he was to meet Andrew and Will on the ninth of September at Orchil Hills. The time had come—they were to forge final battle plans.

Grant glanced around at the country he so loved. The river Forth wound through the valley. Behind that, the Trossachs loomed with the hazy blue of summer, a sharp contrast to their recent snow-capped winter appearance.

In the distance stood Stirling Castle, overlooking the Forth Valley. Commanding the main north-south and east-west roads of Scotland, all knew Stirling's location was why 'twas so important for them to hold Stirling's Castle.

He crossed over a wooden bridge spanning the Forth's lowest crossing point. Beyond that, a causeway ran over marshland to the Abbey Craig.

The rock overlooking the Forth was where the three men met and waited for the next battle to begin.

Andrew said, "Will, I know you're used to a different style of warfare, but I'm convinced this will win the battle."

Will nodded grudgingly. "My only stipulation is we use the device I've developed. Should prove quite handy."

Andrew pointed out, "Although we have many men present, our army remains too small to meet the massive English army head on. Skillful planning will defeat our powerful English enemy. The majority of our weapons are homemade. Most have no armour, and only a few have simple steel skullcaps for protection. I suggest positioning our men so we take advantage of the narrow wooden bridge and the area's swampy ground."

Finally agreeing, they deployed their men upon this craig.

Chapter Thirty-five

Tory worked in the garden when she received word they had a guest. As always, Jamie lay on a large fur making tiny cooing sounds, and Lancelot bounded around the garden chasing anything in his path. It mattered not if it was another animal or something as mundane as a leaf. If it moved, Lancelot chased it and tried to play with it.

The courier informed them, "I have a message I've been instructed to deliver to Lady Drummond." Attempting to brush off dirt she acquired while working in the garden, Tory rushed to the Great Hall to greet their guest. As was usual Highland tradition, she quickly offered the young man refreshments.

While he eagerly ate the proffered food and gustily drank the ale, Tory intently read his message.

The young man told her, "No one else can see the dispatch's contents."

Several men tried to sit as well, but Tory waved them away. They left unwillingly, frowning all the while.

The courier said, "Your husband has been taken prisoner by Edward's forces, lady. He is sore wounded. Your husband specifically requested you join him in his last moments."

"Merciful heaven, of course I'll go to my husband," Tory gasped, deeply shaken. "Let me prepare our men and gather a few belongings. Then we can begin straightaway. I am not certain Jamie should travel yet, but I know Grant will want to see him, too."

She started to rise, but Hamish stayed her with his large hand. "Nay, lady. Naught but you must know of our plans. Edward's men said if you fetch anyone else, they will kill your husband outright."

Tory shook her head. Struggling to collect herself, she implored, "I cannot leave without telling my men. They'd not allow it. And I must nurse my son," Tory added nervously. "I cannot leave him, sir. He is far too young."

"We will wait until dark, lady," the young courier told her, discounting everything Tory told him. "I hear you are good at slipping out of places in the night."

Tory had the grace to blush.

"We go alone, lady, or we go not at all. The choice is yours," he goaded, witnessing her indecision. "Gather some belongings. Not much, mind," he warned as he watched her with grim determination, "since we will have to slip it out with us until we reach the horses outside the keep."

She rose, and Hamish looked at her sternly. "Remember, lady, tell no one aught of our plans. Your husband's life depends on it."

Tory nodded and rushed to the staircase where Archibald stopped her. "What is the lad's message, my lady?"

Tory gulped before answering. It was her only outward sign of emotion, but 'twas enough for Archie to catch, though he made no comment.

She hated lying to him.

"'Tis really naught, Archie. He delivered a message from Erwin. You know, Duncan's aide." Knowing it wasn't the complete truth, Tory couldn't meet his eyes. "Duncan thought of something Grant should know and took advantage of this young man traveling our way. He has asked for hospitality, and of course I told him he could stay the night. Your Highland hospitality, you know," Tory rushed on with forced cheerfulness.

Archibald nodded and let Tory depart, his eyes following her. The troubling thought crossed his mind that his lovely lady was lying, and she rarely did that. One of her traits he fancied most had been that he found her one of the most honest women he'd ever met – even though it had taken him a long time to grudgingly admit it.

The question he didn't have the answer to was why she did so now.

Tory gathered items she felt she must take and had wrapped them in a small bundle when Triona entered the room.

"Good eve, my lady," she smiled and eyed the bundle. "Need you help?"

Tory shook her head quickly. Too quickly.

"Nay, Triona, but I thank you for asking. I'll need no assistance this eve. I believe I'll turn in early." A small knot formed in her stomach. She didn't lie lightly.

Triona stood transfixed, finally shook her head. "Nay, lady, I cannot leave when I know you are not tellin' me the truth of it."

Tory gazed at her in astonishment.

"I know you too well." Triona nodded once, as if affirming her statement. "I have always respected you for your honesty. Pray do not change that now."

When Triona stood gazing at her young mistress, the unspoken words of friendship cut through Tory's heart.

"Oh, Triona, you're right" Disheartened, she added, "Please accept my apology. But the courier said I must not tell anyone."

"Lady?"

Her knees weakening in delayed reaction to the news she received, Tory sat on the edge of the bed. "I'll tell you the whole of it, Triona, but you must swear not to tell a soul." Tory rushed on before Triona could either agree or disagree. "The courier says Grant has been injured and captured. Says Grant is dying, and if I tell anyone, Edward's men will kill him outright! What am I to do, Triona? I cannot let that happen. I love him too much. I must go to him." When Triona said nothing, Tory told her in desperation, "I refuse to let him die. If I go, mayhap I can save him. Pray do not tell anyone what I said. I could not live with myself if something happened because I was too cowardly to travel on my own."

"Where go you?"

"I know not." When Triona looked doubtful, Tory said softly, "I really do not. All I know is Erwin sent this young man to bring me to Grant."

"I do not trust that one, lady. He had the look of evil about him when he was here," Triona warned. "But if I cannot stop you, then God's grace be wi' you in your travels. I'll pray for you and for Laird Grant's recovery." She walked to Tory and gave her a hug. Their relationship had advanced far beyond the point of merely helping her lady dress each day.

They cared for each other as friends.

"Thank you, Triona. Hopefully I'll be able to treat him and we will both be back quite soon. Surely between us we shall come up with a plan of escape."

Tory tried to smile, but the smile never reached her eyes.

Darkness descended as Tory and Hamish stood outside the keep's gate. Letting their eyes adjust to the darkness, Hamish put a finger to his lips and led her past the area where they could be seen from the castle's ramparts should anyone scan the periphery. To Tory's surprise, men waited with horses. No one said a word.

Leaving her alone for a moment, Hamish spoke briefly with the others. Soon, they mounted their horses. Not given her own mount, Tory had to ride with one of them. He said naught, just spurred his mount forward.

When Triona didn't return to the Hall after talking with Tory, Archibald knew for a certainty something was wrong. Sharing his concerns with others, he left the Hall in search of the young maid. He found her alone in the garden, gazing pensively at the stars.

"Good eve, lass."

Not hearing him approach, Triona spun around at the sound of his deep voice.

"Och, Archie, you surprised me. I did not expect anyone to come out here now." She rose. "I'll leave you to enjoy the quietude. 'Tis lovely out here now that Lady Tory tends the garden."

Archibald stayed her with a calloused hand. "Dinnae leave, lass. I dinnae come here to be alone."

She frowned.

Archie added patiently, "I came in search of you."

He'd never been good at conversation with women. They were usually too frightened to speak with him.

Agitated, Triona began tocry. Clearly she knew why he'd searched her out. Archie moved to her quickly. To the young woman's surprise, he wrapped his arms around her in a comforting gesture. His gentle actions seemed totally out of character, even to him.

Knowing time of the essence, Archie prodded, "What is our young lady planning, lass? Dinnae tell me you know not. I know better than that."

Sniffling, Triona looked at him with eyes wide. "But Lady Tory said I couldn't tell anyone." She inhaled swiftly. Her eyes revealed she'd admitted too much.

"Tell me," he said firmly as he wiped tears from her cheeks. Surprise showed on her face. He knew he only showed people his gruff side. 'Twas a defense he'd adopted after his parents had been murdered.

"You could save her life if you tell me what you know."

Triona's head shot up and her hand flew to her mouth. "Oh! Do you think she's in danger?"

Chuckling, Archibald nodded. "Our young mistress attracts danger like honey attracts flies. 'Tis times like this I would much rather fight an enemy I can see than try to figure out what is in our Lady's beautiful head."

Realizing he had no further reason to justify holding her, he backed away. She felt so soft. Och, he'd had his share of camp followers and lightskirts, to be certain, but none had felt like this wee wisp of a girl.

Triona's eyes widened even more. "But she said 'twas Laird Grant that was in danger, not her."

"I do not fancy the sound of that." Shaking off the direction his mind had wandered, he demanded, "Tell me, lass. Every minute she is gone could be another minute she puts herself in grave danger."

Triona looked at him in alarm. "How did you know—?"

"She slipped from the keep?"

Triona nodded.

"Does she not always do some such thing when she thinks she's doing somethin' to *save* someone? Our wee lady has a knack for that, mind."

Triona shook her head in agreement.

"Am I not right? Does our lady not seem to have a penchant for getting into trouble?"

"She said she did not know where she was going," Triona finally admitted. "The courier told her Laird Grant is injured and is a prisoner. Said that weasel, Erwin, wanted her to come so he could take her to Laird Grant."

She shuddered as she said Erwin's name. 'Twas clear to Archie Triona didn't fancy the man. Not many did. No one had ever figured out why Duncan put up with him.

A ridiculous thought flashed through his mind. *I hope the wee lass does not feel the same way about me.*

Archie frowned at the foolish notion and returned to the subject at hand. "I doubt Erwin even knows where our chief is – or Duncan for that matter. He never goes warring with Duncan anymore, always having one excuse or another."

He paced the garden. "And something else doesn't ring true. If Grant were really captured, he'd never send for his lady. He'd do everything in his power to keep her as far away from the enemy as possible."

Giving Triona a quick hug, Archibald said, "I must leave now, lass and ride hot trod to see if I can catch their trail afore it grows old. Be a good lassie, now, and go tell Fergus exactly what you told me. I'll let Colin know where I'm going."

When she nodded, Archie stressed, "Dinnae leave out anything our young lady told you. No matter how unimportant you think it is, there may be some clue she dinnae know she revealed."

Again Triona nodded, but looked worried.

"What's wrong, lassie?" He hadn't meant to frighten her.

"What if Lady Tory gets angered wi' me for telling you what she's doing?"

Triona looked quite woebegone.

Archibald looked at her knowingly. Raising an eyebrow, he said, "I would prefer our young lady be angered with me and be safe and healthy, as opposed to us not knowing and her be injured or dead."

He turned on his heels to leave the garden.

Standing across from two Domincan friars, William snorted. "The English dispatch you to give we *rebels* a chance to surrender? And think you we believe your promises of generous treatment if we but yield?" He cast a disparaging scowl. "I think not! Return to thy friends and tell them we come here with no peaceful intent. We are ready for battle and determined to avenge our wrongs and set our country free. Let thy masters attack us. We are ready to meet them beard to beard."

His intent couldn't be misconstrued.

"Why wait you?" he shot at them. "Return to the English and tell them you think the Scots' army is little more than rabble."

Watching their actions from the craig, Will said, "Their arrogance leaves them little doubt they'll succeed. They think us nothing but farmers posing as warriors."

In the English camp, the Earl of Lennox pointed out, "Heed me. I strenuously oppose crossing the bridge here, since only two people can go abreast at a time. There is a ford but a wee distance away where 'twould be possible for mayhap sixty men to cross the stream abreast. 'Twould be better to cross there."

The Englishmen laughed and ignored his advice.

Realizing he was being ignored, Lennox tried a different tact. "Give me but five hundred horse and a few foot, and I shall turn the enemy's flank by the ford, whilst you cross the bridge in safety."

He turned to Cressingham, Edward's Treasurer/ Tax Collector, a man who was hated by all Scots.

Eyes flaming angrily, Cressingham fumed with his trademark impatience. "I quashed the southwestern rebellion of

Scottish lords almost single-handedly. Foolishly I spared their lives and their lands and now wished I'd done neither. I shall engage these rebels in head on battle."

Shortly after dawn, a party of English foot was dispatched over the bridge, but were soon recalled. Cressingham's impatience increased when he learned the interruption had been brought about because Warenne had overslept.

"I came back because of that old, ailing man? He's no longer in full control over his men." He swore, "Damnation! Why do we thus protract the war and waste the King's treasure? Let us fight. It is our bounden duty."

Frustration and anger rising, Cressingham fisted his hands. "I refuse to wait on him any longer." He looked at the Scots with loathing. "Come men, let us begin and swiftly put an end to this nonsense. We shall have this battle won for Edward before Warrene gathers his men."

Amid raucous shouts of "For God and St. George!" a haughty Englishman proudly carried the royal standard, clearly confident the battle would be short lived.

As they watched from the craig, the English army stormed across the bridge. Andrew reminded the Scots, "Stand firm until you hear the horn, men. Do not charge 'til then."

Though growing impatient as the English drew closer, they waited for Andrew's signal.

"Wait for my signal, then charge with all your might."

From their vantage point on the hill, Grant and his men could clearly see Stirling Castle. A single drawbridge over a deep ditch was the castle's only access.

"The central gatehouse and round gateway towers will be well manned," he reminded everyone. "'Tis imperative we catch men inside the castle off guard while fighting Warrene's men at the bridge."

"I hope the Guardroom Square, Stirling's second line of defense, will be lax," Andrew told the warriors. "I vow, the English assume we'll not survive the battle at the bridge, so they'll not expect us to arrive at the castle." He smiled sardonically. "I doubt they'll be prepared when we make our presence felt."

Grant didn't take his eyes from the unfolding scene. "Andrew, half of Cressingham's force has already crossed the bridge. Give the signal to attack."

Andrew nodded. "*Now!*" he shouted with authority.

346

As Scots' spearmen rushed down from Abbey Craig, the sound of a horn brayed from the slopes. Their piper immediately joined in.

They charged so swiftly, Englishmen were taken aback. Many had scant knowledge the battle had begun. Andrew nodded in approval. His plans were going exactly as planned.

Planning ahead, he ordered, "Alexandre, take a detachment to the ford in case the bloody English try and sneak up on us."

Grant joined Andrew and his men as they raced swiftly toward the unfolding battle, as the skirl of pipes continued.

Andrew capitalized on the momentum. The Scots' fell upon the leading ranks of English on the causeway. He shouted, "Seize the bridgehead and cut away its wooden timbers. That should surprise them."

Jostled from the causeway, heavily armoured horses plunged into the deep mire on either side. Unable to move, they threw their riders to the ground. Amidst these struggles, knights found the ground marshy, not firm like they were used to. Try as they might, they couldn't deploy their war-horses. Nor could they turn back, since the remainder of their own army pressed forward.

They were trapped!

Looking up, the usually unflappable knights panicked when they saw *deranged* men making a full downhill charge toward the bridge.

Encouraged by success, Andrew shouted, "Duncan, follow me." The small group got between the bridge and Englishmen who'd already crossed. They cut off any possible English retreat.

Used to fighting on the offensive, Englishmen were forced to defend their position and were unable to rise to the challenge.

Seeing Andrew's movement to intercept the English retreat accomplished, Will and Grant pressed on with greater force.

Half-formed columns of Englishmen standing on the northern bank soon gave way and cavalry were driven into the water. Too heavily armed to maneuver themselves to safety, they drowned.

The elderly Warrene looked at the ensuing carnage in mute horror. "For the love of God, assist those men in battle. They're being massacred." Those that tried added to the confusion and slaughter.

Shouting insults and obscenities, Scots laughed aloud at their foes' bumbling attempts. Screams of torment from wounded men mingled loudly amidst elated shouts of victory from the Scots.

Soon the English were assailed on every side by spearmen three deep, wielding twelve-foot spears in tight formations. Grant thought the shiltrons William designed looked like oval shaped rings. The oncoming cavalry charge couldn't break the tightly packed ranks of spearmen, and horses wound up impaled or hamstrung by the long spears.

The sound of legions of horses in pain proved deafening.

Many soldiers were injured as well and died torturous deaths. One young man opened his mouth to scream, but no sound emerged, blood bubbling out in its stead.

Amidst the carnage, remaining Englishmen were easily pulled from their mounts and their throats slit. Within minutes, the majority of the regiment lay dead.

Andrew saw Cressingham fighting furiously and quickly shifted his position to move closer to the fray. The danger posed by the man's continued fighting couldn't be ignored. Andrew felt a searing flash of pain, but charged onward.

Wild with rage, Cressingham fought on, shouting obscenities in his wake, but Andrew was the better-trained fighter. His eyes meeting those of his enemy, Andrew dragged the obese man from his horse and slew him. Cressingham's reign of terror came to a bloody end as a rapidly forming pool of blood seeped into the ground.

Finally the wooden bridge parted and crashed into the Forth, and men still attempting to cross the stream drowned. With the bridge destroyed, men standing on the opposite bank looked powerless to help.

The battle was over within an hour.

As was the case in most battles since Edward's bloody course of revenge, the flight of the losing forces became a scene of barbarous slaughter.

Like English armies had consistently done to them, the winning forces rode down fleeing soldiers and put them to the sword. After all the injustices done to them in the past, reason fled and a massacre ensued.

Cressingham's obese body was flayed and William muttered in derision, "Let us send pieces of his skin throughout the country as tokens of our defiance. That is just reward for the likes of him." Sneering, he added, "Take a large strip of skin from his body – from his head to his heel. I vow I'll have a baldric made for my own sword."

Seeing this barbaric action, others were in such a frenzied state they took pieces of Cressingham's skin as well.

Frowning at such brutality, Grant looked toward Duncan. He shook his head and both walked away, feeling Cressingham's death sufficient retribution.

They could find their friend, Andrew, nowhere. He'd protected his country at great personal risk to himself.

By eventide, men crossed the Esplanade into Stirling Castle and partook of a grand victory feast. Gathered within Stirling's Great Hall, "look at the size of this room" was heard by many. When built, it had been intended for great celebrations and occasions of state.

The weary fighters did their best to make this victory celebration worthy of its original intentions.

Kitchens serving the Great Hall were built against the Outer Close curtain wall. When Grant entered to get more food for his weary men, he was impressed with the five ovens.

Glancing around, he noticed several things within the two kitchens Tory would be delighted with and made a mental note to tell her. He turned and saw Duncan smiling.

"Impressive is it not?" Duncan asked as he canted his head toward the massive kitchens.

"Aye," Grant agreed. "I must tell Tory about the kitchen's design. She'd be amazed were she here to see this."

A mischievous twinkle appeared in Duncan's eyes as he looked around. "Aye, and can you not picture the wee lass decorating a Great Hall such as this at Christmastide?"

The two men fell about laughing as they headed back to the Hall.

By night's end a pall settled over the group when they learned Andrew had been struck by an arrow during the battle when he stopped Cressingham.

Though nodding his appreciation of the mens' accolades, he was already in too much pain to participate in many evening activities.

By the next day, his wound had already begun to fester.

"Return to Crieff with me. I am confident Tory's skills as a healer can help you."

Andrew couldn't be swayed. He looked sharply at Grant. "Nay. Unlike you, I love my wife and am not afraid to say so. I must return home. My wound does not look good, and the festering may only worsen."

Grant interrupted stubbornly. "Which is exactly why I wish you to come see my lady wife. Tory can help."

Andrew shook his head as pain glazed his eyes. "Och, Grant. Of course you think your bonny wife can help me. You think the lass can do anything."

When Grant frowned and peered at Andrew curiously, he continued slowly, "Man, when are you going to admit you love the woman?"

Grant merely continued to frown.

"You have for a long time now. Everyone knows it but you – and mayhap your lady, since you've been too stubborn to tell her."

Grant was about to protest, but with flashing eyes Andrew cut him off. "Nay, do not deny it. I know you too well and see through your bluster. I am calling your bluff now. I know how quickly infections set in. I may not even make it home, but I pray I do."

Andrew stopped momentarily and Grant could tell he thought the worst.

"You have been given another chance to return to your wife. Life is too short and uncertain to hide your feelings. For once in your sorry life, be honest with yourself. You're afraid of your own feelings."

Grant snorted in disdain. He didn't want to admit how close to the truth those words were.

"Grant, do not be a witless dolt." He sighed in resignation. "Och, man, go home to the woman God blessed you with and treat her as you should. Some people never feel what you have with each other. Love her with every breath God sees fit to give you. From what you told me of her past, the lassie needs to know you care. You were two lonely hearts who made a connection when The Almighty brought you together. Do not waste that.

"Hold her. Kiss her. Make passionate love to her. But above all, love and treasure her. God gave her to you for a reason, you know. Do not throw such a precious gift away. You know not how many morrows you may have. Take advantage of those you have now."

Grant said nothing, but merely stared as Andrew wearily continued, "Och, Grant, you love her. Do not deny it to yourself any longer."

Grant closed his eyes and inhaled deeply, finally admitting to himself the only thing that held him back was his fear of being hurt. He acknowledged none of that mattered anymore. The lass had stolen his heart a long time ago.

"Och, aye, Andrew. You have the right of it. I do love her."

Andrew said no more and Grant wondered if he'd see him again. If not, this was a parting gift from a friend he held exceptionally dear.

After his talk with Andrew the previous day, Grant was in a hurry to get home. He wanted to see Tory, and had a lot of making up to do. In his heart he knew he'd been unfair to her, even though her present life with him was far better than what she'd had with her father. That would no longer suffice. Suddenly he wanted to give her everything. He'd have given her the entire world if he could have managed it. He wished she were already near so he could run his hand lovingly over her face. He was glad Stirling wasn't overly far from Crieff. It shouldn't take him too long to get back to her. Mayhap, if he pushed himself, he could do it within a day.

Duncan rode beside Grant. "'Tis out of my way, but I appreciate you letting me come home with you. After our recent win, I'm so happy I want to share my elation with friends—and I can think of no one I'd rather do that with than you and Tory."

To him they represented the epitome of happiness, and their home was what he hoped his own would be one day – complete and full of love.

One certainly couldn't call it happy nor loving now. Not with his father supporting the English cause. Duncan wondered what his mother ever saw in the man. *He* never saw anything decent. Certainly not love.

Had it been up to his father, Duncan wouldn't have been home at all while growing up. His father sent him to Clan Kerr far younger than most boys were fostered for training. Duncan thanked God Grant's father had found him there and taken him to Drummond Castle. The horrors of his time with Clan Kerr's chief would forever haunt him. And truth be told, his father could have cared less if he was trained properly in warfare techniques. He only wanted his son out of his sight.

A sickly son proved an embarrassment, after all.

Well, Duncan thought, *I'm not sickly anymore*. Grant's mother cured him of breathing problems while he'd still been a lad.

And, he vowed, some day his father would pay for his heartless behavior.

Grant didn't share his innermost thoughts with Duncan on his return home. Thinking of his talk with Andrew, he knew he needed to tell Tory how much he loved her. She'd brought him such joy in the short time he'd known her.

She also totally exasperates me, he chuckled inwardly. *'Tis probably to be expected with a woman.*

He'd built a wall around his heart after Maeri's death. Now he realized he never really loved her. Not as a man truly loves a woman. He'd merely experienced the growing pains of a young man. What he felt for Tory was so much more intense than he'd ever felt before.

He sighed over the wasted time trying to fight his attraction to her.

Nearing the edge of his lands, he thought of the wonderful gift Andrew had given him. He'd pressed him to admit the feelings he long tried to deny.

Grant feared his friend too injured to recuperate. Were it not for Andrew's skills during and prior to the battle, the possibility existed they might not have won. As it was, the battle had emphatically been won for Scotland – but Grant wondered at what cost to Andrew?

Reaching his destination, he quickly rode under the great portcullis and bounded off his horse the instant he entered his courtyard. Several men headed in his direction to speak to him, but he paid them no heed. Doing something he'd never done before, he left Duncan to fend for himself in the courtyard.

He wanted to see his wife.

Finally his ghillie attracted his attention. "Laird Grant, I needs speak with you. 'Tis important."

As he'd done with everyone else, Grant brushed his ghillie aside. "Not now, Fergus. I wish to see my lady wife. I shall speak with you later." He continued to glance around the courtyard.

Why had Tory not come to greet him? Lately she'd had a special sense about his return. Yet now he saw her nowhere, even though other women poured from the castle to greet their loved ones.

Fergus grabbed Grant's arm to stop him. "Laird Grant, I needs speak with you. *Now*. 'Tis about Lady Tory."

Grant's heart froze. Instinctively he knew something was dreadfully wrong.

"Is she injured? Is Jamie all right?" When Fergus didn't answer quickly enough to suit him, he shouted, "Where is my lady wife?"

Everyone in the courtyard stood stock-still. Glancing at each other, they wondered how they were going to tell their chieftain his wife had disappeared.

Looking uncomfortable, the ghillie said, "Mayhap we should go inside. I think you may need a drink afore this is over."

"*Tell me now!*"

"She is gone, my lord," the man said without further ado.

Duncan quickly strode to join Grant.

"What mean you, 'She is gone?' Where is she? Where is my son?" Grant thought his heart might explode.

Angus rode into the courtyard, looking tired and dirty. Seeing Grant, he dismounted and approached.

"They've told you the news then?" he asked as he flexed and worked knots out of his body from his long journey.

"Nay, they have not!" Grant bellowed. "And if someone does not tell me something soon, I'll cause you all bodily injury!"

"Lady Tory disappeared two nights ago. A courier arrived with a message. He'd not tell anyone the contents, saying 'twas for Lady Tory's ears only. She came up with some cockamamie story of Duncan sending you a message."

"Duncan sent no message. He was with me."

"Exactly. Archie knew that and tried his best to guess what really happened. Your lady tried to act as though naught untoward happened, but you know she is not good at hiding her feelings."

"Only too well."

"Archie told us he would try keeping a close watch on her. He suspected the man got Lady Tory to leave with him and Archie determined to follow without them knowing."

He ruefully looked at Grant. "She slipped out of the keep. I decided to accompany Archie so I could come back if we found them."

"She left willingly?" Grant asked, almost choking on the words.

"Aye," Angus nodded in assent. "Snuck out the gate at night."

"Damnation! The woman is getting entirely too good at that," Grant stormed, his rage and frustration mounting. "I'll make certain this is the last time she does that when I get my hands on her bum! Did she take my son with her?"

He knew his voice sounded ragged with concern. He couldn't stop himself. He wanted her back. He *needed* her back.

Fergus assured him, "Nay, your son remains safe."

Though pleased to hear this, the news gave Grant serious pause. Something had to be terribly amiss for Tory to leave Jamie.

Unless...

Chapter Thirty-six

As they rode through the night without stopping, dawn slowly awakened the earth. Tory rolled her shoulders to stretch her sore muscles and shifted restlessly.

Occasionally she tried to strike up conversation with the young man she shared a horse with, anxious to know about Grant's condition. After receiving only superfluous grunts, she abandoned the effort. She obviously wouldn't discover anything from him.

A feeling of unease settled in the pit of her stomach.

Finally, the top of a formidable castle came into view. Its turrets and crenellations did little to dispel the castle's cold grey appearance. With a feeling of impending doom she didn't understand, Tory rode over the drawbridge and under the massive edifice's portcullis.

Still no one spoke.

Men dismounted and Tory found herself propelled through the windy courtyard past leering glances.

After they entered the keep, Tory had to adjust her eyes to the darkness inside. The castle smelled horrible! She wrinkled her nose at the stench and thought she might become physically sick. She stifled a shudder when she passed beneath a huge cobweb that dangled above her.

She glanced around and saw several men approach. One Tory recognized as Erwin, Duncan's companion. *Thank God*, she thought with a sigh of relief. Although she didn't particularly like the man, she thought now everything would be all right. She thought surely he'd watch out for her and take her immediately to Grant.

The look on Erwin's face, however, appeared far from friendly and a shiver of fear brushed her spine.

"Good eve, lady," he said with a mock bow and mirthless laugh. "Well-come to our humble abode. We were afraid you'd not be joining us."

Tory turned to face the man she saw Erwin look at when he said *we*. A jolt of shock ran through her when she saw his cold, forbidding face. How could this be? He looked like Grant!

He wasn't, of course, but similarities were there. This man appeared heavier and shorter. Startled, Tory observed his eyes were blue rather than grey like Grant's – and he had a scar that ran along the left side of his face.

She didn't stop staring until the man reproached, "Have you not been told 'tis rude to stare, my lady?"

Tory felt appalled at her lack of manners. Shocked and embarrassed, she blushed and lowered her eyes, but the gruff man ground out, "Nay, lady, look all you wish. I'll certainly be looking at you."

Caught off guard at his comment, Tory quickly inhaled a breath. She shrank back, trying to get away from him, but the stocky man grabbed her arm, pulling her closer. "Nay, lady, you will go nowhere."

The man pulled her in front of him and studied her through narrowed eyes. He closely inspected every inch of her, causing Tory to blush profusely.

"Ah, now I see why Erwin has been in such a state to get you here." At her questioning look, the man announced, "'Twas Erwin's idea to fetch you here. The man has been like a rutting stag thinking of you."

"But I came to see my husband," she interrupted, wrapping her cape closer about her. A cold chill settled over her and it had little to do with the castle's temperature. "That man over there told me Grant had been injured."

She pointed to where the courier, Hamish, now stood.

When Erwin and the stranger erupted in gales of laughter, Tory frowned in confusion. "He said Grant asked for me."

The two men looked at her like she'd gone daft.

"Please," Tory whispered tremulously, growing fearful. "Where is he? Take me to him." She watched both men, feeling dazed and confused. Why would they not take her to Grant? Why were they tormenting her like this?

"'*Please. Where is he? Take me to him*'," Erwin mimicked cruelly and fixed her with a steady gaze. "You'll never see the likes of that fool again. Not alive anyhow."

The implied threat in his voice had been intentional.

She also knew her first impression had been correct. This man was inherently evil.

Drawing in a deep breath she jerked her arm, trying to free herself from his hold on her arm. His fingers only tightened, and she felt an overwhelming sense of foreboding.

"Nay, lass," the man who looked like Grant sneered cruelly. "Dinnae pull away from me."

He pulled Tory closer so her face was only a hairsbreadth away. "Allow me to introduce myself. My name is Euan. Euan Drummond."

As his brows cocked, Tory knew her face revealed her shock.

"Aye, I am your husband's beloved brother."

"You lie!" Tory choked out, her throat going dry. "Grant doesn't have a brother."

"I imagine there are a lot of things my dear brother never bothered to tell you," he laughed cruelly. "Actually, we were not on the best of terms when we parted."

He changed the subject and pointed to Erwin. "He told me I needed to kidnap you. It seems he is quite randy where it comes to you, lass."

Tory's eyes widened in fear and flew to look at Erwin.

"He tells me he's wanted to bed you since the night you met."

Tory's eyes shifted once again to Erwin.

"Aye, 'tis true," Duncan's clansman sneered maliciously. "The night we came to your castle. I believe you remember it well. I knew Duncan planned on bedding you. He got that look in his eyes the moment he saw you. But I wanted you, too, so I set about getting him deep in his cups by making certain his goblet never emptied. The man shouldn't have been able to stand by the time I finished with him. With his ego, I figured he'd still try to bed you, but doubted he'd finish. I planned to take over and bed you all night long! He should have been passed out--unable to notice."

Tory grimaced at his crude words.

"I would rather die than let you touch me," Tory uttered before she thought about consequences to her words.

"That can be arranged, my dear," he sneered in anger. Glaring into Tory's eyes he continued, "Then that meddling whoreson Drummond interfered! I knew you were not wed, but Duncan was too drunk to know the difference, so he let you walk away. I wanted to kill him for that! All my plans for naught. A perfect waste of a delectable morsel like you."

"B...but," Tory stammered, her eyes shifting between Erwin and Euan.

"Dinnae try telling me you were wed," Erwin spat out. "I saw Drummond's men's looks of surprise when he said that. You were not wed afore his declaration, but you bloody well were after that with you so sweetly agreeing. I knew right then I would take you away from him some day," he raged as he shook his fist in her face.

She pulled back so he wouldn't strike her.

"Well, that day has come, lass. I had to wait to bed you, but bed you I will."

Once again Tory found herself in a situation she didn't know how to escape.

She pulled away from the blackguard who called himself Euan, but when she tried to bolt from the room, his men blocked her exit. His look of evil intent made her blood run cold.

"Why have you brought me here?" she sputtered indignantly, directing her question to Euan since he seemed to be in charge.

"Erwin told you, lass," Grant's brother answered, a menacing glare on his face. "The man wants you in his bed. There is one wee problem, though." At Tory's unasked question, he responded, "Now I see you, I believe I'll keep you for myself. That should be the ultimate revenge on my dear devoted brother – taking away the woman he loves."

Tory panicked as the boldness of his words sunk in. She tried to run and bumped into several men. They didn't budge.

"Tie her up," Euan gruffly informed his men. "She will tire quickly if she must fight against bonds placed on her."

Tory trembled at the implications of his harsh words.

"But you promised her to me," Erwin argued while Euan gave this order.

The look of hatred Euan shot him silenced him effectively.

"I dinnae say I'd not let you bed her, Erwin," Euan began in a calming tone. "You deserve that. You just must wait a bit longer. Howbeit, after seeing this sweet delicacy, I can see why my brother finally gave his heart away. This should push him over the edge. I've not had the right ingredient to accomplish that afore now. Once he discovers I have his beloved wife, and that I am tupping her every night, my dear brother should finally go daft." He ground out the words as if they left a bitter taste in his mouth. "He will try to find me, and then I shall end his life. I waited a long time for that. You'd not deprive me of such pleasure would you?"

Euan threw back his head and roared with gales of laughter.

Nor was the sexual innuendo lost on Tory. She shivered in apprehension as horrific images flashed unbidden across her mind's eye.

While the two men argued over which of them would bed her first, Euan's men followed his orders and fastened her to crossbeams in the Great Hall. When they finished, her limbs were spread apart. Surely this couldn't be how that detestable man meant her to be fastened! 'Twas indecent and demeaning. Although clothed, her kirtle had been rucked up to accommodate her spread legs. Not only were her ankles exposed, her calves were as well! She felt totally shamed.

Glancing around, she became painfully aware her worst fears were being realized. Men were leering at her. 'Twas difficult maintaining one's dignity while in such a situation, but she was trying her best.

Soon someone approached from behind and skimmed his hand down her back and bottom. She shivered.

Euan walked around to face her. He nodded in satisfaction with a cruel smile. "My men fastened you exactly as I wished." With a hint of unbridled glee, he taunted, "Are you quite comfortable, my dear?"

Angered beyond reason at being so humiliated, Tory spat in his face.

Euan retaliated by slapping her across the face, leaving a dark imprint. He ran his hand down her left side and hesitated at her waist as he said with such sweetness she wanted to throw up, "I truly hope you're comfortable, since this is how you shall remain. Until you willingly agree to let me bed you."

"You will rot in hell before that day ever comes," she venomously spat back.

He mocked, "Och, lassie, I promise afore too much time passes, you will beg me to carry you to my bed." He looked chillingly amused as he imparted what he felt a foregone conclusion.

He paced thc room. "I always get what I want. It may take awhile, but in the end I always win. Your feckless husband should have already told you that."

"Grant never mentioned you," Tory said through gritted teeth. "Meeting you, I understand why. I'd not want to acknowledge the existence of someone as vile as you either."

His face mottled with fury, Euan whirled and slapped a crushing blow across her face. The taste of blood from a fresh cut filled her mouth.

Seemingly out of control, Euan hissed and spat curses. "You may be the treasured wife of my brother, but I assure you I'll bring you down a notch or two within a short time." A fleeting look of annoyance flashed across his face, but disappeared quickly.

Placing a chair in front of her, Euan seated himself and stretched his legs out, crossing them at his boots. "I am sorry I cannot offer you a chair as well, lady, but as I said, you will stay as you are until you beg me to bed you."

Tory gave a very unladylike snort. Trying to divert his thoughts, she asked, "Why do you hate Grant?"

Euan's smile revealed evil as he glanced at his men. "She is quick for a woman, aye, men." Leering, they laughed and nodded their heads. "I knew she must be intelligent for Grant to fall in love with her. He always thought himself intelligent," he added with a short derisive laugh.

He returned his glance to Tory. "Why do I hate my brother? That is simple. He had everything I wanted. He had our parent's love." Euan counted on his fingers to show her the list would be quite lengthy. "He will inherit everything since he is the first born. He got all the women. You name it, he got it. Does that sum it up, or should I continue? I could list reasons all night."

An evil smile settled over his features and cold blue eyes clashed with hers. "Only now I'll take it all away from him in one fell swoop. I waited a long time for this and will enjoy every minute of it."

Euan glanced around the room looking for Erwin. The angry man stood in a corner with a goblet of ale fueling his displeasure. Euan motioned for the sneering man to approach. Without hesitation, he informed Erwin, "I believe I prefer this tasty morsel myself. I know you waited a long time and I appreciate your feelings, but I'll bed her first." He saw the cords in Erwin's neck bulge as the disgruntled man tried to control his temper. "After I bed her and destroy my brother, I'll share her. I'll not forget 'tis because of you she is here."

Euan peered thoughtfully at Tory's uncomfor-table position.

"Who knows, mayhap I'll share her with all my men. That seems a fitting revenge for my brother." He looked at Tory through narrowed eyes to judge her reaction to his vile comments. "Would she not make a lovely castle whore? Would that not be the ultimate key to push Grant over the edge? Knowing I bedded her and turned her into a whore? I must ponder that. It will depend on whether I am willing to share her after I sample her favors."

Euan saw the edge of fear mirrored on Tory's face. He smiled sweetly, as if he hadn't been discussing the destruction of both her life and her husband's. He noted his own lust clearly whetted by the fear he saw in her eyes. He fancied the feeling of power.

Storming from the Great Hall, Erwin was livid with rage. This hadn't turned out as he planned. He dared not cross Euan, but this woman should be his! He'd waited months to exact this revenge and now Euan behaved like a frenzied, possessed animal. Euan didn't want Tory for himself, he wanted to trap Grant. Damnation! He should have seen this coming.

Euan rose and faced Tory. He rubbed his hands slowly up and down the sides of her body and cajoled, "Come, come, lass. All you need do to free yourself is ask me nicely to bed you. I'll be more than happy to oblige your request."

Tory flinched at his touch.

When Tory didn't deign to answer but averted her face, Euan lost his temper. He grabbed her face between his hands and roughly pulled it back towards his and squeezed painfully. "You wretched bi...!" he swore viciously, too angry to continue his verbal onslaught.

He clenched and unclenched his fists to help regain his self-control. "You think to ignore me? I hold your life in my hands."

"Have I offended you, sir?" Tory taunted, knowing she probably aggravated the situation. She didn't care. Her situation seemed hopeless and she couldn't see that irritating him would make a difference. It made her feel better knowing she'd gotten under his skin. When he didn't deign to answer, she smiled sweetly and mocked, "Good! Then I have succeeded in my intent."

She struggled and renewed her efforts at release. As before, they proved unsuccessful.

"Was my brother so wonderful in bed you would prefer to die than bed with someone else?"

"Your brother is kind and loving." Tory gave a derisive laugh. "I doubt you know what those words mean. He took a lonely, broken girl and turned her into a woman who loves him with her entire being. What you did not count on is the fact your brother does not love me." At Euan's frown she continued, "So do with me what you will, but I assure you, if you bed me, 'twill be by force. I'll *never* willingly go to bed with you. And such an action will not hurt your brother."

In an outburst of temper, Euan roughly grabbed Tory. "What mean you?"

She refused to answer. She looked at him with loathing and thought, *if only I could raise my knee enough to slam it into his manhood!*

Riding in the direction he'd been informed Tory had last been seen, Grant cursed profusely. He had no doubt in his mind that when he found his wife this time he'd kill her! She was on one of her harebrained schemes for the last time, and if he had to chain her to his bed to keep her inside his home from now on he'd gladly do so.

The woman drove him mad with her continuous antics. Her usual charming quirkiness now seemed a cause for true concern. Didn't she realize she always got herself in trouble? 'Twas a terrible flaw, that. It must be why God brought this stubborn woman into his life – to correct that flaw. Then again, Grant didn't know if 'twas because God wanted him to watch over and protect her or if He used the lass to totally drive him insane.

If the later, Grant decided the saucey young woman had done a good job of it!

He tried to keep that thought in mind as he pushed both his horse and men to advance. He was unsure from whence the feeling suddenly came, but every passing moment was one closer to Tory being in terrible danger. He sensed it in the pit of his belly, and the prospect of losing her remained unthinkable.

Since he was present when Grant received the news about Tory, Duncan quickly volunteered his services. He rode abreast of his worried friend. "I guess there is no purpose in me telling you to cool down first?"

Grant answered through gritted teeth, "Nay, there is not."

Everyone silently rode behind Grant.

The thought that kept running through Grant's mind was that he might truly lose her this time, when he was finally brave enough to admit he loved her. He feared he wouldn't be fast enough to save her from whatever demented person kidnapped her.

Kidnapped her?

Nay, that hadn't been necessary. The fool woman voluntarily went with her abductor. Again the thought returned – *I am going to kill her! As soon as I get my hands on her, I am going to kill her!*

Please, God, let me get to her in time to save her.

Tory made a futile attempt for the umpteenth time to see if her bonds had loosened. They hadn't. In fact, the bonds were now cutting in where she slumped against them. Glancing at her wrists, she feared they'd soon start bleeding. Not that anyone would care.

These men obviously thought it great sport to see her tied thusly.

Not only did she feel uncomfortable standing, her breasts hurt. She knew when she left home she'd have to express her milk while unable to nurse Jamie, but she certainly hadn't planned on not being able to reach them! She was rapidly becoming miserable.

Tory didn't know which was worst – Euan constantly making vulgar statements or Erwin glaring. She thought both men equally dangerous. She considered appealing to their better natures, but seriously doubted either of them had one.

Somehow she had to free herself and flee. She had to return home before Grant discovered her missing.

Grant!

If he wasn't here as Hamish said, hopefully that meant he was safe. And if she figured out a way to escape, mayhap she could return home without him knowing how daft she'd been. Surely if she begged their men, they'd keep her secret.

Wouldn't they?

Tory fought the sinking feeling in the pit of her stomach.

Truth be told, she knew with a certainty Grant would kill her this time!

As the half light of eventide washed over the castle and streamed through the arrow slits in the walls, Tory heard a loud commotion behind her. Euan's men ran and shouted and she soon heard the unmistakable clash of swords. Before she knew what happened, Euan stood in front of her and glared.

He looked almost apoplectic.

Before she could stop herself, Tory unwisely asked, "What is that commotion?"

Euan grabbed her hair and twisted her head roughly, angling her face in front of his. Before he uttered a word, Tory again heard loud shouts.

Somehow she knew Grant had arrived. How had he found her? Could he save her this time? *Would he really want to*?

Although she hadn't seen him, Tory grew elated and her heart began to flutter.

Grant battled his way into the Great Hall and stopped short when he saw Tory bound from the overhead crossbars.

"Damnation!" Grant muttered sourly. What had the fool woman gotten herself into this time?

A sneer crossed Euan's face and he thundered, "Come any closer, brother dear, and I'll slit your lovely wife's throat."

Grant tried to keep a lid on his self-control. "Release her, Euan. Our battle has naught to do with her."

He spoke as if he hadn't been surprised to see his brother, even though years had passed since he'd done so.

His wary eyes sought Tory's as he surveyed every inch of her body. He saw dark splotches staining the front of her kirtle where her milk leaked, and he felt incensed when he noticed rope marks on her wrists. She also had bruises on her face.

If they had hit her...

"Take your hands off her. Now!" Grant roared as veins in his neck bulged. *Nay,* he thought quickly. He couldn't think like that right now. He must stay focused or Tory could get hurt. Her safety relied on him keeping his wits about himself. He couldn't react in anger, but must carefully plan his every move.

At least she still lived – or did until he got his hands on her and killed her himself!

That had been his one great fear – that he wouldn't arrive in time to keep her alive. Well, he thought, trying to gain control of his emotions, she didn't seem to be overly injured right now. Grant determined she'd stay that way.

"I waited a long time to see you again," his brother said between gritted teeth, "and I now have you exactly where I want you. I know I have your wife where I want her!"

"Release her, Euan. This is atween you and me. Leave my lady wife out of it." Grant glared at his brother. "If you hurt her, you deal with me."

"I dinnae think so. I finally have something you want rather than the other way around."

"'Twas never a contest, Euan," Grant responded stiffly, trying to diffuse the situation.

"Nay?" his brother spat hoarsely. "Mayhap not for you, but why should it have been? You had what you wanted – or so you thought." He gloated smugly.

"What mean you?" Grant slowly edged toward Euan, keeping his expression inscrutable.

Euan laughed sardonically and pulled Tory's hair harder, causing her to wince. "Dinnae move closer, brother, lest you wish damage caused to your lady's person.

"I must admit, I never thought you would give your heart to anyone. It surprised me to hear you took a wife." When Grant didn't comment, but continued to glare, his brother taunted, "After

Maeri died, I dinnae think you had it in you to love someone. You pulled away after that.

"Maeri was a weakling, you know, but she put up a good fight at the end." His look of hatred seemed far worse than Grant had ever seen before.

"What mean you she put up a good fight?" Grant asked warily. "You were not present when those filthy footpads attacked her."

Euan laughed and leaned over and kissed Tory soundly on the lips, hoping his actions would infuriate his brother. It had the desired effect, but Grant tightened his control at the same time he clenched his fists.

If this braggart touched his woman again...

"You know naught of what happened that night," his brother goaded. "And aye, I was *definitely* there."

Stepping forward, heedless of previous threats, Grant glared at his nemesis. "What are you talking about? You never mentioned you were there."

"Why would I?" he snarled. "Why draw attention to myself when everyone blamed you for the chit's death?"

Through gritted teeth Grant measured his words carefully. "What know you of Maeri's death, *brother*?"

"Och, I suppose I can tell you." With added emphasis he smiled evilly. "You will never leave here alive to tell anyone the truth of it."

His eyes bored into Grant's and were returned in kind.

"You dinnae know I took Maeri away from you. Such a silly twit. I never did see what you saw in her – except for her body, of course. Especially her breasts—soft, full, far more than a handfull." He ground out, "But 'twas not her head you were interested in, was it?" Euan only got a glare in response. "Well neither was I. I only wanted to bed her afore you did. And guess what? I did. I got the foolish chit with child."

"You what?"

Grant sharply inhaled his breath as Euan's cruel words continued. "The silly thing wished to wed. Said I must do the honorable thing. As if I would lower myself to wed a lightskirt like her. She proved fine to bed, but naught more. When I refused, she said she'd tell her da and he'd make certain our da made me wed her."

Anger clouded Euan's face as he remembered the night. "The little slut was not going to ruin my plans, so I threatened her. I thought that would keep her quiet, but she was determined we wed. She said she would tell you and you'd make me do what was right."

He stormed, "She shouldn't have said that. She shouldn't have mentioned you at all." His face darkened in suppressed rage.

"Without thinking, I smashed her in the head. I dinnae mean to kill her. It just happened. Thinking of a way to cover it up, I put the twit on my horse and dropped her in the road. Everyone assumed footpads attacked her." Smiling cruelly, he ribbed, "And then they blamed you, since everyone knew she planned to meet you at the dance.

"Och, it did my heart good to see you blamed." He sneered and again pulled Tory's face close. Leaning closer, he mocked, "You dinnae know you had such a noble husband, did you? To take the blame for something he had naught to do with?"

Tory's bleak eyes held Grant's and her expression sobered when she saw disbelief registered on his face. She hated that he was hearing these terrible things. Euan was despicable to put his brother through such pain.

Euan laughed and jerked her head back, and again his mouth closed over hers. Keeping his eyes resolutely on Grant over her head, the kiss proved slow and deliberate.

"This one is so much sweeter, although I must admit she is not biddable. Naetheless, I'll enjoy bedding her much more than Maeri. I plan on keeping your lovely wife, you know." He leaned closer until his lips were only an inch from Tory's. Feathering a kiss lightly, he gave Grant a sugary smile.

Grant struggled to keep a rein on his rage.

"You have two choices," Grant heard his brother snarl. "You can turn around and walk out the door and think of me bedding your wife each night, or you can try and defend her honor – and die in the process. Either way, she will be mine. I waited a long time to bring you down."

Euan knew Grant well, and knew he'd never leave without trying to save his wife.

"This is even better revenge than what happened to Da down at Berwick," Euan snorted.

"Do not mention Da's name," Grant stormed and forced his attention away from Tory. "You were not worthy to be his son. Not after you killed Mam!"

Tory inhaled sharply, fighting back the emotions that threatened to choke her. Never in a trillion lifetimes would she have suspected Grant's mother had been killed! No wonder he never spoke of it.

"Och, Grant," came Euan's sneer, "you are far too sensitive to be a good chieftain."

Grant glared with steely eyes.

"I suppose I shouldn't rub this in, but Da came to Berwick to see me." He gave an exaggerated sigh.

"He what?" Grant roared. His head snapped up and rage swelled in his chest. Euan stepped back to escape his brother's wrath, and jerked Tory's head as he pulled her hair.

"That's why Da went to Berwick? You were his business?" Grant barely choked out the words.

"Aye, big brother. Da came to see me," he gloated. "I needed money to get out of a few wee jams, so I figured I should ask Da. 'Tis only fair I should get some of his money." A sneer spread across his face.

"Only Da came with a proposal instead of money. Said if I would straighten out my wicked ways, he would pay all I owed." Euan laughed in Grant's face, scoffing at that notion. "And he wanted me to come home. Wasn't that *sweet*? Guess he thought he'd try to straighten out his poor wayward son."

Euan paused for impact of his words to sink in.

"What he dinnae plan on was dying. After the massacre, I only had to go to his room and fetch his money. 'Twas quite satisfying, that. No straightening out necessary!" he added with contempt.

Grant couldn't stomach Euan's sneer. Something inside him snapped, and he let his guard down for a split second – just long enough for Euan to take advantage of the momentary weakness.

Motioning for his men to grab Grant, Euan placed the tip of his dirk at Tory's throat. He turned to Grant's associates. "Drop your weapons or I'll slice her throat."

Glancing to Grant for final guidance, he imperceptibly nodded. His men were overpowered as their weapons were lowered.

Ambling over to Grant, Euan punched him viciously in the stomach. "I waited a long time to do that, and this is just the beginning. Och, I will enjoy your death."

Behind him, Tory's eyes widened in fright.

Grant sneered at Euan. "Enjoy it whilst you can, you whoreson. You'll not have the upper hand long. Mark me on that."

"And what miracle do you plan to pull out of your wee bonnet, big brother?" he heckled. "I have you and your lovely wife right where I want you. And soon she will grace *my* bed."

The predatory look in his eyes sent a chill up Grant's spine. He wanted to break every bone in his brother's worthless body.

"This is the last day you shall live. I am tired of having you around. I want everything you have and I'll now have it." He looked at Tory and smirked, but his words were solely for Grant. "Would you fancy seeing me tup your wife, brother? I can do it right where she stands, you know. With ropes binding her as they are, I have conveniently spread her legs. I only need take my manroot out, ruck her kirtle up a bit more, and thrust myself in. Tied as she is, she'll not be able to escape."

Turning his head, he surveyed Grant from all angles. "You dinnae look worried enough, brother. Dinnae you care I'll have your woman from now on?"

Nervous and tense, Tory grasped that opening and tried to distract Euan in a bid to stall for time. She looked at Grant beseechingly and hoped he wouldn't take offense at her plans.

She had to save him, after all.

"I tried to tell you before that your brother would not care if you took me to your bed," she began quickly. Heart pounding, she continued, "I told you he didn't love me. He accidentally claimed me – that's all."

Turning brusquely, Grant narrowed his eyes and glared.

Euan scoffed. "You're trying to say he dinnae fancy having you in his bed? I am no fool, lass."

Looking at Grant, Tory saw he still glared. She assumed he meant her to remain quiet. She ignored him, blushing all the while. "I never said he did not fancy me in his bed, but I doubt he enjoyed it more than any other woman he bedded. I happened to be around." Nervously she worried her upper lip.

"Once I became with child, he probably figured he'd at least have his legal heir." Glowering at Euan, she said, "That is what all men want is it not – a legal heir?"

Euan nodded. "Of course, but I dinnae believe a word you say."

"I didn't really think you would. You think to hurt him by taking me away from him. I say he'll be thrilled to be rid of me."

Glancing over at Grant she added, "He stated many a time I am a frustrating woman and constantly reminds me of what he considers my many flaws."

Grant snorted aloud and mumbled under his breath.

"Besides," she added quickly, her heart racing as she saw Euan glance at Grant. He looked as though he again planned to disagree with her. "If he really loved me we would have been wed in a kirk. Right?"

Euan nodded, indicating he thought her daft to ask such a question.

With a smug smile that said, *Ah ha*! Tory said, "Well we were not. Ask his men. Ask anyone. They all know we never wed in kirk. He claimed me one night. That is all."

The mocking look on Euan's face was one Grant desperately wanted to smash with his fist; however, he could only confirm Tory's words. Blast this woman, what was she doing?

"You never bothered to wed her?" Euan taunted.

"I claimed her, and you know as well as I, that is legal in Scotland. She is my wife."

Grant controlled his temper with extreme effort. He was unsure how much more he could take.

Euan walked over to Grant and slammed his fist into his brother's stomach.

"Nay! Leave him alone."

Spinning quickly, Euan glared. "Dinnae play me for a fool, lass. I thought you said you dinnae love him."

"I said he did not love me," Tory sighed in a choked, hushed admission. "I never said I did not love him. In case you're too thick-headed to be aware, there's a big difference between the two."

"So he wouldn't protect you, but you'd protect him?" He shifted his gaze between Tory and Grant and his mouth twisted in a humorless smile.

"I know not if he'd protect me or not." She saw Grant's face turning stormy and rushed to add, "He should not have to try. Release him so he can return home to raise his son. He will find another woman to... replace me soon enough, and Jamie is too little to remember me."

Her voice broke. How could she bear to let Grant walk out the door and never see him again? For his sake she'd do it, though. She tried so hard to be brave.

She saw Erwin approach Grant, beat him with his fists. Then he pulled out his dirk and began to cut him, small cuts to begin with, intimating what would come.

Suddenly the blade slashed a deep path down the side of Grant's chest.

"Nay!" Tory screamed. "Stop it!"

With an evil smile, she heard Euan ask, "Why should I stop him, lady mine?" At her look of horror he laughed harshly, "Aye, lady. You are mine now. I dinnae need your husband any longer. And dinnae I wish him in my life anymore."

He added to his men, "Kill him."

When men approached Grant, Tory screamed, "Nay! Do not!"

"'Nay, dinnae' *what,* my lady?"

"Do not hurt him," she choked out. Tears formed in her eyes and her heart pounded loudly in her chest. She was afraid everyone heard it. "Oh, merciful heaven, release him and let him leave unharmed. I'll do whatever you want."

She glanced at Grant, tears welling in her eyes. "I promise."

Grant's eyes widened and he scowled. What was this fool woman doing now?

Euan laughed in her face. "You'll do whatever I want regardless of what you promise."

Tory almost bit through her lip. "Please." She looked one last time at Grant to beg his forgiveness and turned to Euan. "You said I would beg you to bed me. Well I am. I am begging. Let Grant live and I'll..."

She had to swallow the huge lump in her throat before she could continue, "...be in your bed from now on. I'll do...whatever you want."

"And if I choose to whore you to all my men?" came the crude response. A glint of evil shone in Euan's eyes as he spoke.

Tory didn't flinch, and the hitch in her voice was barely imperceptible. Only Grant heard it, knowing her far too well.

"Then that is...what I'll do. I'll serve you and your men in any fashion you wish."

Euan walked over to Tory and eyed her cruelly.

"You love him that much?" he questioned in disbelief.

Tory could only nod her head.

"Release her," he told his men.

Having been bound for such a long time, Tory found it difficult to stand. She lost her balance several times, but by dint of will faced Euan.

"Kiss me," he ordered, his fingers sinisterly tracing her jaw line and lips.

370

"Wh...what?" Tory gasped in horror.

"Kiss me. In front of everybody – and not a peck. A real kiss. Like you shall kiss me every day for the rest of your life," he leered.

Tory hesitated, but took the few steps toward him. As she slowly leaned in to try and do as the vile man asked, she heard Grant's feral growl and his one word threat. "Woman!"

She made the mistake of glancing in his direction and knew she couldn't do it. Dear God, she'd failed him. She only wanted to protect him, but couldn't bring herself to willingly kiss this monster. Whether wed in a kirk or not, she'd promised God she'd be faithful to this one man.

And now she'd sealed his fate.

"Grant, I'm sorry. I cannot do it. I thought I could, but I cannot. I love you too much." Breaking into sobs, she rushed on, "But now I..."

She became too emotionally distraught to continue. Walking in front of Euan as she spoke to Grant, she crossed between the two men.

Beet red with anger as he realized she still chose his brother, Euan swung out his fist and smashed it into her face.

Tory walking in front of Euan gave Grant the opening he'd waited for, and watching his wretched brother hit Tory was more than he could stand. Angered beyond compare, he bellowed out his rage.

Breaking into the Drummond war cry, Grant broke away from his captors and grabbed Tory with lightning speed. His companions spurred to action as well, flinging her from man to man until she stood well away of any danger.

Assured Tory was safe as he pushed her toward Warwick, Grant spun around and grabbed a sword from a man next to him. He dashed forward and attacked Euan who finally gathered his wits about himself.

Euan clearly forgot how fast Grant could be.

The two men dueled for what Tory thought an eternity, even though mere minutes passed. The two adversaries were both excellent swordsmen and had obviously been taught to fight by the same person. Grant, however, had demanded more from himself over the years. Although both men drew blood several times, Grant kept himself in peak condition and soon overpowered his younger brother.

With the tip of his blade in his brother's throat, Grant questioned in disbelief, "You really killed Maeri?"

He received a sneer in response.

"And you were responsible for both Mam and Da's deaths?"

Again a knowing look sprung to Euan's eyes, but he answered, "You cannot specifically blame me for the entire Berwick massacre, but aye, Da came there because of me. He still thought he could redeem my soul."

The laugh emanating from his throat sounded more evil than anything Tory ever heard in her life.

"I have almost single-handedly been responsible for the demise of our entire family. Had it not been for your dolt of a wife getting in the way, I'd be rid of you, too. I've hated you from the time I became auld enough to know the meaning of hate."

Groaning over the loss of so many people he loved, Grant pushed the sword deeper in Euan's throat. He not only had a dull throbbing in his side from the deep cut, he had a pain in his heart caused by the loss of so many loved ones. All at the hand of this evil man. Still, he couldn't bring himself to end it. This vile man was his brother.

Euan taunted, "Best you kill me now, brother dear, for if you dinnae, I'll come back with a vengeance, and I'll kill you with my own hands the next time – slowly and painfully. And your wife... you can only begin to imagine what tortures I shall have in store for her after her betrayal this day."

Anger surging through him, Euan tried to rise, and in so doing he swung his leg out to trip Grant. As Grant struggled to maintain his balance, the tip of his sword went deeper into his brother's throat.

The end came swiftly. Holding his bloody sword in his hand, Grant stared down at his only sibling. He shook his head at the wasted life, but Euan had made his own choices. Grant could do naught to change that.

Euan lay dead, and hopefully his evil died with him.

His men were quickly subdued as well. Having no great loyalty to Euan in the short time since he returned to Scotland, they didn't put up much of a fight.

Only now Erwin couldn't be found. He'd obviously slipped out when the fighting began. Leave it to him to once again avoid a battle. Everyone knew, however, that he'd never show his face anywhere in Scotland again, or he'd be a dead man.

Cut and bleeding, Grant walked over to where Tory huddled against the wall. His thick, muscular body towered over her.

Looking up at him, she pleaded silently with her eyes for him to forgive her.

When he said naught, but continued to glare, she said, "Grant, please—"

"Silence!" he roared while he tried to gain control of his emotions.

She was alive. That was all that mattered.

"Do not rage at me, sir," she quipped, trying to diffuse the situation.

"Woman, I am trying to remember why I shouldn't beat you to death." Grant gently touched her swollen cheek.

"You would not—"

"Normally I would not, to be certain. But woman, you try my patience to the extreme!"

Proffering his hand to pull her up, Tory gathered enough courage to reach hers out to take it. In a quavering voice she answered, "I know I do, my lord. And I am sorry." She glanced into his eyes as he still held her hand, "But you are going to take me home, are you not, husband?"

Grant could stand it no longer. He pulled her into his arms and crushed her against his chest. "Aye, my heart. I am going to take you home where you belong.

"And then I'll beat your bum black and blue!"

Wrapping her arms completely around him, Tory looked at him with tears glistening her eyes. A smile formed on her lips. "I know you are husband. And as long as you do it because you love me—"

"Who says I love you?" Grant roared, interrupting her speech at the same time he brushed a strand of hair from her face.

She smiled softly as she brushed a kiss against his cheek. "You do, husband."

At Grant's frown, she continued, "Oh, mayhap not with words, but I am learning to live with that. But you show me every day in your actions. Like you did when you saved me."

She looked through tears she could no longer contain. "And I thank you for that. I truly do." She hugged him one more time before she added, "Grant?"

"Aye."

"I love you, too."

Grant said naught, but smiled broadly.

Tory pulled Grant aside and whispered, "I need a few private moments before we begin our trek home." When she told him why, the look which crossed his face caused her to laugh.

"Och, aye, lady mine. Let us by all means find a quiet room." Grant pulled her behind him up the narrow stairs to find a private quarter. He soon veered into a side room and slammed the door shut with his foot. Quickly divesting Tory of her gown, he remained tentative at first to even touch her painfully engorged breasts.

Tory looked at him with softly pleading eyes and gently whispered, "Please..."

It was all the invitation Grant needed. A surge of heat shot through his body as he aided her in relieving the intense pain caused by built up milk in her breasts. Within minutes it became apparent her need wasn't the only need that had become urgent. Grant pinioned her against the heavy oaken door and sheathed himself within her. His hands on her body were firm and persistent and his lips plundered hers. The door was rough behind her back, but as he so *willingly* assisted her, she happily helped him relieve his own need! Grant threw back his head and shouted his exultation with his release.

The raised adrenaline level of battle always left him with a strong sexual urge as it did most men. That was why so many lightskirts were camp followers. Never having availed himself of services they so freely offered, he felt exceedingly glad Tory was beside him. Merciful saints, how wonderful this woman made him feel.

If she hadn't pulled her daft stunt, he wouldn't have been fighting in the first place.

Threading his fingers through his hair, Grant slowly shook his head. This woman would drive him insane.

Riding back to the safety of their home with Grant's arms wrapped lovingly around her, Tory sighed and asked, "Tell me what happened to your mother." As he hesitated, she cajoled, "Please, my love, let there be no more secrets between us. You made me tell you all the things that hurt me so much. I did not want to tell you any of those things. Let me help you through the things that hurt you, too."

"I do not fancy being needy, wife," Grant grumbled reluctantly.

"Husband, you are the least needy person I know," she told him with great empathy. "There is a big difference between being needy and needing someone. I hope you need me."

Now Grant sighed. With a faint pang tugging at his heart, he told her things he held inside himself for such a long time. "After Maeri died I shut myself away from relationships. I did not wish to be reminded of everything that happened, so I left home." He looked at her with such sadness Tory felt like crying. "I've fought a lot of battles since that day in an effort to stay away. I became good at what I do. I also built a wall around my heart."

Grant stared ahead at the men in front of them, but didn't see them. A faraway expression in his eyes, he continued, "Mam feared I would never wed. She wanted a grandchild so much that on my few visits home she tried every tactic she could think of to leg shackle me with local women. To her dismay, I was not interested.

"One day she and Da received word Euan got a local lass with child." Ruefully he added, "It seemed he had a penchant for that. When the lass' da insisted Euan wed with her, Mam and Da were thrilled and agreed he should do the honorable thing." He quickly explained, "They were not pleased he violated the lass, mind, but that they would now become grandparents. They both envisioned wee feet pattering around the keep."

A wistful smile crossed his face as he thought of how much they both would have loved Jamie.

"Whilst Da remained in the Great Hall talking to Euan and the lass' da, Mam went up the stairs to our auld nursery and got the cradle Euan and I used as bairnies and brought it down. 'Twas her way of telling the lass she well-comed her into our family. She said she planned to have Da take it to our carpenter to clean up and have special carvings placed on it. 'Twas heavier than she remembered, though, so it took her awhile to get it down the stairs."

A frown creased Grant's forehead. "Och, Tory, the poor lass looked so fragile that day and Euan said hateful things to her. She ran from the castle in tears and her da stormed after her, shouting threats at our family.

"When mam arrived back down the stairs with the cradle in hand, she discovered Euan refused to wed the lass after all." It took Grant a long time before he continued.

"Broken hearted, she turned to take the cradle back up to the auld nursery. She so wanted that grandchild. After telling us why she had the heavy cradle, she said not a word to Euan or anyone else. She simply picked it up and headed back up the stairs."

Grant's voice broke.

"No one knew exactly what happened after that. Mayhap her foot accidentally caught in her kirtle. Mayhap she tripped on the steps because she'd been crying so hard over Euan's thoughtlessness. 'Tis what most people thought." Grant gave a derisive snort. "Regardless, she lost her balance and careened down the stairs. The cradle followed and fell on top of her."

Tory waited for Grant to elaborate, but he remained mute. She felt his body tense as he sat behind her and she saw his hands clench into fists. In a voice so low and broken she had to strain to hear him, Grant finally declared, "It smashed her head."

His words, spoken with such painful honesty, were Tory's total undoing.

She turned to hold and comfort him. When she raised her eyes to look at him, he saw they were sodden with tears. She became overwrought with emotion. "Oh, my heart, I am so sorry. Pray forgive me."

Grant remained pensive as he looked at her, his expression intent. Finally he asked. "What are you asking forgiveness for, wife? You had naught to do with it."

Looking almost in pain, her eyes glistened with emotion, "But I made you remember all of that when I took you to see your old furniture." Her eyes widened and a look of total understanding lit her countenance. "That is why you did not want to use the cradle!"

When Grant nodded his affirmation, she clapped both hands to her mouth to stifle her cry of pain. She sobbed so loudly Grant's men turned and stared. Fearing she'd become hysterical, Grant stilled his horse and dismounted, carrying Tory with him.

Together they stood beneath a tree and clung to each other.

Inhaling deeply, Grant leaned his head atop hers, "From that day until now, no one ever went in that room again. Da threw the cradle into the room that day and no one has touched any of the furniture. None of us want anything to do with it. 'Tis tainted.

"'Tis why I said I should have burned it."

Nodding her head in understanding, Tory bit back a sob. She wanted to tell him again how sorry she felt, but was unable to speak. She was bereft of words.

Grant's grief not only overwhelmed him, but her as well. As he'd done for her so many times, she now offered him solace and compassion.

Tory vowed to herself she'd make it up to him. She determined he'd have a fresh beginning just as he'd given her. Merciful heavens, never in her entire life could she have imagined being as happy as this man made her feel over the past year. 'Twas as though he tried erasing her past for her. She determined she'd do the same with his painful memories.

They'd both been silent a long time. Nearing Drummond land, Tory once again turned to Grant. "Will you tell Maeri's family the truth?"

Grant shook his head. "What good would that do? They still lost a daughter. After all this time 'twould change naught."

"But they would know you did naught wrong."

"My family still caused them the pain. 'Tis best to leave the matter drop. We know the truth now, and that is good enough for me. I can finally release some ghosts of the past."

When she still tried to convince him it might be a good idea, Grant sighed. "Leave it be, lass. Leave it be."

Chapter Thirty-seven

The morning dawned bright and clear. Tory stirred when Triona came into the bedchamber to tell her guests were arriving in the Great Hall and Grant wished her to dress and come down the stairs if she felt up to it.

After being cooped up in their chamber for several days, Tory felt more than happy to go downstairs to help. Marveling over the fact she'd escaped her latest fiasco basically uninjured, Grant had insisted she rest. Personally, she thought he'd insisted that so he knew her exact whereabouts for awhile.

She assured him, "I feel fine and can go downstairs."

He allowed her no further than to tend Jamie in the adjoining nursery.

Tory thought he'd been a bit *too* protective. But since he threatened to place a ball and chain around her to keep her safely within his castle, she decided staying in her chamber for a few days might not be quite so bad after all!

"Know this, woman," he snarled, "you will never again leave me. *For any reason.* You have my word on that, and you will sorely regret it if you try." Though his tone sounded fierce, he looked at her with such love she felt overwhelmed with emotion.

That had been only the beginning of the stern, lengthy lecture he gave her regarding her recent exploits. As she thought back on it, Tory giggled. Aye, he was entirely too protective.

And she loved every minute of it.

"Sit, my lady, and I'll brush your hair," Triona smiled. A thoughtful and considerate person, Triona always loved assisting Tory. She brought a lovely côtehardie from Grant that he chose for Tory with careful deliberation. Her lady hadn't seen it yet. For now, Triona busied herself with dressing her lady's hair with soft curls about her face. As Grant had requested, she left her lady's hair down and uncovered, but scattered with small pearls. Tory's dark hair gleamed.

When she finished, Triona helped her into the beautiful cream-colored côtehardie Grant had made from material purchased when they went to the faire. She fastened the necklace and earrings Grant had handed her at the last minute. They were both made of pearls, which was why he wanted pearl accents in Tory's hair.

When he handed them to her, he told her, "They belonged to my mam."

Triona assured him, "They are beautiful, m'lord, and I know Lady Tory will love them."

When Triona stood back to look at her lady, tears welled in her eyes. "You look beautiful m'lady." She rushed on before Tory could say anything. "You always look lovely, mind, but today you are perfect. Come look in yon glass and see for yourself."

She grabbed Tory's hand and gleefully pulled her to the large looking glass Grant gifted Tory with earlier in the year.

Tory stared in awe at her reflection. She'd never seen a côtehardie so beautiful.

She was such a humble person, she didn't realize she was beautiful as well.

Warwick met her as she came out the door. At first he stood gazing at her, then extended his arm with a wide smile on his face and escorted her down the hallway toward the stairs.

Tory could scarce contain her excitement. "Wick, look at this beautiful côtehardie Grant had made for me."

It shimmered with her every movement.

With a flicker of astonishment in his voice Warwick agreed, "Indeed the raiment is beautiful, lass, but it pales in comparison to the beauty of the person wearing it."

When Tory realized what he meant, she hugged him. "Oh Wick, I do so wish you had been my father." She sighed in resignation.

Warwick hugged her back and lovingly told her, "As far as I am concerned you *are* my daughter, lass." He gave her a sidelong glance. "You are the closest to a daughter I'll ever have, and I truly do think of you that way. I hope you dinnae mind how I feel."

As she began to cry with happiness, Warwick put his arm around her shoulder and pulled her snugly against his side, wiping her tears away. "Today is not the day for tears, lass. 'Tis a day for rejoicing and celebrating."

Without further ado he walked her downstairs to the Great Hall. Tory didn't understand what he meant, but felt too happy to question him further.

Entering the Hall, Tory stopped and gasped. It looked beautiful! She couldn't believe the transformation that had been wrought. The large room looked truly festive. Glancing around she noticed it was also packed with hundreds of people.

She turned to Warwick to question him, but he effectively evaded her glance and purposefully strode toward Grant at the Hall's opposite end. Reaching him, Warwick handed her arm over to Grant. Bowing formally, he kissed her gently on her cheek and stepped back.

Tory looked around at everything, and saw Annie smiling and running around the Hall with a small basket in her hands. She laughed with glee and joyfully scattered flower petals over the rushes on the floor.

Tory looked to Grant in amazement. "Grant, whatever is going on? If you knew you were having company, why did you not let me come downstairs and help? I feel horrible I've been resting while all this work must have been going on. You should not have made me stay upstairs."

In exasperation she added, "I kept telling you I was fine."

Grant smiled at her, an impish glint in his eyes.

When he didn't answer, but merely stood smiling, she frowned, "Indeed, sir, why are all these people here? What is the special occasion?" She suddenly panicked. "Oh my, did Cook know they were coming? He must be overwhelmed right now."

She pulled away from Grant to head to the kitchen.

Grant stopped her and answered as if nothing seemed unusual about the event or the large number of guests in his Hall. "There is a wedding here this day, Sweeting, and aye, Cook is well aware of all our guests."

That got Tory's attention quickly. "How wonderful. Whose wedding is everyone here for?"

"Mine."

Tory inhaled sharply and paled, looking at Grant as if he finally lost his mind – or she'd lost hers! She tried to subdue the quiver in her voice and hastened to add, "Nay, husband, you misunderstood. I meant *who* is going to be wed here today?"

Grant looked at her with an impassive face and nodded. "Aye. I knew what you meant. 'Tis I who will wed this day."

Tory looked at him in shock. "B...but I thought you said...*we* were married." She seemed to be having problems breathing.

Grant didn't answer, stared into her lovely brown eyes. The only thought he could get his mind to focus on was that she was an absolute vision. He'd known the côtehardie he'd had the sempstress fashion for her had turned out well, but he never imagined a woman could be as lovely as the one standing before him.

When Grant didn't respond, Tory could no longer stand the suspense. Swallowing before she spoke, she raised her chin defiantly and asked, "May I ask whom you are to wed?" She hoped she sounded unconcerned. After all, she didn't want to break down in front of this entire throng of people.

She had her dignity after all.

"Och, aye," he answered in a tone no different than if they'd been discussing something as mundane as the weather. "I thought about this for quite some time now, and I believe I can hold off no longer."

With a slight quirk to his lips he added, "Although I certainly did try."

When he didn't immediately continue, she strangled out, "And—?"

"I felt it finally time to *properly* wed the woman I love with all my heart." Looking casually about the room, Grant added, "Sometimes a man must do what he knows is truly right."

"The person you...love?" Tory croaked. "B...but you said..." Fighting to maintain her restraint, she could say no more. She felt as if she'd been belly punched. She wouldn't be able to control her emotions much longer. Blessed Holy Mother, she'd thought about this day so many times in the past. Staring up into his beautiful grey eyes, she acknowledged there had been a time when she'd wanted him to wed with someone else, but that had been a long, long time ago. Long before she'd gone and fallen in love with him. Now she didn't want him married to anyone but her.

Stifling a strangled sob, Tory tried to pull away from Grant's arm and leave the Great Hall. "If you will excuse me, milord, I believe I'll check with Cook. I m...must make certain he does not need any help."

Grant arched a brow and stayed her with his hand. When he saw pain fleetingly cross her face, he could maintain his cool façade no longer. A smile almost split his face and amusement sparkled in his eyes. "Och, 'tis you, Sweeting. I am wedding with you."

Her ears must be deceiving her, had to be hearing what she wanted to hear rather than what Grant said.

That's what he told her she always did.

Grant said nothing, but leaned down and planted a lengthy kiss on her lips. In a dry voice, the priest behind them cleared his voice and said, "If I am not mistaken, that usually comes *after* the ceremony."

Tory blushed clear to her toes. They'd insulted the priest! When had he arrived? And Grant had kissed her in front of everyone. What had the man been thinking?

Before she could say another word, with arrogant satisfaction Grant nodded imperceptibly to Father McLeod who stood behind him. The priest spoke, but Tory paid no attention to his words.

"But...you said all along we were already married," she looked at him in confusion. "I do not understand—"

Grant interrupted. "Aye, wife, we are truly wed. I have repeatedly told you Scots law makes it so, but you always said you did not believe me, and would not unless we wedded in kirk. So, I came to my senses and brought the priest to you. I know how much this means to you, my heart. And after this day," Grant said pointedly, reminding her of her recent escapade with his shiftless brother, "you will never again tell people we are not legally wed because it had not been done in a kirk."

Mumbling under his breath that he'd need a drink to get through this ceremony, Father McLeod looked totally exasperated. "May I continue with this blessed event?"

Grant nodded and the priest again began his ceremony.

Without a thought to her actions, Tory looked up at Grant and again interrupted the priest, looking around at everyone. "These people came all the way to Crieff knowing you were marrying me?"

Grant smiled and again nodded.

Rolling his eyes heavenward, the priest once again attempted to conduct his holy ceremony.

Trying not to chuckle, Grant noted the priest looked exasperated at being repeatedly interrupted. Leaning close to Tory, he said, "Aye, Sweeting, everyone knew it was the two of us being wed this day. That is why they are all here. They wanted to be here to see the look on your face – and to help us celebrate."

When Tory's face clearly showed her skepticism, Grant assured her it was true. Glancing toward the priest, he winked at the cleric and laughingly told Tory, "But if you do not stop interrupting the good Father, we will not reconfirm our vows this day after all."

Tory looked horrified when she realized what she'd once again done. Looking at Father McLeod she entreated, "Pray forgive me, Father. Please continue."

Raising eyebrows sarcastically, Father McLeod grumbled. "You mean I have your permission to finish your own wedding ceremony?"

Embarrassed, Tory shook her head sheepishly. She wished she had a hole she could drop into.

When the priest looked doubtful, she assured him, "I'll not interrupt again, Father." Smiling at Grant she said, "I promise."

Deciding he'd best finish the ceremony before his young charge thought of another question, Father McLeod quickly completed the holy event. At the conclusion of his official ceremony the priest looked at them solemnly and gave the following charge, "Remember that love is not blind. In the real world love sees everything and loves anyway."

Grant smiled at the sage advice and asked the cleric, "Have I your permission to kiss my young wife?"

Mumbling under his breath, "Tis probably the only way you will shut the young woman up," Father McLeod agreed.

Grant pulled Tory firmly into his arms. He smiled into her eyes as he lowered his head to claim her lips. The kiss he gave her couldn't be considered a chaste kiss.

A cheer went up from the gathered group and Father McLeod happily pronounced them husband and wife before God.

Shaking his head and again muttering to himself, the priest promptly headed to the closest keg of ale. He felt quite certain he'd earned it this day.

Grant had planned the entire day, including the reception to follow. The young couple walked happily amongst their guests, receiving the many happy wishes proffered. Though too excited to eat anything, Tory made certain none of their guests were wanting.

One thing that caught their attention most as they walked around and greeted their guests was the unlikely sight of Archie gently holding Triona as they whirled around the dance floor. It wasn't something they ever thought to see.

When he got the chance, Grant pulled Tory aside and kissed her soundly. He wanted nothing more than to leave the raucous festivities and take his young bride up to their bedchamber. His men's ribald marriage toasts and the loveliness of his bride in her wedding finery had him once again in a state of total arousal. If he didn't do something soon, he'd find it difficult to continue walking around his Hall!

He pulled her tightly within his arms, and Tory's eyes widened as she felt his desire beneath his kilt.

Wickedly whispering his thoughts into her ear, she surprised him by smiling back and tilting her head coquettishly. When she didn't demure, he grabbed her hand and pulled her behind him, escaping the crowd and rushing upstairs to their room.

In his haste to undress her, Grant tore buttons off her lovely new garment as he removed it. He only wanted to get her into bed. He kissed her as he slowly leaned her back onto the bed, fiercely tearing his own clothes from his body as he did so.

He wanted her now.

He'd given her the ceremony she always wanted and now a primitive part of him needed to claim her as totally his. Even though he had no doubt of that fact in his mind, Grant for some reason needed the reassurance. Kissing her fiercely, he felt surprised when she returned his kisses in kind. His mind shut off then and his body took over. This wasn't the time for gentleness. That would come later. This was simply an animalistic claiming, a base reaffirmation of their love for each other. She was his, and he'd indeed do the claiming. When he entered her, he found her ready for him. Tory was surprised to see his eyes were fierce with longing.

When they were both sated, he rolled off her and pulled her with him. Grant glanced into her love filled eyes and smiled. "I fear I ruined your hair dressing, lady wife. Do you think anyone will notice?"

Tory laughed. "I know Triona certainly will. She spent a long time fixing it. I imagine some of your guests will, as well." When he didn't look the least bit shame-faced, she added, "Not only did you mess my hair, husband, you ruined my new côtehardie. I fear I'll have to wear something else – and I'll be more than happy to let you make all the necessary explanations to our many guests."

At the look of surprise on Grant's face, Tory laughed. He'd obviously not thought about that.

Holding her tightly, he recovered quickly and whispered lewdly in her ear, "I'll tell them you insisted on having your wicked way with me. 'Tis certain everyone will believe that." Grant carefully brushed a strand of hair from her eyes and ardently kissed her again.

Tory playfully punched him in the arm and tried to roll off him. He held her tighter and chuckled. "Worry not about what anyone may say, wife. I am quite certain everyone already knows exactly where we are and what we have been doing."

This time Tory looked shocked and Grant laughed at her expression. He did allow her to rise this time and attempted to help her dress and repair her hair, teasing her about what a magnificent lady's maid he made. Laughing all the while, he helped her into a royal blue côtehardie with shimmering filaments throughout, which sparkled whenever she moved.

After he redressed as well, they walked to the door. Tory stopped and thanked him for the special day he'd given her. Suddenly a bit of uncertainty appeared in her eyes.

Biting her lip and hesitating, she finally blurted, "Grant, do you really love me?"

A smile tipping the corner of his lips, Grant quipped, "Did I not just wed you again, wife?"

"Aye, you did, but..."

"Aye, I do," he interrupted with an almost apologetic smile. "Truth be told, wife, I think I fell in love with you the minute I saw you with all that soot on your face and those ridiculous boy's breeks on you. 'Twas why I tried to be so mean to you in the beginning. I tried everything I could to push you away, when all I really wanted to do was pull you in my arms and make love to you.

"And after this day, woman, I mean it when I say you can no longer tell anyone I do not love you and have not really married you." The look on his face told her he meant it. "I do not wish to ever hear that again.

"You have created a miracle in my life, Sweeting. As you told me so often, you believe in angels – and I believe in you. The two go well together. You are my angel."

"You know I did not want to love you," she told him with a hint of a smile on her face and her dark eyes meeting his warmly. "I told you that before. But I did fall in love with you – a long, long time ago. I...I have wanted so much to truly feel a part of your life for a long time. You made that happen completely today. Thank you."

She looked embarrassed.

Grant's face softened as he finally spoke. "You are not just part of my life, lady mine. *You are my life.*"

Tory inhaled sharply before Grant lowered his mouth to hers. This time he had no urgency in his kiss. She was his. He knew it and she knew it. This kiss was totally a proclamation of tenderness, devotion, and most importantly – love.

Descending the staircase, Grant told her he had one more surprise. When she tried to get him to reveal what it was, he smiled and told her she'd have the surprise in time. He refused to tell.

Joining back into the merriment in the Great Hall, they received several lewd comments about Tory's change of clothes and the flush of loving still on her face. Tory blushed clear to her toes, and Grant smiled proudly. No amount of teasing could dampen the exultation he felt.

They circled the room in an effort to speak with their guests, and Tory suddenly heard tsking noises behind her and a voice she recognized announce, "No lady should ever come downstairs without her hair immaculately coifed. I thought I taught you better than that."

Eyes wide, Tory whirled in stunned disbelief to see the person she knew belonged to that voice.

Seeing her grandmother standing in front of her, Tory stumbled backward. Only Grant's strong arms prevented her from falling. Her hand flying to her mouth, she could barely get out the words, "Grandmum...how..."

Her grandmother slowly moved to embrace her young granddaughter. Alexander carefully held the old woman's arm, bracing her. Smiling into the young woman's questioning eyes, her grandmother told her, "It seems your young husband can accomplish anything he sets his mind to, Sweetheart."

Tory's effervescent eyes swerved to meet those of her smiling husband's as her grandmother added, "He sent several fine young men to fetch me and Ashleigh to the day's festivities. It seems he thought you would want us here."

Stammering, Tory tried to speak as her eyes widened in genuine surprise. "Oh, I do, Grandmum, but how...when did you get here?"

Running her hands over her granddaughter's lovely tresses to smooth the offending wisps, Lady Blackstone looked lovingly at her eldest granddaughter. "We arrived early this morn. Being weary from the long trek, your young man graciously placed us both in a delightful room so we could rest. This old body of mine does not travel well."

"You were here before the ceremony started?" Tory questioned in wonder.

"Aye, child," Lady Blackstone said tenderly, "but I did not wish to take anything away from the ceremony's solemnity. That belonged to you and your charming young man." Smiling at them both, she added, "I asked him specifically not to tell you of my presence. I worried you might not be able to properly focus if you knew I was here. I told him I would announce myself in my own fashion. Trying to keep your young sister quiet is another story in itself. She is so excited to be here, I feared she might spoil the surprise by her constant squeals of delight."

Tears streaming down her face, Tory looked up into her husband's beaming face as she once again hugged her frail grandmother. She mouthed the words 'thank you.'

Knowing the old woman tired easily, Grant led both she and Tory off to a small alcove so they could visit privately. Eyes blurring with tears, Tory noticed everyone in the Great Hall smiling. Had they all known of Grant's surprise?

This was by far the greatest wedding gift Grant could have given her. She'd love this man with all her heart until the day she died.

Soon Annie and her brand new friend, Ashleigh, came running up to Tory. She was so overwhelmed at seeing her young sister she could barely speak. That didn't seem to matter. Ashleigh babbled on about everything that happened on her trip to attend the wedding so Tory barely had time to insert a word. After many hugs and kisses, Ashleigh soon ran off again with Annie. They headed to the food-laden tables.

While Tory sat and spent time with her grandmother, Grant stood talking with guests.

Someone asked Duncan, "Have you ever heard anymore about where Erwin wound up after so completely eluding everyone?"

"Nay, not yet," Duncan frowned as he looked at the men gathered, "but I assure you, one day I'll find him. I regret the fact the man caused so much trouble."

The determined look on his face indicated he meant it.

With a look of disgust at the mention of that blackguard's name, Grant looked around the Hall for Tory. He never let her far from his sight these days. Not after all that had happened. The fear of almost losing her remained too fresh in his mind.

"Knowing that worthless scum wished to bed my wife sickens me. Had I not claimed her that night—"

Looking shamefaced, Duncan looked closely at Grant and informed him, "That would have never happened."

Grant scoffed, "You were too deep in your cups to know what happened."

"Nay, I was not," came Duncan's response. "I knew exactly what I was doing."

Grant didn't look pleased to hear that. He moved away from the wall he'd been leaning against and straightened. "You're telling me you were in control of your faculties when you tried to bed my wife?"

"She was not your wife, remember, but mayhap I should explain myself," Duncan mused as he looked into his friend's angry eyes.

"Mayhap you should," Grant growled.

Running his hand through his dark hair, he began, "I never meant for you to know this."

Grant didn't respond, but his eyes narrowed. The group around the two men grew as tension in the room was soon felt by all.

"I sensed something different about you that day. Something that had been missing in your life a long time. It did not take me long to discover the source of that difference. 'Twas Tory."

"I do not know what you—"

"Wish you to hear my story or not?" Duncan blustered. He felt uncertain about starting this admission.

Grant nodded.

"Then let me talk and do not interrupt. This is difficult enough to tell without interruptions."

He glared at Grant and his glare was returned in kind.

"'Twas obvious you wanted the lass. Your eyes followed her everywhere she went – like they do now."

"I do not—"

"*Wheesht!*" came Duncan's yell, effectively cutting off the interruption. "It made me happy to see you finally care for someone. It had been years since you shut that part of yourself away and I began to think you would never commit your heart to someone."

Grant's glower did nothing to make Duncan's admission easier.

"I decided to give you a wee push."

"You what?" Grant yelled in outrage.

"Gave you a wee push," he repeated with raised eyebrows. "I did not think I would have to carry my act as far as I did. I forgot how stubborn you can be. Nor did I know at the time 'twas your daft plan to give the lovely lassie to me."

The two men glared at each other.

"You put Tory through hell," Grant yelled angrily.

"As did you. 'Twas you she kept turning to for help. You kept pushing her back into my arms. Were I not such a good friend, I would have indeed bedded the lass. I would not have minded that, aye." Duncan pursed his lips as he nodded.

"Friend?" Grant snorted derisively. "You—"

"Aye, friend," he countered forcefully. "I have never forced a woman in my life and will never do so. You should know that."

"Aye," Grant hesitated uncertainly as the truth of the words struck their intended target. "I do, but—"

"But naught," he emphasized. "You were a stubborn, pig-headed auld goat. I thought you would never come to your senses. I had to finally push you past your limits."

"Why ye..." Grant swung and hit him square on the chin. Duncan lost his footing and stumbled into men gathered around them.

When they retreated, he soon sat on the ground and rubbed his chin.

"I thought you sobered up too quickly, but I never thought my best friend would play me for a fool," Grant shot angrily at Duncan.

He spun on his heels and walked away to be promptly stopped with the comment, "Play you for a fool? Never. You would only have been a fool had you let me leave your castle with the only woman you ever loved."

Grant stopped cold in his tracks and turned to look at Duncan who continued to rub his chin. He stood a long time before took a step forward and assisted him. "Och, aye, Duncan, you have the right of it. How is it both you and Andrew knew how I felt afore I did?"

"I think you knew exactly how you felt," came Duncan's response as he clapped his arm around Grant's shoulder. "I think that is why you fought it so hard. You were afraid of wanting her. Truth be told, you came alive again the night you claimed the lassie. It felt good to have you back the way I knew you whilst growing up."

A nervous laughter of relief swept the room as the two men walked away together.

Tory and her grandmother rejoined the group when time for the evening meal approached. She felt amazed at the food Cook had prepared for the festivities.

Her grandmother teased, "Mayhap I'll take that pleasant man home with me to prepare our meals in England."

Tory almost choked on her food! She couldn't begin to visualize the thought of Cook being dragged to England.

As a special treat, Annie and Ashleigh were both allowed to sit at the high table. They giggled and whispered through the entire meal.

After the meal, Grant arranged for music to be played. Soon tables were shoved aside and people danced.

Looking Grant squarely in the eyes, Duncan rose and took Tory firmly by the arm and asked her to dance. He saw Grant's jaw tighten. Before he made it around the Great Table to the Hall floor, a hand on his shoulder stopped his progress.

"Not this time," Grant said, removing Duncan's hand from Tory's arm. Duncan and Grant resolutely stared at each other. With a smile, Duncan nodded and graciously retreated.

Grant spun Tory around to face him. She said nothing, but questions shown in her eyes. "'Tis time to bury a few more of those ghosts, lady mine."

He pulled her into his arms and swirled her gracefully out onto what was now a dance floor. They danced easily together and the love Tory saw in his eyes warmed her to the core of her being. They soon realized everyone else had left the floor and stood watching them. They were the only two people dancing.

For the next several days Tory showed her grandmother and Ashleigh everything about her new home. She joyfully teased Grant, "Grandmum has taken quite a fancy to you, and I think Ashleigh has a major crush on you."

Her grandmother didn't have to ask if she was happy, since happiness radiated on her granddaughter's face. The old woman couldn't remember a time in the girl's young life when she'd seen such a glow on her face.

It warmed her heart to know her precious child had finally found happiness.

Huge castle aside, the main thing the old woman wanted to see was her tiny great-grandson. She spent hours with him. When she tired holding him, she sat and watched as Tory nursed or played with him. He seemed a happy baby, laughing and cooing. He only cried when hungry or needed his nappy changed.

Through eyes wise with the wisdom of her years, Abigail Blackstone watched the interaction between her young granddaughter and her fine young husband. She recounted to Tory, "You would not believe the shock I received when huge men approached me and told me Lord Drummond requested the honor of my presence at the official renewal of his wedding vows with my granddaughter."

She chuckled. "I did not think this old body could handle the shock of seeing such handsome young men."

Holding her stomach as her eyes watered with tears, she continued. "I laughed at them, of course, and told them my aged health would not allow me to travel to some place as rugged as the Highlands." She leaned back in her chair and chortled. "Those young men merely smiled and told me since their lord requested it, they would ensure I had a safe journey through their rugged terrain."

Although a strong-willed woman, even Abigail Blackstone proved no match for men determined to carry out their chieftain's request. Within a day they packed everything they thought she and young Ashleigh would need for their holiday and early the next morn they all set forth on the journey northward.

She informed Tory, "Those fine young men were most polite the entire journey and did everything within their power to ensure my every comfort."

Tory frowned. These were the same men who made life miserable for her on her journey to Drummond Castle.

What a contradiction these Highlanders could be. She thought it might take her a lifetime to understand them.

Although Tory saw it but wouldn't acknowledge the truth, her grandmother was failing quickly. Taking advantage of a rare opportunity to speak with the older woman while Tory gathered herbs, Grant knocked on her bedchamber door and felt pleased when he found she wasn't asleep.

"Enter," Lady Blackstone called in a weary voice.

Pausing only a moment, Grant opened the door and entered the elderly woman's chamber.

"Ah, young Drummond, come in." She smiled as he approached from the doorway. "I wondered when you would seek me out by yourself." She held up her frail hand to stay his words. "Nay, son, let me speak. I must do it before I tire again."

Graciously Grant said, "As you wish, Lady Blackstone."

Glancing around the well-appointed chamber, she told him, "I am dying, son." When he neither acknowledged nor denied her comment, she nodded. "My granddaughter has a wise husband. I see in your eyes you know I speak the truth."

Grant nodded.

"I knew my time was short before I came here, of course. I believe 'tis why I let your persuasive young men fetch me with them to your fine country." Ruefully she added, "There was a time I would have never said that, of course. I, like everyone around me, detested all things Scottish."

When Grant frowned, she continued, "Seeing how well you have care for my granddaughter, I can only come to the conclusion in that matter, as probably in many others, we were wrong."

Grant nodded once in affirmation.

"My granddaughter did not have a happy childhood, young man." She watched him closely to see how he took that news. "Ah, I see from the look in your eyes she must have told you. Knowing my Tory, she did not give you that information easily – or willingly."

The guffaw she received from Grant confirmed her statement.

"I thought so, but the important thing is she did, and you have done a wonderful job of ensuring her future is naught like her past." Tears welled in her eyes. "I thank you for that."

Grant once again started to speak. "Young man, 'tis not polite to interrupt an old woman. Please let me have my say."

Grant remained speechless. He stood twice this woman's size and she had the audacity to tell him to be quiet. 'Twas clear whom Tory had gotten her temperament from.

He didn't say a word, but pulled a chair beside her bed and sat.

Contented, Lady Blackstone continued. "I can now die in peace. It pleases me to know my granddaughter is well loved, and God has granted me an additional blessing. He allowed me the chance to see my great-grandson. I never thought to have that opportunity." Her voice softened.

"But now I must go home. While our home in Berwick is not blessed with the love I feel in your lovely demense, 'tis naetheless where I belong. My beloved husband is buried there. I wish to go back to join him."

Grant nodded his understanding.

"Tory will not be willing to let me leave. I'll need your help to convince her I must."

After agreeing, they continued to chat. Grant wished he'd known this woman longer. He could see a lot of Tory's spirit in her. Telling her of his plans for his and Tory's future, she smiled at his words.

Although she didn't ask him to decide anything on the spot, she asked him to please consider young Ashleigh's welfare in the future.

"Be assured I shall, madam."

Seeing she tired, he rose from his chair to leave. Bidding her farewell, he opened the door.

Lady Blackstone stopped him one final time. "One more thing, young man."

Grant turned to face her. Tears brimmed in her eyes, but she smiled. "Thank you for loving my granddaughter."

Without a moment's hesitation Grant told her, "The pleasure is all mine, my lady. She is the miracle that makes my life complete."

Wearily Lady Blackstone sank back onto her pillow and Grant turned to leave the room.

Those were the last words she spoke to anyone.

Consoling Tory after he convinced her that her grandmother's body must be returned to her auld home proved quite painful. Knowing her grandmother was close to dying and having it happen were two different things entirely. Grant remained loving and patient, remembering his own pain at his parents' deaths.

In time, the love of everyone around her drew her out of her despair and life continued as usual in Drummond Castle. Ashleigh had returned to Berwick for the time being. Tory and Grant discussed whether they should bring her to Drummond to live with them permanently, or if she should be left at the only home she knew, Blackstone Manor.

Jamie took up the majority of Tory's day, and Grant made certain he occupied her nights. Life was good.

After training one afternoon Grant walked into his bedchamber as Tory finished nursing Jamie. The bolt of lust that shot through him felt jarring. To this day it amazed him how much he wanted this woman. He watched Tory send Jamie off with their young nursemaid and immediately knew he wanted more children. Striding toward her purposefully, with a licentious gleam in his eyes, all he could think of right now was he planned on doing what led to those children!

Epilogue

Trudging through the snow, Grant mused it had now been a year since Andrew's death. There was no doubt in anyone's mind his death had been a grievous blow to the Scots. Grant had been quiet all day mulling over past events.

After the English defeat at Stirling Bridge, the surrender of Dundee Castle, and the total expulsion of English from Scotland, there had been great signs of hope throughout the country. There were only two English garrisons that still stood firm – those at Roxburgh and Berwick.

Grant shook his head as he mulled over his knighthood. Who would have believed it possible Duncan, Andrew, William, and himself would all be knighted – and by Robert the Bruce at that. That had been a definite surprise to them all, since they hadn't supported Robert's bid as king. Robert had done them all a favor and knighted them at Andrew's castle, since he was too injured to travel. The four men wanted this privilege to be shared by all.

Due to the injury received at the Battle of Stirling, Andrew had been too ill to attend the Scottish council in Perth in October. The end wouldn't be too far away for his friend. He'd gone to see him a few days earlier, and although Andrew hadn't admitted it, his lovely wife, Adriana, stated she feared he was dying. Grant could tell by looking at him that his life was, indeed, ebbing away.

The three men met often during those few months following the Battle at Stirling. Grant and Duncan always went to see Andrew since he was too injured to travel. Andrew always seemed pleased to see them. He'd honestly not thought to see any of them again once he headed home from the battle. Though admitting it to no one, he knew how bad his injuries were, and Grant and Duncan noticed he grew weaker with each visit.

During the months following Stirling's battle, Andrew and Will jointly signed three letters which were sent out with the closing, 'Andrew deMoray and William Wallace, leaders of the army of the kingdom.'

The news Grant dreaded came by courier toward the end of November. His good friend and comrade had finally succumbed to the mortal wound received at Stirling's battle.

Andrew's wife, Adriana, sent word some of his final words had been about Grant. He wanted to ensure Grant knew how much his friendship meant over the years, and he again reemphasized his pleasure Grant finally wedded Tory. He wanted Grant to know how sorry he was he hadn't been present for the wedding, but his thoughts had been with him – and would be throughout eternity.

After hearing of Andrew's death, Baliol quickly named William 'Regent of Scotland.' Baliol did this even though he remained captive in England. 'Twas an office William held with honor, fidelity, and great dignity.

Grant felt proud of his friend.

As Tory glanced outside, she saw Grant pacing in the snow. From their conversation earlier that morn she knew he thought of Andrew and missed him, but life must go on, and Grant looked far too sad. She determined she needed to do something about it.

Calling her wee son Jamie to her side, Tory playfully whispered in his ear. A huge smile spread across the lad's face and he nodded an emphatic 'aye.' Bundling him up to ward off November's bitter cold, she again whispered to him.

Nodding, the small boy toddled out the door, climbed down the massive steps, and trudged as best as his short legs would take him to where his father stood staring at massive surrounding mountains.

The image of his father, Tory smiled when she saw her son wrap his tiny arms around Grant's strong legs. Jamie tugged to get Grant's full attention, and she heard him asking his father to play with him.

"Da?" Jamie said, a smile on his small face as he glanced up at his father. "Up, Da, up."

While Jamie's vocabulary remained limited, he had no difficulty making his desires known. Both parents doted on him.

Smiling, Grant patted his young son's head. He glanced around and saw Tory framed in the entrance to the huge doorway of their Great Hall. She watched him and their son as they stood together in the late afternoon sun.

Quickly swinging wee Jamie up onto his shoulders to get the lad out of the deep snow, Grant headed toward his smiling wife. Aye, life had allowed sad things to happen this past year, but as Grant looked down into his wife's smiling eyes, he knew God had more than blessed him.

He had his lovely wife, who rarely thought of the horrors of her childhood anymore. She brought him such joy. It had been both a pleasure and an honor to watch her blossom before his eyes. She no longer seemed afraid of anything. Feeling loved, it showed in the glow on her face.

And he had his young son, Jamie. His heir. The lad kept them busy all the time. Grant had never known one tiny person could get into so much mischief.

With a glint of mischief in her eyes, Tory told him, "Our son must take after you, husband. Never would I have vexed anyone so. I have always been the epitome of docileness."

Grant choked as he tried to keep from laughing at her ridiculous statement.

And it was almost Christmastide again. Tory would once again transform his Great Hall into a winter wonderland. Her excitement had grown as time passed and was now so contagious it encompassed everyone in his keep. People in the village had begun to adopt Tory's ideas as well. She always made a special effort to include everyone in her plans. He guessed that was because she'd been so lonely as a child. She felt determined that would never happen to anyone she knew, be they child or adult.

Old Agnes had been the perfect example. The auld crone no longer hid herself out in her forest hut. Ever since Jamie's christening, Tory made certain she included the auld woman in family activities and now Agnes automatically joined in events at his keep. She turned out to be pleasant and seemed to get on *exceedingly well* with Warwick!

Grant would never have foreseen that.

Tory had continued many of the old Scots traditions, to be certain, but she'd also brought new ideas with her as well. What Grant loved best was seeing her reaction to the auld beliefs. He always thought of a few traditions they hadn't yet told her. He loved to watch her expression as she tried to absorb beliefs firmly held by so many Highlanders.

While in most instances his people didn't follow these traditions to the letter, Grant admitted there remained a part of them all that was hesitant to let the traditions go. His mam had taught him to assimilate the new with the auld. Surprisingly, Tory adapted well. She seemed determined their children learn the auld ways, as he had. She felt she owed that to Grant as a part of his heritage.

Grant smiled. Aye, life was good, and it seemed he now had everything he never thought he'd ever have.

As he thought of how perfect and serene everything appeared at that moment in his life, a piercing wail split the quietude of the Great Hall. Glancing down at Tory, she smiled up at him, shrugged her shoulders, and handed him the tiny bundle in her arms.

His wee daughter, Eilidh.

The lassie was a moon's passing old and perfect – a miniature version of her mother. Everyone knew the lassie had their young chieftain wrapped around her wee fingers.

His two children were the delight of Grant's life. He played with Jamie for hours on end and croodled to Eilidh as he never imagined he would. In the past he'd have said that wasn't manly. What ridiculous thoughts he'd had. Anything that brought out the best in your children had to be manly.

He'd never been as happy as he was now, and he owed it all to Tory.

She'd worried at first about Grant's reaction when Eilidh was born. As much as she hated to admit it, there still were times when her father's rejection hit her full force. Though mentioning her fears to no one, she worried nevertheless that she hadn't given Grant another son.

If there had been any upset on Grant's part, he hadn't shown it. He seemed devoted to both his children, and within less than a day Tory relaxed. Surely, no one could have so much love show on his face if unhappy.

She'd put her fears behind her, never to be retrieved again.

With Jamie still hanging onto his muscular shoulders as he held his now cooing daughter in his left arm, Grant put his free arm around Tory and pulled her farther into the Great Hall toward the hearth burning brightly. After being outside most of the day, his body needed the warmth the hearth created.

The three people in his arms were all the warmth his heart needed.

Tory had once told him of the dreams and wishes she'd had before she considered running away from her home in England. Grant hoped they'd come true for her.

They'd all come true for him.

Author's Note

The welcoming beauty of Scotland, and its many castles, is truly breathtaking for those of us who've been fortunate to visit. It's a place I hope to return to time and time again. For those who visit through imagination and the wonder of books, it provides magical legends and endless tales of dashing heroes and bonnie heroines.

While Grant and Victoria are fictional, I've tried to keep Clan Drummond history as accurate as possible. I have, however, taken creative license in using Drummond Castle, since it was actually not built until the 1400s. The inside of Drummond Castle is not open to the public, but the castle gardens I've used throughout this book are breathtaking.

The other thing I've moved up in time is having a Christmas tree as a holiday decoration. Most were not actually introduced to the United Kingdom until several hundred years later, but I believe travelers may have seen them in Germany and taken the tradition home to their families earlier than recorded.

My deepest appreciation to Russ Jimeson, who wrote the article, *Unsung Hero*, based on the book *The Scottish War of Independence* by Evan Mcleod Barron. His efforts made me want to introduce Andrew deMoray to the world. Many know about William Wallace, due to the success of recent movies and books, but Moray has been basically forgotten. A group in his hometown of Avoch has formed the Andrew de Moray Project and is busy trying to rectify that situation and bring Moray to the foreground of people's awareness. Had Moray lived, he would have been just as famous as his counterpart, William Wallace. As is the case with many heroes, history has chosen to forget this brave young man. I hope this book will in some way help to rectify that. Again, I have tried to be as authentic as possible about him, but biographical information is extremely sketchy. The hill where his castle used to set is not well marked or easily visited. I hope someday that will change.

Scotland's War for Independence was a great turning point in Scotland's history. The efforts of men like Moray and Wallace paved the way for further exploits by heroic men such as Robert the Bruce.

Leanne Burroughs

If you liked Grant's friend, Duncan
MacThomas, be sure to look for his further
exploits in the sequel,
Her Highland Rogue
available through online bookstores
and Amazon

Also available from the author:
No Law Against Love

(a delightful anthology with 16 other authors
benefiting the Cancer Society)
- available through online bookstores
and Amazon

About the Author

Leanne Burroughs lives in Florida with her husband of thirty-seven years. They have one daughter, one son and daughter-in-law, one grandson, and two granddaughters.

She enjoys reading, writing, and traveling.
While doing genealogy for her husband, she fell in love with Scottish history. That, combined with her love of writing, led to this debut novel.

If you would like to contact her, please feel free to do so via her website, **http://www.leanneburroughs.com** or by e-mail at **Leanne@leanneburroughs.com**.
She welcomes your comments.

Cover design by
DeborahAnne MacGillivray
Copyright 2004

Leanne Burroughs

Her Highland Rogue

Leanne Burroughs

Printed in the United States
99066LV00003B/201/A

9 780974 624907